See **Dick**
Deconstruct

See *Dick* Deconstruct

Literotica for the Satirically Bent

Ian Philips

With a Foreword by Patrick Califia-Rice

ATTA GIRL PRESS

SAN FRANCISCO

Published in the United States by AttaGirl Press, a division of Damron Company, P.O. Box 422458, San Francisco, CA 94142-2458.
Printed in Hong Kong.
Cover Photo: Rebecca McBride
Book Design: Kiki Carr
AttaGirl Press logo art: Rebecca Davenport
First Edition.
05 04 03 02 01 00   10 9 8 7 6 5 4 3 2 1

ISBN 0-929435-69-9

Grateful acknowledgement is made to the following publications in which these stories originally appeared in slightly different form:

"Walt": *Best Gay Erotica 2000*, Richard Labonté, ed., Cleis Press, 1999.

"Foucault's Pendulous…": *suspect thoughts: a journal of subversive writing (www.suspectthoughts.com)*, Issue 1, July-Sept. 2000. Reprinted in *Best Gay Erotica 2001*, Richard Labonté, ed., Cleis Press, 2000.

"See Dick Deconstruct": *Cuir Underground*, Issue 4, Sept./Oct. 1997. Reprinted in *RE/Porn*, 1997. Revised and reprinted in *Best Gay Erotica 1999*, Richard Labonté, ed., Cleis Press, 1998.

"Harder": *suspect thoughts: a journal of subversive writing (www.suspectthoughts.com)*, Issue 2, Oct.-Dec. 2000.

"Sheldon Smalley Meets His Satan": *Bitch Goddess: The Spiritual Path of the Dominant Woman*, Pat Califia and Drew Campbell, eds., Greenery Press, 1997.

For Patrick Califia-Rice
my Sire in literotica and so many other dark and delicious arts

As the wise old African proverb says and the savvy junior senator from New York is fond of repeating: It takes a village to raise a child. This child—trust me—was no different. So I'd like to thank the following villagers for loaning me juicy tidbits from their ever-so-more-sordid-than-mine lives and for encouraging, inspiring, and even goading me to write and to write well. (And if you find yourself unnamed, it's not because I've forgotten you or your name—you wish! It's simply because I worried you might not be thrilled to see your name included—in the harsh light of print—with all the other charming rogues in this gallery. But I still thank you.)

Aleita, David Alport, Liz Alward, Adrienne Anderson, Charles Andromidas, Jr., Angela of *Raw Vulva*, Roberta Arnold, Avidan & his two mommies, Ellen & Stephanie, Biagio Azzarelli, Dr. George B. & Michael McG., the men of Dr. B.'s Monday Night Stitch-'n-Bitch, Glen Baird, Randy Boyd, Tala Brandeis, Elise Braverman, Bill Brent, Fairy Butch, Lady Anne Campbell, Linda & Carmen Catalano, Justin Chin, David Christensen, M. Christian, Camillo Cimis, Randy Conner, Sarah Conner, Dana Cory, Jim Coughenour, Dame Esther E., Dossie Easton, Bruce Elsperger, Woody Ever, Michael Thomas Ford, Frankie & Mama Rose, Dan Freeman, friends and faculty at both Earlham and St. John's Colleges, Chenda Fruchter, Bruce Gatta, Ed Gatta, Robert Goins, Mark Guillory, David Hambly, Janet Hardy of Greenery Press, Kai Harper, Doug Harrison, Karen Heather & Xochtlquetzal George, Christine (Hillie!) Hilliard, Drew Holweger, David Howley, little Johnny Jackoff, Matt Kailey, Rob Kahn, Scott Knell, Dr. Kohn, Krandall Kraus, Gil Kudrin, Garland Richard Kyle of the (sadly) late and always great *modern words*, Dr. Julie L., Chad Lange of *asspants*, Robert Lawrence, Asa Dean Liles, Peter Limnios, Warren Longmire, Bill Maguire, Leah Mayers, Marty McCurdy, Carol McDonnell, John McGourty Jane Megginson, Kevin Michéal, Robbie Micheli, Kyra Miller, Mark Moody, Chris Murchison, Felice Newman & Frédérique Delacoste of Cleis Press, Miss Betty Pearl, Mary Peelen, Jim Pelfini, Elissa Perry, Felice Picano, Marge Poscher, Martin Pousson, Carol Queen, Alex Ralston, Reilly, Matt Rice & Blake Chatman Califia-Rice, Wendell Ricketts, Thomas Roche, Brian Schulz, D. Travers Scott, Simon Sheppard, Mikal Shively & John Mudd, Martha Silverspring, Vikki Sinnott, Mr. Sloan and all my other English teachers at Holland Hall, horehound stillpoint, Michelle Tea, Laura Trent, Glenn Turner, David Valentine, the infamous Ms. Sarah Wersan, Greg Wharton of www.suspectthoughts.com, Anne Williams, Pam Williams, Stormy Williams, Christina Woolner, and Mark Wunderlich.

And many special thanks to the following psychic wet nurses and tribal chieftans: the Furies (to serve is to honor as the Vulcans say); Auntie Virginia and Old Horny (for all your behind-the-scenes miracles); my mom, Lynne, and my sisters, Gretchen and Heidi, and their respective hubbies (for honestly encouraging me to write even when they knew what I was writing and that they may never get to see it); the Alpha Females of AttaGirl Press: Louise Mock (for being my patroness and fellow Aries cheerleader) and Kathy Pratt (for "christening" me a witchbitch and still helping me figure out computers) and Rebecca Davenport (for her biting Yankee wit and introducing me to Gogol) and Erika O'Connor (for introducing me to those wonder siblings Amy and David Sedaris); Rebecca McBride (for making art with your cover shot); Jen "the Incredible Bawd" Williams (for embodying Pan, Hecate, and Ruth Vitale all at the same time); Kirk Read (my bold, soul sister who is giving birth to her feisty and brilliant baby, *How I Learned to Snap*, as I type this and who endlessly tries to coax this shy girl to live it up, loud and proud, as she does so well); Richard Labonté (for the many labors of love he has performed—like shepherding many of these stories into print—as the one, true gray eminence of queer lit); Drew Campbell (for looking so fetching in a bow tie and being my master editor and font of erudition); Kiki Carr (for bending me to her femme will and masterful design sense); Gina M. (is for Master) Gatta of AttaGirl Press (for being a writer's dream and running with this manuscript that no other publisher would touch with even a ten—no, make that twelve—inch, irradiated pole); Patrick Califia-Rice (for *Macho Sluts* which launched this ship and for being the god/dess father/mother to my baby and the best friend a wicked little witch like me could dream of); and Yo (who sat on my lap and purred while I typed all these stories save the last—incarnate soon so we can do that novel).

*Life is short,
and* **Art** *long....*
—Hippocrates, *Aphorisms*

The lust of the **goat** *is the bounty
of* **God.**
—William Blake,
"The Marriage of Heaven and
Hell"

Stories

Skullfucking

A Few Words About See Dick Deconstruct

by Patrick Califia-Rice

> "... the sex we have is precisely that which initially separates us from the rest of society in the most fundamental way. It is the first essential reason we are alien in this world and therefore it can't be ignored. Its impact is simply too great to be shunted aside.
>
> "One of the reasons we constantly return to sex is—I think—that we are always needing to know if this is enough to justify what we go through because of it. Often that's an emotional issue: are these emotions worth it? But because the repercussions are so enormous it becomes a political and social issue as well."

—John Preston,
"Epilogue: On Writing Pornography,"
Forbidden Passages: Writings Banned in Canada,
Pittsburgh: Cleis Press, 1995.

Before I let this twisted collection of queer satire and elegantly phrased filth mess with your head, I have a confession to make. I can't possibly be objective about this book, which was written by my best friend, Ian Philips—bawdy raconteur, gracious host, eclectic scholar, wounded healer, merciless proofreader, and devoted servant of the Furies. Three years ago, we decided to constitute a Novelist's Support Group of two. I have read more than a dozen drafts of some of these stories, just as Ian patiently waded through several versions of the tales that make up *No Mercy*. (The least I could do to pay him back was let him borrow one of my characters. But I'll let that be a surprise.) I still haven't written the novel that was hanging over my head when we became the Queer Quill Twins (and neither has he). But we are both workaholics. The only way we can procrastinate when we are supposed to be writing a book is apparently to write *another* book. Hence, this volume you hold between your two hands, which ought to be sweating, if they know what's good for them.

It's a strange sort of adultery—productivity without virtue; passive-aggressive progress in spite of oneself. Since Ian and I also suffer from severe religious damage as a result of childhood indoctrination into bizarre fundamentalist cults, we know all about the goad of guilt, which serves mostly to drive us off the path that leads to other people's idea of heaven. And we both suffer from an inability to feel that we've ever done anything meaningful or worthwhile, given how far from divine perfection we fall short each time we leap for the sky. In fact, one of the things we have had to do in this convoluted relationship is to establish a Compliment Quota (no more than two per phone conversation or one face-to-face) because we simply can't listen to or trust anyone who says too many nice things about us or our work. During Rough Draft Hell or any of those inevitable periods of self-loathing when it seems to every writer that they ought to burn every single page they've ever labored over, we have each allowed the other to keep the faith in our dreams and aspirations. Thus, no pages are destroyed, and the evil spirits can't get to us over the mounting heap of manuscript. I trust his red editorial ink, and he trusts mine.

The fact that Ian and I know each other well enough to finish one another's sentences should not, however, make you think that I don't know whether this is a grimoire for good gay witches or the Other Sort. There's a lot of false mythology about writing in our culture. For one thing, there's the notion that the only way to find out if your work is any good or not is to let it sink or swim, like the defendant in a witchcraft trial, before the harsh critics and editors who are self-appointed guardians of the bibliography of worthwhile literature. In fact, many of these people (second-rate teachers of creative writing classes, self-absorbed publishers of prestigious poetry and short-story journals, puritanical editors who work for corporate publishing houses, and their long-tongued protégés) are on a mission to *prevent* the development of new writers. They do this by scoffing at anything that might actually attract an audience, by demanding unreasonable revisions, by keeping their standards mysterious, by dictating fads that put words to fashionable misuse, and by echoing the hateful inner voice that will convince us we are gauche and self-deluded if we give it any credit.

I think what any writer, especially a new one, needs is at least one person who can weed the mistakes out of a piece of writing without destroying the entire garden, someone who absolutely believes in their talent and wants to help it to grow. Fortunately, there are some editors and publishers like this, but often such people are to be found among our friends rather than literary professionals. The desire to tell a story is pretty much a universal human instinct, and the ability to tell a story well on paper is not as rare as we've been encouraged to believe. And artists don't have to be solitary creatures. In fact, we do much better when we flock together and encourage one another. (This also makes it possible to share information about the bad eggs who write those snotty rejection letters, edit our work without permission, or "forget" to sign our checks.)

It's been a great pleasure to work with someone who has Ian's sharp and merciless mind. He is a tireless critic of sacred cows of all sexual orientations. Whether he is lampooning the predictably virile dialogue of porn videos and "straight-acting, straight-appearing" personals in "Man Overboard!" or going after the uniforms and other stereotypes of the leather community in "The Color Khaki," or meting out the dark goddess's justice to a homophobic televangelist in "Sheldon Smalley Meets His Satan," Ian always recognizes pretension and hypocrisy. His satire is well-aimed. These are some of the funniest pieces about queer sex and politics that I have ever read.

Humorists will often target people or experiences that everybody already agrees are despicable or expendable. Instead of being a powerful weapon for questioning the legitimacy of power, such humor becomes a further punishment for the downtrodden and a conservative pillar that holds up the status quo. There's none of that here. Even when he is skewering the slavish academic worship of postmodernism (in "Foucault's Pendulous..." and "Story of the I") or mocking the smugness of the gay "sexual ecologists" in "The One, True Lord of the Dance," Ian's righteous indignation springs from a conviction that gay desire is a healing and wonderful thing. Indeed, such desire is, in the worlds that he creates, powerful enough to defeat Old Scratch himself. (See "The Devil and Mrs. Faust.") The right people are the heroes in these stories, and the right people get left high and dry without a spanking or a bareback ride.

These stories also tickle me because they reach beyond the limits of gay male experience to include lesbians and transgendered characters. "Walt" is already a classic among FTMs who don't often see their experience reflected in erotica. This tale of a queercore kid who gets picked up in a sleazy backroom bar by a poetry-spouting, transgendered bear of a top has been featured in a *Best Gay Erotica* collection. I only wish I could have seen the looks on the faces of biofag readers when Joe gets into Walt's pants and decides to stick around and see what other surprises are in store. And what juicy little dykelet would not thrill to see that patron spirit of wild women, Lilith herself, strap it on for a horny housewife like Ruth Faust?

Because of this polymorphous perversity, rumors have circulated that "Ian Philips" is in fact a pseudonym for a lesbian porn writer, or that he's actually an FTM himself. When confronted with these rumors, his usual response is, "I'm flattered." While Ian's work is sexually explicit, it certainly doesn't follow the usual preset scripts of pornography. This critical approach to gay male popular culture accentuates the humor, thoughtfulness, and wicked heat of these pieces.

Not all of these stories are funny. Some are bitter or full of grief. The last story in the book, "Memento Mori," is particularly moving, and was for me the most difficult to read. Because of AIDS, Julian has endured the loss of most of a generation of friends and lovers, and the description of the impact this has had on his old age is done with a delicate and accurate touch. I don't like thinking about death and all of the pleasures that we lose when we give up our mortal bodies. Without the piquant passages of graphic S/M sex, it would be difficult indeed to follow this tragic tale of love found too late and given up far too soon. I'm not sure who I liked better, the master whose body is betraying him by harboring cancer, or the mostly-silent submissive we first meet clad in cordovan leather, being used as an ottoman. After enduring volume after volume of dumb smut in which dominance is equated with moronic (and therefore supposedly butch) brutality, how refreshing it is to encounter an extremely intelligent sadist who has more than a passing knowledge of Rome's ancient history and her most indecent pagan poet.

Several of Ian's characters have been radically altered by their experience with the pandemic of HIV infection. The unpleasant reality of AIDS has been a challenge that most porn writers haven't handled very well. Many, if not most, choose to simply ignore it and create a fantasy world where there are no evil consequences for fucking without protection. They argue that nobody can get sick from reading about or jacking off to fantasies about unsafe sex, and tout the value of such porn as escapist entertainment which burned-out activists surely need and deserve. While I'm sympathetic to these arguments, I also know that human beings are not drawn exclusively to pretty or wholesome erotic experiences. A story about sex gets more interesting when it includes the more confusing, disturbing, or paradoxical aspects of Eros. If you want to do more with a piece of sexually explicit fiction than simply turn the reader on, I think you have to face some of the uglier realities of sex, and somehow acknowledge or react to them in your narrative.

A handful of gay porn authors have done what they think is the principled thing (or what the stray politically correct publisher requires), and imposed safer sex upon their fiction. They argue that fantasizing about high-risk behavior makes it more likely that people will engage in this conduct. Their intention is to help other gay men to eroticize latex and other forms of safer sex. But the precautions taken in these stories are usually described in such a self-conscious and heavy-handed way that it diverts attention from the action and wilts the reader's growing excitement. In *See Dick Deconstruct*, AIDS appears as a harsh fact of life, and its impact is handled in a realistic but more complex way. There are no simplistic positions about AIDS in this book, and no easy answers.

If there's any form of human sexuality which has suffered from reductionist thinking and the laziness of knee-jerk reactions, it's sadomasochism. S/M has been used as a metaphor for just about every nasty thing that human beings can do to one another. A sexualized interest in dominance and submission or pain has been held out as the rationale for or psychological underpinning of totalitarian governments, torture of political prisoners, the oppression of women, the institution of slavery, capital punishment, the celibacy of the Roman Catholic clergy, child abuse, etc., etc., etc. Extreme S/M appears in these stories as a metaphor as well, but here it is employed in a more interesting fashion.

In "Walt," the bioboy is on the receiving end of some heavy-duty tit torture. He is thus held away from Walt's body (so we never learn if the transman has had chest surgery or not), and his breasts are marked for sexual use in a way that both underscores the distance between the two men (as top and bottom, trans versus genetic man) and their similarities (as people who have nipples that may be erogenous zones). In "See Dick Deconstruct" and "The Writer's Life," beautiful boys are spanked or penetrated to punish them for taking the privilege of their good looks for granted. The fact that they receive so much attention also, unfortunately, confirms their superior status. But their response to this domination equalizes things somewhat, giving the older and less handsome characters access to these beauties and a measure of power over them. The ability to elicit arousal from the bottom (like the sadism of Julian in "Memento Mori") is equated with a greater wisdom about human nature, which is bitter, but also very useful.

Rather than being used as a synonym for persecution or oppression, in several of these stories, S/M dynamics are used to attack nonconsensual hierarchies of power and privilege. In "The Color Khaki," no mercy is shown to whiteboys' racist fantasies about "appropriate" conduct for big, bad, black topmen. Rather than Robert Stoller's "erotic form of hatred," in "Memento Mori," the sensual act of carving poetry upon the beloved's body makes palpable the way love changes anyone it touches. And indeed, the lasting impact we have upon one another may be the only immortality we will enjoy, when we are disempowered by death.

Without preaching, Ian frequently uses his interest in spiritual matters as a theme. Christian notions of good and evil get their comeuppance in "The Devil and Mrs. Faust" and "Sheldon Smalley Meets His Satan," while "Beloved of God and Man" and "Harder" acknowledge the homosexual subtext in Jesus' love for his disciples, the discipline of monastic orders, and the yielding of penitent to priest. A knowledge of the Hindu pantheon is useful to follow all the references in "The One, True Lord of the Dance," and the collection as a whole addresses our attempts, as mortal and moral creatures, to deal with our fear of extinction and fill our chilly existential sense of emptiness or aloneness with the presence of an Other. The power of pleasure and its potential to create transcendental experiences is recognized, but so are the limitations of physical delight and the occasions when a fading orgasm reminds us that we cannot escape ourselves. *See Dick Deconstruct* is about love as much as it is about lust. The glory and frustration of trying to love one another is played off against the dilemma of trying to achieve some sort of relationship with a divinity who is by turns uncaring or uncooperative and then unexpectedly magnanimous.

See Dick Deconstruct is dense, flavorful, and chewy as a chocolate mousse cake or a rare roasted leg of lamb. There are many layers to these stories. Every time I read them, I notice a new line of dialogue or a quip that I'd overlooked before. These stories combine the author's knowledge of ancient history, psychoanalysis, queer theory, Christian theology, the iconography of modern pornography, American literature, gay popular culture, Michel Foucault, lesbian-feminism, the semiotics of S/M, the interaction of race and class with sexuality, Georges Bataille, the tenuous connection between the word and the deed, and probably a dozen other topics that I missed. It's not a book for the stupid or the faint-hearted. Nor is it a book for people who like their sentences short and snappy. These stories linger over their characters and their biographies, take their time to build up the setting where the action takes place, lovingly detail dialogue and the inner states that accompany it. If you come away from most erotic fiction disappointed with its thinness and predictability, this is a book that you can sink your teeth into.

But I wouldn't want you to think that *See Dick Deconstruct* is so abstract or "heady" that it lacks more ribald rewards for the reader. The usual mind/body split is not too evident in these pages. As well as being funny and thought-provoking, these stories are also very sexy. The interrogation scene in "See Dick Deconstruct" and the preppie ordeal of the bottom in "The Color of Khaki" are priceless—hot as well as hysterical. These stories will keep you busy in many, many ways for far longer than one usually expects to be affected by a collection of short fiction.

Author's Note

Patrick Califia-Rice is the author of several works of fiction, poetry, and queer theory. He is currently working on *Speaking Sex to Power,* a collection of essays from Cleis Press, and *The Code*, an erotic novel about an S/M relationship between an FTM and an old guard top, set in San Francisco during the late '70s.

See **Dick**
Deconstruct

Walt

for Matt Rice

San Francisco. Saturday night. Almost midnight.

I was at The Hole in the Wall. Alone.

I know, I know—I'm making it sound like a bad thing. And it wasn't. No way. I'm just trying to picture it in my mind so you can in yours.

Okay, Saturday night. So I wasn't bummed really. Or scared. It's just I'd never been there before without my roommates—the guys.

They'd gone skating. This time somewhere in the Mission. Alex told me that once they were sweaty enough and tired of falling—they're still not that good—they planned to go South of Market. Find an alley. But where there weren't so many yuppies with lofts. You know, the kind who'll call the cops if you even fart too loud in *their* alley. Then they were gonna put their decks—no, no, you know, skateboards—in a circle. But since there's only three of them, I guess it'd have to be a triangle. Anyway, they're gonna put their decks in front of them. And then, at the same time, they're gonna drop trou and whip their dicks out and circle jerk. I guess it's cuz they heard someone at the bar telling about how he and some friends christened his Harley by pissing on it.

I thought the whole thing was a little weird. And I don't have a skateboard anyway. So that's where they were. And me, like I said before, I was alone, for the first time, at The Hole in the Wall.

It's not like I was scared. It's just—you know how at parties, like in high school, and you're trying to act like what you thought was cool but you couldn't even begin without a plastic cup of beer in your hand. Except you're older. Okay, not much in my case. And now the plastic cup is a bottle. You know, a prop. Well, I guess a bottle isn't prop enough for me. I needed the guys. I mean, if you saw us, you'd see me talking to three guys who looked like they're playing pinball at the same time—like one person. And the whole time you'da been looking at us, I'da been cruising you.

Sounds like I'm hiding. Maybe. It's not like I'm ugly or anything. Brown hair. Brown eyes. I keep my goatee trimmed real close. I've got a big mouth. Honest. And a big nose. I don't like it. But this hot guy told me it was "classical." He said I have a Roman nose. Makes sense. I'm Italian. Okay, my mom's dad and my dad's grandparents are Italian. So I try to remember what he said and how sexy he said it when I get self-conscious. Like Saturday night.

I know, I know—BFD. What's my problem? Especially when most guys just want you to have meat on your boner. No sweat, then. I don't mean to be bragging, but I gotta big, fat dick. What can I say, it came with the body. And when I used to fuck around with "most guys," I scored all the time. But what gets me hard, you know, dick-pointing-to-the-sky-rock-hard, is men with meat on *all* of their bones.

So? Shit. I forgot to tell you I'm real skinny too. So, I'm always thinking, since I'm so skinny, those guys won't want me. They'll throw me back in the water just like my dad does with any fish he thinks is—his words, not mine— "a runt." Okay, it probably doesn't help that that's his nickname for me too. And I'm not that small. It's just my dad's 6'1" and I'm 5'8". And, I guess, if you put only 130 pounds on 5'8" worth of bones, you gotta runt.

Whatever. By the way, none of what I just told you was to throw me a pity party. I swear. It's so you'll know why I didn't tell Walt to go fuck himself when he came onto me. Even if he did seem a little crazy. Hell, he *is* crazy.

Great. Now I want my men big and crazy.

Well, right now, I just want Walt.

• • •

No, he isn't one of the Naked Guys or that guy that barks. Though they were all there last Saturday night. But maybe you've never been. Sorry. I keep forgetting I'm supposed to see it so you can see it. Okay. The Hole in the Wall. It's like that bar—you know, the one in Star Wars. Honest. Except this time everyone's a fag and horny. They call it a biker bar. I guess it is. There's always a bunch of guys there who look like they're Hell's Angels. But, to say it's a biker bar, you gotta include mountain bikes with the Harleys.

Right. Saturday. It was packed. Two deep along the bar and three around the pool table. In the back—you know where that mural is of the great daddy bear riding a Harley and his boy into heaven—the one right beneath the sign that says "Booty Juice Rules"—back there, it was so thick with bikers and bears and boys it didn't take much to guess what was going on.

I looked across to the bar. Then looked up front again to see if my guys had decided to show up after all. Nothing. Then I looked straight ahead again. And two blue eyes were staring back. Staring right through me. This blond bear was cruising me. Heavy cruising. No looking away. No blinking. But there was something odd about him. He had the cruise down, but, even though his thick lips never moved, I could tell he was grinning at me. With his eyes. You know. Like that cat in *Alice in Wonderland*. The one that had the shit on everyone and just smiled, driving them crazy cuz they all feared just how much he knew. Yeah, his face was a lot like that cat's. Then the eyes, the smile, the face, him—they all moved toward me.

His belly pushed guy after guy out of the way. Kinda like those big rocks in streams that water has to split itself in half to get around. Except the stream was men heading for the bar or the john. And the rock kept moving toward me. God, my eyes musta been bugging. I almost had to bite my tongue to keep from grinning back. I wasn't nervous anymore. Okay, maybe still a little. But, mainly, I was stoked to be singled out by such a hot man. All I could think was *Please, sir, don't stop.*

I braced my butt against the ledge that runs along the wall. I didn't want to start shaking. But I was getting so excited. *Omigod. He's getting so close. Is he gonna kiss me? Yes, c'mon, daddy bear. Closer. C'mon.* Then I shook. *Omigod. Did I just say any of that out loud?*

I'd been shouting in my head to hear over the electric guitar solo going on above our heads. Some riot grrrl—I think from L7, maybe Tribe 8—was making her guitar shriek like the first chick offed in every slasher film. Okay, I lied. The music was hella loud, but I was shouting in my head cuz I was nervous—yeah, nervous enough to be shouting out loud. But no way anybody coulda heard it. Walt sure didn't. He just kept coming. Till his thick gut was pressing hard against my belly-flopping stomach. He was only a few inches from my face. He leaned in. *He's gonna kiss me.* I closed my eyes. I dunno why. *You're such a girl,* I screamed to myself. But I didn't care. I waited for his bristles to poke my lips.

Then I felt them. On my ear! He was snorting in my ear. Okay, breathing. But he was a heavy breather. Like a crank caller. Like a bull.

My ear prickled and burned till my whole face musta been red. Then, his body gently crushed mine and he whispered, "*I sing the body electric.*" And I felt it. The current coming from his fingers as he grabbed my shoulder blades. "*The armies of those I love engirth me and I engirth them.*" His hands dropped slowly along my spine. I thought—I hoped—he was gonna shove them down my pants. But they kept going till he'd pushed my butt from the ledge and held a cheek in each hand. "*They will not let me off till I go with them, respond to them.*" Then he pulled one hand from my ass and dragged it around my hip. If he was going for my dick, it wouldn't be hard to find now. It was making as much of a pup tent as it could in 501s one size too small. I breathed in. Closed my eyes tight. He found it. I had a raging boner by the time he mashed his palm into my crotch and said, "*And discorrupt them, and charge them full with the charge of the soul.*"

After one hard, slow squeeze, he pulled his hand from my dick and up along my stomach—totally belly-cartwheeling now—and over my chest till he held my chin. I felt his breath now before I heard it. My lips grew warm. *Please, kiss me.* I waited. He waited. I opened my eyes.

"It's Walt."

"Hey, Walt. I'm Joe."

He laughed. A burst that softened as it fell down the register. *God, he's cute.*

"No, Walt Whitman. That was from a poem by Whitman."

I think I've seen just one picture of Walt Whitman. He was a really old dude. Probably sixty or seventy years old. Maybe not. Back then, life was rougher. He mighta been forty. But that Walt didn't look like this Walt. That Walt—Walt Whitman—he looked like Grizzly Addams' friend. You know—the old guy, not the bear. What was his name? You know. Well, it was the same guy that played Uncle Jesse on *The Dukes of Hazzard*. This Walt didn't look like either of them. Okay, maybe he looked like Grizzly Addams. But my Grizzly's a few inches smaller and so's his beard.

Now all that thinking I just did really happened in a second. Well, as long as it took to get one good look at his face. Okay, I'm not sure. It coulda been longer. I'd been drinking. Good thing too or I never woulda had the balls to do what I did next.

I leaned up to his ear and grabbed his dick. *It's hard too.* Then I said it. "Wanna go to my place and fuck?" I felt his whole body shake. He laughed till I thought it was the laughter lifting me in a bear hug.

• • •

We held hands the whole cab ride to my house. I didn't let go of his paw till we got to my room and I had to plug in the strings of pink flamingo lights on the wall above my futon. It was just them and the lava lamp across the room. Enough light to tell where the buttons in our jeans were.

I looked up from the outlet and there was Walt. He was grinning for real now. He'd propped all my pillows up against the wall. Then scooted his whole bulk into his new chair, pulling most of the blanket up under his ass. He was patting his thigh. His thick fingers thudded against his thicker leg. It was a drum beat I couldn't ignore.

I bent down and tore at the laces of my boots. Yeah, it was light enough to see a silver button, but there was no way in hell I was gonna untie a little black knot fast. I think I said one of those strings of "shit's" out loud. Finally, I got both boots off. I marched up and onto my bed, straddling Walt's legs. I tried to kneel down slowly but he grabbed my hips and tugged. My ass fell hard onto his lap but I didn't even knock the wind out of him. Nope. He wasn't even fazed. Just pulled me in closer and kissed me.

His lips were heavy and wet. Mine slipped around on them, scratching against the edge of his beard if I rolled too far, till he had my mouth and me anchored to his tongue. He tasted so good. Honest. Like really dark beer.

He slipped his hands up under my shirt. It wasn't difficult. It'd come untucked and it was a velour pullover anyway. A real deep purple. They were warm—his hands. He fanned them across my chest. *"The curious sympathy one feels...."* He slipped them under my arms. I jumped back. I couldn't help it. It tickled. But he kept talking, *"...when feeling with the hand the naked meat of the body."* He lifted my arms, then his, and, with it, my shirt up and over my head. *One cool move.*

"Was that Walt, too?"

He smiled. *God, he must know every poem Whitman ever wrote!* He didn't say anything—just placed a palm right on top of each nipple. Then he arched his hands so only his fingers and my skin were touching. I watched them and waited. They looked like they were gonna play the piano. He dragged them real slow down to my stomach. I was shaking. A big quivering shudder ran up and up and then down my spine. He was getting closer to the rim of my jeans, to the buttons. And my dick was getting closer to rock hard.

It was show time.

But when he got to the denim, he stopped. He pulled his fingers into a fist, leaving only his thumbs against my stomach. He traced his thumbs out from my belly button like a potter smoothing clay on a wheel. And, trust me, I was spinning. They met up again on my back. Suddenly, thumbs and fingers and hands were all trying to go down my pants. But they were too fat and my jeans were too tight. Walt could barely get the tips of his fingers in.

He chuckled. I smiled. I was embarrassed. Excited. Leaving one hand waiting at my waist band, he took the other and started fumbling with my top button. I sat up on my knees, sticking my butt up like a cat. *Pop.* One free. His hand slid under the denim. *Pop.* It was at the tip of my crack. My dickhead jumped out. *Pop. Pop. Pop.* His fingers slid into my butt crack, digging for my hole, while my dick sprung up to my stomach like one of those flowers in time-lapse that comes up out of the earth in full-bloom.

Before my cock could cool in the open air, Walt had it in his grip. His hands were fuckin' huge. This one held almost three-quarters of my dick. He squeezed. I groaned. He squeezed even harder. His thumb stroked my sticky hole again and again. Quickly, it was sliding back and forth. He breathed more words in my ear. "*Without shame,*" his thumb kept counting out the beat, "*the man I like,*" back and forth, "*knows and avows*" back and forth, "*the deliciousness of his sex.*"

I was "unnhing" by now. Which isn't bad. It sounds hot. It feels hot. It's just if he kept thumbing and I kept "unnhing" I was gonna shoot way too soon. So I grabbed for his dick. It was long and hard against his thigh. I tried to squeeze it real rough-like. *Shit, this fucker's thick.* He barely noticed. So I pulled on it. I couldn't tell if he was moaning or laughing.

I gripped it harder and yanked it. He got quiet. He stopped thumbing me but didn't let go of my dick. My other hand was still holding onto his ledge of a shoulder. I let go and made a grab for the back of his head. I pulled him in till his open mouth was on mine.

There's no better way to say it: we were sucking face. No shit. I thought he was gonna swallow my head like a Tootsie Pop.

Somehow I was able to keep up the tongue-wrestling match we had going while I unbuttoned his flannel shirt. *Plop.* I broke the vacuum seal. I gulped down a breath and then dropped my face into the brush of his beard. His hairs pricked my lips and tongue again and again as I dragged them down his face to his neck. Walt's hand had long let go of my dick and joined its twin on my ass. He held each cheek tight while thumbing my butt crack. As I pushed my mouth down his neck, I inched my hole toward his thumbs. I was sitting on them by the time I got to his chest. His skin was smooth with sweat and sweet-smelling. Then, finally, I found it, that patch of dark blond hair. I matted it some more with my face. I was getting real close to his meaty tits.

Okay. I know the minute I said "meaty" you were thinking I meant the usual two sirloin steaks circuit queens either grow or have glued onto their chests. Nope. In fact, "meaty's" kinda lame since I'm a vegetarian. I just mean those big, thick ones you can really suck on. Like the monster man-tits in *Bulk Male*. You know, they look like two huge mudslides on Pacific Coast Highway 1.

And Walt had them. We're talking El Niño mudslides. With the biggest, pinkest nipples I'd ever seen on a guy. I sighed in awe, and that got Walt's thumbs to wriggling at the edge of my hole. My ass sent a quick message up my spine to my brain. If I wanted any nippage, I was gonna have to totally scrunch down on his thumbs. Two holes filled in one move—yeah, it was a sacrifice I was willing to make.

I stuck out only the end of my tongue and moved in. I flicked it against his fat nipple. A butterfly kiss. Walt shook. The futon creaked. My asshole danced over his thumbs as they took turns jabbing it and each other to get in. I quickly locked my lips 'round the tip of his tit and the Waltquake stopped.

His thick knot stiffened between my lips. He growled and I sucked. Then I pulled away till I held the tip of his tit in my teeth. I bit down, real gentle-like at first, then not-so-gentle-like.

Walt belched out something that sounded like "Ah, shit!" My asshole was pulling around empty air. His thumbs were gone. He tugged at the back of my head with both his hands and pried me loose like I was some kinda tick.

I slipped free, dragging my tongue down through the trail of hair to the edge of his jeans. I kept expecting his belly to shake like that bowlful of jelly under the weight of my tongue. But it was one solid block of fat and muscle. I was leaking some serious precum now.

I reached for his belt buckle. My hands fumbled like I was a kid, up since 4 a.m., tearing into his first Christmas present, finally, at 9 a.m. *Got it!* Now for the button fly. Top button down. Then another. My whole body was shaking. I wanted his dick. Now. To let him know just how bad, I gripped it hard and squeezed.

Suddenly my face was swallowed in the palm of his hand. He tilted my chin up from his crotch till our eyes met. "*Whoever you are holding me now in hand,/ Without one thing all will be useless,*" he smiled just like that cat again. "*I give you fair warning before you attempt me further,/ I am not what you supposed, but far different.*"

I guess if I was really listening to what the words meant, I might have stopped then and asked him just what the fuck he was talking about. But he used so many words. Some pretty. Some weird. Some really vague. They all sounded like what a genie in a fairy tale says, or a fortune cookie. I didn't really care. I just wanted to see his cock and suck it. Talk later.

I shoved my fingers under the tight waistband of his black underwear. It was leather. A leather jockstrap. *Kinky.* I had to see his dick bad now. *Please, let him have a Prince Albert.* My asshole twitched. *Amen, sister.*

I kept pushing down. At some point I knew my hand would find that odd spot in the damp, wiry hair and soft fat of his mound where a hard, thick stick grew. But I kept pushing down. *Where was it?* It's supposed to be just south of the belly button. Then my fingers slid over another curve of fat and into this warm, wet crease. I panicked.

"Where's your dick?"

"You pushed it out of the way for my cunt."

"Your cunt?" I yanked my hand out of his pants as fast as I could. "How can a man have a cunt?"

"I just do."

My face was swallowed again by his hand. For a sec, I got scared he was gonna crush my head like a walnut. But, instead, he held it real tender, like I was this little baby bird that'd fallen out of its nest.

Then he let go and grabbed my hand. I started to wig when he tried to push it back down under his jockstrap. He just held tight and shoved my fingers into his sweaty and steamy bush. "*Have you ever loved the body of a woman?*" I watched him pull my wet hand up his stomach and onto his stiffening nipple. "*Have you ever loved the body of a man?*" My fingers were almost cold and he pulled them up and into his mouth. He sucked till they were warm, then dragged them out over his soft, wide lower lip. *"Do you not see that these are exactly the same to all in all nations and times all over the earth?"*

"Is that another poem?" He smiled again. "Could you just fuckin' stop with the poetry crap." My dick was shrinking like a dying balloon and I was cold.

"Stop and listen to their words. Feel them. They're so beautiful—like you."

I forgot what I was gonna say. Then I blurted out, "You tricked me."

"You tricked yourself."

Okay. Reality check. Yeah, I thought right then about telling Walt to get the fuck outta my house. For a sec. Or two. Maybe a minute. I was kinda shocked. Alright, I was pissed. But before I could say anything, my dick had to go and put in *his* two cents. Well, more like his eight-and-a-half inches.

Walt, my dick and I both agreed, really was—even with a pussy under his dick—one of the hottest guys we'd ever seen. Honest. I wasn't that drunk. And, my dick reminded me, the last time *we* got laid was two weeks *before* finals and my last final was almost two weeks ago. Hell, that's a month.

I snapped out of my head just in time to see Walt groping around in his pants for his dick. "Here," he pulled it loose and it flapped up between us. "I'll keep it on the whole time. Okay? You just get it wet and I'll fuck you with it. All right?"

I stared at it. It was pretty realistic, for a dildo. You know. You could tell the head from the shaft. It had veins. Even smelled like skin from being in Walt's pants. But I knew it'd taste like silicone.

"He's hot," my dick shouted. *"A month. Thirty fuckin' days and no one's touched me but you!"*

Walt pushed me off and stood. Snapped his fingers and pointed to his feet. I scurried over and tried to make a go of it.

His dick was about eight inches long and six around. It was hard. And Walt knew how to face fuck like it really was his. In a few minutes, he was shoving it down the back of my throat. He was a rough, mean fucker and didn't care if I was choking and sobbing. I shoulda been happy. Real happy. It felt good. Honest. But something was missing.

I know you thought I was gonna say "a real dick." Wrong. It's just the more

I sucked, the more I thought. And the more I thought, the more I knew that no matter what he did with that dick, he couldn't feel me and I couldn't feel him. I mean I'm pretty good with my tongue. But it was wasted on his dick. I wanted Walt to feel how excited I was by him. And I wanted to feel, from the surge of his skin and blood, that he was excited by me.

You have to understand this. You just do. It's real important. Really. So you'll get why I did what I did.

Okay. First, I raised my hands off his cock and onto his belly, pushing it, pushing him, to lie back on the futon. I started to get up off my knees while keeping the dick in my mouth. Of course, now I can see it would-n'ta withered in the cold air if I'd popped it out of my mouth. So, maybe it was out of habit. Or respect. Whatever. There I was crouching with his dick in my mouth and hoping he'd figure out what I wanted him to do next.

Maybe it was the luck of the first date, but he did. He squatted down till he could sit on the edge of the futon. He laid back. All this time, I was still casually blowing him and waiting. He hadn't been on his back long before he was tweaking a nipple real hard and sliding his other hand down his heaving belly toward my head and his dick and his cunt. He stopped for one rough tug on my head to remind me to keep up the pace. And then, it was under the band of the dildo harness. You know, the leather jockstrap.

He grunted. Low. He moaned. Lower. He snorted. He sighed. Still, he was a long way from orgasm. But he musta been getting hard under there. Or flushed. Whatever he called it. I didn't care. I just knew each loud breath was a good sign. So I started "unnhing" again. I wasn't hard or anything. Walt wasn't even touching me. I was doing it cuz I thought if we're both making noises he won't hear me popping his harness open.

Walt told me later that some have velcro fastners. Thank God his didn't. Velcro makes such a fuckin' racket. I never woulda surprised him. Well, I think I surprised him. Hell, only he knows for sure.

Of course, I wasn't thinking any of this then. I was just doing.

Snap. One down. I wasn't sucking his cock anymore. Just pushing on it so he'd think I was. *Snap.* Two down. I needed to get the dick out of the way now. I thought of pulling the harness up and over it. But I woulda had to yank the back side of it down and out through his butt crack first.

Not too subtle.

So I crawled up onto the futon alongside Walt. Then I tilted the dildo at an angle and pulled real gentle. You know like in the "Grinch Who Stole Christmas" when he takes the candy canes from the sleeping babies. And Walt didn't notice either. And me, all I was thinking was that I had to see his cunt. I had to touch it. With my hands. Hell, with my face. I don't know why, except, like I said before, I had to feel him getting it up for me.

I pulled back the leather triangle. And there it was. The first cunt I'd ever seen. Honest. Its lips were big, fat, wet, and pink—real pink. The pink of bubblegum. Not that hard, dry pink of Bazooka Joe, but the soft, squishy pink of Bubblicious—before you bite into it.

I watched his fingers to find the clit. And there it was, under this thing that looked like the awning on some fancy apartment building. A little dick head with wings, no bigger than a thumb or a Vienna sausage, you know, a cocktail weinie. Honest. I'm not trying to be mean. That's just what I thought of first. I didn't think it looked gross. Just kinda weird, kinda different, kinda cute.

"Well, boy, whatdya think? Too small fer ya."

For a sec, I thought it was my dad talking to me about some fish. Or me. *Why is size such a big fuckin' deal?*

"Well, boy." A hand yanked hard on my hair. I snapped out of my head. This wasn't my dad. He never touched me.

"Hey," the hand let go and slapped my head, "you asleep?"

"No, sir. It's no runt, sir."

"That ain't no pig yer talkin' about. That's my dick, boy." The hand rubbed the top of my head, mussing with my hair. "Be more respectful."

"Yes, sir."

"Well, go on now. You kin touch it, boy."

You'd think touching a dick that was a clit woulda been weird to me. But it wasn't. I wasn't even thinking that. I wanted to know what it felt like. What

I didn't get was why Walt was talking now like Festus on *Gunsmoke*. You know, some old prospector or something. I guess cuz it made his voice sound deep. Like Darth Vader's. It was odd but hot.

Whatever, I sighed to myself.

Walt grabbed hold of my dick. He was sliding his thumb up the underbelly of my dick. "Ah, fuck," I said out loud. The thumb had found that magic spot right were the dick meets the dickhead.

Then he let go so I could scooch down. I put my face in and it felt like his cunt was giving me a big, slobbery kiss. My cheeks were sticky, but I kept going. I puckered and aimed my lips for where I thought I'd seen it last. I was gonna try and get it all in my mouth with one suck. *Won't Walt be impressed with his pussy-eating virgin.*

"Fuck!" He grabbed me by the back of the head and yanked me out. "Listen, boy. I may call it a dick and you may think it's a dick. But it ain't just like *your* dick. So don't be getting all riled up to tug at it like it's your teenage peter in a circle jerk."

"I'm sorry," I mumbled.

Good thing it was dark. I was blushing. I felt so dumb.

"First rule, tonight, no fingers. We'll work up to those." I suddenly got excited. He was already talking about a second date.

"Next rule, use your tongue. But think of my dick as a thousand times more sensitive than either of your nipples." He gave both a hard twist and I jumped. "Okay?"

"Okay."

"And five hundred times more sensitive than your dick." He stroked the underside of my dickhead lightly and I shook. "That's more like it."

I sighed and gave him this real goofy grin. *God, I'm such a 'tard.*

"Now, kiss me." I did. I went all out. *What the hell*, I figured. Might as well let him know that when I kiss I like to get my face wet and my lips sore. Minutes, maybe hours, later, he pulled out for air.

"You're a fuckin' good kisser," he gasped. "Now, do it again." I leaned in and bumped my lips against his finger. "But this time, my tongue is my dick."

I know my eyes bugged this time. Walt just laughed. "Geez, that sounded way too much like a paper I wrote in school." I think *he* was blushing. "Okay, I want you to *pretend* my tongue is my dick. And I want you to use your tongue to get it off."

I almost had "but" out of my mouth.

"Don't worry," he said. "I'll do a little old-fashioned operant conditioning to let you know when you're doing it just right. Trust me. Now, close your eyes." I couldn't even blink. "Trust me. Close your eyes and feel the force, Luke." I laughed.

"Feel it." Walt rubbed his thumb beneath my dickhead. I closed my eyes. "Kiss me." I barely had a chance to really mush lips or even get them wet when he goes and shoves his tongue into my mouth. *So much for fuckin' foreplay.*

I wasn't ready. I just poked his tongue with mine. Then his thumb pushed down from my piss slit. I poked it again. The pressure grew less. So I touched it lightly. The thumb was gone. *Fine.* I jabbed it from underneath. He left my dick waving in the air—alone. *Oh-kay.*

I was getting pissed, and panicked. *Whaddaido?* Then an idea.

I pulled my lips back from his tongue until I sucked only the tip. Walt stroked my dick. I kept sucking. Stroke. I prodded his tongue with as much careful force as he was using to rub my cockhead. Stroke. Then I got creative. I lapped at its underbelly as it curled away from me. I kept at it. And Walt repaid me by rubbing his thumb in circles below. I was gonna "unnh." His tongue pulled away.

"Good. Now git down there and suck my dick, boy." A final flick of his thumb, as if he hoped to get a spark from my own dick.

I knelt into his cunt.

"Close your eyes."

I looked up.

"Close'em." I did. "Follow your instincts. Follow the heat." I inched closer. "Remember what I've taught you, Luke, and someday you may just become half the Jedi pussy-eater your sister Leia is."

I opened my eyes and gave him a look that said, "You are *so* weird." Of course, the longer I stared the more it said, "You are so weird, but *so* hot."

Walt was grinning back. He gave my hair a yank. "Okay. Close'em."

I leaned in toward the heat. The smell. Somewhere between micro-brewed beer and musk deodorant in a really sweaty armpit.

"Now lick my lips. Go on." A few mouthfuls of hair and then I touched skin. "Now, suck my dick, boy."

I kept expecting to taste salt. You know how precum a lot of times tastes like when you drink a plain margarita and the rim's all crusty and you take a sip and all you get is that sting of salt with a little tequila.

That didn't happen.

And I thought the first kiss from his cunt was wet! He drooled on the bridge of my nose, then all over my cheeks as I pushed my face in. I stuck my tongue out slowly into the hot, sticky-sweet darkness. Walt's dick didn't leap out to greet me like it had in his other mouth. I was gonna have to dig deeper. So I stretched my tongue till it bumped up against a hard, hot rock of flesh that wouldn't budge. But it sure did shiver. Then Walt's whole body, wrapped around my head, did the same. I thought he was trying to twist my head off with his thighs. *Captain, I believe we've just made first contact.*

I brought my tongue back to his clit. I pushed against what had to be the clithead. A steady pressure. Then pulled away. Then back, but longer. Walt shuddered. *Now,* I thought, *time for the fancy stuff.* I did an under-belly lap. Then again. Then a side-swipe. I knew I was doing something right 'cuz I couldn't hear a thing, his legs were crushing into both sides of my head *that* hard.

I had to breathe soon. So I flicked my tongue against the tip a few times. He dug his back into the futon and squirmed. His legs opened and I lifted my face out of his crotch long enough to gulp down some air and hear him grunt, "*All things please the soul, but these please the soul well.*"

It may not taste like spunk, but cunt juice cools about as quick. Before my face could harden into a smile, I plunged back down. I got into a real pussy-eating rhythm after a while. Some slow and steady tonguing followed by spurts of tongue acrobatics. Not that different from cock-sucking really. And I didn't hate it or anything. It's just after a while I got bored. My tongue can only feel so much. It was time to send in my hyper-sensitive probe. Just one thing—Walt had originally thought he was gonna fuck me. Now I had to let him know, real nice, that there'd been a *temporary* change in plans.

I dragged the tip of my tongue across his clit. I lifted my head and said, "Fuck."

"Fuck," Walt groaned.

"I wanna fuck you." I dragged my tongue back over the clit. It was getting so hard I was afraid it might pop.

"Fuck."

"I wanna fuck you." I wriggled my tongue against the head.

"Fuck," he grunted. I kept on flicking my tongue. "Fuck me." Man, I've seen guys with sensitive dickheads, but…if Walt had had balls, they'da been blue by now.

I pulled up leaving his cute, little dick pointing into the cold, cold air. Then I really startled him.

"I said I wanna fuck *you*." I bent down and gave it a few laps of my tongue like a cat. "Right now. *Here*." I lapped one more time, hoping."I've never done it before."

He pushed my head away and sat up. "Fucked a man?" He sounded nervous, hurt. I shook my head. "Oh, a pussy."

"Yeah. A real man pussy."

"A what?!"

"You know. Like in the personals. A man pussy."

"Asshole," he said, real serious.

"Huh?" I said back, real casual, but I was so scared I'd pissed him off.

"They mean asshole."

"I'll fuck you there if you want. But I'd really like to fuck you in your man pussy. Then you can fuck me anywhere." He laughed, then grew quiet as I put his hand beneath the super-swollen head of my cock. He gripped it hard till a bubble of precum popped out of my piss-hole. My dick head was red, bright red.

"Okay, but to get my cunt really wet, I need a lot of tit torture."

"Sure," I said. I couldn't wait to chew more on his soft, thick, hairy tits. I leaned forward. My chest bumped up against the palm of his hand.

"Oh, no, boy. Not mine. Yours."

He shoved both his hands into my armpits and heaved. In one move, he dragged my body up along his legs and held me in mid-air like a baby and plopped me down so I was riding his lap. He bent his head toward my nipples, but there was no way he was ever gonna reach them unless he had the tongue of a giraffe. The hands were back and I was hovering. This time I was lowered till I was on my knees, straddling his thighs.

"Much, much better," he said. *Yeah, for you*, I thought. I was totally naked with my balls dangling in the wind.

It wasn't that cold, for a San Francisco night, but I was shivering anyway. Suddenly, I felt the warm weight of his palms pressing into each of my asscheeks. He pulled me toward his mouth.

Okay, my nipples are nowhere near as big as Walt's. But they ain't the size of dimes either. Or "innies." But it still took him a few tries to get one snug between his teeth.

He bit, then licked the sting away. Another longer, sharper bite. Again. I sucked in my breath. He snorted back. I think he was laughing. He moved over to slurp on the other nipple. And hard. So hard I started to freak he was gonna draw milk or blood out of it.

Then the heat was gone. The pressure was gone. Walt was reaching for his pants. He swung for something glinting in the shadows. A chain. *Probably to his wallet*, I thought. *What's he want with that? Condoms? I've got plenty of those.* He tugged and it slithered out of its nest in the jean's pocket. It crashed hard on the floor. It wasn't a wallet. It looked more like two high-tech clothespins held together by a bicycle chain. I flinched from the back of my scalp to the balls of my toes. Tit clamps! They rattled as he dragged them across the floor. The heat rolled back toward me.

"*I am the poet of the Body and I am the poet of the Soul.*" His broad tongue squashed one nipple then another. "*The pleasures of heaven are with me....*" He sucked in what I thought was my whole right pec, holding it between his lips while his tongue poked my aching nipple. I was wriggling. Then he did it all over again to my left tit. I was really squirming and sighing now. He pulled away and his spit grew cold and my nipples harder. Like goose bumps. *"(A)nd the pains of hell are with me,"* he hissed. Then I did. Something thick, heavy, bit into my nipples. Both of them. Not like a pinch. Not like teeth. Heavier. And it didn't let go. *"The first I graft and increase upon myself, the latter I translate into a new tongue."* He got his tongue up under one nipple wetting it. It was one hot ache. I thought there'd be steam. Then he dragged his stinging beard over my tightening, shaking skin to the other.

At some point, he musta stopped again to talk. "Boy, you're getting yer Uncle Walt real wet." He yanked the chain. My chest burned. "Now it's yer turn."

He wrapped his fingers slowly around the chain and pulled it toward him. The pressure built, I threw myself ahead of it and landed on his face. Our tongues were pushing, then slipping in sync with the moving of his fingers between my legs. He pushed my dickhead into the tight hat of a condom. My skin was hot and dry while the latex was cool and wet. He tugged and rolled it down my boner. In my head, I kept jumping back from my tongue to my dick.

Somewhere I heard what sounded like a baby with the runs. He was getting the bottle by my bed to cough up some lube. I kept kissing as he greased up my dick. I felt that odd, solid cold of the lube where the condom ran out and my skin started.

He guided me between his legs. I sank in. Slowly. The lips of his cunt—warmer and softer and wetter than any mouth that had ever blown my dick—were rising up on both sides to pull me deeper. He slapped my butt and pushed me in all the way. I pulled out and the warmth fell away. I pushed back and it thickened against my cock.

I wanted to start out slow. Go so far, so fast. Let my hips keep time. Really get into feeling my butt tighten then relax. Rock on my hips. Each thrust I'd dig a little deeper. I wanted to work up to slamming his cunt with the full length of my cock. You know, do his man pussy just like I like having mine done.

And it did start out that way. But Walt was up to something. He didn't sigh or groan or snort. He just smiled that cat smile. And it got wider and wider as I began to get a rhythm.

I was thrusting and thrusting and thrusting. The sweat was welling up at my hairline. Then the first trickle down my back, then my forehead. I was getting a pretty good fuck going, I thought. But Walt just smiled and looked so fuckin' content, so calm. Like he was coming onto X or something.

I was startled, but relieved, when he spoke.

"*Ebb stung by the flow…*" I closed my eyes. I was trying to feel the fuck, shut out the words. "*(A)nd flow stung by the ebb, love-flesh swelling…*" Then, outta nowhere, Walt arches his back, his belly, up, and I thrust down—*bam*—to the bone under my bush. I gasped, but Walt kept on talking. "*(A)nd deliciously aching…*" I heard his back hit the futon. At least the bed was groaning. "*Limitless…,*" his fingers dug into my ass, "*limpid jets of love…,*" and pushed me and my dick as far into him as we could go together. "*(H)ot and enormous…,*" he squeezed my hips with his palms, "*…quivering jelly of love…,*" and almost popped me back out, "*…white-blow…,*" only to push me down again and pull me out again. "*(A)nd delirious juice…,*" he blurted as he slapped my ass down into him.

Now I was pumping. Really pumping. It sounds stupid, but, at that moment, I *am* my dick. And I think I'm banging the hell out of Walt's cunt when he goes and really does it.

"What's that grimace fer, boy." He was panting. "Ain'tcha having fun?"

I grunted this deep wild moan. And bared my teeth. I was trying to smile. I think.

"C'mon, boy. Whoop it up." He reached toward me, my chest, and ripped the tit clamps off with one jerk.

I was stung. The air was cold. It felt like a sharp slap. The jab of a needle. Then stinging hot. Like a sleeping foot waking up in one second. Burning. Breaking out in a cold sweat. I was choking. Couldn't swallow. I'd forgot how to breathe. I couldn't get air in or my scream out. Then Walt smacked my butt and I coughed it up. And somehow, I was able to holler and fuck at the same time. I was mad. Raging. I was gonna bang him till he broke in half.

Well, that's what I was shouting. Walt was getting pretty red-faced himself. And gushing sweat. Looked like he was gonna have a baby or something.

I almost jumped out of him when he reached down toward his cunt. I thought he was gonna grab my dick and get me to fuck him even harder. But, without looking, he stopped at his clit. He must have felt the heat. Hell, I could feel its heat. And it was as red as the end of a cigarette.

I was still huffing and puffing. Squinting all my tits' pain into the pounding of my dick. And I was gonna make sure he felt every inch of it. But I was also on auto-fuck. Kinda. Watching his hands, hearing his voice.

"Bridegroom night of love..." He was almost barking the words out. *"(W)orking surely and softly..."* He pressed his finger down onto his clit and rubbed a circle 'round the head. *"(I)nto the prostrate dawn,..."* He never let the finger up. He was groaning now. *"Undulating into the willing...,"* he dragged his finger up the underbelly, *"and yielding day,..."* He pushed his finger back down. *"Lost in the cleave of the clasping..."* He ground his finger 'round and 'round and mashed it up and down. If that had been my dickhead I woulda come by now and hard. Hit the ceiling even. But Walt kept panting out more words. *"(A)nd sweet-flesh'd day."*

Under the flickering of his lids, I could tell his eyes were rolling. Like a mad dog. And all this show was getting my slip-'n-sliding dick so stiff I knew if I didn't come soon it was gonna snap.

"Ah, fuck." Another Waltquake had begun. This was gonna be The Big One. "Ah, fuck." The bed was rocking and creaking. He was thrusting his hips as high as he could and lifting me with him. "Sweet...fucking...day!"

And then, I think I'm still pumping. But I'm not. It's Walt. His pussy's yanking on my dick. I don't mean squeezing like some virgin butthole. I mean like a hand. A big man's hand. That does it. I shoot. And shoot and shoot. And his cunt keeps on squeezing all the cum out of my dick. Like so much so that any part of me that isn't coming is freaking the condom's gonna explode. Next my arms are wobbling like some newborn colt's legs. Then they finally give way and I fall onto Walt's chest, into Walt's arms.

• • •

I was so tired I couldn't open my eyes. The spit kept hitting my face. It wouldn't stop. Then it was gone. Walt had stepped in front of the showerhead. The water made an even louder hiss against his back.

"Wake up, sleepyhead." Water plinked here and there against my chest as Walt bent down to my face and kissed each eye. He pushed his lips up against mine till he'd opened them and coaxed out my tongue.

I heard his hands fumbling behind me in the shower caddy. I know, I know. We had it on the wrong side. Alex wanted it opposite the showerhead. And it made sense cuz almost everything in it was his. I should have said something to Walt when I heard this loud, farty squirt and felt the loofah sponge on my back. *Man, is Alex gonna be pissed.*

Then wham. The sponge was pressed up under my balls. I almost jumped into Walt's arms. No way was I gonna tell Alex now. Walt rubbed it real gentle all over my crotch. Pushing my dick away from my balls and my balls away from my dick.

All of a sudden, I felt like I was sitting on the sponge. Kinda. We'd been kissing this whole time so I was living in my mouth at that moment. But I was pretty sure he was washing his way back to my asshole. And I was totally sure that if he planned to shove that sponge any farther, he was gonna have to lift me up or come in through the back door.

"Gotta gitcha clean, boy, before I kin gitcha dirty. And I like to git mighty dirty when I fuck."

Okay. It wasn't Walt Whitman. But it was getting me hot.

I inched closer to the heat of his body. I could feel the steam. I knew I was close. I leaned in. Bingo. Even with my eyes closed, I could find his tits. I nudged and rubbed till my head was happily between both.

Another one of those sick, farty squirts. My ass was gonna be awash in Alex's European body gel. *Shit. I ain't stopping this. I'll buy him a new one tomorrow. I can't believe he pays fifteen fuckin' dollars….*

"*We two boys together clinging,*" Walt said over the hiss as he began to soap my butt. "*We two boys together clinging,/ One the other never leaving….*"

I kept my eyes closed and let my hands slide down his tree-trunk of a back till I could dig my hands into his ass. I pulled us together as tight as I could. Walt chuckled and kept murmuring, kept soaping my crack. And I kept repeating, "*We two boys together clinging,/ One the other never leaving....*"

Foucault's Pendulous...

for Peter Limnios

had the dream again. The dream I have every night. And maybe this really was the last time. That's what he said: it would be the last. But, God, I hope not. Not after last night.

The dream always begins with utter darkness. Not just the dark of night in some huge city where the buildings blot out the stars. Not just the dark of the earth above this basement in a basement where I always awaken. No, it is the dark that is without light, a dark so dark it is no longer dark. It is the void...

Until, as always, someone lets there be light.

In this case, lights. Two caged light bulbs.

As my eyes wobble into focus, I'm sure I've died and gone to paradise. I'm in the secret VIP playroom of the Mineshaft—Valhalla to a race of warrior gods who will never walk the face of the earth again. God, just thinking about it now and my dick is as tall and hard as the World Tree.

I guess, before this dream gets any weirder, I should use this moment of clarity to contextualize this story's dreamer, i.e., me.

I'm afraid I can't use my real name in case anyone on my thesis committee reads this. I can't even describe myself. Sorry. I'd never get lucky again at another MLA conference if I did. What I can say is that I'm working on my doctorate in comparative literature. And that I've rather cleverly used both my BAs in Religion and Philosophy and all my field research at rest stops throughout the tri-state area of Indiana, Ohio, and Kentucky to write my master's thesis on the queerly coded semiotics within the Odin saga. I know what you're thinking: the myth cycle of the cruisy area is pretty out there for a thesis. Still, here I am at Columbia.

Here *I am* in New York.

In my dream, however, I'm in the New York I've always longed to visit. The New York that has almost been eaten away, not by the city's billions of rats, mind you, but by a single mouse. The billionaire mouse that ate Times Square.

In my dream, it will always be 1977.

The bunker smells of beery urine mixed with Crisco mixed with poppers mixed with the thick, snuffed-out candle smell of spunk. It is one vast crotch, bathed in all these unguents and unwashed for a week and a day, overripe and ready to fall.

I pretend that the enormous rectangle of glistening black leather I'm manacled to is the top sheet from Mr. Benson's bed and I'm his newest slave. I've run away and wait for him to find me here. 'Please, Sir,' I whisper as my asshole gasps and gasps from the removal of the latest fist attached to the latest forearm the size of Popeye's. 'I am so unworthy, Sir. Please come and reclaim your property. Don't let that square-jawed, steely-eyed neo-Nazi abduct me and sell me to your age's wicked stereotype of the sex-crazed Arab sheik. I long only to be a white slave to you, Sir.'

I stop, swallowing my next words. I sense, somehow, a new presence. I crane my neck. My head aches from the poppers which only makes the music—once again they're playing KC and the Sunshine Band's "I'm Your Boogie Man"—louder and louder. I look toward the only other light in the room besides the one above, highlighting my body. It spotlights the doorway. In it, there stands a tall, thin man in a very odd leather outfit.

He wears a black leather replica of a herringbone-patterned tweed suit and a white leather turtleneck. His eyes are two squares of light. Glasses. On his head, the standard issue leather bike cap. He takes it off as he enters the room. It seems the gentleman handballer has arrived.

As he moves closer, I realize he's also wearing a black leather toupee. *How odd*, I think. He doffs the wig and then the silver-studded black leather scales fall from my eyes.

It's Him! *Michel, ma belle.*

He steps to the edge of the sling. My asshole and I shudder. He speaks.

Something is wrong. I know he is speaking French and I know, up until this moment, that I have been fluent in French. But he's speaking now and I can't understand a word. I strain to listen as if my ears are plugged thick with wax. I try to crane my neck even further so I'm closer to his mouth. I hear nothing except the blood gurgling along the veins in my temple. That and Rod Stewart's "Tonight's the Night."

I must appear very bewildered for he stops and looks into my eyes for the first time, looks over my entire body for the first time. He commences anew, and this time I know I look like a strait-jacketed inmate in a cell at Bedlam rather than an academic bound to a sling in the Mineshaft's cellar. For this time when he speaks, words—honest-to-God words—appear, like subtitles, before him.

They spell themselves out across his chest and I read them. And, as I read them, they break into a smoke of letters that encircles his head and then trail off, broken, around the room, bumping against the ceiling and into the corners.

I squint. Despite the ringing bells the poppers have set off in my skull, despite the off-key voices singing along to "Don't Leave Me This Way," I concentrate. I see only the words and, finally, I hear them.

Monsieur Foucault has come tonight to plead with me. *He* is pleading with *me*. It is urgent, he begs, that I stop the endless references to him in every discourse, every journal article, every personal ad, every phone message. It is imperative that I stop the endless troubling of his shade with phallocentric masturbatory reveries like this one.

I look up at his face. His mouth is a thick line. A vein, like a small garden snake, wriggles beneath the skin of his forehead. His cheeks are red and sunken like the hollow of a brightly painted bowl. I say I am sorry. Truly, *I am* very sorry.

The ends of his mouth slump. He sighs. He pities me, he says, but tonight it is I who must pity him. I have no idea, he chastens me without even having to wag a finger, what my Foucault-centric obsession is doing to his death. Here he had planned to enjoy several decentered, yet industrious centuries, as a professor in the Academie de l'Elysée.

Yes, he reads my eyes now as I've been reading his chest, it is *that* Elysium, the true Champs Elysée—that supposed paradise where he is now haunted by the virilizing dreams of the living. And, like ghosts here, you, he points to me, and your kind shadow me there. The reddening snake on his forehead has begun to dance. I am ruining his death, he shouts.

De Sade, at the mere sight of him and his following flock of boyish ghosts, laughs so hard now that he can no longer enjoy a quiet night of whist and brandy cordials with the Divine Marquis and the Borgias, Cesare and Lucrezia. And Bataille and Nietzsche, whenever they pass him on another of their peripatetic conversations, no longer stop to invite him to walk the gardens with them. Even the American, John Preston, he laments, refuses to fuck him because he feels it's demeaning to fist a man whose legend valorizes the desire-driven and genitalized jerk-off fantasies of so many twenty-something post-gay geekoids like me.

Suddenly the anger, the blood, the life drain from his face. I fear he will cry, perhaps even sob. Elton John is now singing "Love Lies Bleeding." Instead, he raises himself up to his full height and asks, if he were to pleasure me once, would I swear never to dream of him again.

I nod so vigorously the leather sheet flaps beneath me and the chains twist as if they were holding up a child spinning in his swing.

He slips an arm from his jacket; hands pull it into the shadows. He removes his glasses; more hands take them. He raises his arms; even more hands gently tug the white leather turtleneck up his torso and across his sharp Gallic chin, cheeks, nose and over his large cranial dome, as smooth and milky white as china from Limoges.

I choke when I see the T-shirt he's wearing. It's a classic wife-beater. No sleeves. No collar. A reminder perhaps of his solidarity with the workers of the world. But in the center of his chest is emblazoned a child's drawing of a mustachioed man and the slogan: Hello Nietzsche. I pause and read it again. That's actually when I choke.

It's Nietzsche. It's Nietzsche with a shock of black hair, two black button eyes, a huge mustache that looks as if a black Pekingese crawled in under his nose and died, and, oddest of all, this cartoon Nietzsche is smiling—no, beaming.

My choking finally dies down to several coughs and a sputter when a huge blue and white drum of Crisco on a dolly as red as any hanky in the room is wheeled in and placed just beneath Nietzsche's lips. The hands retreat. Now Foucault himself smiles.

He dips the tips of his fingers in the vat of vegetarian lard as if it were a fingerbowl. He dabs the Crisco onto his face with the cold calm of a drag queen preparing to remove her makeup and return to the drab world of strip malls and minivans. He grabs a fistful and then another. He lathers it on. In minutes, I no longer recognize my Michel. His head is an egg plastered with white cake frosting.

If he has done this to repulse me, he's failed. No matter what beastly form he assumes, I know what beauty lies below. For below the skin, the thick cartilage and muscle, the hard bone, there it will be: his brain, gray like a rainy April morning over the Champs Elysée, with synapses sparking, showering the dark crevices with brilliant colors, more magnificent than any nighttime spectacle of fireworks and lasers above the Arc de Triomphe on Bastille Day.

My swelling dick rolls back and forth on its warm rug of pubic hairs. It is a Thirties starlet writhing on a circle of black satin sheets, forever captured in the retina of the camera's eye. We luxuriate in our dreams, my dick and I, until my dick jumps. Now I jump. Warm, sticky hands pull at the lips of my still-gaping hole. I assume they're his hands until another pair pushes at the mouth of my ass then another pair and another pair. A final pair shoves itself up inside me like an enormous dildo.

By now, my pelvis should have snapped like a wishbone. It doesn't. My hole, my ass, my cock, my thighs, my belly all grow warmer. Perhaps the Crisco is really a topical anesthetic or, in the evening's earlier flurry of fists, an epidural was administered that I have, contrary to all laws of nature, forgotten.

I don't know; I don't care. All I feel is the pulsing of my sphincters—two warm rubbery bands holding together the bundle of forearms. Then, slowly, the clasped hands bud within me. A crack. I feel the shift and the wet heat of what I can only imagine to be the Crisco melting out of the blossoming hands.

I want to open my eyes. I want to see him, see all the others. But I can't move; the hands around my asshole, within my asshole, bind me to the sling. I only "see" the melting pad of butter-flavored Crisco that is the vibrating yellow of the light beyond my eyelids.

I am growing sickly dizzy. The theme from *Star Wars* is now being played for the third time. Its chemical equivalent, a smell like an exploding drug lab, punches me in the left and then right nostril. I try to guess how many pairs of hands are swinging the little vial of poppers under my nose. My sinuses rip open and then my brain.

My head is empty; my body is full…

My entrails are falling! I'm shitting all my intestines! I shriek, out loud, or so I think. Another pair of hands strokes my throbbing forehead and temples. I'm panting. I'm sobbing. I'm empty. The flower has been plucked; the arms have left me.

I gasp. Four, ten, twenty hands push at my hole. Another drug lab explodes in my face. The big ball pushes against whatever is left of my boyish pucker. I want to faint. To scream. To howl.

But I no longer think. I am remembering these words only now as I tell this. At that moment, I have no mind.

Yet, my decentered self knows that these are not hands. Too smooth. They lack the odd-shaped knobs of knuckles or bony points of fingers or the blunt knives of fingernails. I know it is *his* head. He is crowning within me.

I am breath. I breathe in and swallow more of his hard, warm, stinging skull. I breathe out and hold him in my ass's embrace. I breathe in and my bones break and my skin tears. I breathe out and my blood aches and my nerves weep. I breathe in. I breathe out. I breathe in…

I scream and I scream and I scream. The pride of every great French profile jabs the first, then the second, burning rings of fire that were once my sphincters. The nose, his nose, drags closer and closer to my prostate.

His head stops. I will my body to suck in more. More. More. No luck. But, some part of me knows, if I am patient, I will get lucky, more lucky than I have ever been or will be.

For he has not finished with me. He presses his face deep into the walls of my rectum, until his beautiful big nose pokes into my prostate. He rubs his nose once. Every hair on my body gets hard. He rubs his nose again. I shudder. My spine is a wave of hot gelatin.

He rubs his nose one last time and I sing. An original aria to bring the opera queens in the stalls and troughs and slings several stories above us to their feet. Garbled bits of "La Marseillaise," the "Internationale," Rita Coolidge's "(Your Love is Lifting Me) Higher and Higher," an improvisational Gregorian chant, and the "Ode to Joy" from Beethoven's Ninth Symphony.

And deep within, I hear something. No, it is someone. My Michel! He is speaking within me. There is discourse even in our intercourse! I draw in the air around me to sing my aria's final refrain and then I realize he is singing. *He* is singing with *me*. I swear I hear "…did I ever tell you I'm your hero? I am the subtext beneath your sling."

I bellow triumphantly, my alveoli bursting and my lungs tattering, "I am spread atop the cockhead of God!"

For the encore, there is only one thing left to do: I shoot. But not the usual spunk that looks like several strands of white Sillee-String™. No. This time I come words. His words. Some of my favorites of his favorites. I clench and spurt out *panopticon*. My balls throb. Then my whole dick sneezes out *psychologico-medical armature* and I'm grunting for breath. A final pop. *The desexualization {i.e., the degenitalization} of pleasure.* I pass out.

When I wake, his words are brittle and stuck to the hairs of my chest. I look into the shadows, into the light for him. He's gone…

Until tonight, I pray.

Forgive me, mon seigneur. I did not know how impossible last night's oath would be to keep. Please, Michel, come soon.

I'm sorry, my beloved brain, but now I only love you more.

See Dick Deconstruct

for Richard Labonté

I'm thinking of an image. It's from one of those stories where Our Father throws Lucifer out of the house for good. I can't remember which.

Maybe *Faust*.

Maybe *Paradise Lost*. It doesn't matter. All I remember really is the image.

It's of the future Satan sitting among us and forever looking back toward the one place to which he would never be able to return. And this, of course, leads to more stories. Ones where, to soften the pain of remembrance, The Fallen One tries to stick it to The Man by sticking it to one of The Man's favorites.

Think Job. Think Jesus.

In a way, this is one of those stories.

Sort of.

I have no idea what The Man or any other god thinks about my little boy. But I do know that before we met he was fast becoming a darling of the Academe. Not any just any old university. The Academe—site of all discourse and inquiry located in that great metanarrative in the sky.

I'd seen his name several times before he told it to me that night. He'd been a contributor to various anthologies. Ones with glossy covers in garish colors drawn on a computer. Covers that promise a mondo-pomo-homo-a-go-go world within. Then you turn the page. Instead it is only a book filled with straggling bands of menacing, jibbering words from the clans Tion or Ize. Words which must wander those pages forever at war—sometimes even with their own in the same sentence. Leaving behind a field of white, strewn with participles dangling, dying.

To be honest, I don't know if it was just dumb luck or synchronicity that led me to answer his personal. And, after what I did to him our first night, he's the one who'll want to dig up Jung and ask him whom or what to thank. I merely made the most of a moment.

His personal? Something about a Queer, White Dork, this weight and that height, goatee and glasses. Has a hard spot for hairy, horny daddies. Grooves on the transgressive in theory and praxis. Then the standard blah, blah, blah.

I had no plans for what we'd do if things clicked. Not even after I recognized QWD's name. My inspiration came only after he offered me a cigarette.

I smiled and shook my head. His brand, not his offer, had surprised me. American Spirit. This boy had spent a lot of his time and someone's money redecorating his mind in early '70s French cultural critique. I'd expected Gitanes. Or maybe, in the down-and-dirty spirit of Genet, that he'd have rolled his own. But no, he smoked American Spirit—filtered. He'd been out here on our brittle bit of the Rim of Fire longer than I'd thought.

He lit up. A real feat since we were sitting outside this cafe on Market Street. That shouldn't mean anything to you unless you've been to San Francisco in the summer. It was late afternoon when we put our first pints on the table. And a late summer afternoon in San Francisco means that the fog flying in over Twin Peaks uses Market Street as its landing strip.

So as gust after gust touched down, he lit up. On the third try. And, by then, he was curled so tightly around the cigarette he looked like a foetus hugging its heart.

He sucked a few times on the burning paper and then spoke. I had the masculine signifiers he wanted—bulk, a beard—or so he said. But, he added, I was smaller than the men he'd been with before. And I thought, *Yes, I am small; beware the small.*

I know. I know. You probably don't give a shit what we said or what I look like. You only want me to describe my dick and what it did. I won't. Call me a tease, but we both know one man's dick is another man's dink is another man's dong. Besides, I'd rather give your puny little imagination a workout. So maybe I have one. Maybe I don't.

The boy and I kept talking. Through several more beers, cigarettes, a course of spring rolls and pad Thai, then along the streets and up the stairs to my apartment and down the hall to my bedroom.

We stopped beside my bed. I put one of my short, thick fingers to his lips. I stepped back. "Strip."

He nearly beamed. Quickly, he gripped the bottom of his terrycloth shirt of many colors and yanked it over his head and down his arms. His nipples stood out on the pale skin. Two dark dots. Alternating patches of muscle and bone. All strung together by a few hairs running from his breastbone to the rim of his shorts. He knelt and unlaced his Airwalks. They'd been the color of wet sand, but in the unsteady light of the room's candles I could barely see the whites of their laces or his socks. He put them all against the wall and returned to the spot beside my bed. He unbuttoned his shorts, let them drop, stepped out of one leg and, with his foot in the other, kicked them over toward his shoes. I could forgive this smiling eagerness to please as a bit of nervous excess, but that kick smacked to me of precociousness. My suspicion was confirmed when he tried to lock eyes with me as he tugged his white cotton briefs down over his budding cock and then his thighs. He had to look down once he got to his knees. As soon as his underwear was at his ankles, he raised his back so I could get a good view of his dick. It was long and fat like an animal's snout. It flopped against his balls while he shook one, then another, foot free.

It'll do, I thought.

I looked up and met his eyes. "It's interesting how it's often the choices made with the least thought that carry the most damning consequences." He blinked. "Like your high kick. Very precious. I don't like precious." His eyes widened. "Maybe I should just send you home...." He blurted out something. The beginning of a plea. I jerked my right index finger to my lips. He swallowed a paragraph of yet-to-be-spoken words.

"What—no one's ever spoken to you in the conditional? I said 'maybe.' I said 'should.' You'll stay as long as I want you to stay. And that might even be the whole night if—if you obey my one rule: you may speak; but each sentence may have only three words; and each word may have only one syllable. Otherwise, you can jabber away at the cab driver on your way home. Agreed?" He nodded. "Are you sure you don't need me to diaper that mouth with a gag?" He shook his head so hard his balls swung from thigh to thigh.

Always the student, I thought, *craving tests. Good, we'll begin with the hardest one first.* So, I decided to take a few long minutes and bind him tight with the one thing I knew he feared most—silence.

It began when my face stiffened into a stare. He smiled nervously for the first few seconds. I think it was a minute before I even blinked. By then, his lips had filled in the gash of teeth. We listened to our breathing. To the sputtering of the candles. Finally, I turned and walked out of the room. I left him alone in the squirming shadows. It would be three, maybe five, minutes more before I'd return with a wad of pink fabric tucked in my right fist.

I tossed it toward his feet. The wad fluttered up into the air and blossomed into a pair of pink silk panties, a size 5 women's, a snug fit even with his narrow hips. The one-petaled flower fell fast to the ground. "Put them on."

He crouched to pick them up. He fumbled trying to get the crotch going the right direction. He stepped out of one leg and turned the material around the pole of his other. The panties slipped up his calves and over his knees. Then, he had to tug slowly up along his slim thighs, over the ass I'd yet to see, and around his resistant cock. The waist band snapped at his hips and the dick was plastered against the right side of his pelvis. He looked up. Either the material chafed or he was pantomiming defiance. I didn't care.

"Take off your glasses."

He nearly chirped. Something about no longer being able to see.

"What's to see?"

I walked up to him, pulling a strip of leather out of my back pocket. I let it hang out of my right hand, though I doubt he could see this. I got behind him and lifted it above my head, then over his. I tied it around his eyes. I stepped back in front of him. As I pressed my hands close to his eyes to adjust the blindfold, I could smell his face. It was bitter with smoke and fear. I lingered long enough for his cold skin to feel the warmth from my breath.

I moved away. "You've talked a lot tonight. Most of it, I enjoyed. In fact, by dinner, I felt like I was back in school. Shooting the shit at three in the morning with a paper due at ten." I paused to cross the room and return with my butterfly knife.

"I just have one question. It's about what makes a man. You seem to know. Well, you did in that article for *Homosex(e)*." He started as he realized how naked he'd become. "What was your thesis for that one? Something about 'penetration being a mode of production in the manufacturing of the masculine.'" I stopped to let his own stilted words limp over to him.

"I'm sorry. Here I am contextualizing my question and I haven't even asked it. Let me try this again. First, I'll introduce some givens, then the question." I opened my left hand, "This is a dick," I said while I pushed my palm flat against the pink panties and then his prick until each were mashed against the wall of pelvic bone. I waited for his dick to stiffen and push back. Hand and cock then began a little dance until the hand had shuffled the tip of the dickhead up and under the strangling elastic waist-band. Below it, a swelling pink stem was pointing toward the ceiling.

"Then," I said as I plucked the head, nearly in full purple bloom, "to use your own terms," and I pulled flower, stalk, and the taut rim of the panty out to me as far as I could—I almost lifted him up off his feet— "there's what you called the concretized phallus." And now my right hand and its knife reached into the gap between his dick and his belly.

I turned the knife on its side and stroked the dull edge of the cold blade up the shaft, prickling with hairs and goose bumps. "Actually, anything with a point'll do." My left hand slowly let go so that only the knife held his cock and the overextended waistband in place. "So here's my question. If I took this," and I flicked my left index finger at his dickhead, as if it were a marble and this were a game. I paused to feel it thud against the warming metal. "If I took this and left you with this," I pushed the concretized phallus against the cock that was trapped on the other side by my finger, "would you still be a man?"

I waited.

The muscles of his stomach flinched, shaking the skin that rippled the air that stirred the hairs on my arm that held the knife. I hoped that this was his answer. I waited. It was.

I almost smiled. I was beginning to enjoy our date. For now I could spend the rest of it teaching him the deeper meaning of his wordless response.

I pulled the knife out in one stroke. The panties snapped his prick back in place. He gasped. He was stung but uncut. I grabbed both his hands and pulled them toward me and the bed as I jumped up onto it. I rolled off the other side still holding him. I let go and he lay facedown across it. I took his left hand and tied it to the left post of the black metal headboard. I moved around the bed knotting and cinching his three remaining limbs to the three remaining corners. Then I stood. Breathing deeply. I'd worked fast and was winded. I'm sure he could hear my snorts over the thudding of his own heart.

For the first time, I saw his pink ass. I jerked the waistband down and under the curves of his butt. The smooth, round, white cheeks plumped like breasts lifted by an underwire bra. I cupped them with both my palms. They grew warm. *Pap. Pap. Pap.* Three swift slaps to warm them more. I allowed a few moments of silence. Enough time for his ears to stop ringing. So he'd be able to hear this. I yanked the tail of my leather belt out of its buckle so hard that it creaked. Next belt and buckle slithered into my hand. The treated and tanned skin groaned as I bent it, then snapped it taut.

"You cocky little fucker. Answer me." The dead animal's hide slapped across the hide of my little live one. The echo of the clack somersaulted around the room. The candles wavered. But he said nothing. This boy who, in print, had never made his point in under 15,000 words said nothing. I was growing quite excited as I realized there might be a spark of brilliance in him after all.

"Or maybe you can't." I began to punctuate each sentence with the end of my belt. "Not because you're too dumb." *Thwack.* "Not because you're too smart." *Thwack.* "But because you're one of those pitiable scholars who can't speak without citing someone else." *Thwack.* "Must explicate." *Thwack.* "Must legitimate." *Thwack.* "Must use the f-word." *Thwack.* "Foucault." *Thwack.* "Foucault, Foucault, Foucault." *Thwack, thwack, thwack.*

His ass was pink again. Almost roseate. I took my left hand and let my fingers survey those patches that even in this dim dark shone. "Such a hot ass," I said. I lowered my head toward it. My tongue slipped and slid over the nearly hairless skin as if it were ice. Ice that seemed cold and smooth, but my tongue grew warm against it, felt its throb. "Such a hot ass," I said again and left the room.

The kitchen isn't far from the bedroom. A few feet. He must have heard me open the mouth of the freezer. Heard it sing its one long, cold note. Heard the spine of the ice tray crack in my hands. "Miss me?" I think he moaned some answer. "Miss this?" I dragged my tongue back along the trail left by my belt. I'm certain he was groaning when I took my tongue and pried at his crack, digging deepest near his hole. He tried to push his ass closer to my face. So trusting for one I'd thought so critical.

I lifted my head. Now, before my saliva could dry, I pressed down the melting cube. His butt muscles clenched. I retraced where the tongue, first of my belt and then of myself, had been. His whole body tensed as I pushed the cube down between his cheeks. "Such a hot ass," I whispered. I nudged the ice over his hole. It was sweating its own lube. I took my thumb and ground it into his asshole. He rolled his head over the pillow, biting at it. "Go ahead. You still have your dick. Be a man and scream." He tried to kick me off. Maybe he yelped. I dug at the decomposing ice cube with my fingernail. It plopped out. I slid it down toward his balls, leaving it to melt.

He began to twist against his ropes. All this show to shake off a shrinking chip of ice. I grabbed the scruff of his neck. Then I gave his butt a swift, sharp blow with the belt. He was still.

"You lied to me." I struck him again. "I've read everything you've been able to get published so far. You posited yourself over and over as a master theorist. Acted like you could demystify any obfuscation thrown your way. Like you were going to deconstruct the cosmos. Down." *Thwack*. "And down." *Thwack*. "And down." *Thwack*. "Until your praxis led to your dick. But why'd you stop there, boy?" *Thwack*. "What's so fucking special about your dick?" *Thwack*. "Is it magical?" *Thwack*. "Is that where you keep your male essence?" *Thwack*. "Your fucking trans-historical male essence." *Thwack*.

My left hand pulled at his hair and shook his head while my right hand flung the belt over my back. "You fucking hypocrite." *Thwack*. "You're nothing but a fucking," *thwack*, "closeted," *thwack*, "gender essentialist." Mid-stroke I stopped.

The harder I had hit, the higher his ass had leapt. On the last stroke, it jumped up to meet the belt. "No," I said out loud. I wasn't going to let him take control of the scene. This was about my revenge. Not his pleasure. Not tonight. Not on our first date.

I climbed onto the bed. I sat on his butt. Even through my jeans, I could feel the warmth of his skin. I sat there a moment, like a hen on her almost-hatched egg. I sat there a little longer. *Soon*, I thought with instinctual certainty, *soon*.

I leaned over his back until I was crouched over him, my belly pushing his head deeper into the pillow. I untied the left hand, then right. I crawled off him and the bed. I untied the left leg, then right. With both hands, I dug for the waistband that had now burrowed under the cheeks of his ass. I took the elastic and scraped it up along the skin. Before I let go, I gave a final yank and, *snap*, his panties were pulled up.

He began to mutter, reciting a rosary of "no's." He must have thought I'd untied him to send him home.

I tugged the ropes and the boy over to the chair and down across my legs until I felt the smooth fabric and the stiff cock slide across my right leg. I stopped when I had his dick bent over my knee just so. As if it had been scaling the outer wall of my leg and was now stuck, unable to heave the balls over.

Keeping the ropes in my left hand, my right hand was left alone to tear down his panties for the last time. I could feel the faint pulsing of his cock. It wouldn't be much longer before he wet himself. A few good slaps. So I decided to take my time. I ground my palm into the small of his back. Then I turned it on its side and started to push at that firm pink border wall. It gave a bit. A budge more. Then it recoiled, scooting my hand back to where it began.

Once more. This time I rolled my hand back onto its palm and let it curl into a fist. I plowed against the panty's waist. My knuckles, like the broad lip of a shovel, tried to lift it. Instead, they pushed under the rim and over the warm earth of his ass, until all momentum was lost and my hand flattened again, this time over that long fissure venting heat from its deep hole.

It was a pleasant moment. Unexpected. I dragged my hand out to try yet again. I placed my knuckles half on skin half on silk. The boy squirmed a bit. I felt his cock flatten against my leg. He was growing impatient, insecure. Good. I would go even slower now.

I took my knuckles and rubbed at the edge of his right hip. Several tries and I got the rim to fold over on itself. I moved my hand toward the left hip. I did the same there. Soon I had the elastic turned in and out all along the edge of his butt. Now I would knead and roll and knead and roll the panties down as if I were making a pie crust. By the time I had them tightly under the ledge of his ass, I'd left his skin stinging, throbbing even, where the elastic, like a crude lawnmower, had torn out some of the few black hairs. And, though I was pleased, I could feel that my little man's interest had waned.

"Don't fall asleep on me, boy." I slapped his cold butt hard enough that my baby had to fill his lungs with air. "Do I bore you? Afraid you'll drift off before your queer elder passes the staff along to you?" I felt his body hesitate. He actually thought of answering me. "Oh, is that it?" I yanked the ropes and his wrists to the floor. I let my voice drift back in time and up an octave. "Fuck me, daddy, sir." Possessed, I began to bounce him against my knee and whack out a beat while I said, "Yes, sir.

Yes, sir. Fill me full."

I stopped. His skin shook. His cock quivered. I leaned toward his left ear and whispered hoarsely, "I will, young man, but when I'm good and ready. Do I make myself clear?!"

I tugged the ropes again. His dick slid over my leg until his balls where flat against the side of it. "Huh?" I let go and he slunk back. I pulled again. "Well?" Then several more times until I knew these slow kisses between his silk and my denim must have been burning his dick. I could feel it swelling. I let him slide back and forth over my leg several more times as I kept shouting, "Do I?" The last time I didn't let go of the ropes. His cock and balls could barely teeter on the edge of my quite warm thigh.

"Now, you're going to tell me the truth. Aren't you, my queercore kid?" I slapped his ass twice. My palm stung. "You're going to tell me just how much of a lying essentialist hypocrite you are. Aren't you?" And I began to whack at the fleshy underbellies of his cheeks. Soft, fat, some muscle. I kept whacking all the while I kept shouting. "Aren't you a liar? Aren't you? Aren't you a fucking closeted essentialist? Queer theorist your ass. You never read Judith Butler. Did you? Did you? No, you hunched under your covers with a flashlight reading Judy Grahn and diddling yourself. Didn't you? Huh? Didn't you!"

By hitting the undersides of his butt cheeks, I'd been lifting his ass with each swat. Forcing him to rub his cock over and over against the hard muscle and bone in my leg. Making his own body first slap his balls and then mash them against the side of my thigh. So hard and so fast that the silk and denim were close to sparking. Even if I'd wanted to stop beating on his beet-red butt, it wouldn't have mattered now. He would've kept on humping my leg like the precocious panty-wearing dog he was.

Now, for every word I would speak, I batted at him with whatever strength was left in my nearly numb hand. "I know you read Mark Thompson's *Gay Spirit* over and over and over...." A "yes" spurt out of his mouth. "And over and over and over...." Another "yes." "Until you were weeping and clapping for faeries."

"YES!" He bucked forward and then rocked back on the fulcrum of my leg.

It shook wildly, then he did. And did. And did. He was spewing a loud stream of "yes's" now.

I waited. He moaned, a low, hoarse sound, while rolling from side to side. I let go of the ropes and let my left hand stumble about until it found my knife again. I passed it over to my aching right hand. In a series of jerky, sawing strokes, I cut up the left side of his panties. When I reached the waist, they sprang apart. Now I leaned forward and cut open the right side. I put the knife down and steadied the boy's butt in my hand. With my left, I reached under his panting chest and pushed him up. Next, I grabbed the soaked front of his panties and pulled. My right hand felt the back end come slithering from both sides into his crack and up the crevice toward his balls. I watched his face contort as the fabric brushed up and up his still-too-tender shaft.

I gave a gentle shove to his left shoulder. He started slowly to drop down onto his knees, dragging his drooling dick along the denim, leaving behind a silvery streak like a snail's.

Once he landed on his knees, the real dumbshow began. Bobbing up and down like a puppet with a broken string. One awkward attempt after the other to balance the weight of his body on his calves without letting them actually touch his butt. For a minute, it was amusing. Certainly more arousing than his striptease. But he kept on squirming and I grew bored. I bent sideways and fumbled along the floor. I was looking for the other thing I'd brought back with me from the kitchen. My hand patted the rug until I saw it glint in the candlelight. It was one of those tiny spoons used for cracking the boiled shell of an egg and scooping out its jiggling white insides.

I opened my left hand and dug around in the pink wad with the spoon. I slid it under a shimmering blob of come. "Open wide." I turned toward him. Even with the blindfold, I could sense his blank stare. "Your mouth, brainiac." He hesitated then dropped his jaw. "Here comes a little spoon for my little man. Filled with man essence. Your man essence. Eat up." I rested the spoon's cold underbelly on his lower lip. Instinct—and that even crueler master, desire—made him do the rest.

"That's it. Eat up all the sacred man essence. We wouldn't want your sex to grow up without a gender, would we? No, we want your sex to have a gender," I said as I wrapped my hand around his plump cock and squeezed. "A manly gender."

I scooped out an even larger dollop. And, while he sucked down that spoonful, I smiled to myself. I was nearly humming by the time I made him lick the still-sticky insides of his panties. And it wasn't because I knew my little man was ready to be fucked. It wasn't even because I knew, from that night on, I could have this little man as I long as I wanted him. It was simply because nothing soothes the forever broken like breaking another.

I See Vienna,
I See France,
Sigmund's *I See*
Underpants

for Dr. B. and Michael McG.

I've never had a dick up my ass, I tell my shrink. Dr. Horney smiles. Says it's an important rite of passage. I can barely hear him over the moaning. Butch needs to vocalize to get hard. He's yanking his cock. Soon, it'll be stiff enough to stick in me.

Dr. Horney, his first name's as weird as his last—it's Kermit—jots a word or two on his big, yellow pad.

Butch leans in to kiss me. His breath stinks. He's been sucking at my poop chute like it's a straw clogged with chocolate shake.

When I first saw Dr. Horney, I was having wicked panic attacks, shuddering like I had a fever and then running home to the lightless dark under my comforters. He prescribed Xanax and said I had a bad case of existential angst. All I knew was that even in crowds I felt so alone I wanted to die.

I got better after I started seeing Dr. Horney outside his office. The first time, I held a bottle of gerkins. Should I get these, I thought. "What does Scott want?" He startled me. I didn't know he shopped here. He even helped me push my cart and carry my groceries to the car. I turned to thank him but he had gone.

We never talked about that unexpected appearance. Fifteen minutes into the following session, I just had this gut feeling he didn't remember it. Like he's a sleepwalker or something. To be honest, I can't tell which times he's asleep. During our session? In the car ride home? I don't say anything. It's cruel and dangerous to wake a sleepwalker.

This is his first time to come along on a date. In fact, I wouldn't be here— on my back with Butch grunting between my legs—if Dr. Horney hadn't concluded, in his professional opinion, that Butch would be a good fuck.

I turned to thank him. Dr. Horney was crouched between the legs of this old guy with lips as black as the rims of his glasses and giving head to a big, unlit cigar.

What does this all mean, I panted. Butch had finally gotten his fat, red head in my redder hole.

Dr. Horney slid up the cigar and faced me. His left eyebrow arched up to his hairline. He handed me his yellow pad.

Sometimes a dick is just a dick.

The Devil and *Mrs. Faust*

Yer never gonna believe this story. I don't blame ya. I have a hard time believin' it an' it happened t'me. I mean how often does the Devil talk with a Jew?

What? Oh, sure, Pat Buchanan an' half of Idaho want ya t'think it happens every day. Right after the Devil calls one of us, we triangulate with our other cells in Moscow an' Jerusalem. Actually, if ya play a video tape of the Academy Awards—any year—backwards, all his instructions are there for the year to come.

Trust me. Whatevuh y've learned about Jews an' the Devil in Sunday School or yer Rotary Club an' yer Junior League meetin's is all wrong. We're talkin' total crap here! This don't happen every day. T'be honest with ya, I think this was the first time. An' first time out, he *shtups* one of us.

Actually, I *shtupped* the hell outta him.

Alright already. Stop with the eye-rollin'. Hear me out an' then close yer mind. Just listen, will ya?

In the beginnin', there was this fuckin' *schlimazel* an' his saint of a wife. That's me. My name's Ruth. Ruth Faust.

Again with the eye-rollin'. Wait an' hear my whole name an' then roll away. Ruth Faust, née—that means "born" if yer a girl—Ruth Marie Vitale. What gives? yer askin' yerselves. Whoeva heard of a Italian girl named Ruth?

My mutha, née—don't ya just love that word. It sounds like somethin' outta Shakespeare. What? Ya don't think I ever read the bastard. Hey, don't let the plain speakin' ways of my people fool ya. What people? New Yorkers, ya *schmo*. Greenlawn, Long Island, t'be exact.

Anyways, I've read the complete works of Mr. William Shakespeare three times in the last year. That's right. I said "year." Okay, okay. Hold the phone. I'll get to that if you stop rushin' me.

My mutha's name when she was born, in case yer still interested, was Estha Rosenbaum. Guess what? She's a Jew. An' 'cause of that, I'm a Jew in the eyes of good ol' *Eretz Yisrael*. I could make *aliah* —that's Hebrew for returnin' to the muthaship—in a second an' be putzin' aroun' Tel Aviv's equivalent of the Walt Whitman Mall t'day.

My *tata*, Sal—that's Sal, not Saul—his family came over on the boat about a hundred years ago from Palermo. That's in Sicily, by the way. That's right. I'm a *Sicilian* Jew. Don't fuck w'me. Unless ya want yer bed, yer house, an' yer world t'be seriously rocked. Even the Devil'll vouch for that.

I wasn't always so in ya face, though. Actually, I'd never talked back to anyone till two years ago. Honest to Gawd.

Hey! I said enough already with the eyes.

Na, since I was a kid, I've always been the good little girl. The problem was that, on the inside, I wasn't really good. It's just that I was afraid of gettin' caught doin' all the dirty stuff I was thinkin' about doin'—*all the time*. An', on the outside, I wasn't ever little. That's right. I was fat. I still *am* fat. The only difference is that now I'm fat with a fuckin' vengeance. But I'm gettin' ahead of myself here.

Back then, I was just fat. An' shy. An' a girl. It couldn'ta been worse. Except at home. I mean, me an' my parents didn't hold hands all day an' skip aroun' the house. But they loved me. I think they worried about me bein' so quiet 'cause they weren't. No way, no how. But that didn't matter. In their eyes, I was their beautiful daughter, Ruth Marie. An' as for the fat, they were unusual for the time. They never said a word. I mean, how could they. The food don't fall far from the table, if y'know what I'm sayin'.

So, home was alright. Hell was anywheres other kids where. Gawd, kids can be such fuckin' shits. Like at school, durin' recess, in the third grade, I'm finishin' up my lunch, bitin' into my Charleston Chew an' dreamin' of what it'd be like to touch Bobby Randall down there, an' Joey Fusaro comes over an' starts in on me. Don't ask me what he said. Either yer fat an' y'know or yer not an' y've said it. Or whaddabout every afternoon in tenth grade, after gym an' after fingerin' myself to the point of no return—twice—in the showers while thinkin' about Scott Jacobs bonin' me, an' I have to walk back to my locker past Mary Kilpatrick an' hear her wonderin' aloud to her _girls_, Brigit O'Shaughnessy an' Shannon McQuaid, about why it takes so long for me to shower. Y'know. All that _blubber_ needs time to hose off or some freakin' shit like that.

You'd think things woulda gotten better in my junior year when I gave up on food an' just swallowed pills an' washed 'em down with Diet Cokes. I lost seventy pounds by senior year.

T'be honest, I lost many things my senior year. That's when I met my future husband Kurt. Kurt Faust. A little too Aryan Nation, I know. But I fell in love with him, not his name. Trust me, the last name coulda been worse. Thank Gawd, it wasn't Waldheim.

Actually, he's _Dr._ Kurt Faust. He'd want ya to know that. What my _schmuck_ of an ex-husband—I'm gettin' to that—wouldn't want ya to know is that, after ten years of tryin' an' failin', he had to make a deal with the Devil t'get his tenure at S.U.N.Y. The one in Stony Brook.

I'm not shittin' ya. I swear. The original Slick Willie. Lucifuh.

So where was I? Oh, yeah. Senior Year.

Kurt'd just transfered in. Instant misfit. We met for the first time when we sat next to each other in band practice. What instruments? Trumpet. Don't laugh. I had amazin'ly strong lips. Still do, just a lot lower.

An' did I mention he was cute? Little did I know I he was a *putz* in *mensch's* clothin'.

Lookin' back, it's so obvious I was naive. Not in the stupid way where ya get what ya deserve. But in the sad way where ya settle for somethin' that's so-so 'cause ya can't believe you'll ever get anythin' better. If y've been there, y'know what I'm talkin' about. If ya haven't, forget about it.

When I saw Kurt all I saw was the *mensch*. This really kind, gentle man. He wasn't the first guy to kiss me. C'mon, my life was never *that* pathetic. But Gawd, could he put his embouchure to good use! An' no, he wasn't the first guy to fuck me. But he was the first to really look at me while he was poundin' away. Askin' me is this good for me? Do I like this? How about that? An' he was definitely the first to go down on me. I bet he's still got little dents in his head where I dug my nails in.

Maybe that was all show. He gave me head so I'd give him one of my "famous" blowjobs. Yeah, I had a reputation, at least among the football team, for doin' things their girfriends wouldn't. That's right. No gag-reflex. No shit. I musta practiced my way through a field of cucumbers the summuh before my senior year. *An' I swallowed.*

Or maybe the reason he was so sweet was 'cause he still believed he had everythin' ahead of him. Hell, he was seventeen. He hadn't failed yet. He'd never even fucked up. Never lost anythin' really special.

Not till April 3, 1977. That was the day the doctuh told my mutha, who told my fathuh, what I'd already learned two weeks before, pissin' on a pink plastic stick in the bathroom. I was pregnant. Go ahead. Say it. Y've been dyin' to.

Oy!

Feel better?

Yeah, there was lots of tears. An' shoutin'. An' more tears when I finally told Kurt. But he did the *mensch*ly thing an' asked me to marry him. An' I was seventeen too an' wait-listed at Hofstra—can ya believe it? Hofstra!

An' I was scared. I was in love. I said yes.

In May, we graduated. In June, we got married. In July, we got our own apartment. Both our parents helped with the rent. In August, I miscarried an'

I lost my baby.

Okay, I don't mean t'be flip or nothin', but let's just say I knew about Hell long before I met the Devil. An' that's all I plan to say about the "Summer of '77."

Kurt got his first degree. I got a job as an office manager for this lame-wad office supply company. I also got back the seventy pounds I'd lost an' then some. Next Kurt goes an' gets his master's. An' then, in the four years it took him t'get his doctorate, my mutha—Gawd rest her soul—died of cancer an' my fathuh—Gawd rest his soul—lasted about a year longer before he died of grief. That left just me an' Kurt. In other words, I was alone.

I missed 'em somethin' fuckin' awful. Still do.

So, yeah, right. Where was I? Right. Kurt gets his doctorate. In what? History. With a special emphasis on that magical moment when the Gawd-awful Middle Ages turned into the ain't-it-friggin'-swell-t'be-alive Renaissance. What was the word he used all the time? Oh, yeah. "Liminal." It was a *liminal* moment. I think it means "doorway" in Latin. You know, "threshhold." Like what you carry a bride over. Or that invisible boundary you have to cross t'get from bad to worse.

Which, Kurt an' I did some time in 1997. Our twentieth anniversary—can you fuckin' believe it? Twenty fuckin' years.

Now'd be a good time for ya to roll yer eyes.

Thanks.

I don't know why we stayed t'gether that long. I mean, I guess in the beginnin', even after the baby died, it was 'cause I was in love with him. But from August 17, 1977, Kurt Faust hated me. I mean, in his *cocka-mamy* mind, I was the fuckin' cunt—his words, not mine—who trapped him in marriage an' then killed his child. But he needed a maid so he kept me on. I see it now. I didn't wanna see it so much then. I told ya I used t'be very different.

Take sex for example. Not like I wanted to have sex for a long time after the baby, but at some point the jones comes back. I mean, it's part of bein' human. I used to try all the time t'get him as hot-an'-bothered as

I was. But he'd push me away. An' then, for some gawddamned freakin' mysterious reason known only to him, he wouldn't. An' when he was done, I wished he hadn't bothered, the *schlub*. You know. Like I'd be goin' down on him an' right when he's about to burst, he goes an' pulls it out an' shoots all over himself or the bed. The same with fuckin'. It's like he never wanted his precious gawddamned fuckin' seed anywheres near me again. An' goin' down on me? Gettin' *me* off? You can *so* forget about that.

Right, 1997. By then, we'd been livin' in Smithtown for almost ten years an' Kurt'd been teachin' in the Department of European Languages, Literature an' Culchah at Stony Brook where he spends alla his time runnin' the tenure track like a rat in a wheel at the pet store. We'd stopped havin' sex altogether an' didn't even talk. Wheneva he was home, he lived in the downstairs den: *his* office, *his* study, *his* space. Occasionally, he opens his door an' shouts out some command, which I ignore, or some complaint, which I also ignore. Why bother? I'm mean, it may take milk a few days to go sour. But, with Kurt, it took twenty long years. An', Gawd, by 1997, he was the foulest *farbissener* there ever was.

What? *Farbissener*? You know. A bitter ol' fuck.

Oh. What's with all the Yiddish? ya ask.

Now ya ask.

Yeah, yeah. I've heard it all before: if I'm a *Sicilian* Jew, how come I never go an' blurt out a really killuh insult about my ex in Italian. I mean, it's obvious I'm not too fond of him nowadays. For good reason too. An' the language has got some fuckin' perfect words for a man like Kurt Faust.

The answer's simple.

Pretty much everythin' was *verboten*—you know, *forbidden*—in Grandma Renata's house, 'specially swearin'. An' my dad's dad, Grandpa Giancarlo, died when he was just a kid, leavin' him alone with his five olduh sisters, each one a nun from birth, an' his holy terror of a Mutha Superior. An' the rest of dad's family lives in Jersey an' he only saw 'em wheneva there was a funeral or weddin'. Sure, he learned a few dirty words from his cousins. What teenage boy can't say "whore" in at least two languages? *Gabiche?*

Gawd, I can hear him doin' it now in my head. He's yellin' from the reclina in front of the TV to my mutha in the kitchen about his cousin Vito's third wife, Concetta. "You like *her*? I *hate* her. What? Huh?! 'Cause the *butanna*'s a freakin' hoo-uh, Esta, that's why!

Yeah, my *tata* Sal could curse with the best of 'em. But he never learned how to swear the way yer supposed to in Italian. Rapidfire. Arms an' fingers shootin' off in the air. Which means I never learned how to swear like an Italian, like a *Sicilian*. Which is too bad, cuz Italians can curse as good as they cook. *An'* fuck.

But, boy, whadda mouth Bubbe Rachel had on her. That's my mutha's mutha. An' if ya wanted to talk to her ya had to learn to give as good as y'got. By the time I was six, she had me swearin' up such a blue streak, I could make even *her* blush every now an' then. I wish she were still alive to see just how much *chutzpah* her little *bubeleh*'s got now. She'd totally *kvell*.

That's Yiddish for "cream in yer jeans." An' ya will too if ya let me finish my story. Okay?!

So, one night in 1997, Kurt comes all the way outta his office an' speaks to *me*. Okay. Speaks *at* me. He tells me he knows that I think I'm some hot-shit witch. Which I never said or thought, yet. But it was no secret either what I was doin' in my freetime. An' there were all those trips an' checks to the Magickal Childe in New York. Who knew the *schmendrick* still paid attention to the outside world? An' then he goes an' says the most fuckin' outrageous thing eva. He says he needs *my* help with a research project of *his*.

Yeah, I looked just like ya. My mouth all open wide. Oh, did I forget to tell ya I'm a witch?

Well, *bubeleh*, I am. I'm a fuckin' amazin' witch. An', maybe, if ya keep bein' a good listener, I'll give ya a ride on my broom when I'm done tellin' ya my story.

What? When did I turn into a witch? Listen, ya don't just turn into one. What are ya? From California or somethin'? This ain't *Bewitched* we're talkin' about. Ya can twitch ya nose all ya want, but you'll look like a friggin' rabbit with a coke habit an' that's about it. Na, it's just like everythin' else. Y'gotta start out knowin' nothin' an' then work yer ass off.

For me, that was when I joined this monthly women's encounta group. The year's 1981 an' I'm 22 an', as ya can imagine from what I've told ya so far, very lonely. Yeah, we did that rite of passage for the repressed housewife. Y'know the one: ya squat over a hand mirror an' read between ya lips. Gawd, I can see the rest of their faces now. Some of 'em look so shocked, like they'd just asked to go down on the woman next to 'em (a request that, at the time, I'm sorry to say, would have had me runnin' for the car). Actually, Mrs. Scaduto does. Run for the car, that is. I'm already hikin' up my dress an' pullin' down my panties before I hear her car door slam. By the time she's floorin' the car into reverse an' then grindin' the gears over to first, I'm done wedgin' the slightly steamy mirror between my thighs.

You'd think I'd be all hesitant to do this shit in front of strangers. Wrong again. First, the mirror was nothin' new. The summuh I was thirteen I wanked off in front of the mirror every day. An' takin' a peek at my twat. No problem. What? Yeah, I know it took me a long time t'get over how others saw my body. I was there, Einstein. But I never was ashamed of my twat. Don't ask me how or why the Angel of Penis Envy passed me over. All I know is that me an' my twat have been best friends since I was four.

What's with the face? Oh, don't even try. A lot of well-meanin' women over the years have "counseled" me—that's Joyce's word—Joyce Krieger, she's the one that started the group. Anyways, they 've counseled me to call it by any other name. Sorry, "ladies." Sorry, Joyce. But I'm gonna call my "female mystique" a "twat" till the day I die.

Why? That's easy. I hate all the other words. "Vagina." It's too clinical. It makes me dry up every time I hear it. All I see are stirrups an' cold, shiny speculums. An' "vulva." It's a great name for a drag queen an' that's about it. An' "pussy." Puh-leez. If I was a size two, maybe. But t'me, it sounds so high-school, y'know. An' "cunt." Y'gotta scrunch up yer mouth just to say it. It's too tight an' angry. An' that ain't my twat. No ways, no how. "Twat." Y'gotta really stretch yer mouth to say that. Wide. An' it is. An' deep too. Especially mine.

So, after a year, the group kinda turns into this witches' coven. Or, as Joyce, who's known to witches far an' wide t'day as High Priestess Morganna Moonblood, calls it, "a circle of goddesses." The first meetin', I feel kinda stupid. Joyce keeps wanderin' aroun' the room with that same damn mirror an' makes us tell our reflections, "Thou art Goddess." But it's still better than waitin' aroun' for Kurt to come home from classes an' pick an' complain his way through whatevuh I'd cooked. Which, at that point, he's done every night since our weddin', unless it's somethin' *über*-german like bratwurst. Then he *fresses* his way through it like a pig at a trough.

Finally, after months of *kibbitz*in', we go an' "celebrate" our first ritual. The minute we get sky-clad, y'know, naked, my twat's hooked. But it ain't till we're spinnin' aroun' the room chantin' to the witches' gawddess Hecate an' I can feel the encouragin' laughter of Bubbe Rachel that the rest of me lets loose. It was the closest I'd come—in twenty-three fuckin' years—ta the Big O without havin' to use my killuh hands.

An', even if I don't believe much in the high ritual mumbo-jumbo (*O sea-swept watchtower of the watery West...*), I really took to the idea of spells. It's just like cookin'. I started borrowin' all of Joyce's Llewellyn books. Ya probably have no idea what those are. They're like those ol' time school books for "Today's Wiccan." Y'know, see Jane cast a spell on Dick.

Wiccans? Jeez, I need a freakin' vocabulary list here. More Yiddish yer thinkin'. Wrong. Y'know, Wiccans. They're like the Unitarians of pagans. A pinch of this an' a dash of that with lots of so-so songs an' endless conversations filled with bad, really bad, puns, thrown in for good measure. I'm sure you'd know who I'm talkin' about if ya saw of big gatherin' of 'em. There's always some ol' hippies who like to do arts an' crafts when they're stoned an' lots of middle-aged formuh Dungeons & Dragons warriors who wander aroun' in homemade armor convinced they're extras on the set of *Excalibur* an' tons—literally—of some of the ballsiest fat women, like yours truly t'day, in search of finally gettin' the respect an' righteous bonin' we so deserve.

Sorry. I'm gettin' way off track here. Where was I? Oh, right. Spells.

I kept it kinda simple in the beginnin'. Y'know, a little prosperity spell—a few green candles slicked up with some fast money oil—ta have enough cash t'get the shoppin' cart through Waldbaum's without havin' to *schlep* the Tupperware bin with all the coupons in from the car. Or my favorite—one I made up myself—the be-there-now spell. I'd use a little incense, the cigaratte lightuh an' ashtray, an' start chantin' as I'd head the car toward Burguh Haven. An', nine times outta ten, by the time I drove up to the winduh, that gawd Rick—Jesus, I can see his face an' his plastic name badge even now an' I get wet—Rick would be waitin' to hand me my double cheese-burguh an' fries.

Hey, stop lookin' at me like that. I told ya I was "happy" in my marriage. *Real* happy. I was fuckin' giddy by the time my twentieth anniversary hits me. Come to think of it, it was a week after that blessèd day when Kurt goes an' asks *me* for *my* help.

"What's the project," I asks.

"You wouldn't understand, Ruth. It's very complicated."

"Try me," I says.

Boy, does he look pissed. He knows he's gonna have to tell me.

"I've translated this text in medieval German...."

"When'd *you* learn medieval German?"

"In graduate school. When do you care? Just shut up and listen, okay?"

"Y'know," I says glarin' at him, "you got a fuckin' attitude!"

"What now, Ruth?"

"Forget it!"

"Fine."

"Fine! Y'know what, yer right I don't care."

"Good. That'll make this all the easier."

"Sure will, 'cause I'm not helpin' *you* with nothin'!"

"For fuck's sake, Ruth, don't go and fly off the handle. Jesus, you're always so emotional. Just listen. This could help us both. And you know we need help."

"No shit, Sherlock. I mean, *Dr.* Sherlock."

Now he's givin' me that frosty stare he's gotten so good at.

"All right," I says. "I'm listenin'."

"It's a ritual for summoning the Devil."

"The Devil," I laugh. Then I look at him. "Oh, for Gawd's sake, Kurt. The Devil? What are ya, some teenage deliquent?"

I was nervous. Not hysterical, but spooked. I mean, I didn't really believe in the Devil or Gawd or any gawds or gawddesses then. What can I say? My family was only half-Jewish. An' that half was so Reform we was non-practicin'. The other half was classic recoverin' Catholic. In fact, if it hadn't been for the time Grandma Renata got all worked up to have me baptised an' confirmed, I never woulda known enough about the Devil t'be scared of him now. I had to spend a bunch of Sundays goin' to Mass with my aunts an' havin' to sit at their kitchen table for hours afterwards learnin' all about "my father's faith." Then Grandma Renata died an' they got all distracted. But those Sundays was enough to creep me out for years.

"Go ahead," he shouts. "Think I'm crazy. I don't give a shit. I'm not the one who plays witch with a bunch of frustrated housewives on the weekend while my husband's out in the real world busting his hump to make something of himself."

"Poor baby," I says but he don't hear me. He just starts pacin' back an' forth.

"No matter how hard I work, nothing comes of it. No matter how many articles on the *quattrocento* I publish, no matter how many stupid freshmen humanities courses I teach, I can't get those assholes to notice me. Ten years. Why can't they see that I'm this century's Walter Pater?!"

"Who?" I says. I'm gettin' scared 'cause now Kurt's standin' talkin' to the wall.

"My career's in the toilet unless I get tenure. I can't transfer. I can't do a frigging thing. And those old farts just keep passing me over. They're hellbent on passing me over. Hellbent! So, fine. I've tried everything else. Now, I'll get Hell to help me for once.

"Here," an' alla the sudden he turns back t'me an' throws a piece of paypuh on the floor. "Get me all these things by this date at this time...or else." Then he storms off an' I hear his door slam shut.

I got him what he wanted. Yeah, I was afraid. I told ya before I was very different from how I am now. But mostly, I was curious. I knew there was no way he could pull this off. But maybe it would calm him down. An' I'd never been in his sacred space since the day we moved in.

The list was pretty simple. A lot of plants an' spices with names you'd imagine for summonin' the Devil: hellbore, devil's dung, poison parsley, dragon's blood, toad flax, ghost flower, hag's tapers, bad man's plaything, clove root, pukeweed, naughty man's cherries, witches broom. I ground up a bunch of 'em for a powda an' the rest I boiled down into this oil that fuckin' reeks. It took a week t'get that smell outta my kitchen.

By a few minutes before the witchin' hour, I'm ready. I'm sittin' at the kitchen table tappin' my nails so fast it sounds like machine guns are goin' off. Finally, the clock says it's midnight. Midnight, Saturday night. The Devil's open for business. Don't that explain a helluva lot, I thinks.

I grab the tupperware with the incense an' the jar of oil an' walk through the livin' room an' down the hall to the den. I knock on the door. It's real warm. What the fuck is he doin' in there?, I asks myself. Then I hear all this fumblin' an' the door opens just a crack an' I see the forehead of my no-goodnik husband, all pasty white with his thinnin' hair plastered to it. Then his little bird-like eyes. He's all squintin' an' shit like I've shined a flashlight in his face. But all the light's comin' from the den. He musta bought every fuckin' black candle in the tri-state area.

"What?" he barks.

I almost sound off. Then I check myself. I wanna see more. So, I says, real polite, "Here. It's all the shit ya wanted for callin' the Devil."

"Oh," he says an' opens the door wider. I push the tupperware into his hands an' try to wedge my fat ass into the room. Kurt stumbles an' the door flies back. But I just stand in the doorway. Not 'cause he's put a curse on me or somethin'. It's the smell. Gawd, it's like a moldy gym bag someone took a crap in. He musta painted the winduh shut when he painted all the glass black. I look aroun' an' there's books stacked in piles everywheres—on the desk, on the TV, on the couch, on the Lazy-Boy—an' paypuhs an' boxes of paypuhs stacked on top of 'em an' pohstuhs an' cut-out pitchuhs of all these paintin's of fat women. That fuckin' *schlub*. An' then there's all these candles. I never seen such a fire hazard. I can't believe the house ain't burnin' down right that gawddamned minute. I'm gettin' ready to blow an' let him know just what I think of this toilet when I look at the floor.

I almost bust a gut laughin'. But, by some miracle, I keep a staight face. He's used like a hundred cans of Morton Salt to make this complicated circle in the carpet. There's a pentagram—big surprise, huh?—an' some real crazy symbols I never seen before.

"Give me the oil," he screams now that he's back on his feet. He's shakin' an' flappin' his arms over his head. Gawd, he's even thinnuh than when I first met him.

"Sure. Here. Take it." I hand him the jar. Thank Gawd I put a lid on it or he woulda spilled it all over the carpet. He's twitchin' somethin' awful. Like he's got the DT's.

"Leave," he says in this creepy high voice. "Leave now. And don't open this door no matter what happens. Heed my warning, woman, or be damned."

"Okay, ya fuckin' freak," an' I pull the door shut so hard the frame rattles. I decide to go upstairs an' pack before the place catches fire.

I guess somewheres in the middle of packin' I fell asleep. Outta nowheres, from far off, like in a dream, I hear this awful classical music blarin' away. An' it keeps comin' closuh an' closuh. Then it hits me. It's not in the dream. It's like that moment in yer sleep when ya figure out the noise is comin' from yer alarm clock an' ya wake up. The same here.

Shit, Kurt, I think. I roll over. It's friggin' five in the mornin'. The music's even louder now that I'm awake. "Gawddamn it, Kurt," I shout at the top of my lungs. But it sounds like I'm whisperin'. I sit there waitin' for the sirens. Someone musta called the cops by now. Nothin'. Just this music that sounds like some kinda demonic John Phillips Sousa march.

"Fine, at least the house's not on fire, ya bastard" I scream. An' I stomp, skyclad, all the way downstairs to his door. I think I'm gonna have a seizure 'cause the hallway light's all wonky an' flickerin' on an' off real fast. I yell for him to turn the fuckin' music off. I yell for him to come out. To go to hell. I'm coverin' my ears an' I'm still goin' deaf here between all the brass an' timpani an' me screamin'. Then I decide to bang down the door. I try an' nearly burn my hand off.

"Kurt Faust, what the fuck are ya doin' in there?"

Alla the sudden, silence. But now it was too quiet. Somethin' really bad musta happened, I thinks. An' when the gawddamned strobe light ovahead lets me, I start seein' these little whisps of smoke comin' out from unda the door. An' I smell more of that awful reekin' gym bag. "Christ, Kurt, ya set the house on fire!"

I guess the "C-word" set somebody off 'cause the music comes back. Not so loud, but you can still hear it thuddin' away from anywheres in the house. An' it goes on for two weeks like that. That damned music an' little clouds of smelly smoke. A full freakin' fortnight as Shakespeare would say. Come midnight Saturday I start gettin' worried. I'm thinkin', maybe that smell's from a dead body? What if it's Kurt's dead body? How'm I gonna explain that to the cops?

Next day, Sunday mornin', the music stops again. For good. I know 'cause I can hear my nails—the ones I haven't bitten off—rappin' against the outsides of my coffee mug. An' alla the sudden, this little man appears. He looks sorta weird.

Oh, yer back to the eye-rollin', huh? Alright already. I know, I know.

Weirda than all that's happened so far? Kinda.

First, he really *is* little. No talluh than Bubbe Rachel was. We're talkin' 4'11" here. Secondly, he's dressed all in black: little shoes with silvuh buckles, some kind a panty hose or tights, these silk lookin' shorts that come to his knees an' are wrapped tight aroun' his legs with little bitty bows, an' this fancy jacket with all these buttons goin' up the front. But best of all, he's wearin' this huge white collar aroun' his neck. It looks like this cheese wheel made of lace or somethin'. An', on top of that, there's his head. It's kinda shaped like an olive. Y'know, pointy. But not the color of an olive. Na, it was—what's the word? oh, yeah—"ruddy." A little bit of mud mixed with a little bit of red. He's mostly bald with some white hair an' a goatee. An' he's got these sparkly little green eyes. Like he was a real handful when he was young. Y'know, some sophisticated ladies' man. Or a really classy *faygeleh*. I can't tell for sure.

I guess I coulda been frightened or startled even. But I was just relieved. The fuckin' music had stopped. He wasn't Kurt. An' he didn't smell like a gym bag. Not at all. More like lemon verbena. Y'know, like he'd gone an' splashed Jean Naté all over himself. Like I said, he was classy. An' he was real polite.

The first thing he says t'me is "Do you mind if I smoke, madam?"

"Knock yaself out," I says.

Next thing I know, he's pulled out this long silvuh cigarette holduh, like a silent movie star. Outta thin air, he takes a cigarette. Puts it in the holduh an' touches it with the tip of his finger. It starts to glow. He comes up to the table, motions with his hand if it's okay to sit, I motion back "sure," an' he sits down an' smokes.

When he's done, I find out he's this nice little ol' Greek man named Mr. Mephistopheles. An' then he goes on to tell me he's my husband's servant. That's when I freakin'*plotz*.

That's Yiddish for "shit a brick."

"Yer his what?!" I says. An' I goes an' hits my fist on the table so hard the coffee sloshes outta my cup. "Tell me this, Mr. Mephistopheles, what does my *schmo* of a husband need with a gawddamned fuckin' servant when he's got a gawddamned fuckin' slave?!"

"Mrs. Faust, have I offended you?" he says as he takes out this big frilly white hanky an' wipes it once over the table an' it's like it's some magic paypuh towel 'cause the coffee's all gone.

"*Mrs.* Faust? What am I? His mutha?! Listen, Mr. Mephistopheles, ya can either call me Ruth or Yer Majesty but never call me Mrs. Faust, ya hear?"

"Yes, Your Majesty." An' the little flirt winks at me while he pockets the hanky.

After I get us a plate of Stella D'Oro Swiss Fudge Cookies an' some fresh coffee, he proceeds to tell me that Kurt really went an' pulled it off. He got the Devil to show up in *our* house. An' that, Mr. Mephistopheles, points out, is very rare. The Devil usually sends him to do all the bargainin' an' the paypuhwork. The Devil told him that Kurt was one of the most promising hellbounds he'd met this year outside of George W. Bush.

"So where's Kurt now? In Hell?" I says all hopeful.

"Oh, no, Your Majesty. Not for quite some time. The Master is in Florence for the next year with his girlfriend."

"What?" I screams an' I drops my cookie into my coffee. "Mastuh?! Florence?! Girlfriend?!"

"Oh, I am sorry, Your Majesty, but your husband has a lover named Gretchen." Then he goes an' puts his hand in the arm of his jacket an' pulls out a friggin' polaroid. "This was taken here in the house. In the master's study," he says as he hands me the photo.

I know I'm gonna shit anotha friggin' brick when I sees the photo but I look at it anyways. There's Kurt, about to fuckin' burst with joy. An' there she is. Gretchen. This blonde *shiksa* dressed like she's workin' Oktobuhfest. Swear to Gawd. Big boobs in this tight blouse an' dirndl.

I wanna kick over the table or rip up the gawddamned photo or somethin'. But I don't. I just hand it back to Mr. Mephistopheles.

"So all that music an' noise was the Mastuh an' his girlfriend?" I says.

"I am afraid so, Your Majesty. I do apologize for the loudness. That was my doing. Only inside the Master's study could one hear Master Wagner's operas in their titanic glory. I did a little bit of sophisticated necromancy to prevent any words from within being heard without. But, as always, the sin of Pride in my work blinded me. I had not taken into account that cries of pleasure are not always words. So, I had to increase the volume on your side to drown out the Master and the Mistress.

"The Mistress," I says, slumpin' over my coffee. "Thanks, Mr. Mephistopheles, yer a real pal."

"I truly am sorry, Your Majesty. While I understand the Master's desire for power and glory and tenure, I cannot fathom how he could ignore a woman of your caliber."

"Me either, *bubeleh*. So the Devil gave him his tenure?" I asks.

"Why, yes. Not only does the Master have full tenure now, but he is also the leading light in Renaissance Studies as well as an authentic Renaissance man."

"Well, fuckin' A for the Mastuh," I says. "He's finally got his stinkin' tenure." Thank Gawd, I whispuh all silent to myself. I never have to hear that *alter kocker* bitch about that again. Maybe I never have to see him either. That perks me up.

"Hey, Mr. Mephistopheles."

"Yes, Your Majesty."

"Ya wouldn't get in any trouble if ya showed me the contract, would ya?"

"Well, I'm not supposed to do so. First, may I ask a question of Your Majesty?"

"Sure," I says.

"Is Your Majesty considering offering her soul to the Devil as well?"

That stumped me. I hadn't thought about it. I'd just wanted to see how long before Kurt was roastin' away.

"Maybe? How much worse could Hell be than here, huh?"

"I'm afraid quite a bit much."

"Yeah, I figured. But ya still don't mind showin' me the deal?"

The sweet little ol' man smiles at me. Then he puts his finger to his lips an' digs aroun' in the arm of his coat again. He pulls out this little plastic box an' puts in on the table. The minute he does it swells up into one a those fancy schmancy laptop compuruhs. He opens the lid an' turns the screen t'me so I can read while he goes an' lights up anotha cigarette for himself.

A course, it's all in written in fuckin' lawyer. So, I have to scroll down an' down t'get to any good stuff. Well, good stuff for Kurt. As I'm readin' it, all I can think is, "I'm dyin' here." Basically, it says as long as Kurt's alive, he's got all Hell's demons at his friggin' beck an' call. He can have anythin', no matter how awful. Tenure. Blondes. World domination. Worst of all, he gets to live t'be a 175. The only good part for me comes after he croaks. That's when he gets the four-star treatment in Hell—foreva.

But a hundred an' thirty-eight years—thirty-seven from a hundred an' seventy-five; y'do the math!—is nothin' compared to all eternity. Boy, he really got screwed.

"What a stupid *schlemiel*," I says out loud. "I can't believe he signed this. Wait. Yes, I can. Jesus, Kurt!"

Once I say the "J-word", Mr. Mephistopheles starts gettin' all fidgety in his chair. "Sorry," I says. "Hell's friggin' bells, Kurt! That better?"

"Quite, Your Majesty. I personally do *not* have a problem with you-know-who's name, but *He* does," he says, pointin' at the floor. "It has been written into all of our contracts that we writhe and moan at the merest utterance of Our Lord's latest Arch-Rival. At the risk of appearing vainglorious before Your Majesty, I must admit that I used to be quite good at it. I would even toss in a round or two of hissing. But, after a thousand or so years, I have grown weary of trembling with fear. Now I merely wriggle."

"Ya did fine, *bubeleh*."

He smiles again an' takes a long drag on his cigarette.

"Mr. Mephistopheles."

He nods his head all eager an' smoke shakes outta the cornuhs of his mouth.

"I gotta question for ya. Ya really gotta do whatevuh Kurt says till he bites the dust."

"Yes. Quite so, Your Majesty."

"I'm not talkin' the typical deal-with-the-Devil stuff like invadin' Poland or gettin' an Oscar. I'm talkin' the really pissant stuff."

"Yes, yes, that too!"

"Ya mean if he asks ya to cook him his food, clean his clothes, even flush the toilet for him, y'gotta do it."

He takes anotha long draw from his cigarette an' stares up an' out through the winduh above the sink, as if he's really interested in the new shingles on the Nachmann's roof. Smoke's curlin' slowly outta his nose, like the little roots ya see when ya repot houseplants.

Then, he sighs an' goes an' says, "Yes."

"Oh, ya poor *farchadat dybbuk*," I says. "Do I know how bad a job that is!"

An' once I'd said that, I got t'thinkin'.

My life's a freakin' shambles. Kurt—the *putz*—has sold his soul to the Devil an' is gettin' it on in Italy, of all places, with some bimbo named Gretchen an'

Gawd-knows-what-else.

But that's not the worst of it. Now I'm even more alone than before 'cause I don't go to the coven nomore. Joyce an' I had a little partin' of the ways about a month before Kurt gave it up for the Devil. I—always the *meshuggeneh*—thought we could take turns bein' the high priestess. Y'know, rotate it. My "sistah goddesses" ended up takin' her side too. So I told 'em they could all rotate *this* an' left. Which means now the only person I can talk to other than myself is a demon named Mr. Mephistopheles.

Not that he ain't nice an' all. But he works for Kurt. So I goes an' decides right there I need a demon of my own. Someone who'd do all the wifey crap I'd been doin' for years an' was sick to death of.

Hell, I think some more to myself, if Kurt can do it, why can't I? I mean, I'm the witch in this fuckin' madhouse. *An'* I'm a *Jew*. I know I can finesse a way better deal outta the Devil than that clunkuh Kurt settled for.

So, the next Saturday night at midnight I'm settin' up an altar in the kitchen. It's a little cramped over in the breakfast nook by the table 'cause my altar's three TV trays crammed with gawddessey *tchotchke*s an' red candles an' four or five of my spice racks with all my incenses an' oils.

I was just gonna pick a few an' mix 'em up in a bowl. The problem was I didn't have a free bowl anywheres on the altar. So, I goes an' turns t'get one off the kitchen table. That's when my big, fat *tuchis* hits the trays an' knocks everythin' to the floor with a big crash.

The sound scares the shit outta me an' I nearly ram the table through the swivel chairs an' the half-wall where the side counter is. An' I can feel all this heat behind me. The room's gettin' all smoky, quick. "Gawddamned freakin' dammit," I scream, smashin' the bowl on the table. I turn expectin' to see the wall on fire or somethin'. But instead, there's this really butch dyke commando starin' back at me.

She's about an inch or two talluh than me. Y'know, like 5'5" or 5'6". Her hair's black like mine but she's cut hers real short. In a crewcut or somethin'. Actually, since my hair's been down to my ass since I was thirteen, I put it up that night 'cause I didn't want it t'get in the way. If only I coulda done the same thing with my ass.

Anyways, she's got these fuckin' beautiful, light brown eyes with dark eyelashes. An' the most gloriously Semitic *schnoz* since Barbra's. An' this skin that's as tanned as mine is pale, somewheres between the color of a garlic-stuffed green olive an' a perfect black Kalamata. Speakin' of stuffed, she's gotta this brick shithouse of a body that's nearly burstin' outta this dusty ol' beige muscle T-shirt an' these black-brown-an'-gray-spotted camouflage pants. I mean, we're talkin' fuckin' killuh biceps an' great breasts an' this beautiful little belly—she was probably aroun' a hundred pounds lightuh than me, about a 180—an' wide hips an' monster thighs an' thick calves that were laced-up in a fierce pair of boots.

Sounds like I had the hots for her. I checked with my twat. We did.

Whoa, yer thinkin', when did that happen? I thought ya said youse was gonna run for the door, like Mrs. Scaduto, if yer women's group asked ya to chow down on anotha of yer sistah gawddesses.

I did. That's all true. If she'd'a grabbed me then an' there an' pushed my face into her crotch I probably woulda bolted. But I wasn't that surprised by my attraction. Hell, I was thirty-seven. In my friggin' sexual prime. Still am. An' let me tell ya, that many hormones makes ya honest. I mean, I could admit I was curious. Christ, I'd thought about foolin' aroun' with other girls as far back as high school. An' since I hit my thirties, I'd even gone to bed a few times an' wanked off thinkin' about doin' it with a room full of hot women. So, like I said, it didn't surprise me—t'think about it.

A course, I was still sorta in a bad mood from knockin' everythin' over an' a little shook up from havin' yet anotha person appear in my kitchen outta nowheres. So, I kinda lit into her.

"Who the hell are *you?*" I says.

"Your mother, Ruth," she says.

"Right, right. Sure y'are. My mutha always dresses like she's chasin' after Rommel."

"No really. I *am* your mother."

"Great. I'm tryin' t'get a devil of my own an' instead I get some *meshuggeneh* dyke with maternal instincts."

"*Bubeleh*, the name's Lilith."

"Oh, fuckin' Christ Almighty. A course, I get Lilith the baby-killer!"

"Ruth Marie," an' she goes an' grabs my face in her hands an' says all serious, "I'm only going to say this once. Okay?" I nod. "I'm no baby-killer and neither are you."

An' then I goes an' starts t'cry an' then she does an' we're huggin' an' bawlin'. Jeez, it was so freakin' *Lifetime*. But, honest to Gawd, somethin' did change right at that moment.

We talk for a few hours while I make us cups of coffee an' we work our way through a Entenmann's pecan ring. By the time we finish off the second box, I've told her as much as I've told youse so far.

"Oh, *bubeleh*," she says, pushin' away her plate, "he's worse than the first one."

"What? Y'think I'd do this a second time an' pick *him*," I says. "Trust me. Kurt's my first *an'* my last husband."

"No, no," she says. "The first man. Worse than Adam."

"Listen to *you*. That a dyke like *you* should know from Adam."

"Trust me, I do. I told you I'm Lilith. I was his first wife."

"No shit. Ya really *are* her?! Ya don't look anythin' like I imagined ya would."

"Most deities don't."

"Oh," I says. I mean, how the fuck do ya respond to that?

"I've changed my look some since the last time someone summoned me."

"Oh."

"Yes, it's been a while. Congratulations."

All I can do is shrug my shoulders an' smile. What a *schnook* I am!

"This is also the shape I take in dreams nowadays. Do you remember any of them?"

"Huh? Ya mean we've met before?"

"Yes. I come in the night to women who dream of regaining their lost strengths. I show them just how they can do this. I also keep them warm while they sleep. Very warm."

"Oh, really," I says an' my voices goes an' squeaks. "But I read that all ya did was run aroun' givin' head. Great head. Come in the night an' drink guys dry."

"Our pasts have a lot in common."

"No shit," I says, noddin' my head.

"Our futures have even more."

Omigawd, I'm thinkin', she's makin' a move on me. An' what do I do. I blush. That's it! My twat knows what's in store an' she's sittin' tight. Well, actually, she wasn't tight at all.

So Lilith pushes away from the table an' comes over t'me. She stretches out her arm. Y'know, invitin' me to take her hand. My twat says, "Take it, ya *schlemiel*." I do it. She pulls me up into her arms an' gives me this fuckin' tender, wet kiss. By the second one, I got my tongue in her.

Next thing I know, she leadin' me upstairs to my bedroom, undoin' my hair, strippin' my dress an' my bra an' my soakin' panties off of me between kisses, an' then she pushin' me back onto the bed where she licks her way down to my breasts an' aroun' an' aroun' my nipples, takin' these little hurts-so-good bites into my high beams, an' then she's lickin' her way over my big sighin' gut an' into my twat.

Fuckin' A!

Even Kurt, when he loved me, was never this good. She sucks her way aroun' my lips. She pushes that tongue of hers into me to drink up every drop of my juice. That tongue! *Oy!* Does she know how to use it. Even how to put just the right amount of pressure for just the right amount of time on my clit. Listen up, people. Too much an' I'm gonna kickbox yer head away. Too little, an' I'm gonna fall asleep with my thighs wrapped tight aroun' ya. Gawd, I sound like freakin' Goldilocks here, but it's true. An' all the squirmin' in the world won't wake me up once I gets a good snore goin'.

A course, none of that's happenin' with Lilith. Not on yer life. Goldilocks is takin' her lickin' 'cause it's just right. An' then, it gets even better. I have The Big O to end all Big Os. I'm shakin' an' screamin' like a porn star. But I really mean it.

"Feel better?" she says as she slides outta my twat an' up my belly.

"Um-hum," I muttuh. We kiss.

"But...?"

She's like a friggin' mind reada or somethin'.

"You haven't been fucked in five years."

"Six."

"I think I can definitely help you out there." She pulls this duffle bag outta the air an' takes it into the bathroom.

Boy, do I start gettin' excited all over again. I'm imaginin' she's gonna go an' get Rick for me. Or maybe take his shape. Then she comes out with this harness strapped aroun' her ass like she's ready to climb a mountain or somethin'. An' there's this big, fat dildo wavin' at me from where her twat used t'be.

I musta made a face. A pretty bad one too. Somethin' that said, "Yer kiddin', right?"

All I could think to say was, "Nothin' personal. But I like boy bits for fuckin'. Y'know, real ones."

"I know."

"Oh, okay." I was confused. "So, then, ya don't mind, y'know, gettin' me some or, um, maybe turnin' yerself into...."

"I don't do men anymore."

"Oh, sure, right."

"I'd seen so much of that pillar of salt that the other goddesses used to call me 'Lot's Wife.'"

"Oh, o-ho, yeah, pillar of salt, that's clevuh," I says, stallin', tryin' to think of what to do. Then, I figures what the hell an' goes for broke.

"But ya could turn yerself into one, right?"

"I've done it a few times. Parties mainly. But," an' she starts to walk toward the bed, her dick floppin' ahead of her, an' I'm slowly scootin' on my ass back toward the headboard, "that's not your fantasy."

"Oh, it's *not*," I says all surprised 'cause I *am*.

"No," she says. An' she crawls up on the end of the bed an' wades on her knees through the sheets an' blankets an' gets to my legs which I got drawn up against my chest an' she pulls 'em down an' then pushes 'em apart with her knees an' rubs her dick up an' down my twat's fatter-an'-juicier-than-eva lips. "Not tonight."

An' was she right. What can I say? If ya get the right demon with the right dildo, anythin's possible.

So, later, we're snugglin' in bed, talkin' about my idea to make a deal with the Devil but keep my soul by bettin' him I could give him the best blowjob he's ever had. Lilith's holdin' me from behind in her big arms, just listenin' t'me go on about what I'm gonna do when I win. Then, she kisses my neck an' I forget what I'm sayin'.

"*Bubeleh*," she says, "the devil's dick is cold. Icy cold."

Somewheres I remember someone else warnin' me about this. Right. It was Auntie Teresa. She was the smartest of my dad's sisters. I'm mean, she's read Dante's *Inferno*, for Chrissakes, an' that's how I learned the devil lives on the ninth floor in Hell. An' it's freezin' cold. Like an eternity of Januarys in Minnesota or somethin'.

"And," she says loudly to catch my wanderin' attention, "whatever you do, don't let him stick it up your ass. That's his favorite. You'll never melt him that way."

"So, I'll just microwave him with my twat," I says.

"It's a hot one, I'll grant you that. Lots of juice. But, it won't be enough."

"Get outta here."

"Trust me. But I think I have just the plan to put the *kibosh* on him stealing your soul. We'll have to tag team him...."

"We?" I can barely say the word. I'm gettin' all *farklempt* here, an' fast. Thirty seconds till I'm bawlin' again. I mean, she's bein' so freakin' sweet t'me an' it's been so long since anyone's talked t'me like this. Not since my parents died. But I gotta know what her plan is. So I take a deep breath an' stifle the waterworks for t'night.

"Won't the Devil recognize ya?" I says.

"I doubt it. We travel in very different circles," she says.

"Oh."

"Hey. You want to hear my plan or what?"

"Sure. Let me have it."

"You're insatiable, Ruth Faust." She kisses me an' slips me her tongue an' then—guess what?—we fuck for the second of thirteen times that night.

Hey! What'd I tell ya about the eyes? It'd been six long, *dry* years.

The thirteenth time was the craziest of all. She asks me, all nice an' everythin', to eat her out an' I do. This from the woman who says she only likes boy bits. Well, like anotha crazy Jew once said, we're all a bit polymorphously perverse.

So, I push Lilith off of me. I chew aroun' on her neck some more an' do a bit a nippin' an' tuckin', if y'know what I mean, on her breasts. Hey, great tits are great tits! No shit. I've always gotten kinda warm when I spot a awesome rack. But my twat knows I should be pokin' my tongue somewheres else an' she drags me down to Lilith's dick. I deep throat it on the first go—I told ya I have no gag reflex!—an' give it my high school special. A heavy suction swirlie. I grip the dick really firm between my lips—no teeth—an' every time I get to the head I let my tongue go wild. A few bobs on a teenage boy an' he's creamin'. Shit, the last time I did "Fat Ruth's Special" on a guy, Kurt *was* a teenage boy.

I'm startin' t'get nostalgic here, so I stop before I bite her dildo in half.

I pull it outta my mouth an' help her get it off. Boy, fuckin' a girl ten or eleven times in one night can make ya ripe. She smelled like a big, hairy wild animal an' dirt ya just dug up in yer garden after a really light rain. It was makin' me wild. It was makin' me wanna dig.

I look up at her an' grin. "*L'chayim,*" I says an' she laughs. Then I press my mouth, my tongue, my nose—hell, my whole gawddamned face—into her shakin', steamin' twat an' go to town.

Despite all my enthusiam, I gotta admit I didn't do so hot. The first time. I didn't suck neither, mind ya. Na, wait. I did suck. A lot. But I fumbled here an' there. I kept gettin' all shy with her clit. I mean, I know what I like. I just never done it from that angle before. But I got better. Lilith's a fuckin' amazin' teachuh. *Oy,* my tongue got so strong an' so fuckin' suave, if it was possible an' it wouldn'ta hurt like hell, I coulda gone back in time to that night an' tied a knot in her clit just like a cherry stem. Yeah, I was that good. Actually, I'm even better now.

Remember that, okay? It's important. 'Cause eatin' twat is the key to Lilith's plan.

Next Wednesday, it's gettin' close to about four. The usual time that Mr. Mephistopheles an' I get t'gether for coffee an' cake. Lilith thinks he might recognize her an' blow everythin'. So, she takes off to visit a few of her musician friends. I'm puttin' the pecan ring out on the table when I can smell him comin'. I take in a deep breath. The room's startin' to smell like pecan ring, cigarettes, an' Jean Naté. I'm feelin' better already.

After our second slice, anotha cup of coffee, an' a cigarette for us both, I'm finally feelin' relaxed enough to go for broke.

"So, Mr. Mephistopheles," I says while I exhale, "ya remember when ya asked me if I wanted to sell my soul to the Devil?"

He's mid-drag so all he can do is arch his eye-brow an' grin.

"Well, I'm ready. T'day. Ya ready to write up my deal?" I stub out my cigarette. Next thing I know, his silvuh holduh's cigarette-down in the ashtray an' he's pullin' the laptop outta his sleeve.

"I'm ready, Your Majesty," he says.

So, I goes an' tells him what I want an' he types it all into his computuh.

Basically, I want all Kurt got. But I wanna live t'be 300 years ol' an' I wanna be in my sexual prime—y'know, 35, for the rest of my life. An' when I kick off, it's gonna be all peaceful like. In my sleep. With all my great-great-great grandchildren aroun' me.

An' when he's done typin' all that I says, "There's somethin' else but I gotta tell it directly to The Man."

"Oh, my, Your Majesty. I would advise you against that. I promise you I can arrange all the details of a soul transfer. Not to boast, but I am quite good at it. Legendary, if I might add."

"I believe ya, Mr. Mephistopheles. It's nothin' against ya. It's just that I don't wanna give The Devil my soul."

"Oh, dear me. He's not going to like this. No, not one bit."

"I wanna make a wayjuh. If I lose, he gets my soul. If I win, he gives me all

I asks for an' that's that."

"I see. And what kind of wager is Your Majesty making. A contest of wills, bodies, minds, appetites, depravaties...?"

"Alla that. It's sex for Chri—" an' he starts to scrunch up his shoulders an' quiver so I stop myself. "For Satan's sake. I'm bettin' I can make the Devil come."

"Oh, Your Majesty, that will never do."

"Whadda ya mean?" I says all nervous now. He has to agree to my wayjuh or I'm royally screwed.

"It's just that, well, it doesn't take much effort for My Lord to—how does one put this to a lady of your caliber?—achieve his ends."

"Ya mean, come, right?"

"Exactly." An' he goes an' leans across the table to whispuh into my ear. "The Great-and-All-Powerful Satan has a bit of a problem with what mortals now call "premature ejaculation." It has actually proved quite convenient over the ages. Oh, my, especially when the Borgias were in the Vatican! Why, every gala orgy Pope Alexander VI threw, the more and more Borgias would show up to make a wager much like yours with Him.

"I personally would have been exhausted. But not My Lord. A few minutes with a hundred or so people meant he could be done in hours instead of days or months. And when he was through, he was more refreshed than when he had begun. Why, that rascal, Cesare, even after he'd lost his soul, was still begging My Master to sodomize him as often as possible. And, kind soul that He is, The Bright Star would oblige and ream that rakish boy fifteen or twenty times at every one of his father's bacchanalias. Yes, My Lord may be a tad hasty with his delivery but he has no problem whatsoever with recovery...."

At this point, I'm so fuckin' lost. I have no idea what he's talkin' about. I don't know nothin' about the Borgias yet. So I decide I have to clarify myself or give it up. Now.

"Hey, Mr. Mephistopheles."

"Oh, oh. I'm sorry, Your Majesty, I was waxing on. Do forgive me."

"Forget about it." He bows from the waist an' I watch the lace cheese wheel tilt to the table an' back up. "I meant to say I can make The Devil come after his longest go-round ever...." Here I remember somethin' Lilith told me so I adds, "An' there'll be warm fluids."

"Well, well. That's a wager after all. I can't see him passing that up. It's never been done before. A very bold move, Your Majesty."

"Sure. Thanks," I says.

An' the ol' man starts to type away again, mutterin' aloud "warm fluids" an' gigglin' to himself.

That Saturday, aroun' midnight, Lilith an' I are waitin' up in my bedroom for the Devil to do a walk-on. I look over to the clock by the bed. It says 12:01. I turn back an' there's this little green ball in front of me.

It's like this tiny thundercloud. All bubblin' an' shit like someone's tryin' to boil it. I wanna start laughin my ass off 'cause all I can think is this *schmekel* of a cloud *is* the Devil? It musta read my mind 'cause next thing I know, it's growin'. An' the bigger it gets, the worse it smells. "Christ," I yell an' the cloud freezes for just a moment. Now it stinks even worse. Like a fuckin' dump—I mean a honest-to-Gawd garbage dump—filled only with rotten eggs an' rancid garlic. I scream to Lilith to open the winduh. As soon as I do that, the *farshtinkener* cloud goes poof an' it's like it blew up. There're just pieces of it floatin' aroun'. Same goes with the stench. An', in the middle of *my* bedroom, there stands none other than the Devil himself.

T'be honest, I was expectin' a real lump. A bug-eyed golem with waxy skin an' big tufts of hair sproutin' from his shoulders. Instead, I get this curly headed, blond *boychik* with hypnotic blue eyes an' these red lips that beg t'be chewed, wearin' this *schmatte* of a red robe that barely covers any of his skin. Creamy skin ya wanna lick from head to head to toe an' back to head, if y'know what I mean. He looks like a cross between a Hitla Youth an' Christopha Atkins in *Blue Lagoon*.

Gawd, I wore that video ragged one summuh.

Anyways, this *pisher*, once he's shook loose his cloud of shit-stinkin' smoke, goes an' drops the robe an' I see he's got the biggest *schmuck* I ever seen. Swear to Gawd! Makes Kurt's look like a dinky *schmendrick*. All I could think was, Jesus Christ, if he sticks that thing in me I'll fuckin' *plotz*. My twat, on the other hand, she don't give a damn. She's already droolin' through my panties onto my inner thighs. An' in the end, I always agree with my twat that what she should want, she should have.

"So, you're the next contestant to best the Devil," he says, just oozin' smarm.

"Yeah, I guess I am," I says.

"Splendid."

"Y'know, my girlfriend fucks me up the ass all the time. She likes to pretend we're *faygeleh*s runnin' aroun' the woods on Fire Island."

The Devil grinned.

"Don't get me wrong. I'm with the *faygeleh*s here. I think butt-fuckin's hot."

"It *is*, Mrs. Faust," he says, comin' as close as his all-of-a-sudden-stiff-as-a-two-by-four-*schmuck* lets him. Believe me, it was close enough 'cause poster *goy* has got day-ol' vodka breath. We're talkin' cheap vodka. The Maneschevitz of vodka. "Just wait till I'm inside you. No one does it *quite* like I do."

"Oh, sure, sure," I says, backin' away from the fumes. "I've heard yer great. Hell, my girlfriend says she'll even join us if ya like."

"I'd like that very much, Mrs. Faust" he says. "But I didn't know there'd be another here to make a deal."

"Oh? Oh no. She don't want nothin' from ya. She just wants to hang out. Watch. Maybe play. We never done a three-ways before."

He turned to Lilith. "You don't wish to try for vast riches," and Lilith shakes her head, "world domination," she shakes it some more, "immortality?"

"It's overrated," she says.

"Oh, the high and mighty Christian, are we?"

"Yeah, right," I laugh. "She just wants to have sex with the Devil."

He stared at her. "What an odd woman. But what Devil would I be if I denied any of God's children a moment of ecstasy with me. Just remember the deal's between me and your girlfriend."

"No problem."

"Okay then. Shall we begin."

"Sure," I says. I start takin' off my clothes. I catch the Devil eyein' my breasts as I pull off my bra.

"Y'know," I says. "I was wonderin' if I could work up to you plowin' my ass."

"Work up? My dear Mrs. Faust, didn't my underling inform you? I don't do foreplay. No fondling of the breasts, no matter how impressive they might be, no cunnilingus, no anal-oral contact. Why, I don't even use lube."

"Oh, I didn't know."

"Would you like to cancel the wager?"

"Na, na. I'm just curious why no foreplay.

"I'm not a big fan of traditional sex."

"*Bubeleh*, where have *you* been? No foreplay is about as traditional as sex gets."

I don't think he likes me. He gives me this really lame-ass smile.

"If you must know, Mrs. Faust, I'm an aficionado of the asshole."

"Oh," I says, havin' no idea what he's talkin' about.

"I find it a painful challenge for the contestant."

"No lube. I bet."

"Yes, Mrs. Faust, you have made a bet," he says all impatient like. "So, if you don't mind, I have a very busy schedule. Please, just pull down your panties and bend over. This won't take long but it will hurt very much." He starts laughin' like some little boy who's had way too much sugar.

"Sure, sure." An' I'm standin' there slippin' my underwear off an' I stop. "You like challenges, right?"

"Obviously, Mrs. Faust."

"An' you think the asshole's the hardest."

"Look at my devilhood," he says pointin' to his *schmuck*. It grows anotha foot right then an' there. "Now compare that with the average asshole and I call that a challenge."

"I guess."

"What, Mrs. Faust? You had something else in mind."

"Well, in my experience," an' I goes an' nods my head toward Lilith, "nothin's more of a challenge than eatin' a woman out. 'Specially a real butch one like my girlfriend."

The Devil looks back at Lilith like he'd forgotten she was in the room. "I wouldn't know," he says.

"Whaddya mean ya don't know? Yer the friggin' Devil. Y'know as much as Gawd."

"More," he adds, all bitter soundin'.

"More. Sure, more. But then ya musta eaten out a woman some time."

"Never."

"What? That's crazy. Was it 'cause you didn't enjoy it when you was a woman?"

"I've never been a woman, Mrs. Faust. I'm the Devil."

"Oh, yeah, yeah. Right. I know ya ain't a woman. No more than yer the hung-like-a-fuckin'-horse *ganef* standin' before me. But ya musta a taken the shape of one before?"

"No. I never have."

All I could think was "Don't that explain everythin'." But I goes an' says, "Feh!", an' pull up my panties.

"'Feh,' Mrs. Faust?"

"That's right. Feh! Yer not the Devil. Yer just one of his little guys pretendin' t'be. I'm not gonna do anotha gawddamned thing till ya get me the Devil."

"What? Don't be an idiot, Mrs. Faust. Everyone knows I'm the Devil. I often take a pleasing appearance. Look at me! I know you're pleased. And my penis! Everyone knows it's colder than ice. Please, touch it."

"Ice, schmice. I bet every demon in Hell has a fuckin' icicle for a dick. I want the Devil. The big-D Devil. Lucifuh."

"I *am* Lucifer. The Bright Star. Look at me! Don't I look like a fallen angel to you?!"

"Maybe. But I need more proof."

"I don't give 'more proof,' Mrs. Faust!"

"Fine, ya *shaygets*, then the deal's off."

Next thing I know I'm coughin' my lungs up. There's smoke everywheres. I screamin' to Lilith again to open a winduh. Then, it's gone an' there's the Devil doin' his impersonation of a woman. He's—she's—I'm no fuckin' good with these pronouns here—the Devil's turned himself into one of those scrawny supermodels that looks like they got a teenage boy's body with little round breasts glued on. Jeez, I'm thinkin', I'm learnin' way more t'night than I ever wanted to about who the Devil thinks is really hot. No wonder he came to Kurt first.

"Is that the best ya can do?" I laugh.

Oh, is *he* pissed. There's this big puff of red smoke an' then it's gone an' I'm starin' at Betty Bazoombas.

We're talkin' the American Porno Queen Dream. Trust me, I know. I've watched hundreds over the years. She's aroun' 5'10" an' weighs no more than a 135 pounds. That's 5 pounds for her bleached hair an' 15 pounds for each boob. 40 Double D. A course they're implants. Jeez, it's the Devil for Chrissakes! Only he could have tits that huge an' a waist as big aroun' as one of those starvin' Hollywood actresses arms an' not fall flat on his face.

Did I mention, he's wearin' 6" stilletos an' still not fallin' over? I can't even stand in freakin' 1" heels. While he coulda probably danced a jig in those shoes on wet grass if I'd asked. An' get this, 'cept for the heels, all he's got on is a little gold ankle bracelet with a pentagram. I swear, nothin' else. That's right. The Devil's butt nekked in my bedroom. Oh, oh, an' he's gone an' shaved his twat. Yeah, all that's left of whatevuh bush he had is this teeny, tiny Hitla moustache. What's that? Y'know it. The perfect porno pussy.

"Can I call you Lucy?" is all I can think to say.

"No, Mrs. Faust, you cannot," he says.

"And don't even think of calling me Lyle," says this man's voice behind me.

I look to see what new demon's snuck into the house now an' there's Lilith. She's gone an' turned herself into a guy. Same feachuhs. A little talluh. A little thinnuh. Same killuh *schnoz* an' a *schmuck* to match. That's right, people. A big flesh-an'-blood dick.

"Whoa," I says. Lucy looks back an' I hear him sigh. I know he's drippin' too. I can smell it. It's like this strong spice, y'know. Turmeric. Yeah, that's it.

"What?" Lilith says. Her voice is real sexy an' suave soundin'. Like Frank's.

Sinatra, ya dope!

"Oh, this," she says. "Just a little shape-shifting I do for parties." We're both starin' open mouth 'cause Lilith is one hot guy. "Hey," she says, tryin' t'get our eyes outta her crotch, "up here."

"Huh?" Lucy an' I says at the same time.

"Let's party, girls."

Lilith goes an' walks into the middle of the room, her dick bobbin' along up in front, until she's standin' before Lucy.

"Go ahead. Touch it, " she says. "You know you want to."

I nod my head without thinkin'.

"Whatever do you mean, boy?" says Lucy.

Gawd, the Devil's got the right-soundin' voice—all high an' breathy. But he sure as shit don't talk like no porn star. Sounds more like one of the Three Fuckin' Musketeers.

"It's colder than yours ever was," says Lilith.

"Impossible."

Lilith takes Lucy's hand an' wraps it aroun' her *schmuck*. The Devil makes a hissin' sound. Like some angry snake.

"Ow. It's too cold. It's too cold," Lucy says, tossin' his hair an' makin' all these whimperin' noises. What a whiny fuckin' girl! "It's burning me."

"I bet." Lilith thrusts her hips a few times so her dick's pumpin' away in Lucy's hand.

Lucy shrieks as he tears his hand away. He's cryin' an' jumpin' from one foot to the other an' wavin' his hands in the air an' blowin' on them like he just got done playin' Twistuh on top of a electric stove.

I can see his hands. They look fine t'me. Didn't even muss up his French manicure nails. The bitch. Guess it's not quite like bein' human an' stickin' yer fuckin' tongue to a frozen pipe.

"How did you do that?" he asks my man Lilith.

"It's just a matter of practice," she says, playin' with her balls—we're talkin' real low hanguhs here. "I've had more time than you."

"That's impossible. Only God Himself is older than I!"

"Oh, Lucy, do ya have a lot to learn t'night!" I says.

"Mrs. Faust, *what* did I tell you about calling me Lucy?"

"Sorry, Yer Devilness." I turn my back for a second an' roll my eyes, hard, an' mutter a curse or two. Gawd, I wanna tear that bitch a new one.

"Not only," Lilith goes on, "is my dick colder, it's also harder and longer than yours."

"Oh, please, man!" Lucy says as he puts his hands on his hips an' tosses that hair of his. Gawd, it looks so South Shore.

"There's only one way to find out."

"Never," he says. He goes an' throws his big hair about some more. Y'know he's secretly wishin' I'd go find a fan from the attic an' bring it back to the bedroom an' spend the rest of the night aimin' it at him so he wouldn't have to keep that wind-swept look goin' by himself. I swear to ya. I can hear him whisperin' the fuckin' suggestion in my head. But I don't.

"C'mon," Lilith says. "You know you've always wanted to experience what it feels like for those wretched sinners impaled on your icy spear." Lucy starts to giggle like she's some nine year ol' girl at a slumber party.

"For once, you have the chance to experience that torment yourself." And Lilith now's yankin' on her *schmuck* as she talks. "You've seen them writhe and you've heard them shriek for centuries, but you have no idea why. In your head, you think you do. But in your body, you feel nothing. You're empty."

"What nonsense. Why, it's pure projection." Lucy's talkin' all quiet like now 'cause all she can do is stare at my girlfriend's king-size dick.

"Perhaps. Maybe more than you know. It's possible I was once good at giving torment myself. But that doesn't change the fact that you're still curious." And Lilith swaggers over to the bed an' lays herself spread eagle on it. Her long dick's pointin' to the ceilin'.

"C'mon, Lucifer. You know you want to sit on it."

So guess what, the Devil does just that. But not without makin' a total fuckin' production of it. He can't just walk over to the bed—who could in those heels? An' he can't just take 'em off neither. Na, he has to lift off the ground about four feet an' then hover over to the bed. Ya can tell he's havin' a hard time with the new body 'cause he's floatin' back an' forth over Lilith's dick, tryin' t'get his favorite hole lined up with it.

He's just about got it when Lilith goes an' says, "I need you to be facing away from me."

"Why," he says, soundin' real hurt. "Do I not please you?"

"You look great," Lilith says. She better be lyin' is all I have to say. "It's just that I have something special planned for you and it only works if you're straddling me the other way."

"Special?" Lucy says, all curious.

"Very," she says.

"For me?"

"Yes, for you."

That does it. Alla the sudden, Lucy's turned around an' squattin' on Lilith's *schmuck*. No foreplay. No lube. Just the way he likes it. He must, 'cause he's makin' these really scary cooin' sounds for every little bit of dick he takes up his ass.

"You don't mind if my girlfriend helps out," Lilith says, givin' her dick anotha thrust. "This is *her* deal with the Devil after all. She really wants to lick your clit while I savage your asshole. I promise you, it's right up your alley. You've got extreme pleasure and pain fighting it out throughout your body. A very delightful experience. But it might be too much for you. Being a virgin and all."

That does it. Lucy turns his head aroun'. Just his head—hey, y'knew he would—an' says, "Call me a virgin again and your girlfriend loses her bet."

"Okay, Lucifer, calm down." An' Lilith goes an' lifts her hips an' the dick slides in deeper. Lucy makes this happy-soundin' grunt an' turns his head back. Lilith ignores him an' just keeps on talkin'. "I'm just saying you're good at what you know and after you experience this you may want to add it to your repertoire."

"A clever save, young man. Oh. Oh, oh! Oh, yes. Your penis is growing *colder* and *colder*!" An' the Devil squats down further on Lilith with a few more happy, piggy grunts. "But I must concur. I have been growing fatigued with the old routines. Well," he says, glarin' at me, "are you going to minister to my vagina or not?"

"Ya mean eat your pussy, right?" I says.

"I assume so. That is what the rustics are calling it nowadays?"

"Who ya callin' 'rustic,' *Teifel?*"

"Girls, girls," says Lilith, laughin'. Yeah, sure, *she's* havin' a good time all right. All *she's* gotta do is sit there with her dick hard. *I* gotta eat out the Devil.

"My apologies, Mrs. Faust," says Lucy. "Would you please eat my pussy?"

"Eat it?" I says, psychin' myself up. "I'm gonna devour it. Yuh're gonna come so hard...."

"How would I know in *this* body?" he says all snippy.

Lilith an' me, we just laugh. "You'll know. Trust me, " I says.

I look over at the clock again. 12:27. It's time t'get this show on the road. So, I take my panties off an' put 'em on Lilith's face. She likes that. Musta made her dick harder or somethin' 'cause Lucy's gaspin' an' "ooohin'" big time now. I crawl up onto the bed where Lucy's squattin' on Lilith's flesh-colored popsicle. He don't even wobble on his heels. We're talkin' fuckin' amazin' calf muscles an' lots a black magic here. Just keeps pushin' his ass lower an' lower an' spreadin' his legs wider an' wider so his pussy lips are open an' waitin' for my killuh tongue.

By some miracle, I get my body into this *cockamamy* position where I can get my face into her twat without knockin' everybody off the bed. It looks like a real twat up close. Smells a helluva lot better than that cloud did too. But there's somethin' odd about it. Maybe the lips are too perfect, too perky. But then this is a pussy, not a twat, I reminds myself. They're supposed t'be perky. Maybe it's the clit. It kinda glows. Not like Rudolph or nothin'. It's real faint like. But it definitely glows. Then it hits me. If somethin' glows, it should be hot. But all that's comin' outta this pussy is a chill little wind.

Shit, I thinks. How'm I gonna get warm fluids outta this ice box. I tries to calm myself down. The cold could be comin' from Lilith's *schmuck*. A big part of me's afraid my tongue's gonna freeze to Lucy's cunt but the rest of me says I gotta play this out to the end. I've come too far to quit. Even my twat's givin' me her two cents an' tellin' me t'get in there already. I put my lips to his lips an' start lickin' my way aroun'.

"Oooh," says Lucy with this throaty little growl. "That's new. I want more.

What else can you do? Well? Do it!"

The fuckin' cunt tries to grab me by my hair an' mash my face in his pussy but I bat his hands away. Then I goes an' blows on his clit. Real light. He likes that 'cause it shuts him up. I touch it with the tip of my tongue. It ain't ice, thank Gawd. It's cool, but it ain't ice. I got a shot here after all.

So I start takin' turns between my fingers an' my tongue with the Devil's clit. I'm suckin' here an' rubbin' there like my life depends on it. An' it does. But it's gettin' harder an' harder 'cause Lilith's got a really good fuck goin'. Lilith's slammin' her dick into Lucy an' Lucy's nearly jumpin' up an' down on Lilith. Which means his pussy's bouncin' all around an' I'm gettin' a friggin' crick in my neck.

I pull my head out for some air while I give the Devil the finger, an' hard too. The clock says 12:37. Ten minutes. Only five more an' we're home free.

My finger musta done somethin' right 'cause we're gettin' some juices flowin' finally. I lick my finger. Not cold. Not warm. Somewheres in between. Like a really hot bath an hour later. What's that word that sounds just like this water feels? Huh? Tepid. Yeah, that it. His juices was tepid. If I wanted warm, I was gonna have to pick up the pace. Fast.

Lilith musta knew I was flaggin' 'cause she goes an' gives me a boost. She puts her hand between my legs an' starts playin' with my twat. Strokin' it. Rubbin' the juicy edges. Draggin' her fingers teasin'ly between my lips. Givin' little flicks of encouragement to my clit. An' boy'd that make a born-again pussy-eater outta me. I was tonguin' like a madwoman. Then Lilith goes an' slaps my ass hard, an' again. Now, I'm tonguin' like a very mad woman.

"Why does *she* get her ass slapped?" says Lucy. "I want *my* ass slapped."

Jeez, I thinks, whadda whiner. Just shut up an' come already.

Lilith's hand disappears. I hear her tryin' to slap Lucy the same time as she's fuckin' him. Must be like battin' away two tetherballs. Y'know. Whatevuh. All that matters is that Lucy likes it an' he does. He starts doin' really impressive deep-knee bends. Gawd, don't that kill my neck.

But I keep on bouncin' along an' eatin' the Devil's pussy. Even when he stops alla the sudden, mid-jump.

There's several things that tip me off to Lucy havin' his biggest O. I mean, I'm busy in his twat so I can't be lookin' aroun'. His juice is still lukewarm. So I gotta push my face in deeper an' lick harder. But I'm close enough to hear it all. Like Lucy's hole squeezin' Lilith's dick. Yer asshole don't do that unless y'got a majuh case of the shits or yer gettin' the fuckin' of yer life. It's makin' this awful cruchin' sound. Like yer walkin' on ice an' it starts to crack. Pretty gross, huh? I thought so too. But whatevuh gets the Devil off, y'know.

Then there's all this wailin' an' cryin' an' shit—from Lucy. He's in heaven—so to speak. Gawd Almighty, is he loud. C'mon, y'knew the Devil was gonna be a screamer. He's yellin', "Yes! Yes! Yes! I AM THE ANTI-CHRIST!" Honest. Whadda freak! An' it ain't hurtin' Lilith neither. She's just moanin' all happy soundin' while she's shootin' all these ice pellets—how else does a fuckin' icicle come?—inside of the Devil.

Then, I dunno why, I goes an' does somethin' completely *meshugge*. I bites into Lucy's clit. Boy, does he scream now. A course the *putz* likes it rough. What was I thinkin' before? Forget the tongue. Go for the teeth. An' I do. An' how.

It'd'a been easier to pull a bone from a Rottweila's mouth than get me to let go of Lucy. An' while I'm chewin' his clit, I'm lickin' the tip from inside with my tongue. A modified "Fat Ruth's Special." An' that's when I feel the temperature risin'. My face is gettin' wetter an' warmer.

Then he goes an' has anotha Big O. Fuckin' A! Am I lovin' Lucy now.

When the Devil's done shakin' an' shriekin', I stop bitin' his clit an' pull my face outta his still-throbbin' lips an' lick my own. "Well," I says, "whadda we have here? Tastes like warm fluids."

"What? That cannot be," Lucy moans.

"Lilith whadda ya think?" She pulls her big icicle outta Lucy's ass—Jesus Christ, whadda sad sound he makes when that happens—an' leaves the Devil squattin' over nothin'. Then she slides out from between his legs an' rolls over t'me an' starts lappin' at my face.

"Tastes like warm fluids to me. Here taste this, girlfriend."

An' Lilith puts her fingers into Lucy's twat an' then goes an' rubs the sticky juice all over his face.

"No, no, no," Lucy shouts, makin' a big tadoo about it an' tossin' his bimbo hair aroun' again. "This is *not* what we agreed to."

"Hold the phone, *Teifel*, this is just what ya agreed to. I make ya come after yer longest go-round ever. Which I did. With the help of my girlfriend. An' it was all totally legal as ya would know bein' the fathuh of all lawyers."

"What?" the Devil says. He sounds all tired an' dizzy. He's wobblin' a bit as he stands up on the bed.

"That's right. There was nothin' in yer contract that said I couldn't have help or that ya had t'be a man. I said "the Devil." There was no mention ever about "he" or "she." Just "the Devil" comes. That's it."

I hear this weird noise. Like snifflin'. I looks like Lucy ain't far off with anotha round of waterworks. Time to close the deal.

"An' I also said specifically, an' I quote, 'they'll be warm fluids.' End quote. I didn't say you'll come warm fluids. I said you'll come an' there'll be warm fluids. You did. There were. The end. I win. Now fork it over."

Next thing I know, the walls are runnin' with tears. Lilith an' me are on the floor. Lucy's hair is touchin' the freakin' ceilin' an' he ain't far below it, arms spread wide like he's You-Know-Who on the cross, his heels just danglin' in the air. What's this nut's obsession with Jesus?! The bed's hoverin' next to us an' spinnin'. I'm waitin' for some hurricane wind t'kick in. That an' some loud organ music.

Instead, Lucy's face turns redduh an' redduh. An' he makes the fuckin' awful high screechin' sound without openin' his mouth. Then he belches out in this terrifyin' monster voice, "Oh, Christ!" an' disappears in a little cloud of the same ol' *farshtinkener* smoke.

Next thing I know, there's this light tippy-tap goin' on at the door. "Come in," I shout. An' Mr. Mephistopheles pops that big white collar of his aroun' the door an' then I see his head. He's givin' me this fuckin' sly smile an' smoke's all curlin' out, as usual, from the end of his long cigarette holduh. He pulls it outta his mouth an' purrs somethin' like,

"Congratulations, ladies. You've won."

So I'm all screamin' an' shit an' bouncin' on the no-longer-hoverin' bed an' Lilith's laughin' her ass off an' Mr. Mephistopheles asks, "Mistress?" Lilith has to slap me on the *tuchis* t'get my attention. "Hey, what's that for?" She tells me he's talkin' t'me. To *me*. Mistress. Well, all right. I can do "mistress." So I says, "Yes?"

"Mistress, if you'll be needing anything in particular tonight, do let me know."

"Well, y'know Mephi—can I call ya 'Mephi?'" I says, climbin' down off the bed.

"I would be honored, Mistress."

"Great. You know what I could go for right now?"

"No, Mistress."

"Rick at Burguh Haven. Y'know, aroun' 1981."

"An excellent choice, Mistress."

"An' make sure he brings enough double cheeseburguhs an' fries for both me an' Lilith. Ya okay with eatin' meat t'night, *bubeleh*?"

She starts laughin' her ass off again. "It's been a while," she says, "but why the hell not."

"That's what I'm thinkin'. Why the hell not!" An' I goes an' grab her by the dick. It ain't no icicle now.

"Y'don't mind keepin' this a little longer?" I says.

"Longer?" she says.

"Y'know what I mean." She gives me this nasty grin an' pulls me in to slip me some tongue. Did I mention I love tongue?

Eventually, I tear myself away. I gotta breathe sometime, an' I can feel Mephi watchin' us. Not that I mind bein' watched. But in Mephi's case, I know it ain't doin' a thing for him. I remind myself to order him to have a go with Rick when Lilith an' I are done with the Burguh Gawd. Hell, I bet he's gone without it longer than I have.

"Hey, Mephi," I says, turnin' to him. "Y'got all that?"

"Oh, yes, Mistress." An' he closes the door an' then opens it an' there's Rick, naked except for this big bag of burguhs an' fries. Boy, did we *all* pig out that night.

By the next afternoon, I've divorced Kurt. Mephi an' Rick had to go to Florence t'get him to sign. Good riddance was all I could think. He an' that Gretchen bitch an' the Devil deserve each other.

By sunset, I had a new house in Sag Harbor an' I got one for Lilith next door. We spent all night testin' out the beds in both houses. In fact, for the rest of that year I was testin' beds an' bodies all aroun' the world.

This year I've been fuckin' *an'* readin'. Yeah, William Shakespeare. That's right. Him an' every other bastard that still got somethin' in print.

A course, now that y'know I got all these super*mensch* powers I bet ya wanna know what I'm gonna do with 'em next. A fair question. I don't know. But I've been thinkin'. An' it's gonna be big. It's gonna be very big.

Peace in the Middle East? Ya had to ask? A woman in the White House? A course. But it won't be me. I've got bigger matzoh balls to boil.

Y'know, come to think of it, I might as well put one in the Vatican too. Just to shake things up a bit. Maybe a Madame President in Bejing an' Moscow. It's the second Madame Prime Ministuh for Israel that's gonna be the real trick. Y'think I'm kiddin'. I should know. I worked on a kibbutz one summuh. Some of those *sabra* boys are to die for, trust me. But ever try talkin' to a *muy macho* Jew. *Oy, vay iz mir.* All I can say is this shrew's gotta helluva lot a tamin' t'do.

But I said really big. End world hunguh? Such a question. A course. What am I, a monster? Somethin' much *bigger*.

Like, for example, turnin' all those fat farms in the strip malls into pleasure palaces for us plus size women. Gawd, how I've hated that name "plus size." Like we're one plus anotha woman. Talk about yer Addition Doublin' Disorduh. Na, I wanna turn that plus into somethin' good. That's right, people. I don't want my weight watched. I want it worshipped. An' that goes double for my twat!

But that's only the beginnin'.

For now, just remember my name. Ruth Vitale. Yer gonna be hearin' it any day now.

Hey, ya want anotha slice of the pecan ring? Good. Then we'll take a ride on my broomstick like I promised ya.

Troll

Beware.

I am no longer able to mask my need. I am a hungry ghost. The Buddha, if you had bothered to listen, would have warned you about me.

You see me as grotesquely fat. A glutton who feasts on the rich drippings and excreta that fall from the lives of my aloof betters. You. The Almighty Beautiful. But my balloon of a belly is light with the gas of incessant and unvented hungers. Worse, the accident of birth, this descent into unchosen flesh, has delivered me into a body whose mouth has been cruelly twisted into a slit. I will never devour the spew of incandescent stars that I dream each night might fill me.

Still, I must eat. I beg to be fed by your cock, rigid with disdain. All you hear slipping through the crease between my dry lips are the sighing hisses of my sweet entreaties. It is a comic yet infuriating sound. Like a life's worth of mail pushed in handfuls through a slotted door.

You see me as completely alien. I loom off the horizon. I am lust's greatest obstacle. Your Scylla and your Charybdis. Freakish creatures stretching their slippery fingers to snag your heroic prow and swallow your bobbing flesh in our gaping whirlpool mouths. Shoals of pink-striped fat and thinning hair to run your odyssey aground.

I leer sidelong at your silhouette and grab for you. I await, with ridiculous expectancy, the return of another's unsteady heat. I mutter as I trail in your wake, echolocating you with my hands. The warmth of your spittle when you turn and tell me to fuck off reminds me, as it waters my face, that I am still alive. I am not alone.

I defy more than common decency. Your small gasps and blank stares are meant to remind me I am ugly and not wanted. But I will never believe anything you say. I know who I am. I am not ugly. I am something far worse to you and the other hoped-for phoenixes who self-immolate from every Friday's dusk until each Sunday's sunrise, certain that something miraculous will grow from your cooling ash.

My offense is that I believe we both are no more than men. Men made brothers only by our own hungers. And if there are no gods, there can be no monsters. I am ordinary. I am turning to dry gray dust without fire. I am old. And someday, I will have you. Despite your slaps at my unabashed hands. Someday, if you live through youth's fiery night, you too will be old. You will be me.

I wait for you.

The One, True
Lord of the Dance

for Gil Kudrin

The deadline was Monday morning. It was Wednesday. All Mac had left to write was the introduction. Before Monday. Four days. Then email it with the manuscript revisions to Jeremy.

Jeremy Plotkin. His editor at St. Sebastian's, *the* gay press of note—this year. Next year, its parent company, Veber, Strauss, and Theroux, Publishers, might become a division of the Güttenberg syndicate or Murisaka Industries. And neither über-publishing house was known for being a patron of gay artists, even a media *wunderkind* like Michael A. Corrigan. But that was next year—maybe.

Today St. Sebastian's was riding high. Seven Lavendar Literary Award nominations this year alone. And one win. The Lavvy for best gay non-fiction had gone to him, Michael Andrew Corrigan, for *The Yellow Brick Road Goes Nowhere.*

His first book had mapped out the political horizon from the right to the left. It had spelled out, in CAPS, the triumphing ideological myopia of the Religious Right and contrasted it with the bumbling factiousness of the left. Then, with all the bravura he'd brought to the barricades as an AIDS activist, he'd thrown down the rainbow-hued gauntlet. In his tour-de-force conclusion, this brazen twenty-something had challenged all gay men—and lesbians and bisexuals and transsexuals too—to stop looking off toward that very same horizon he'd just surveyed for two-hundred-and-eighty pages for any signs of a cavalry rescue: "The shimmering promise of SALVATION, let alone ACCEPTANCE, let alone ACKNOWLEDGEMENT, from either the American LEFT or RIGHT or CENTER is no more than a MIRAGE OF HOMOPHOBIC SELF-LOATHING!!!" (p. 285).

As these words rang out over the heads of his imagined audience, Mac smiled. Then he looked down to see the one rival writer he hated so much he wouldn't even name him here in his mind—that fatuous cipher! that damned Ewok in overalls!—standing in the front row, waiting to fillip him verbally on the nose as he always did. The creature grinned, looking all the more pop-eyed, and shouted out, in front of everyone, at *his* Pride parade, "Hey, Mac, are you ever gonna finish that *second* book?"

He flinched, now open-eyed, as he listened to the echoing laughter.

Today was Wednesday. Tomorrow was Thursday. He had to get writing.

Why did he always save the introduction for last? Each time, he'd been stumped. How could he condense what had taken him several hundred pages to detail and defend? How could he put all those words back into their box and wrap it up with the introduction? Especially with this book.

Keep it simple, Mac, Jeremy had said over and over in phone messages and emails. *Why this new book?*

That would be the one and only question he'd have to answer for those few who read introductions: novice reviewers who wanted to skim more than the dustjacket blurb but less than the whole book and undecided readers who didn't know if they wanted to spend $22.95, minus the mega-chain miracle discount, to buy it in hardback.

So far, he had an outline. That had to count for something. And it was a simple one. Only five coffee-stained and pizza-grease-dappled legal size pages.

Of course he'd begin with a nod to his first book. He paused and corrected himself—his first and award-winning book, *The Yellow Brick Road*.

Then, he'd tell, briefly, of the new questions that had made his sleep so fitful and the new answers that had left his mornings so red and bleary in those two years after his soon-to-be bestseller had gone off to the printers. And of how, one after the other, these unwelcome guests had led him to the sobering realization that queers must stop seeking the Promised Land, that "somewhere over the rainbow," altogether and take stock of where they were in the here and now. If they did this, they would agree with him that it was time to rebuild the wasteland of contemporary gay consumer culture before them. Make this desert of dessicated and clichéd desires bloom.

Thus his second book and, he felt, his masterwork: *Out, Up, and Away.* Or, as St. Sebastian was billing it, "Corrigan's bold Marshall Plan to help the queer nation of the 21st century move away from the current mass-marketed lifestyle that has been obsessed solely with what gay men can and cannot do with their genitalia."

In his own words, and he rarely bothered to hear any others, the book was an "URGENT unwrapping of gay liberation's EMPTY GIFT that is today's 'gay lifestyle'" (p. 15). For what good would it do them if—and this was, he'd admitted, a big IF—if the politicians and policy makers finally transmuted all the base metal of their community's human rights demands into the solid gold of law when a few cock-crazed gay men still held the "movement" hostage to their antiquated gay liberation dictum: *penem cupio ergo sum.* Or, as it translated roughly, despite his three years of Latin at Our Lady of Sorrows High School, *I want dick, therefore I am.*

And so, for five hundred more pages, he'd torn at their penis-plastered paper. Until there was nothing left to tear. Until he'd finally ripped the remaining scales from the queer community's eyes. Until they saw—as he saw—that they had been betrayed by their very own phallus-worshipping fifth column.

For this wasn't just a simple matter of some aging activists-turned-academics writing in unread journals their learned conclusion that we are post-AIDS and can thus revive the Seventies' glory days of ALL FOR SEX AND SEX FOR ALL! No, "their poisonous pedagogy" (p. 152) had spread beyond the tower and its ivory walls. Now generations that had been spared the worst of the AIDS pandemic were running off to be consumed in bacchanalian tribal cults.

Like the Radical Faeries. Most people had never even heard of them. And they preferred to keep their societies secret. But Mac had been to a drumming circle once, and he had sources who'd attended their orgies deep in the woods. Weeklong excuses to smoke pot and watch waifish glitter-dusted boys drop their skirts and dance naked in circles before they all jacked-off while rolling around in mudpits under the full moon.

And the Faeries, like their whimsical name and attire, were a lighthearted Dionysian hoedown when compared to the true *bête noire*, The Circuit. A series of drug-drenched dance parties where every gorgeous male model and male-model wannabe again danced, nearly naked, in circles but skipped the jacking off altogether and went right to having UNPROTECTED ANAL INTER-COURSE while they rolled around in lavish hotel rooms all across America.

Worst of all, now lesbians, the only role models left to queer kids of the life-giving rewards of commitment and community-building, were succumbing to this madness. God, just the other day, he'd heard from one of his dyke pals from ACT-UP. She'd said her ex-girlfriend, a mousy young thing, much too young, he'd always thought, for Rachel, was gaining quite the reputation in her new hometown of San Francisco for her "all-grrrl" Xstasy-driven slumber parties that began with spin-the-bottle and escalated into a seething pile of pussy-eating and fisting with nary a dental dam or finger cot in sight. It wasn't technically a barebacking party, the real "San Francisco treat," but it wouldn't be long before lesbians either showed up on the Circuit or turned the innocent bare-breasted joys of their music festivals in Michigan and Bloomington into something far more sexual and sinister.

Yes, for FIVE hundred pages he'd written, poured his soul onto paper—well, actually, into his computer—providing countless examples like these of "what constitutes our most queer and present danger" (p. 32). And for five hundred pages he'd offered "bold, do-able, workable solutions that raise queers up from a rag-tag assembly that craves only sexual congress to a united front, empowered by its embracing of diversity, which can lead, by more than just example, our country's Congress" (p. 17).

Five hundred pages.

Until his jeremiad culminated with his soon-to-be-often-quoted warning: "The WILLFUL ignorance and WANTON indulgence of our gay urban masses will lead not to the organized extermination of queers— for how much more organized does that CENTURIES-OLD process of eradication need to become as long as straight men, ALONE AND IN ARMIES, bear arms to protect the sanctity of their self-treasured ASSHOLES. No, our chemical-driven pleasure-seeking and the attendant soul-consuming ennui of living lives without meaning will instead lead to the SELF-INFLICTED EXTINCTION of any desire for queers to rejoin and revitalize the greater American society with our hard-won insights, learned in life-long committed partnerships between equals, of how it is possible to live the dream of democracy daily. For, if we do not add our names and pledge our lives to this new social contract, we will become, once and for all, the DESPICABLE AND TRIVIAL people our ENEMIES have always claimed us to be" (pp. 587-588).

Yes, there it was. A warning as chillingly accurate, he thought, as Cassandra's had been to Troy. But unlike Priam's cursed daughter, *he* — after a chat with Larry King and *The Times* (New York, London, and L.A.) and then a five-week book tour—would be heard. And, a year from today, he would be celebrating—with his life-partner whom he would meet at a welcoming party in L.A. thrown by Ellen and Anne—his second Lavvy nomination and his second Lavvy win.

Two-for-two.

He heard the soft, mechanical sigh. His computer had closed its one eye and gone to sleep.

Today was Wednesday. Tomorrow was Thursday.

The radiator issued its first clunking hiss. It was 4:36 p.m. He looked out his window. The monthly column, the odd freelance assignment, the book royalties, and even rarer lecture fees had afforded him a room of his own but not one with a view. Already, he couldn't see the brick wall across the airshaft. It was mid-December in Manhattan and the pale sun had set.

Instead, he stared at a ghostly negative of himself in the glass.

The reflection forced a thin-lipped smile. Mac returned it. The man was an faint facsimile of himself. Yet, he too was handsome in that rugged black Irish way. A collection of contrasts. The window's juxtaposition of his white on the night's black made it easy for him to make out the bold features he knew to be his own.

His skin, from afar, appeared unblemished and the color of pristine sand. At the uppermost edge of the craggy shoreline, small jet black waves of hair crashed and halted, except in two small tidal pools above his eyes and a wet patch that ran along the breakwater of his square jaw. He smiled warmly now, pleased with this impromptu homage to his seafaring ancestors. But it had grown too dark, and he sat too far away, to determine if this man shared Mac's more subtle accents: the fine powdering of fawn-colored freckles, the clear aquamarine of the irises, or the slight flush of pink in the cheeks that blossomed into two red roses with the third beer.

He turned to a closer mirror, the computer's screen, a bubble of humming tar. The face from the window had grown more solid though it wobbled a bit here and there as it would on a sheet of mylar in a Coney Island funhouse. He searched this smaller, dimmer night sky and still couldn't see even one freckle. Instead, he found a constellation of lines. Creases at the edges of his eyes and around his mouth. Like scaffolding, they held up the large bags under his eyes.

That was it. He couldn't go out again, not even to hop down to Macy's to buy more Clinique concealer, not even to go outside his building, turn the corner at 22nd and 8th, and walk down to Big Cup where he'd sip his less-than-big cup of coffee outside while he shivered and smoked and cruised the Chelsea boys—no, not until he'd slept a full night. And he wasn't going to sleep until he'd finished this introduction.

He stopped to listen to the rattlings of the steam pipe. It was getting hot. He stood and peeled off his maroon Boston College sweatshirt. He'd bought it after he watched his big sister—a right wing with a wicked awesome left shot—play her first hockey game for BC. And then he'd worn it to every home game. And each time he did, she would score in some miraculous way that'd make his dad stand up and dance, his mother cry, and

The One, True Lord of the Dance

his grandmother cross herself.

And, since then, he'd worn it every time he wrote. Throughout his senior year at Our Lady of Sorrows where he'd written for the school paper, edited the yearbook, and been class valedictorian. And, when he'd won his own scholarship to Boston College, he took it with him and wore it up to the day he received his honors degree in English. He packed it when he moved to New York, where, after a year of forgettable part-time jobs, he wrote his first piece of journalism for a brand-new queer four-color glossy that so impressed the editor it scored him his own column. And from those columns he'd scored a three-book deal. And out of that deal, he'd published one book, written a second, almost, and won one Lavvy. And he was going to score two more. If…if he wrote his introduction.

He looked down at his pecs. Two squarish slabs of lean muscle. But from his solid earth had grown a field of cotton. Little balls of fuzz from the inside of the sweatshirt were stuck to his skin. He brushed them away as he observed his torso in the window for any signs of betrayal or, worse, mutiny since his workout yesterday. Nothing seemed amiss. A respectable six pack and, with his gray USMC shorts slung as low as they were, he could make out his obliques. He flexed. His biceps weren't too small. He flexed again. His triceps looked quite firm. His neck, however could be thicker. It was reverting to its original state of pencil thinness. He'd remedy that as soon as he could go back to his two-hour-six-days-a-week routine at American Fitness—the one over on 8th. And he could do that as soon as he finished this fucking introduction.

He needed inspiration. The introduction was his call to arms. He had to warn the others about the seriousness of frittering away their power. Get all those Pinocchios, desperately trying to be real boys and delighted as their woodies grew and grew, to leave behind the Isle of Lost Boys, the Carnival of Pleasures, before they were all turned into asses. Or worse, CORPSES!

But, as this day dragged on, he realized he couldn't sound that alarm unless he was OUTRAGED. He'd have to rewatch Greg's bootleg video tape of this year's Circuit—six hours of panning over and through the crowds at the Black Party, the White Party (all of them), and, of course, Black and Blue. He fiddled with the remote until he'd rewound the tape and cued it to begin after those first, seemingly endless, thirty minutes where Greg gets ready with the girls for the big dance.

The sound quality on the video sucked. Just the watered-down beat of the bass line. As if his friend had recorded that element separately from the street outside. He needed music. No music, no men, no Circuit.

He slipped several home-mixed CDs into the carousel. He'd start with some Susan Moribito from the Morning Party and build up the beat with some Junior Vasquez, David Knapp, DJ Abel, and—*oh, yeah*—some Neil Lewis, Monty Q, and—*gotta have this one*—Victor Calderone and then go deep with another CD or two of the dark, drum-driven, three-in-the-morning music that burns you hard like your fourth hit of X. He arranged his headphones, pushed play on both remotes, and sat down on the edge of the couch.

He lit up and sipped at the bitter end of a joint he'd been nursing all day. As far as he was concerned, he was clean: no more coke, no more crystal, no more Xstasy, just pot, his balm in Gilead, a necessary evil; hell, if ever he did move to the country like he was telling others to, if he ever did break off his fuck-buddy relationship with New York—every few months The City would notice him and screw him over royally—then he might even grow some himself.

He flicked the burnt tip into the ashtray and looked beneath lunch's cold cartons of Mu Shu Pork, pancakes, and miniature plastic tubs of plum sauce for that dog-eared copy of *Circuit Boyz.* Tan skin shimmered as he turned the pages. Tan skin shimmered on the TV screen. Twisting. Punching the air. All solidly. One unmoving block. No hair, no muscle out of place. He stared at the TV. His eyes were following the camera following a succession of bouncing crotches.

Bouncing, blurring crotches. Blurring, bouncing crotches. He and his eyes grew dim as the TV and the room attached to it started to spin.

For one reeling minute after the other, he was the pen, the paper, and the Spirograph he had doodled furiously with for hours each Sunday after church when he was eleven. Then the pen fell out of his hand, the Spirograph slid off the table, and the paper dropped down into the void.

He'd passed out.

When Mac came to, he sensed something was not as it should be. All was complete darkness. No light. But there was music. A familiar-sounding music that comforted him with its sameness. But it wasn't Susan Moribito. Of this he was certain. He'd been to enough Morning Parties to know. It wasn't dreamy, giddy, sunny enough. But it didn't matter. It had the universal Circuit beat. 138 per minute to be exact. The musical equivalent of a Möbius strip.

And as the beat looped in and in on itself, layers and layers were added to it. The drum machine tapped out the same frantic code. The bass funked out the same few notes. A keyboard played the same two or three chord progressions. And laid over that were samples, remixed and straight-up, of divas, some legendary and others never-to-be-known, testifying.

Why, he'd said in his circuit days, as he'd mix himself another drink from the jugs of vodka and juice at the improvised wet bar in Greg's hotel room in Miami, Palm Springs, Atlanta, San Francisco, Montréal, New York, *why would you ever want to listen to that music when you're stone cold sober? And why the fuck would anyone want to be stone cold sober?* A rousing battle cry that always elicited cheers from Greg and his other circuit brothers as they waved him over for a few more lines.

Mac jolted. This shriek. He recognized it. It was Donna Summer. Throwing back her head and howling in the middle of MacArthur Park as she realizes that the pile of crap she's nearly stepped into is the very same cake that took so long to make and which some fool has left out in the rain. Then the instrumental bridge. Then the shriek. And again. And again. And again.

Christ. Anything was possible now. Whitney Houston. Céline Dion. Even that remix of the Gordon Lightfoot cover he'd heard everywhere during his visit to San Francisco last summer. He shivered. He was nowhere near high enough to survive the minimal camp of "If You Could

Read My Mind." He searched the crowd. Now he panicked. There was no one else there. No faces. No socks with the tell-tale bulge. *Shit!* He had to score a few hits of anything. And fast.

He walked on. Suddenly, Donna was gone. Her voice, the keyboard, the guitar had all collapsed in on each other like a red giant going supernova. Out of the cosmos-creating explosion, a new voice, a new star, burned as it arced between the black emptiness of his ears. Then the star spoke. *Life* .... She sang. *Love* .... The Great Cosmic Mammy reached out to her little jumping, arm-waving white baby boys—hidden from Mac out there, somewhere, in the shadows which surrounded him. *Lifting* .... She rocked them, hugged them, swallowed them safely within her somethin' fierce voice. *Higher* ....

Mac walked faster. Halfway through her hymn for the fourth time, Mother was drowned out. She'd been washed away in wave after wave of drum beats. Then, out of the new sea and onto the new beach came Woman. The Woman. Welcome here only as a voice. Singing. A voice singing for each and every man. She moaned with the silly sweetness of love's first desires and wailed with all the dried, blood-black rage of its inescapable betrayal.

The ghostly vocals faded off as he ran deeper and deeper into what he imagined was the room's, the stadium's, the universe's center. The music grew mechanical to mirror his mood. It was driven. It was desperate. He would find others. He would get high. He would have a good time. And, hell, since he was here, he might as well get laid.

But, to do any of this, he had to find a man.

He'd been running long enough and hard enough now to be winded. Then it hit him. He stopped and panted. A wall of wet heat, as if some enormous demon were cooking a rainforest and had briefly dropped the oven door to add more rain and a few animals. He knew that kind of heat well. It came from several thousand almost-naked men dancing skin-to-skin.

He pushed his way into the center of that dark fire.

The music had been reduced to the whir of two noise boxes. A rogue Korg organ from a Pentacostal church and a drum machine, that staple of Eighties pop who'd used his years out of the limelight to travel and sample a variety of world beat sounds.

At first, the two bantered back and forth, making meaningless conversation. Then their X kicked in. They snorted a bump of crystal and pocketed the K for later. Next, they ran off to some rundown motel along the old interstate. Once in their room, they climbed up onto the bed and got it on. Plastic grinding against plastic. And, when other, more organic, instruments might have fallen back for a breath, that rascal Korg went and slipped a quarter into the rusting silver box bolted into the nightstand. The organ laid back, jostling out the same chord, while the drum machine rattled about the bed faster and faster and faster.

And just when any addled eardrum would have prayed for the machine to break, the drumroll grew louder and louder until the whole body wanted only to scream, until the X-fueled and crystal-hyped heart struggled to keep up with the beat. But this perpetual-motion machine of sound drummed on as it bounced and rolled around the bed in wider and wider and wider circles. All a man could do was to throw up his arms and stomp his work boots on the ground and grind his hips in tighter and tighter spirals. And Mac did.

His ears rang from the shrill squealing laughter of the instruments, distorted through rows of unseen six-foot speakers toward which he pushed his way deeper into the slick, pulsing center. The heat coiled around him. He could barely breathe. His knees jangled from marching in place on the hard floor. His arms ached from punching the air. His dick and his asshole pulsed in sync with each other and the beat.

Suddenly, finally, the quarter ran out, the bed froze, the drum machine toppled off the bed. A second of total jarring silence. A blinding flash of light. Then another. Lasers beams shining here, then pivoting and strobing over there. Hundreds of them. Angels on acid skywriting. Then Mother spoke. *Oh.* And there they were. *Oh.* Thousands of her baby, barechested boys swaddled with the smallest strips of gold Lyrca. *Oh.* Mac was in the center of the largest Circuit party ever. *Oh, don't you know.* He was home.

Oh, don't you know I'm tweakin'! The organ, which had just finished awkwardly, but silently, sliding off the bed, let rip with the stirring prelude to an old Gospel standard. *Don't, don't you know.* The drum machine revved up. *Don't, don't you know.* From out of the depths of the motel room's shag carpet, they wailed away in another holy, fervent round of speaking in tongues. *Oh. Oh. Oh. Don't you know I'm tweakin'!*

The room roared with a hundred-thousand-voiced howl. *Tweakin'! Tweakin'! Totally a-peakin'!* Upheld hands shook and twirled their glow sticks. Other, less-extroverted, hands hoisted bottles of water to drying lips or pushed gum and plunged lollipops into open, waiting mouths. Mac stretched his tired arms higher, hands spread wide open, and joined in the song. Somewhere between "totally" and "a-peakin'" the floor decided to move six inches to the left. He righted himself before he met the ground. Seconds later, his brain ran over from where it had been left standing.

What the fuck? he thought.

He looked down. In the flickering light, he made out the floor. It was awash with condensation from the damp air and even-damper bodies as well as gum wrappers and the remaining sticks from the well-sucked candies, one of which poked out from beneath his shoe.

His shoe? He knew something was very wrong. He'd had the same feeling when he was sixteen and driving the family car. Some fucking tourist ran through the five-way intersection. Only born-and-bred Bostonians should be allowed to drive in Boston was all he could think as he and the rest of the family saw it coming and watched, waiting. Slowly the seconds ticked out until the impact. Then the car hit. Just as now the awful realization collided with him. His shoe was a *shoe.* Not a tawny workboot, not even a passé pair of Doc Marten's, not even the clueless white gym sneaker. It was a dress shoe. Worse, it was a wingtip.

In the dull light, he made out an even duller sheen that surrounded his body. He dragged his dumbfounded gaze back up his leg and across his torso. He was wearing …. *No!* The humiliation. He wished he had let himself fall to the ground so he could now crawl his way back to his apartment in New York, back even to the introduction he'd left waiting. He was wearing…a thousand dollar—two if it was from Barney's—burnt sienna business suit with…a robin's-egg blue dress shirt and…a midnight blue tie with enormous white dots. All he needed was a cell phone and he was ready to meet a date at the Townhouse and size up each other's stock options.

Joseph, Mary, and Jesus. He'd never get laid here now. If these queens saw him, they'd drive him out, laughing all the way. He started to faint. *Wait. This has to be a dream. Pinch yourself.* His fingers grabbed at his arm. He winced and then wobbled. Wooziness wasn't far off. If this were a dream, it was a true NIGHTMARE! The wobbling grew steadily into quaking. He was going to cry. He was in the middle of The Circuit Party of All Circuit Parties wearing a business suit encased in plastic like the furniture in his grandmother's sitting room. Plastic or …. He raised his fingers to his nose and sniffed. *Oh, Mary, Mother of God.* It was latex. He was at a circuit party in an all-body condom. *Please, Merciful God, let me die now.*

He waited. But all that happened was that the earth lurched back six inches to the right. Again, he caught himself before he landed on all fours. Something or someone had danced into him. If it had been a body, he couldn't tell. All he felt was the rubber holding in his own heat and sweat. He straightened his back and turned.

"Sorry. Got any gum," yelled a frantically chewing mouth holding up two wide eyes with pupils the size of quarters.

"No," he shouted back, the vein in his forehead swelling.

"God, cool it on the crystal, girl! You need some K. Wanna bump?" the mouth screamed.

This half-assed rubber suit, this ditzy queen, the heat, the noise—Mac was in shock. Otherwise, he would never have answered, braying even louder than before, "No. Leave me alone."

The eyes blinked, stuggling to refocus as they inspected Mac from head to toe and back again, then blinked twice more. The shoulders shrugged. The mouth spoke. "Suit yourself." And the remainder of the body pushed its way past him. Mac turned and watched the crowd swallow him whole.

Suddenly, the drops of sweat trickling down his back chilled and Mac froze. Not because he'd seen a crowd of men consume yet another man—

no, that was one of the most promising possibilities in a crowd like this one. It had been the convergence of angels around a singular head rising above the horizon of bobbing boys.

He jumped to see better. A heroic bust of a god backlit dramatically. He jumped again. A sweetly impish boy's face bonnetted by a halo of exploding white, like a camera's flash in the enormous dark. He readied to jump again and wavered. He felt the small bite of self-consciousness. He was the one and only man wearing a suit under a sheet of latex. He was also the one and only man jumping up and down. One queen a-leaping as that bitch Greg would say. But was he the one and the only one who realized just who this Man was that moved among them? He jumped for the third time.

Perhaps, he thought as he fell back to earth, this vision was only a mirage of his own making. The angels were, as he'd clearly seen, only the lasers and the halo was just their light reflected back off his platinum blonde hair.

Perhaps.

Then again, perhaps it truly *is* Him.

The wall separating Mac from his mysterious Man-Among-Men must have been, on his last leap, only twenty dancers deep. He was coming closer. Then there was light. A light that would not fade but grew brighter. Mac could see His face now from where he stood.

The Man towered over the others. He must have been six-and-a-half feet tall, at least. Beneath the thick forest of gold-glinting hair dropped the broad cliff face of his forehead. It rested lightly on the dark, well-tended topiaries that were his eyebrows. And below these, set not too-deep, were the sexiest eyes Mac had ever seen cruising a crowd. They not only smoldered, they commanded.

Come. Follow me.

For a mere second Mac was certain that their eyes had locked. He recoiled from the gaze and nearly swooned. He knew now why prey froze in those final moments before the greater beast devoured them. He knew now why St. Teresa had writhed in such agonized ecstasy when she was pierced by the arrows of Our Lord. Then he blinked and the gaze went elsewhere. The Man had turned to talk.

Vowing to commit every detail of Him to memory for future, lonelier late-nights, Mac memorized His profile. The ridge of His nose, like an unbroken outcropping of stone, jutted over the soft swells of his lips. Though he was still too far to see for certain—he'd need to be close enough to chew them—Mac imagined they were the rosy pink of a cockhead dawning from its foreskin. What he did see was that the black shadow of His goatee circled them, keeping His lips in a state of obscene fullness. The dense stubble also softened the cleft where the two massive jawbones that framed His face met.

The Man laughed. His tongue rolled out and pulled the hard candy head of a lollipop back into His mouth like a great wave heading back to sea. Mac's dick quivered with envy.

It *must be* Him.

The Man sucked vigorously. The force caused His cheeks to collapse and swell with a pulsing urgency that echoed throughout Mac's veins. Mac watched The Man's own jugular rise and sink with each thrust. It was a thick as the root of a tree. Encircling the base of His trunk of a neck, there was a tight string of small stones that appeared, with each passing of a light, to be some depthless shade of blue. The polished pebbles grew larger and bluer as they walked nearer and nearer and Mac craned his neck higher and higher. Until they were so close, Mac could see them shudder, slightly, with each step. Until they were so close, Mac could have leapt up one last time and cradled himself in His waiting arms and slipped his fingers under the stones and up against the warm, beating skin.

The Man parted the sea of ruddy dancing children and rose up, a pillar of flesh, before Mac. He wore only the necklace and a pair of glistening motorcycle boots. To the casual observer, He was naked; to the art historian, nude; to Mac, a miracle of God.

While his brain decided whether to faint now or wait, Mac's widening eyes could no longer restrain themselves. They began their descent.

From the roots of neck, each trapezius sloped down like a mountain's foothill, smooth and solid in the light of the high desert sunset. They rested on the round rocks of His delts, boulders that not even the archangel Michael could roll away. And from beneath these stones grew biceps and forearms the size of a man's, of Mac's, thighs and calves. And through all, a rope of a vein threaded its way down until it flowered in a wild profusion of vines that clustered in His broad hands. Mac giddily imagined that just two of The Man's fingers could split him wide open. His asshole awakened and yawned with joy.

And His chest. The Man's chest was like the breast plate of a Roman soldier in those Sixties gladiator movies Mac had watched as a boy on late Saturday afternoons with a pillow wedged into his lap and over his wicked hard boner. Just thinking the "B-word" and his dick sprung up deep with in the layers of cloth and rubber like a once-sleeping dog who's heard the clink of its leash and is barking and spinning in circles, ready to be let out. The aroused pup grew even more impatient when a light stalled in the cleft of The Man's breast. This was no armor's exaggerated rendition of the godlike perfection of the male warrior. This was the godlike perfection itself. Each pec was a burnished gold discus the size of a chariot wheel and embossed with a nipple as wide as a child's palm that ended in a tip as thick as the ends of Mac's own fingers.

Both Mac and his dick sighed.

But his eyes were insistent. So they climbed down from the mountainous crags of His pecs and ran swiftly along the well-packed and deeply furrowed earth of His abs, hiked up the broad plain created by His chiseled obliques, and wandered out to the close-cropped hedge of pubic hair to peer down at the awesome cascade of muscle falling below them. To have called this waterfall of flesh a dick would have been a gross understatement. Like saying Madonna was merely an entertainer.

For it was the length of a dong and the girth of two pricks. It was, in other words, a prong.

It was fat. It was huge. Mighty veins coursed down the shaft like rivers after the spring thaw. Down to the head, as pink in its perfection as a prize-winning rose. A rose the size of a small man's fist.

It is Him, Mac thought as he gazed at His cockhead. The Him whom he'd always sought. The Him whom they'd all sought. The One, True Lord of the Dance.

The One, True Lord of the Dance

Mac's heart flopped and shook like his great-uncle Seamus who, somewhere toward the end of every family wedding, would tap dance drunkenly—all three hundred pounds of him.

The blossom of the flower of all manhood moved closer. Mac couldn't look away from It. He readied to fall to his knees and open his mouth. Then, It just stopped and hung far out of his reach, taunting him. No, he thought as he struggled to read the *mot juste* from the imagined pocket dictionary in the failing light of his brain. Tantalizing him. Just like in that old print in Jeremy's apartment where a frenzied sonofabitch is treading water, neck deep, and grasping for the retreating branch above his head. But it's not the branch he wants; it's the golden fruit, the prize he's going to eye for eternity because it will always be an inch beyond his reach. After all, it is hell.

The fruit bounced slightly on the bough. *An apple. Yeah.* He smiled as his own dick stiffened within the latex cocoon. The head *was* the size of a red delicious. But It wouldn't come any nearer. Impatiently, he looked up.

The Lord smiled. The edges of His lips and the whites of His teeth were stained blue from the lollipop. He waited for Mac to return His smile. Mac, however, stared blankly into the endless dark depths of The Lord's eyes. He heard only Their persistent, insistent command: *Come.* The Lord ceased to smile, cocked His head, effortlessly lifted His eyebrow, shrugged His shoulders, and moved to turn away.

No. No, Mac thought, slapped awake when The Lord's eyes released him. *I will come. I will follow. I will be with You.*

Mac knew his body, even at 36—though he told dates that he was a ripe 28—could turn heads. He'd seen it in his window tonight—or was that yesterday now. He tore at the rubber. Wriggled out of the jacket. Unknotted the tie. Fumbled with button after button of the shirt. Yanked at the belt, then the zipper. Tugged off pants and socks and boxers. Shucked and peeled away all that smothered his skin—all that hung in the electrified air between their bodies, between him and The Answer to twenty years of silent prayer. Until he stood before The Lord slick, flushed, and naked.

Mac's own dick, though it was but a fraction away from the personals' Revised Gay Standard Measure of seven inches, suddenly seemed so small as he looked up to see The Prong. But he didn't care. He didn't want to fuck The Lord. And he didn't want to be sucked off by The Lord. He didn't even want to suck The Lord off.

He wanted one thing. The Lord's Prong. Inside him. His own body no more than a flag flying from His Pole. His heart pierced by His Prick. Pumping and pumping the pounding muscle full of white, hot jism. Until Mac's blood was cum. Until he choked from the ecstasy, only to be reborn and fucked again.

Forever and ever. World without end. *Amen.*

Mac turned and straddled his legs and arched his butt up to polite applause. His ass had been his obsession ever since that night at the baths when a god had passed him over and this talking white prune, old enough to have served Miss Dorothy Parker cocktails at the Algonquin and clawing the doorframe of her cubicle just to stay upright, cackled out to all within earshot, "Boys with big boxes seldom accept passes from guys with flat asses." And so, one of the two hours he spent in his two-hours-six-days-a-week routine was devoted to exercises to plump and sculpt his ass. Then there was the daily application of exfoliants, moisturizers, and, of course, the unforgiving razor.

The clapping from the surrounding onlookers, as all things must, began to dwindle and then died. Music filled the empty space. In the few seconds of darkness between the laser bursts, a voice rang out. A sample of Barry White or Isaac Hayes or Shaft or Superfly, some Supreme Mack Daddy, saying, "It's a vibratory thang." Mac peered his head through his legs, the receiver waiting for the quarterback.

But The Lord just stood there.

"Man, I've got one hot hole that needs plugging," Mac growled in his best imitation of Eartha Kitt.

"You what?"

"My hole…"

"I can't hear over the music."

He hadn't planned to shriek, but a shriek is what decided to come out along with the words, "Fuck my hole, Sir. Please fuck my hot hole."

The music stopped. The dancing men stopped. Only the lights, still tripping, kept raving on.

"C'mon. It's so tight," pleaded Mac.

A circle of a thousand queens closed in around them.

"Pfff," a square-jawed brunet said.

"Tight," laughed an identical other.

"I've fucked her hole," said a third with a fiery red crewcut. "It's like throwing a hot dog down a hallway."

The Lord laughed and waved Mac's ass away as if it were coughing out the most sulfurous of farts. But Mac continued to grip his ankles and hold it up and out to Him. So The Lord walked around him and disappeared through the still-laughing crowd into the fields of now-waving arms beyond them.

Mac watched The Lord's ass, two mounds of flawless muscle the size of basketballs, piston away from him. He sighed, stood up, and turned to face the circle's remaining inner ring—The One, True Chorus of Circuit Queens.

He looked at them. He couldn't think of any other word to call the hundred-or-so men but "chorus." They were a crowd. A crowd who moved as one body and spoke with one voice. A chorus. As ancient and as Greek a concept as active and passive.

In all honesty, though, he couldn't say they were one body. Not even one body type. There were a few ectomorphs and endomorphs bobbing about in this sea of mesomorphs. Still they were, each one, an attempt to embody one archetype: The God.

That was their allure, their comfort. Each promised the possibility of being that one step closer to perfection. To Him. Each had one perfect part: tits, lips, abs, eyes, biceps, jaw, delts, chest, glutes, dick. The lords-in-waiting would have two or three, maybe four. The One, True Lord had them all.

To the untrained-yet-understanding eye, this chorus of men and their parts weren't exactly interchangeable, but they were remarkably similar. To a master classifier, one who'd spent three years on The Circuit cataloguing, like Mac, the differences were subtle but telling, often damning.

The cylindrical bicep of that one on the far right, ridged with its one perfect vein sealing the meat within the skin like a ripe, shining pod encasing a muscular pea, measured eighteen inches while the one in front of him was a less impressive sixteen inches. He compared the flat, natural fullness of the lower lip seven men to his left with the collagen swell of a man two rows in. He sighted four varieties of the Abercrombie & Fitch chiseled square pec. A dozen more of the porn star/leather daddy/power lifter rounded pec or classic "man tit." Even a few obvious implants and one that, if it was silicone, was the work of a master craftsman.

Then there was the cut of the Raymond Dragon short versus the cut of the latest from Jocko for showcasing the cut of the cock and the heft of the balls. He could even spot those few plump pouches enhanced by cockrings.

Mac could have even determined which of the chorus had baked their melanin-rich or melanin-challenged skin in the rotisserie of the tanning both. He could have singled out the few who dared to be seen flushed with the garish red underhue of one-too-many-hours by the pool. He could have eyeballed the men in the second and third rows who'd been to a master electrolysist or suffered under the uneven eye of a waxer. He swore he could even see, in the semidarkness of the laser flares, the imperceptible—until you'd been stung— spines of the shaver, stubbling the brown desert of their chests like the Saguaro National Forest to the east and west of Tucson.

But the hallmark of the master classifier is not the magnitude of his scope nor the distance from which he can detail minutiae; it is all about the amount of time it takes to make a complete catalogue. Tonight, slightly dazed from his brush with The Godhead, it took Mac thirty seconds.

I'd let him and, maybe him and him, do me, he thought.

His asshole shuddered. He imagined its pursed mouth looked like lips, pressed tightly together, holding back a cough. It clenched and a wave of jittery heat fanned up through his bowels, swelled in his chest, climbed his neck, and leapt from the top of his head. His ass had cleared its throat. Now, it spoke to Mac.

How you disappoint me, Michael Andrew Corrigan. You just let slip past my mouth the one man to whom I have sung my siren song for twenty years. Twenty fucking years! Now, you listen to me, Mister. This is no time for a beggar like you to get choosy. You will take any and all of these nice, hung men who will have you. And you will take them in any and every way they will have us. And you will take them until I tell you I can't swallow any more. Do you hear me, Michael Andrew Corrigan. Do you, Mister?

His asshole squeezed him so hard from within that Mac gasped. "Will somebody fuck me?" he cried. "Fuck me now! I need all of your big, fat dicks inside me."

Not to be outdone in repetition, the music began again.

Mac rubbed his ass cheeks between his palms. "I feel so hot." The chorus stood still. "So?!" His eyes shot about the crowd, staring down any who'd match his gaze. He realized he was going to have to work it harder after all the catty chatter to get even one of them hard.

He would have to use the classic gay porno foreplay move for signalling "I'm one hot fuck." During his years on the Circuit, he'd used it only as the night wore on and the drugs wore down. But it had never failed. He hummed "You Can Ring My Bell" to himself.

First, he twisted lightly on his nipple. Then dug into it with his fingernails. He bit his lip for effect. He pinched and turned the nipple again and again between his whitening fingers. He rolled his eyes up into his head and closed them. *The first hook is cast.*

Now, eyes still closed, he took his free hand and clutched the long throat of his cock. With each twist of his tit, he yanked his dick further and further downward. A teasing preview of how big it was to become *if* .... As it lengthened, he opened his eyes and locked on the first face he saw—the Daddy with the gray eyes and silvering temples. Mac didn't look away. His hands didn't stop. *The second hook is cast.*

Daddy obviously liked what he saw. His Lycra shorts were now, not one, but two sizes too small. Daddy squeezed his swell with a successively firmer and longer grasp. Then, he broke away from the grip of Mac's eyes and bent down to stick his fingers into the top of his boot. He pulled out a condom. In the flash of the lasers, it shone like a runaway mylar balloon in the mid-afternoon sun at Fire Island's "Morning Party" or Austin's "Perfect Day."

"No." Mac had let go of his tit and prick mid-pinch and mid-pull. "Ride me bareback."

"You?" Daddy now stared Mac down.

"Yeah, Sir. Fuck me raw, Sir."

"Mac Corrigan wants to bareback?!" He bent down and placed the condom back, deeper, in his boot. When he stood up, he walked as close to Mac as Mac's jutting erection would allow. "You? Our so-called Redeemer. 'A lone moral voice in the desert of the post-gay consumer and the circuit queen.'"

"Who the fuck said that?" asked a voice from behind him.

"Larry Kramer," Daddy said without turning his head or breaking his stare.

"Who?" the voice asked again.

There was a collective sigh throughout the chorus. An unspoken acknowl-edgement that said, *Yes, all of us are beautiful; and, yes, some of us are dumb.*

"It can't be Larry," chimed in a new voice. "He would have said that only about himself."

"He's right. I'm certain Mac wrote it about himself in an Op-Ed piece for the *Times*," said another voice tersely.

"Cocky sonafabitch," said yet another voice.

Daddy's gray eyes fell down and jumped back up to Mac's. "It doesn't look like it from here."

"Then it's Mac," laughed a fourth voice.

"It does appear to be the same Mac," said a fifth.

"I told you all I've had that hole," blurted out a sixth and quite excited voice. "I never forget an asshole, no matter how fucked up I am."

Daddy turned away from Mac. It was that redhead with the crewcut again. He looked around at the field of quickly sprouting arched eyebrows. He smiled like the fox caught after swallowing the cock—or, in tonight's case, the twentieth cock. He tapped a finger to his throbbing temple. "Photographic memory." The eyebrows began to wilt back to the earth. "It's him."

Daddy walked away from Mac and back into the chorus. As he did, the redhead—a tall queen, four down from Mac's right, with a mustacheless goatee that drew the eyes away from his deviously small blue eyes and down to his plump suckable lips—pulled two long leather jump ropes with silver handles out from his still burgeoning basket. He handed one and then the other to the two men on either side of him.

The first, a clean-shaven boy, distinguishable only by his actual youth and a pukka-shelled choker, gripped his two handles gingerly as if the silver might still be molten. The second, a dirty blond whose hair, Mac noted to no one but himself, had more highlights than the waiting room of a dentist's office, sniffed his handles hungrily. The redhead's lips parted and he smiled. He patted the blond on the head, while whispering loud enough for all to hear, "Maybe you'd like to sniff that trail back to its source a little later."

"Maybe." The blond then punctuated his promising nonchalance with the tight-lipped, come-hither grimace of a veteran cruiser.

"Not," said the clean-shaven boy as he placed his handle in the outstretched hand of the blond's doppelgänger, down to the highlights.

The redhead was briefly startled and then politely positioned himself between Blond One and Blond Two and their tautening rope. A bronzed brunet leaned in over it as if the rope were a fence between two Forties row houses. Mac almost expected the redhead to peel his shorts off and peg them onto the remaining rope while the two men gabbed away.

"Where'd you get these?" said the brunet, plucking the rope.

"The Black Party," said the redhead, throatily.

"Yum."

"I wish he," and the redhead pointed his head in Mac's direction, "could have dreamed us there." He shoved both hands into the front of his shorts and reassembled his bulge. "This Lyrca really chafes."

Several heads around them nodded and "un-huh"ed.

"And Lycra," the redhead had subtly moved his hand from his dick to his ass, "doesn't do my ass justice like leather."

"Whaddya mean?" exclaimed the brunet in sincere disbelief. "It's so tight …."

"Yeah, I can even see stubble, dude," snickered the clean-shaven boy.

With the swiftness possible only to an enraged movie alien, the redhead whipped his head alone toward the boy and spat, "Fuck *you*, Don Ho."

Out of the crowd came a few finger snaps.

"No, fuck *you*, Steroid Mary! The only thing your Raymond Dragon's lack are landing lights into your mangina."

A dozen more fingers joined in the snapping.

"You are *such* the vile bitch." He looked away from the upstart child and back toward the choir. "I like a bit of mystery, okay?" He raised his hand into the air, and, as he now spoke, his double-ringed index finger spun like the antenna on an orbiting satellite. "And nothing, am I right, my sisters, leads the horse-hung to drink like an ass sweet with the scent of leather and sweat."

There were so many fingers snapping so hard, Mac surveyed the crowd for castanets. The music took its cue from the crowd and from all around them an exuberant woman, accompanied by an acoustic guitar and a cheering, clapping soccer stadium, sang out, "¡*Vamos a jugar a la playa! Todos los días son días de fiesta.*" Within seconds, the Korg and the drum machine were off to the beach and kicking up sand.

"Ladies, ladies. Please. We're losing focus here," said a laughing, mischievously male voice.

Mac rapidly rescanned the crowd to see what face, what body, what dick this voice belonged to. The crowd obliged and opened up to let the new man enter. The hairs on the back of Mac's neck stood up as he watched the lord-in-waiting materialize. Mac stammered out something and almost, remembering a long-forgotten custom, crossed himself.

It was *him*! Carlos. The hunky hotty of a boyfriend to that doe-eyed blond doll Billy. Not that Mac ever, seriously, contemplated spending over fifty dollars for anything with a two-inch penis. Until he'd seen Carlos all trussed up in his leathers. He might have been plastic but he was no giddy boy like Ricky Martin. No, Carlos, was all-*hombre*. And now, merciful Father, he stood before him—lifesize. Six feet tall. Which meant his dick was a foot-long schlong. Mac began to grin giddily himself and wag his little *bombón*.

¡Vamos a jugar a la playa! Todos los días son días de fiesta.

Erasmo could feel the small man's eyes, two clouded blue stones, appraise his body. He heard him gasp to himself and mutter "*¡Ay, papí!*" It happened all the time. These sudden assumptions that demanded the reassertion of race. They sprang from a single seed out of a groundless ground: a fervent need to believe that the further they flung themselves beyond the crushing gravity well of their icy white sun—the center of their universe and, they assumed, his—the hotter and wilder the encircling darkness must be.

¿Que pasó, papí? Each frozen man would quickly reach for a warming word, a sound to spark heat from this dark new man. When they'd exhausted their ten-word Spanglish vocabulary, they grew colder and nervous. Nervous people speak only in questions. Rarely, however, did they ask his name. Erasmo. Never his full name. Erasmo García Rivera. Or where he came from. Lawrence, Kansas. His parents had met, fallen in love, and raised a son and a daughter while they taught, and still teach, Nineteenth and Twentieth Century Latin American Literature at KU. No cold man wanted to hear that story. Though it would have answered their urgent questions. Why don't you have an accent? He did, but it was flat like Kansas, not rich like Corinthian leather. Or why won't you say something dirty to me in Spanish? First, he hated the usual refrains to the usual fuck songs, and secondly, he'd learned from the pinching-fingered chidings of his first teachers and the pointing-fingered ridicule of his classmates to speak Spanish only with his *familia*.

¡Por favor, papí! And when he would not play *Señor Muy Macho* and backhand them across the bed, the floor, the limo seat and tear at their pants like a rabid dog and push his dirty dark hairy uncut dick into their clean smooth white asses and rape them without care, without lube, without condoms like the fucking *putas* they playacted they were, these men would do what men have always done well—remake him, body and soul, with their eyes and their words, words drawn from the only places they might have encountered his kind outside of their kitchens, their nurseries, their lawns—the "Mexican" restaurant and *taquería*.

¡Ay! Chíngame, papí. He watched the little man begin his inventory. Erasmo's skin was no longer brown; it was the color of thick honey coiling

in the steaming fold of a *sopaipilla* or of warm caramel drizzling over a quivering mound of *flan*. His eyes were no longer black; they were *negros* like the beans boiled until soft and stuffed in burritos. His hair was a *mole* sauce, exotic, with a hint of the bitterest chocolate. His lips, tender and full, like cooked *plátanos*. His tongue, glimpsed through the rows of teeth as white as refined sugar, was a slice of freshly macheted mango. It would taste in his mouth like a just-cut stick of *caña de azúcar*.

¡Vamos a jugar…!

And as each man, as this man, sucked on the imagined sugar cane, his eyes would plunge to Erasmo's crotch. For there, tucked in his shorts, was the fabled ripe uncut cock, sealed tight beneath the puckered tip of foreskin, smelling like the deepest, dankest hold in a beat-up banana boat, filling with the thickest *crema* for the lucky man to scoop out with his little pink tongue. *¡Que pinga loca, papí!*

Erasmo grimaced. Some day, he knew their *papí*—the beautiful one these men dreamed off every time they saw a shade of brown darker than their own beige—would come, but for *him*. He would walk up to Erasmo, their eyes locked, until they were lips apart and he would say only, "*¡Que rico!*" Then he would take Erasmo's face in his hands, kiss him long *con cariño*, before he backed away smiling, tugging Erasmo's *huevos*, and leading him off to his palazzo in South Beach where they would fuck and fuck and fuck while each recited Neruda and García Lorca to the other happily ever after.

¡Vamos! ¡Vamos! ¡Vamos! ¡Vamos! ¡Vamos! ¡Vamos!

The drum pounded out the words faster and faster until it spun out to sea and was silenced. Alone, the organ bravely played on.

Erasmo sighed and cleared his throat until his eyes refocused. "Ladies, please. Show Mac what you've been working so hard on."

Mac struggled to return from the hold of the magical banana boat. He blushed a bloodied pink, like a slice of rare steak, when he realized the lord-in-waiting and the rest of the Chorus were eyeing his recently resurrected hard-on.

The redhead laughed in a string of honks and then rolled his eyes. "Okay, girls, this is it," he said as he readjusted his basket with both hands for the final time. "Assume the position."

The two blonds moved out close to the redhead and dropped the limp cord in front of his feet.

"Now I need someone else with a big bounce-worthy bulge," the redhead said. "Hmmm. Daddy," he pointed to the butch with the gray eyes and silvering temples that Mac had driven away earlier. "Yes, you, Sir. Would you mind helping out your humble boy? I'll spit-shine your boots later and you can polish my hole?"

Daddy chuckled and returned the redhead's brazenness with a wicked grin. The man took his place in the center and the ropes started to turn slowly. Like a rusted windmill on some Dustbowl farm that's hit with the first breeze after a week of still heat. This mysterious breeze, however, picked up speed fast. A few revolutions of the rope and it was a gale. The cords spun over and under and over and under the jumpers. The redhead broke out with a chant.

> *Mac, Mac, gotta bareback*
> *When he calls you lover*
> *He wants to fuck sans rubber*

Mac cringed as the crowd roared. But he wanted to cut himself out of his skin as everyone joined in on the following verses.

> *Mac, Mac, gotta bareback*
> *Slip it in raw and let it cook*
> *Very next day, you'll be in his book*

> *Mac, Mac, gotta bareback*
> *What a two-faced little guy*
> *Makes the lesbian caregivers cry*

Then the redhead leapt back and forth between the two ropes at each new line.

> My mama heard him say he's sick of being gay
> And fags are whores; but he's the bore, o K-
> hole operator, can you connect me with Tina
> She owes me a bit of G and loves to suck mi pinga

If steam really could come out of an enraged man's ear, this would have been the time for it. But it can't, so it didn't. Instead, Mac's face grew so red it looked fiery enough to fry an egg—preferably both of the redhead's. And he began to pray fervently for him to trip and strangle himself.

> How many men here won't fuck Mac?

The redhead kept leaping between the ropes but now he was patting Daddy's ass each time they shared a jump.

> 1, 2, 3, 4, 5, 6, 7, 8, 9, 10, 11, 12, 13, infinity, infinity infinity, infin...

That was it. Mac reached out and drew Blond Two's end of the rope tight. The redhead tumbled into the chorus.

There was no politeness in the clapping this time. Just a long, honest, vigorous round of flesh slapping flesh. And a few shouts of "Brava" and one call for "Author!" toward which the now-standing-but-staggering redhead bowed.

"Well done, girls," Mac hollered through his cupped hands. The sounds, the smiles, dribbled away. "Have you considered," he added now that he had regained center stage, "taking that Off-Broadway? Lose the shorts, call it '4 Naked Guys Jumping Rope,' and it'll be sold out before it opens."

The redhead's eyes widened with further hurt. "Do you ever stop bitching, Mary?"

Mac smiled wanly and spit out, "No, dear, I'm gay."

"Suck my dick, Corrigan."

"I'd have to find *it*, first."

The redhead's face ripened into the color of a plum. There was a flash of silver in the lasers. And before Mac could scream, the redhead was garroting him with the jump rope.

"Jesus, Stevie." A second later Erasmo had the redhead's neck in the crook of his elbow. He tightened and lifted him up off his feet. Stevie let go of the rope and fell back against Erasmo. Erasmo let his arm slide down Stevie's chest until he held him by the waist.

"Go," Erasmo shouted.

Mac waited for *Papí Suave* to release the idiot Red Queen so she could dart back into the chorus. But *Papí* didn't. He just shouted louder.

"Go. Hello! Speak English? I said go. As in get the fuck outta here."

Mac, after all tonight's indignities, was finally stunned. "Me?"

"Yes, you. You're no longer welcome here."

"Oh, fuck that shit! And fuck you, Juan! Like I ever felt welcome here. Tribe of brothers my ass!"

"Tribe of brothers? Mac, you're the one who used to write that New Age shit for *Circuit Boyz*." Erasmo pulled his tightening arm and fist away from Stevie's stomach before he heimliched him. "And, my name isn't Juan, Mic. It's Sir."

Mac went white and then opted for red as blue veins began to bulge from his forehead. "Jesus, Mary, and Joseph! What is wrong with you fucking people? I just want someone to fuck me and then I'll go. How hard is that?"

"Harder than you think," said Erasmo. "We've all read your new book."

Mac's eyes glassed over. His dick hung its head. His right cheek twitched. He blinked nervously until he'd gathered enough speed to blurt, "But it's not even out."

"We get the gallies faxed to us here. Such a waste of paper."

"Yeah, what's your next book gonna be, Mac?" shouted the redhead as he pushed his way into the crowd. *"Virtually Straight?"*

The entire chorus snapped their fingers in Z formation.

"Well, screw the book," he screeched, frightened by the growing silence. He'd wanted to say calmly, dryly, "I can't believe *all* of you can actually read," but he didn't. He couldn't. He wasn't going to leave his final circuit party with blue balls. "Screw *me!*" he begged. "C'mon, guys," he wheedled. "Just one last zipless, condomless fuck for the road."

"When sex pigs fly, darlin'," said a smiling Asian boy as he sidled out of the crowd. His musculature was so chiseled and his skin so polished that it wasn't implausible, at least to Mac, to believe he'd been sculpted from some precious stone the color of the coffee candies his grandmother had kept in an ornate glass bowl in her aforementioned and much plasticized living room. Mac smiled back and thought, *Thai. Such a friendly people. So accommodating. And such good food.* His eyes started to glaze as he smelled from far behind his eyes a plate of chicken *satay*. "Bring on the peanut sauce," he mindlessly mouthed.

The next thing he knew, he was ready to black out. A warm vice had clamped tight around his dick and balls. The sweet, smiling face loomed before him and whispered, "You call me Thai Stick, darlin', and I cut it off. The appetizers *and* the entree."

An icy, sickly sweat broke out along Mac's forehead. The grip tightened.

"Are we clear, darlin'?" the white teeth said.

"Very."

"So glad to hear it." And the clamp was loosened, but not released.

"Joey?"

"Yes, darlin'." Joey turned and his teeth-grinding smile relaxed. A hulking man who looked like a mustachioed strong man from a turn-of-the-century circus clomped out of the Chorus. His head was small, dwarfed by the swollen muscles below, and bald and gleamed like a pale pink canonball.

"Oh, Bill, you big ol' strappin' sugar booger. Did you want to hold his leash for a while?" Joey gave Mac's pud a hard yank and another twist and Mac yipped like a dog struck by a car and then came a groan and with that gust of breath a soft "please, fuck me" escaped as well.

"You are one sorry-assed dog, Michael Corrigan. I can't believe you. You're so doggy desperate you're gonna break The Great Chain of Fucking, the holy order that has scripted every shitty gay sex plotline, that holds all the gay circuits together, and pick an Asian 'boy' to fuck you!" Joey's fingers dug in and his fist tried to crush all that it held. Tears collected at the edges of Mac's eyes. He wriggled clumsily as if all the bones in his body were breaking. "But, then, who could blame you, Mac? I am your *last* choice!"

Mac shrieked for the second time that night.

"Joey," sing-songed the giant. "Let him go. He's not worth it."

Joey laughed unnervingly loud. "Hell no, baby doll. How often do you get to have a Gay White Moron by the nuts *and* tell him just how fuckin' sick you are of him and the other gatekeepers of desire lording it over you."

"Mac?" the giant asked further. "I usually don't interfere in scenes, but, if you don't go now, I'm afraid Joey might Lorena Bobbitt you with his bare hands."

"No," Mac stammered. This fierce touch, as painful as it was, was all he'd received tonight. And he wanted so desperately now to be touched from without and within. "I want him to fuck me. Rip me a new one, Joey."

The grip grew soft with disgust.

"Um, yes," the giant continued, "well, I guess as long as we're all safe, sane, and consensual...."

"I ain't fuckin' consenting to none of his shit," Joey smiled stiffly.

"Oh, yes, well, my...," the embarrassed giant muttered as he tried to regain his thoughts. "That's too bad, Mac," he blustered on, "because Joey's one amazing fuck."

"Why thank you, darlin'."

"Oh, of course. You really are. So, um, Mac. I guess it really is time for you to leave."

"No," Mac shouted. "I'm not leaving this fucking freak show until one of you comes up my ass."

"Okay, well, um, yes," the giant said as he contemplated the image. "That's a very succinct stating of your needs, but may I ask you why *you* of all people would want that?"

"Sugar bear, it's as obvious as a dick that grows." Joey squooshed and squeezed the lump of flesh in this hand. "It does grow, darlin'?"

"He's a horny little hypocrite," groaned the redhead before he went back to pinching the tit of the Daddy.

"He's human," said Blond One who'd been quietly holding the hand of Blond Two since they'd stopped jumping rope.

"No, no, it's simpler than that, girls," chimed in Blond Two. "It's because condoms are little rubberized grim reapers. And only the French can think about death and stay hard enough to fuck all the time."

"Omigod," sneered Mac. "Camille Paglia has finally gotten her wish and become a gay man."

"Such a silly boy," Blond One said. "His name isn't Camille. It's Kevin."

"Thanks, Khamryn." Blond Two patted Blond One on the head who barked out a "woof".

"Yes, well, okay, yes," the giant spoke. "Kevin's got a point."

"And how," grinned Khamryn. Kevin giggled and they both kissed.

"Ahem, yes, well, I see." The giant was completely flummoxed. He turned to search the crowd. He found Erasmo and pleaded, with his eyes alone, for him to intervene. Erasmo nodded for him to go on. "Alright then…so, Mac, why can't you teach us how to be more like the French?"

"Yes, how do we do it?" asked the Chorus.

"So spill it," Joey barked. He felt a surge in his hands. "Eewh, not that."

"C'mon," cried out the Chorus.

Words rolled in Mac's mouth like broken teeth. He tried to spit something out. The men watched. He looked like a hooked fish dying in the bottom of a boat.

"Maybe we should leave *her* alone," Joey stage-whispered to the Blonds. His grip started to slip.

"No, please don't go." Mac reached down and grabbed Joey's wrist. "We queers have been alone too long. By ourselves before we came out. By ourselves when we come out. Here I am in the middle of a city of millions and all I feel is alone. For a few hours…"

"Ooh, you're an ambitious piggly wiggly," Joey cooed.

"Please." Mac clutched tighter. "Right now, I need to know I'm not alone. And I won't be sure unless I feel you—one of you, all of you—in me. Every vein, every hair, every pore. I need you to leave something of yourself behind. I need to feel your cum burning within me. Burning away at me. Making me feel new again. Alive."

"Well, well now," said Erasmo, "don't you make the dirty deed sound magical."

"Transcendental," said the giant.

"Radical," Blond One chimed.

"Revolutionary," Blond Two echoed.

"Freeing," the giant sighed.

"Free to fuck you and me," Joey hissed through his clenched, smiling teeth. "But, darlin', haven't you heard? No freedom comes from fucking."

"Yeah, Mac, you should know that," the redhead grunted while Daddy tongued away at his ear. "Remember? Oh, God, yes. You wrote, and I quote...do it harder, Sir. Ram my ear."

The redhead was now redfaced as well.

"I'm sorry. You said, 'What have we won if we someday find ourselves free to fuck when how we fuck only frees us to die. We are free only when we have freed ourselves from this compulsion to define our being by a catalog of sex acts.'"

"God, you really do have a photographic memory," said Joey.

The redhead would have smiled, mostly likely, to hear himself vindicated if he hadn't fallen into a full liplock with Mac's former Daddy.

"So, that's why you came back. One last fuck to set you free, darlin'? Well, then, sugar, let me help you."

Joey's hand opened and Mac's dick and balls slithered along his palm and down his fingers and fell back to Mac.

"You're free to go."

But Mac wouldn't let go of Joey's wrist.

"Shoo, run along," said Blond Two as he tried to help Joey pry Mac's fingers away.

"Off to the country," enjoined Blond One as he began to pull Joey away by his other arm.

"You'll be safe there. No one fucks there." Joey snarled.

"Oh no, Mary, rest stops are for resting," added Blond Two. He was now using both hands to tug at Mac's whitening fingers.

"Don't you mean arresting?" Blond One said between puffs. He'd stopped yanking on Joey's arm and had wrapped his arms around Joey's waist, pulling him back again and again and again onto his swelling crotch.

"Ladies, don't go tangential on us," interjected Erasmo, impatient to hurry along Mac's explusion from Paradise.

"Yes, you'd best...head...instead...to...the...suburbs...unnh...yes...yes," Blond One puffed on.

"Puh-leez, if there ever was a fuck-free zone," said a nearly beaming Joey.

"Maybe you can burn off some of your horniness with a mall-raising," added Blond Two, unaware of just how much his boyfriend was helping Joey.

"Better yet, get your Republican gal pals to shut up and finally build that log cabin," moaned Joey, his head thrown back against Blond One's shoulder.

"Go on, now. Go," a flustered Blond Two muttered after he'd looked up to see what was wrong with Joey.

"Yes, darlin', go on," said Joey to Mac and, perhaps, Blond One. "Nothing to see here but mindless hedonism. The *danse macabre....*"

A loud cheer, then applause, rose up from the farthest rows of the chorus. Heads turned, one after the other, away from Mac. When the men saw who it was, they bowed and made way. Who could this be, Mac wondered. He could barely make out the figure of a man at the far end of the human corridor. This must be their Lord of Lords. But he seemed so much smaller than the One, True Lord of the Dance. He was sinewy where The Lord had been colossal. He looked somewhat out of place as he strode past the walls of muscle. As he came closer, Mac grew nervous. Their Lord of Lords looked somewhat familiar. In fact, the closer he came, the more familiar he looked. An itinerant laser that had been wandering throughout the Chorus paused to spotlight his face. Mac dropped Joey's wrist as his dick deflated, his balls shriveled, and his whole skin crawled.

It was *him*!

No Lord of the Dance, he. No lord of anything, this one. Well, maybe of darkness, he thought. Yes, it *was* him. His bitterest foe. His one, true archnemesis. Rolf Erickson. The SexPublican.

Mac actually looked at Rolf this time instead of performing his usual take on Diva Depature #180: scrunching one's face in revulsion, whipping one's head to the side in disdain, pirouetting on one's pumps (here Mac always substituted the latest in butch footwear), and storming away through the crowd in a huff. He surprised himself further by feeling a small twinge of sadness as he noticed the bright-eyed boy from Minnesota he'd picked up ten years ago at an ACT-UP meeting was no longer either.

His reddish hair—now he understood why he'd loathed that redheaded brat Stevie at first sight—had darkened. It hadn't thinned like Mac's. In fact, he'd grown a faint beard. But all his hair was going gray much faster. Even Rolf's eyes were grayer than Mac remembered. His six foot frame seemed broader and tauter. His slight arms and slim legs now bulged, stuffed with an assortment of small round and oblong muscles. He'd obviously joined a gym; he probably had a personal trainer. Even the necklace he always wore had changed. He'd been there when Rolf had bought the silver skull bead in memory of his friend, *their* friend, Joe, and threaded it around his neck. Now, it was hung with a hundred heads of the beloved dead.

But one thing had not changed. His body was still a canvas of a thousand unconnected brown dots that an unseen painter had flecked along his legs, his arms, his chest, his face, and, if memory—disoriented as it was tonight—still served, his nine-inch dick.

Rolf and his nine-inch dick. Mac shivered and the memories shot before his eyes.

Their first night had consisted of the requisite first-date foreplay of drunken fumbling between beers. To this day, however, Mac couldn't remember if it had progressed to sucking each other off. They were pretty shitfaced. But he did remember giving him Xstasy on their second "date" and sucking his cock and rimming his asshole for hours.

Mac cringed. Not for that event—it still made his tongue hum—but because he felt that the following three months they'd spent together had sparked Rolf's transformation into the sex-crazed creature of the dark he'd become.

A SexPublican.

What do we want—public sex! When do we want it—now!

What had he done!

Hey! Hey! Ho! Ho! Monogamy has got to go!

What he'd said had been so simple.

Silence=Beddeath! Action=Life!

Stay with me tonight.

Rolf—somehow, certainly not from him—got the idea that Mac had invited him to live with him as a boyfriend. Forever. But Mac was positive that all he'd said the next morning was that Rolf was welcome to keep staying the night until he'd gotten his shit together.

And so what if, each of those nights, he'd encouraged, and sometimes demanded and even begged, Rolf to fuck him. It just meant he was horny and that Rolf was hot. That's it. And maybe some Saturday nights through to Sunday mornings he wouldn't rest until his own warm earth had been tilled five or six times. Who could pass up a corn-fed farm boy hung with a prize-winning corncob? Okay. Rolf never lived on a farm. He'd grown up in Minneapolis. But he had canvassed for the Democratic-Farmer-Labor Party. And, at twenty, which was merely six years younger than Mac then, he was young enough and naive enough to have been mistaken for a wide-eyed farm boy fresh from the Port Authority.

And, best of all, he really knew how to give a good plowing.

But it all fizzled like a spent cock when Mac found, through a writer friend of his, a sublet in the East Village and told Rolf that he could move in at the first of the month, then only a week away. Rolf, oddly, overreacted. Like he'd been betrayed. Like he was being thrown out. Like they were lovers.

Mac quickly corrected him that they were ACT-UP brothers, comrades, you know, fuckbuddies. And Rolf, that drama queen, told him to "FUCK OFF." He didn't even move into the sublet Mac had offered so graciously. Then, not long after that, came the St. Patrick's demo. Rolf had stomped on the host. Now,

Mac hated the Church for a lot of reasons, both political and painfully personal reasons. But desecrating the host was literally one step too far for him. He knew Rolf had done it deliberately to get back at him. They never spoke face-to-face again. Instead they sparred, but only in the press, like the bitterest of divorced couples.

After Rolf, Mac had sworn never to sleep with someone *that* young again. And he'd done so well until he picked up Brian at last year's NGLTF "Creating Change" conference in Pittsburgh. He winced. Brian. Now he too was a SexPublican.

"Excuse me."

Mac started and turned to see who had spoken to him. He almost choked on his tongue. It was The Lord. He tried to speak, to smile. But The Lord merely looked over him and grinned at someone in the distance and ran away from him. Mac spun around only to be startled anew. The chorus had swarmed the spot where Rolf had stood last. Mac watched, his crest falling, as The Lord and His Ass bounded solidly into the thick of the crowd. Soon the golden head set below the horizon.

Mac's heart sank. A cheer rose up from The Chorus. The Lord had returned to dwell in their midst.

Mac had never felt so alone.

He shuffled to the edge of the burgeoning circle. There must have been five hundred men huddled together. And around them, thousands more swayed and twirled and shook to the loudening music.

The Woman, still determined after all love's betrayals, returned once more. She'd grown bolder after a few Seagram's 7s. She'd also burned her way through a pack of unfiltered cigarettes; her voice crackled with lust. She growled from the darkness above them. *Take them shorts off.*

The Korg had obviously been drinking with Her. It let loose with a roll of blues chords it must have learned in a New Orleans bordello during its long musical exile. *You heard me, boy.* A whipcrack boomed and echoed like summer thunder. A man's voice, lifted straight from a Falcon Video soundtrack, imitated the requisite gasp of first thrust and groaned throatily. The organ and the just-arrived drum machine fell in line and began to plink and snap away at The One, True Score for all porn films.

Take them shorts off. The porn star grunted and yeahed. And thus began an endless call and response between The Woman and The Ecstatic Echo, punctuated occasionally by the crash of her cosmic whip. *C'mon. Take them shorts off.*

Mac pushed at the arm of this man and shoved against the hip of that man. Not one would budge. He pinched this plump rump and that. Nothing. Rubbed here and there. He couldn't even find a chink in the great wall of men to peer through. Once again, he was the short man out. He turned and slumped down until he was ear-level with row after row of knee pits.

He skulked there until he felt a tremor in the legs around him. They twitched and shifted as they took The Woman's words to heart. Them shorts were coming off. He turned his head and strained to catch a glimpse of The Lord through the crowd. Nothing. His lower lip began to tremble. A thousand competing moons now orbited around Mac's head. And on one of them—any one but his own—The Lord was destined to land tonight. Sister Mary Patrick was right, he thought. I've finally gone to hell. Then came the most beautiful smell a cocksucker could dream: the crotch funk of an army of willing and able young men. Except each and every one of them kept his stiff, bare back turned to him.

Mac quietly cried as The Woman purred out his thoughts.

Let me be your sweaty jock. Let me hold your big thick cock.

It wasn't much longer before the Amen Corner behind him joined in the singing. It sounded like a gay men's tent meeting or gym. There were labored breaths. Sweet, soft groans. Garbled moans and joyful cries of "fuck him" and "harder" and "yeah, oh yeah." He closed his eyes and tugged on his lonely dick. It was hot and hard from tonight's constant humiliation.

Suddenly, as if he were in his favorite recurring dream, he felt two enormous hands grab him on either side of his ribs and lift him to his feet. One hand dropped away to take his own, then raised his arm and spun him until they faced each other. It was Him. The Lord took Mac in His arms and hefted him up to His mouth. He kissed him; even His still-blue lips were muscular and they swallowed Mac's own.

The Lord's tongue snaked into the small opening and writhed until it was spread wide. Quickly, He pulled away from Mac's gaping face to feed him His long, fat index finger. He gave him another. And another. Until Mac was nursing greedily on His four fingers while His thumb stroked the hungry child's pulsing bottom lip.

When they dripped with spit, The Lord withdrew them. There was no time for Mac to abhor this vaccuum. The Lord replenished it. Mac licked the great slab of thick, wriggling muscle and pulled at it with his own tongue as if he were trying to swallow it. He gasped, nearly choking on it, when, unexpectedly from below, came the cool, wet finger of his God to rub the lips of his asshole.

There was a cursory tracing and slickening of the puckered mouth. Then the finger popped its head in, looked around, and invited another phalange and the first knuckle to join it.

Mac nipped wildly at The Lord's fleshy lips as the shock of His finger's blunt thrust burned its way out from Mac's bowels to the goosepimples that dotted his skin. He swore he could feel the dulled sting of the manicured nail and each wrinkle and hair in the skin and the bumps and ridges on the hard knot of bone. He squirmed against the huge arm cradling his back and stuggled to sit on the other and ease his way down to the second knuckle.

As Mac's ass grew comfortable lodged on one finger, a second intruded. They rolled about to make room for a third, and Mac nearly bit down on The Lord's swirling tongue when the impatient fourth barged in. As eager as they had been to enter, once in, they decided to stay put and wait until the rectum officially welcomed them and made more room.

It did, and soon almost all was well. The fingers were gliding easily against the smooth walls of his chute. But the thumb, bent and excluded, banged angrily at the tender edges of his hole. No matter how The Lord twisted and turned, it was the same. Mac jumped with each lunge. Then the hand of The Lord grew still. It had found what it had sought. The pad of the longest finger brushed against a small smooth-shelled nut. The bundle of nerves felt each and every whorl of the fingertip.

Mac let The Lord's tongue slip from his mouth as his head tilted back onto his shoulders. The Lord stroked and stroked his prostate. Mac grunted strings of vowels. Short *a*s and long *o*s and flat guttural *u*s. He languidly offered up fragments of words and broken bits of oaths and prayers. Then, as rapidly as they'd intruded, the fingers departed. They had to make way for another.

Mac could feel it, wider than The Lord's four fingers together, pushing against his still-too-tightly gathered purse strings. It had to be just the tip of the glans but it was tearing the circle of muscle. He panicked and drew the purse even tighter. He feared The Lord was going to rend him quite asunder and his innards would sashay right out onto the dance floor. Mac tried to calm himself with a breath and then another. He boldly attempted a spell of sympathetic magic.

As above, so below.

His mouth yawned and his hole widened. He aped a full-on howl and it nearly gaped. Then a battle yell. Anything to swallow the crown whole. The Lord plunged deeper into his open mouth while His cockhead pressed on. Mac's spine shifted upwards, bones jostling his skull, setting off sparks and fires all along the body's electrified third rail. His hips splayed; his pubic bone buckled. *Schplop.* Why are the most intimate moments accompanied by the oddest, most awkward sounds, he pondered for a millisecond. The head was in. He choked as if it had lodged up in his larynx.

Tonight, at last, Mac was learning his limits, his utmost capacities. He'd reached the one for width in minutes, but he'd prayed there would be days to learn the scope of his body's depths. He imagined the hours it would take The Prong to slither its way up the base of his spine, to coil its fat shaft around the bones, to wend its way upward, until, groaning, it slipped from the topmost branch down to his heart, swallowing it in slow, throbbing constrictions.

The Lord, however, had different desires. He arched His hips and pushed as fast and as far as He could into the little man. Mac hissed like a pricked balloon. In time, the hole relaxed its crushing grip on His enormity. The Lord prepared Himself to charge into battle.

Even if Mac hadn't been a candle burning wildly at both ends, aware only of his own conflagration, he still would have been likely to miss the signs of The Lord's preparations: the nearly imperceptible rise in His left eyebrow and the subtle wry curl at the edge of His lips between kisses. And, regardless, it wouldn't have stopped The Lord from charging. With one long hard tug, He pulled Mac all the way down onto Him.

Mac tore his mouth away from The Lord's and cried the loudest he'd ever heard any man cry. It felt like every nerve in his body was unraveling, shooting off a fireworks display worth of sparks from the tip of its downed line. He waited for The Lord's prick to lunge out of his wide mouth, pushing the pain ahead of it. It never came. Before the cold sweat that had washed out and over Mac's skin could dry, The Lord was piercing him again and again with the short sharp thrusts of His spear.

It only took Him a few minutes to build to ramming speed. The Lord dandled Mac on His dick like he was a baby riding Daddy's galloping knee. The stubble at the base of His cock rasped Mac's insides like the tongue of a large wild ravenous cat. It tore Mac wonderfully and he yowled from the ebb and flow of bittersweet pain. He grew to want more. Harder. Now. He began to squat and jump on The Lord's thighs, dancing at the end of His Prong, until he resembled those loose-limbed puppets that cavort and jangle on the end of stick.

In one swift, unexpected move, Mac found himself yanked completely off The Lord's cock, his hole panting in the cold air, and then shoved right back down. Mac wailed, his head flopping about his shoulders. The Lord pulled out again. Then He drew nigh and thrust His sword, with all His might, in to the hilt. Mac gnashed his teeth and wept. Once more, The Lord withdrew. He poked about the yawning hole and missed it. He rutted frantically against Mac's crack or jabbed him furiously in the balls and thigh. One of His blind lunges finally found its mark and He rammed The Prong as deep as it would go. Until the thrashing, impaled man sat on The Lord's slight tuft of pubic hair.

The Lord slapped and rubbed that bit of coarse fur against the jiggling ass, giving it the buffing of its life. And all Mac could do was receive and receive and receive His bounty as he babbled unending nonsense that sounded like he was speaking in tongues.

With a yell that drowned out the music's crash and Mac's chatter, The

Lord came inside him. His white-hot cum geysered like water spraying from a broken hydrant after an earthquake. It burned Mac as it raced through his body, hotter and faster than his own surging blood. He willed every cavity in his body to store this precious gift. But there was too much. The fiery translucent quicksilver seared his lips as it poured from his convulsing hole.

Mac had never felt less alone. He sang along with the porn star. *A mighty fucker is our God.* He howled with the choir. *Praise The Lord.* He had been truly filled with the spirit of The Lord. *Amen.*

The earth, however, had not been satisfied. Even after The Lord's massive flow had been staunched and His prodigious member pulled free, the world continued to quake. And it was this, despite all he'd endured tonight, that Mac considered to be the most odd. For he knew he yanked himself pretty feverishly when he masturbated and this time was no different—*oh, God, yes*—but he'd never jerked himself so hard the floor shook and shook and shook. *Omigod, I'm gonna blow the biggest wad ever.* Or so he thought if thought were possible in such moments.

The current reality was that the legs that had been backing him up were stomping and buckling as the cocks they were attached to shot and spit. Still churning his unspent stick, Mac rolled onto his back, smack-dab into several warm, wet spots, and opened his eyes. He looked up into the canopy of distant faces to see countless dicks, dangling and dripping, which started to back away and grow smaller as they turned cold. More and more bodies staggered aside. He tipped his head back, dipping his hair in yet another puddle, to see into the clearing. A second upside down face, flushed and grinning, stared back at him.

It was The Lord's. He lay sprawled and panting over an enormous lumpy bed of black velvet—Mac gasped—bean bags! With one hand now forever wedded to his dick, Mac leapt, after a series of odd contortions and near-slips on the slick floor, to his feet. Teetering behind, the blood rushed up to his head to greet him. Together they both saw Rolf pull his glazed corncob out and strip off the long, shriveled condom and place it on a silver tray held by the only circuit boy still wearing shorts. The little skulls strung around the SexPublican's neck glinted in the swirl of lights.

Mac shrieked for the third and final time that night.

It was *true*. The second law of homodynamics. Or as it was known in New York, Chelsea's law of phallic entropy. *The bigger the dick, the bigger the bottom.*

The first law? He'd verified that one when, at 19, he fell in and out of love in three weeks. *All verbal agreements between men are non-binding.*

"Sorry, Mac," Rolf said without looking at him, "but you're too late for a three-way." Mac had never heard such girlish peals of laughter from so many men's mouths.

I'm gonna be sick, he thought. Mac and his body, except for his unflagging dick, wobbled back to the floor.

A second short-clad boy appeared with another silver tray piled high with steaming white cum towels from which, with a pair of gleaming tongs, he picked one and placed it in Rolf's waiting hands before he began to move again throughout the crowd. Rolf wiped the dick and chest of The Lord and then his own. He placed the towel on the first tray with the condom. The first boy curtsied and backed away.

Rolf cleared his throat. "Dear brothers, adieu. Now that we've come, we must go."

"No's" bounced about the crowd like beachballs at a summer rock concert. A few towels flopped on the ground in protest.

"Now, now, boys. Keep a stiff dick up." Bleached smile after smile flowered in the field of glistening faces. "Until we meet again—in the re-opened bathhouses of San Francisco!"

A hearty "hurrah" rose up and the crowd pulled the bean bag bed apart to let them pass.

"To the barricades, my brothers," Rolf shouted. "To the bathhouses!"

A solitary black velvet bag remained in their way. The Lord easily lifted a laughing Rolf into his arms and carried him around the obstacle to the cheers of The Chorus.

Hey! Hey!

Ho! Ho!

The Lady and His Lord have got to go!

And when The Couple had walked a good fifty feet, they came to the next obstruction: a small pink angry man crouching in the middle of their path. Rolf motioned for The Lord to put him down. The Lady looked at this odd little man who was cradling his rock-hard dick from the stares of the court.

"Good to see you and Paddywhack are still in love," said Rolf.

Mac blushed. Laughter drowned out his curses. The Lady started to walk on but turned and came back.

"You think this queer world is so simple. You always did. Good: people like me. Evil: everybody else. I don't get it, Mac? I know you're smart. But are you always going to be too fuckin' *insecure* to be intelligent?"

A part of Mac wanted to jump up and coldcock Rolf. But it couldn't coax the rest to leap one more time tonight. Instead, he slowly got to his feet.

"I mean, you and this barebacking obsession." Rolf appraised Mac quizzically. "What's up with that? Yeah, sure, there's nothing like skin-to-skin. And I have *you* to thank for that priceless knowledge."

There were gasps and twitters throughout the crowd. The Lady held up His hand and there was dead quiet.

"Honest. I really thank you for that. Sure, right now, out there in the real world, two guys are getting it on raw. Some are drunk. Some are high. A lot are both. Some don't give any thought to what could happen. Or they don't want to. Can't. It's too terrifying. Instead, they just plow away. And if you're still working through your messiah complex, I wish you good luck trying keeping these magnets apart.

"Oh, educate them you say?" Mac tried to stammer out an answer to the rhetorical question. Rolf cut him off. "They're plenty too that have read and talked and thought about it. Maybe too much. And in the end, they're just as desperate to join in the dance of the inevitable. My solution? Grow up. You. Me. Everybody.

"This nightmare is bigger, harder, and gonna go on longer than my boyfriend's dick." The Lord tittered nervously along with many others. Mac choked on his guffaw and coughed.

"You've got two of human nature's strongest drives, the need to get rich and to get off, helping that fuckin' virus on its merry way. And one of them's got to give or we all go. But it won't be sex. You're fighting the wrong drive, baby.

Rage for a cure. And not just some drug company's golden egg of a vaccine. A cure. Don't look at me like I'm crazy, Mac? Yeah, I know it'd be easier to find God, the great No-Show, and get Him to explain evil than get the board of a multi-national pharmaceutical company to grasp the pricelessness of the less-profitable act.

"But fighting sex? That's insane. Cuz, as long as men have dicks and a lifetime supply of testosterone, sex—especially public, piggy sex—ain't never gonna go away. You of all people, Michael Corrigan, should know that."

"Here. Here," shouted various members of The Chorus.

"Your rhetorical skills have improved since you moved out," Mac said glumly.

"Yeah. A lot of things have gotten better since we broke up."

Mac screwed up his face into a bitter smile.

"You never could wrap that altar boy mind of yours around the fact that a loud, proud sex pig can have ethics."

"Like you, I guess," Mac smirked.

"Yes, Mac. Not all us pigs are like you."

"Ouch," Mac cooed.

"Contrary to your rantings, dear, not every one believes we're post-AIDS or post-any-other-modern-ill." The anger was draining from Rolf's face, leaving him with the look of a sad, beleaguered boy. "Trust me."

"Ha. That'll be the day."

"You just don't get animal magnetism, do you?"

"What?"

"Magnestism. Hello!" Rolf's index finger lept back and forth between him and The Lord. "He's negative; I'm positive. Hello. Magnetism."

"I get it," Mac said coolly, attempting to fake as much nonchalance as he could after the impact of Rolf's bombshell. Somehow, his little farm boy had seroconverted.

"Yes, you keep on scripting life like a one-act morality play and you will get IT," Rolf continued.

"Get what?" he asked, having heard only the last few words.

"Don't 'get what?' me, Michael Corrigan. You know all-to-fucking-well what I mean. The big A. And as much as I know you like to drink, Mac, the new cocktail ain't no cocktail."

"God, Rolf, what do you think I am? A child?"

"Yes," Rolf paused to look him directly in the eye. "Yes, you are."

Mac rolled his eyes in response.

"Christ, Mac, a few months of being a good boy for the media and here you are, back for some bad boning. And, you know what's really pathetic, you don't even care that much about the boning. You just want it to be bad. For the simplest, stupidest of reasons. Good—necessary but dull. Bad—deadly and hot."

Rolf stopped; he looked startled, as if he'd just been violently awakened.

"Oh, Mac," Rolf sleepily shook his head. "I should have know better." He sighed and ran his fingers through his dark burgundy hair. "Of course *your* dreams would have sermons in them. And of course I—you perverted piece of shit—would be the one you choose to deliver them!" Rolf's voice quieted to a hoarse whisper. "Well, fuck you, Mac. And the day you finish fucking yourself raw, do us all a favor and go to hell."

He spun on the heels of his Doc Marten's, took The Lord's hand, and strode off. Their court, confused, rustling as they pulled up their shorts and murmuring loudly, scurried after them.

The music stopped. The Voice, the drum machine, and the Korg were no more. But there was no silence. Instead, there was the din of several thousand disgruntled gay men who had to leave a party before their drugs wore off. With all the catcalls directed his way and the surrounding commotion of the disoriented pushing their way toward some distant, unseen door, Mac failed to notice the EMTs until they bumped into his still-jutting erection with their stretcher.

He was too confused to curse and even smiled faintly when he saw a familiar face, and body, sitting astride the cot on wheels. Erasmo chuckled when he realized the extent of Mac's bewilderment. "Admit it, Corrigan. You'd have felt cheated if you went to a circuit party and some naked boy clutching his dick wasn't carted off in an ambulance."

Erasmo chuckled again and it sounded much louder this time in the growing quiet of the room. "Nighty-night," he said as he waved at Mac. "*¡Pendejo!*" He threw back his arm and snapped.

Darkness.

Mac came to. He waited for the bright blurs about him to slow down and focus. He was alone. *Fuck.* In his room. *Fuck.* On his couch. *Fuck.* He looked down. There it was. Old Reliable. Hard in his hand. *Fuck.* He looked up. Greg's face watched him from the TV and laughed. He turned to join his friends on the floor. *Fuck.* With his free hand, Mac ripped the headphones away and they clattered across the floor.

"Fuck," he shouted to hear a voice. The garbled soundtrack of the video jabbered away softly. He strained to make out the song. It was that damned giddy remake of "Perfect Day." He squeezed his dick with his fiercest stranglehold and tried to fuck his fist. The much mishandled skin burned.

"Fuck, fuck, fuck," he screamed. He thought of spitting in his palm but his mouth was too dry. He fumbled with his hands, both of them, about the coffee table. He grabbed the tubs of plum sauce and smeared his dick. He almost laughed, he almost cried, when he saw what he'd done. It was the color of bloody shit. Like he'd been fucking on crystal all night long. He looked away before he was cheated out of his orgasm again.

"Fuck," he cried plaintively. The cold goo squished through his fingers as he wrapped them once more around his cock. It grew warm as he began to piston. And soft. Like the greasy mouth of a babbling drunk he would have been grateful to find this late in the night.

"Fuck," he grunted. "Fuck. Fuck. Fuck. Fuck. Fuck me. Fuck...me. FUCK...ME!"

He shot and hit the TV screen. Greg and his merry, dancing men raised their arms wildly over their heads, ecstatic to find it's raining semen. Then the screen flooded with wriggling gray dots. The tape had ended. The only sounds were his breaths and the computer's eternal hum.

Mac wiped the plum sauce and cum off his dick with some napkins, pulled up his shorts, stood, and walked over to his desk. He looked at the clock.

Today was Wednesday. Tomorrow was Thursday. The deadline was still Monday morning.

Man Overboard!

for E. Alward

go ahead...you've got eyes...take a look...a long, hard look...here...lemme come closer...you want it, don'tcha...un huh...you're drooling...

hey, faggot, who told you to move...you can suck my **man** tool when I say suck it...

poor sonofabitch...gotta get your lips around my ten inches of salami...huh, cocksucker...won't my **man** meat taste good...look at it...think you can swallow this fucker...ever seen so many veins popping from a cock...yeah, my dick's in a fucking rage...wants to push your pussy lips open...plow your tight **man** hole...then blow its wad deep inside you...

you'd like that, huh, faggot...go ahead...touch yourself...yeah, show me you're **man** enough...you're gonna have to get a helluva lot harder than that...nice...nice...oh, yeah, now that's a boner...good faggot...

now get over there and get Johnny up...no...no hands...be creative...you big city faggots are supposed to be creative...stop looking at me, dumbfuck, and use that pretty mouth of yours...that's it...go for the **man** titties...yeah, suck 'em...umm...nice...Johnny's got big, hard **man** tits, huh...go ahead, chew on his nipple...harder...hear him moaning...Johnny likes you...

okay, untie his gag...yeah, use your hands...but I want you to pull it out with your tongue...awww...look at my little pussy boys kissing...yeah...lick his face like the dog you are...Johnny, you like the puppy I brought home to play with you...yeah, Johnny likes the puppy...

hey...faggot...that's enough kissing...get down there and chew on Johnny's jock...Johnny spread your legs...more...as wide as the ropes'll let you...awww...that hurt, boy...Daddy's ropes biting into your skin...good...yeah...that's it...sniff that basket, puppy...shove your nose into his big bulging **man** basket...yeah, smell his **man** funk...get a good whiff of all that dried splooge and piss...that's right...that's my boy's lucky jock...I've never let him wash it...till now...

stop grinning, faggot, and start licking it clean...get it wet...suck it...ummm...taste him yet...pretty bitter piss, huh...get a dried chunk of his thick spunk...ummm...now get his dick out and lemme see how a big city faggot sucks cock...yeah, that's it...bite into it...nice...pull it out and let my boy's balls flop out...no, you're not done yet...I said I wanna see you suck his dick...so suck his dick, cocksucker...you'll bite his shaved balls when I say so...next time I won't kick your ass so lightly...I'll just mash your lame-ass nuts under my boot...

now get that dick out and suck it...that's it...tug at the **man** pouch...good puppy...keep tugging...I see one fat dickhead...that's it...bingo...pull it out...now swallow it...I wanna see puppy chow down on Johnny's **man** meat...all of it...what the fuck kinda cocksucking is that...his dickhead ain't no lollipop...hey...that's enough of that kissy stuff...and save all that licking for *this* dick cuz you're gonna want it wet when I shove it in you, faggot...

Christ, just swallow the **man** fucker...what the fuck's wrong with you...you give head like a virgin on her honeymoon...don't tell me I got the only faggot from the big city who can't deep throat...you better say goodbye to that gag-reflex, dumbfuck...cuz it'll been gone after you get a workover from this jawbreaker...yeah, it's gonna shove your tonsils out your ass if you don't take my boy's dick down to his balls...NOW!...

ah, did I scare you, little girl...poor baby...poor little cocksucker...not sure what the mean old neighbor **man**'s gonna do if she don't suck the jizz outta his boy's cock...well, shit, Johnny, look at that...we got a sword swallower after all...feels good huh, Johnny...yeah, take that **man** shaft, faggot...good, Johnny...stick it in him...harder, boy...real hard...**man** hard...make your Daddy proud...I wanna see that fat dickhead of yours trying to push through his cheeks...

you...faggot...better keep trying to swallow that mouthful...you stop, even to breathe, while I'm untying Johnny and I'm throwing you out that door...you hear...you can walk back to the city naked for all I fucking care...ah, Johnny boy, someone give you a ropeburn...good boy...you like it when your Daddy twists your little boy titties, don't you...hurts **man** good, huh...yeah...makes you want choke that sick faggot with your big boy dick...yeah...that's it, son...show him who's running this fuck...yeah, the big city cocksucker thinks he's sucking your boy cock...but he ain't...naw...cuz Daddy's boy is **man** fucking his face...yeah, **man** fuck his faggot face, boy...show him who's the **man**...

better watch out, cocksucker...Johnny's bucking hard...he's gonna fill your mouth with a few quarts of his **man** cream...and I don't have to tell you who his **man** cream belongs to, do I, faggot...good...get Johnny's big **man** boy cock outta your mouth...yeah...that's right...leave his stiffie out to dry...cold, huh, baby...you want something warm inside you, huh...well, I've got it, boy...and if you're good, you'll get some too...

so what are you waiting for, faggot...crawl over here...pull off your jock...did I say you could stand up...pull it off already...now get over here...lemme see you tug at your own **man** balls...go ahead...yeah...that's it...tug 'em...pull at your **man** nuts...yeah...now get rougher...yeah, you can pinch your **man** tits too...but I wanna see that other hand down there jugglin' some **man** *huevos*...nice...oh, yeah...real nice...now let's see you do that with some king-sized **man** eggs...

yeah, that's right...these king-size **man** eggs...crawl over here, faggot…sit up…yeah, you like it when I slap you in the face with 'em…hell, I could knock you out with 'em…you're gonna have to use both hands, boy…ah, yeah…shit that feels good…now put 'em in your mouth…suck that huge **man** sac…yeah…ever sucked on **man** nuts this big…oh, yeah…suck those **man** nuts…stuff 'em both in your **man** mouth…do it…you better get used to **man** choking if you're gonna take this **man** rammer…and you are, faggot…you are…oh, yeah…that's right…suck those big **man** balls…oh, yeah…**man** suck 'em…

hey, Johnny…you come before I tell you to and I'm sending you to your room without a fucking…stop **man** playing with yourself and get over here…suck some **man** ass, boy…no, you've gotta earn the right to eat out this **man** hole…first, I wanna see you eat the faggot's **man** cunt…that's it…I want it real **man** wet before I plug it with my **man** fuckpole…how's that feel, **man** puppy…**man** good, huh…why don'tcha show your Master how **man** grateful you are to have Johnny **man** eating you…

that's right…**man** lick your Master's **man** balls…lap 'em up with your whole **man** tongue…lap 'em up…good **man** puppy…ah, yeah…lap 'em up with that big fat **man** tongue…yeah…

hey, Johnny…Johnny…you still tongue-fucking the faggot's **man** twat…or d'you fall asleep down there…let Daddy see you **man** cram that pretty **man** face of yours further up his hairy little **man** crack…now…before I make you…further, boy…tug his **man** balls too…twist 'em…that's it…ah, yeah…get **man** puppy so confused he **man** bites…that's it **man** puppy…**man** bite that big **man** dick…harder…harder, you dumbfuck…it's all **man** gristle…it can take it…**man** bite it…gnaw on that big hard **man** bone…yeah…oh, yeah…sweet Jesus, yes…yes…**man** bite me…shit, that hurts so **man** good…ah…good…**man**…puppy…now you're ready…to suck it…

man swallow it…all of it…now…**man** swallow this **man** pole…un huh…that's it…down to the thick, black **man** bush…nice…get that **man** nose in there…get a **man** whiff of some heavy-duty **man** musk…yeah, un huh…nothing smells as **man** good as a real **man**'s crotch-funk…oh, yeah…

now…lick my **man** piss slit…yeah, shove your **man** tongue in the little **man** hole…now get that wet **man** tongue right up under my **man** dickhead…oh…ohhh…oh, yeah, **man**…right there…yeah…right there on my **man** joy button…lick it…yeah…oh, yeah …**man** jab it…you heard me…**man** jab that big **man** joy button with your **man** tongue…oh, God, yes…

now…**man** suck down all my **man** meat…yeah…**man** suck that big **man** dick…yeah…**man** suck it…yeah…**man** suck that big **man** dick…you like **man** sucking that big **man** cock, huh…yeah, you like it, **man** cocksucker…yeah…**man** suck it…yeah…**man** suck that **man** meat…oh yeah go, **man** cocksucker…go…

oh…oh, yeah…I'm gonna **man** fuck your **man** mouth…gonna **man** fuck your **man** mouth, faggot…**man** fuck it with my **man** fuckpole…oh, yeah…umm…**man** fuck your wet, hot **man** mouth…umm…yeah…fuck, **man**, yeah…oh, yeah…I'm gonna **man** fuck your **man** hole, faggot…yeah…I'm gonna shove my ten-inch **man** dick up your **man** ass…yeah…ten fucking **man** inches…fuck yeah, **man**…I'm gonna **man** plug your **man** pussy, faggot…**man** plug it with my ten-inch **man** hose…yeah…

now lemme see that little **man** ass of yours…yeah, lemme see your **man** boy twat…yeah…hey…whoa…slow down, **man** cocksucker…I'm gonna bust my **man** nuts…I'm saving my **man** buckets of **man** milk for your little pink **man** pussy…yeah, you'd like me to **man** whack your **man** face some more with that big **man** fuckstick…but it's going up your **man** ass, faggot…all ten **man** inches…

Johnny, you done yet…then get over here and get that fat **man** tongue of yours up Daddy's sweaty **man** ass…wait…faggot, **man** thank Johnny for getting your **man** hole ready for his Daddy's **man** donkey dong…well…**man** kiss him, dickhead…it's just your own **man** shit…suck it off his **man** tongue…awww…what a cute little **man** couple of **man**-shit-eating queers…

now get over here and **man** suck my **man** butt, boy…yeah, **man** lick my **man** crack…yeah…get my **man** thick **man** ass hairs **man** wet…yeah, **man** chew on 'em, boy…that's it, boy…**man** bite Daddy's **man** butt…**man** rub your pretty **man** face in Daddy's **man** crack…**man** kiss my **man** hole…oh, yeah, boy…tease that hot **man** hole…**man** tease it with your **man** tongue…just like when you used to clit flick your girlfriends in high school…ahh…now, **man** shove it, boy…good, boy…ah, shit, boy…you're getting **man** good at **man** eating Dad out…good boy… **man** fuck Daddy with your **man** tongue while he **man** fucks the faggot's **man** hole…yeah…good boy…

now, faggot, get up on the **man** bed…shove that little faggot **man** ass of yours up in the air…poor faggot…your **man** butt cheeks are so cold…lemme get you **man** warmed up…yeah, you like it when your Master **man** whacks 'em…what d'you say…harder…you want Sir to **man** spank your **man** ass **man** harder…okay…now they're **man** warm…

man spread those pink **man** cheeks, faggot…don't make me **man** pull 'em apart for you…nice…oh yeah…that's real **man** nice…fuck…your **man** pussy's tiiight, faggot…shit…don't tell me I got me a **man** piece of virgin **man** ass…just my **man** thumb…not even two **man** fingers…I've got myself a big city faggot with a cherry **man** ass…oh, faggot, you are so **man** mine…better bite **man** hard into that **man** pillow, you poor sonofa**man**bitch…cuz here comes the **man** rammer that's gonna **man** pop your cherry **man** ass…

oh, yeah…**man** suck in that meaty **man** knob…unnh…unnh…just try and **man** push me out, faggot…unnh…unnh…UNNH…oh, Christ, yes…it's in, Johnny…Daddy's gonna **man** pop the faggot's **man** cherry…unnh…unnh…oh, suh-weet…oh, faggot, I am so gonna **man** tear you up tonight… you ain't felt no **man** pain yet… unnh… unnnnh… unnnnh… unnnnh… ahhh…that's it…tighten your **man** ass around that **man** long, **man** hard **man** shitpoker…you **man** crying yet, faggot…go ahead…scream your **man** heart out…

man scream, faggot…lemme hear you beg for it…**man** beg for it, you **man** pussy **man** bitch…you know you **man** want it…you **man** want Sir to **man** give it to you **man** long…and **man** hard…real **man** hard…real…real…real **man** hard…yeah…**man** take it, faggot…take it…c'mon, you sick **man** fuck…**man** take that **man** big **man** dick…yeah, take that, **man** pussy boy…and that…and that…and that…ah, shit, **man**…my **man** nuts are gonna **man** burst…get ready, faggot…cuz I'm gonna **man** pump you **man** full of my

man hot... **man** white... **man** thick...**man** juice...yeah...**man**...pump...you...**man**...full...**man**... fucker...*whee ooo*...I'm...gonna...**man**...shoot...my...**man**... sperm... yeah...*whee ooo*...yeah...unh...fuck...yeah...**m a n**...till...it...*w h e e ooo*...**man**...gushes...out...your...fucking...*whee ooo*...**man**...pussy... **man**...lips...unnh...*whee ooo*...yeah...*whee ooo*...yeah...*whee ooo*... OH, **MAN** YEEAAAHHHHH!!!!!... *whee ooo whee ooo whee ooo whee ooo whee ooo whee ooo* ...

• • •

He jolted awake. The sirens were several blocks up the street now. He blinked. *Shit.* He'd fallen asleep before the final scene of *Verbiage à Trois 2.* He looked down. Blinked again. *Fuck.* His dick had shrunken and fallen asleep on his thigh. It looked glazed from the lube. The TV hissed. The screen swarmed with gray dots. A red 3:43 jumped out and back and out again from the shadows. *Fuck. Fuck. Fuck.*

He flicked off the TV and rolled onto his belly. He punched down the pillows and dug his fingers under the blankets and yanked, pulling and kicking until he'd wedged himself between the strata of sheets and comforters. Squinting his eyes, he reached his hand toward the light and twisted it off. He rolled over. His crotch slimed the sheets. *Fuck.* He rolled back, away from the cold, sticky spot.

For the next few minutes, seconds, he staggered outside the black room of sleep, all the while stringing a few words into one sentence, one thought. *I'll shower my **man** body in the **man** morning.* He repeated it, maybe out loud, maybe not. And, with that, he found the door open and stumbled in.

Harder

for Greg Wharton

A whip-crack. Then you. Scuttling, crabwise, for the furthermost corner.

Tonight, we play at love's games. One tailored to our taut, well-oiled, black hides. I call it "Harder." It could be said that it is childlike in its simplicity. It could be if one were an amnesiac, forgetful of just who needs cunning most to survive. Still, it is true that it is a simple game. There is only one rule, stolen unrepentantly from a textbook of Newtonian physics. For every action, there is an opposite, equal reaction.

Already, I have lied. My reaction is never equal. It is—as long as I love you—exponential. You will call out; and I will reply—harder.

I lay down the whip's tip at your knees. Twice. You do not flinch. Your chest swells and your jaw tightens. You no longer crouch; you kneel. If you sweat, it flows unseen down your spine into the warm, dark crevice of your ass. I sidewind the long leather braid before you. It roils rattleless on the floor. Then, the black serpent arcs and strikes at your right nipple. You shriek—staccato, soprano notes—like a boy twenty years younger.

Your legs splay and you flop onto the backs of your calves, your bare ass kissing the floor.

I fight the curling of my lips. I swallow a hiccup of laughter. I have caught my prize-winning leather boy unawares. The whip bites again, just above the silver glint of your left tit. Now, on cue, in character, you bellow like a bull pounding the haunches of its staggering mate.

I watch silently, amused and mildly aroused. By not prefacing the pain with our standard scales of blows and curses, I have made it new again for us both. This enchants me. My prick thickens alone in the chrome cocoon of my codpiece. This enkindles me. I have decided it will swagger well outside the reach of all your wet lips tonight. Instead, I will surprise you and surprise you and surprise you until you break. This enraptures me.

The reddening welts on your chest fashion an arrow that directs my gaze downward through the latticework of your abs to your crotch. Your cock strains against the threadbare jock, dyed a light shade of saffron from soaking so many nights in our beer-bitter piss and flecked brown and black with old stains of come and blood. I drop the single tail. I must make tender what is so stiff.

I approach, my boots crunching softly on the grit of the basement's concrete floor as if it were newfallen snow. The cables of muscle that anchor your shoulders to your neck quiver. The delicacy of this motion belies their bulk.

Your eyes meet mine. In this room's dim light, they are the color of wet stone. They ask to speak on your behalf. They accuse. They cajole. They beg. It is a sight no less dramatic than the processional of old mothers whose skins are like weathered tarps, crawling the mile on their brittle, arthritic knees to the Shrine of Our Lady. It would be a moving sight if I were compassionate like Mother Mary. But I am not. I have become like Our Father. You remember Him, Brother. You remember how we prayed to Him for hours together in my cell. How we suffered in agony, abandoned into His Almighty Silence. How His cold quiet drove first me, and then you, out into this new wilderness. Naked and afraid.

There is something about the pleading in your eyes that keeps my gaze. I have never seen such fervency except in the clenched faces of the old women who lined the marriagebed or the deathbed when I'd assist Father Bernard with the blessing of it, the blessing of them. And, at that moment, I realize that you still pray. Despite all He has done to us. Despite all I have done to you. You still have faith in us both.

Again, you have surprised me tonight. So, again, I must surprise you. I will intercede and answer your prayer. I will be your Father. I will take you up into my shadow.

The palm of my hand slams into the raspy stubble of your cheek and the unyielding bone of your jaw. You have forced me to speak. So I remind you that our love will never be equal for the simple reason that you are not my equal. And yet, I go on to tell you, I have, in my mysterious way, chosen to love you. You lower your head and ask my forgiveness.

I reach into my right boot and withdraw my buck knife. I push down onto the back of your neck with my other hand. You bow before me. I lean across you and, with one stroke, slice the waistband of the jock in two.

I put the knife away and grab for the crop. I look down on your broad bent back. Your clear skin, stretched across the blocks of muscle, is so beautiful I want to open it up. Instead, I place the tip of my spit-shellacked boot beneath your chin and lift it and then you onto your ass. I bend my knees until we are almost eye-level. I yank the remnants of fabric away from your groin. Your dick and balls leap out, either to defend or invite attack. I stuff the wad of reeking cotton into your mouth. I have never gagged you before. Unasked, you look up at me.

Some would attribute this act of defiance to the folly of youth—a boy's mistaken belief that he is a man when he is not. They might laugh it off. Or shrug their shoulders and roll their eyes. I am not one of these people.

I kick the steel toe of my boot between your legs, beneath your balls. You cough out the jock. You are choked by lamentations. With infinite grace, I press the sole of my other boot into your crotch until I meet the resistance of the metal cockring and your pubic bone. I twist my foot hard to the right. You yelp. I grind it back to the left—harder. You moan. I tap with the crop at the edges of your reddening cock and balls, whatever is not crushed in my impromptu vice grip; for a brief moment, I am reminded of our other life together and I see this morning's burning overflow of batter around the mouth of the waffle iron.

The head of your dick juts out at an odd angle. It is the hue of a newly baked brick. I swat it lightly several times. Then I take a single whistling stroke at the underside of your most exposed egg. Your head lurches backwards and I watch calmly as you gnash your teeth. Before our game concludes, I hope to have made you grind all that professionally bleached enamel down to a fine powder until it cakes in your mouth and stains your lips a deathly shade of white.

I lift up my left foot in an act of mercy. You are unworthy. But how else can I hit the swollen shaft of your dick? It stiffens under the blows until it points heavenwards like two hands pressed together in a solemn show of piety. You, however, no longer pray piously to me, your new Father who art on earth before you. Your lips contort and spit out curse after curse. Each more outlandish and impotent.

I think to strike your lips with this short fiberglass stick entwined in leather. But I want them unblemished. They are thick enough. Swollen, they are obscene and useless. For when we have played our game out to its lovely end, I will make you—because I love you—suck out whatever rancor remains in my thudding heart.

So, I slash instead at the lines the whip has burned into your skin. Across them. Up and down them. Each strike produces a note. At first, I am hellbent on hearing your complete octave range. After the first arpeggio of groans, however, I am bored. I will have to work harder for that unmanly wailing.

I punch one of your pecs and you flail backwards. I hit the other and you topple forward. I tug what I can of your close-cropped hair. It is futile. My fingers slip through the wet stubble. I content myself by digging my finger-nails into the edge of your left ear. I haul you across the uneven floor. You scream as you hobble on your knees behind me for I am scuffing and tearing your custom-made chaps. You had to take on that second, thankless job of editing yet another anthology to buy them. This is your first night to wear them.

We have come now to my own custom-made extravagance—a low-standing, wide-beamed sawhorse, swaddled in leather and studs. I lift you up by the tip of your ear. You are almost as tall as me. I press my chest into yours and back you into the end of the sawhorse. I pull away and your sweat turns cold on my skin. I plant my hand above the arroyo that runs between the two mesas of your breasts. I push you backwards. Your butt lands on the beam and your back arches as it descends. Your head hangs off the opposite edge. You will have to strain and lift your neck to see what I will do next.

I cuff your wrists and ankles to the horse's legs. I leave your body to adjust its new wounds and old aches to the awkwardness of this position, to the rigidity of the wood and leather. I return with an antique medical kit. I lean down toward your face. You expect a kiss or a curse. I blow the first gray layer of dust off the old bag. I watch to see if it powders your flushed face. There is too little of it. Instead, you cough.

I open the case and there sleep the pride and private joys of my long-dead mentor. Sounds. Sticks and twigs made of metal. Yet another forgotten medical practice, like cupping, like bloodletting, that can still bring more pain than it cures. I dislodge the smallest and thinnest one. I hold it up in the hopes its dull reflected light catches your eyes. You pull your head up and out of gravity's mouth. The veins in your neck and brow look like ropes threaded under the skin of a mansize marionette. You asked me once what these rods were for and I told you. You shook imperceptibly at my descriptions. In seconds, I knew you were drowning in the undertow of those tidal forces, attraction and repulsion. Later that night, you questioned if we would ever play with them. Tonight, you will have your answer.

As I swab the sound, I see you recall that evening. I grab your rigid prick. It is redder than your face. It too is a patchwork of distended blood vessels the color of bruises. I tap the head of your cock with the hard metal. Only a two-year old can spit out more "no's" in one breath. I grip you all the tighter and slip the spikelet calmly into your piss slit. I must go slowly. I have no desire to bend or break your video-worthy dick. I must wait until each new convulsion subsides before I can slide it deeper. I counsel you to offer up the pain. You respond in Latin. I know this is no small feat for a boy born after Vatican II. I am impressed. Almost. But then I have always known that we share a love of ancient things. And nothing is more ancient than pain. When your cock resembles a freshly skinned animal, skewered and ready for the fire, I stop.

I reach for my softest flogger. It looks like hair on a rag doll and feels like felt. I slap your chest in a series of lazy eights. Each strike is less hard. You look dazed. The welts sting but all you feel is your cock throbbing around the indifferent metal rod. I swat your fat shaft with no more force than a horse in a treeless pasture at noon brushing flies off its backside. You howl. The restraints nearly snap. The sawhorse almost bucks you off. I swat your dick again. And again. Like that song says, I am killing you softly.

The wooden horse lurches sideways, away from me, in one strident scrape. My nerves are jangled and strung tight. I hate that nails-on-a-blackboard screech. I drop my flogger and retrieve the buck knife. I move toward you until I loom over your face. I deftly toss the knife from my right to my left hand. I strike your face with my free hand. Then, with even more grace, I lob the knife over your head and into my waiting, open hand.

You try to shake off the blow. Your eyes struggle to refocus. When they do, I watch them grow comically wide. I have raised the blade high over you chest and am poised for the fatal thrust. You scream, pathetically, for help much as I imagine little Isaac must have on that lonely mountaintop. But, unlike Father Abraham, I have no god to sacrifice you to other than myself. Worse, your new god cannot bring you back from the dead.

My hand and the knife drop to within a quarter inch of your quaking skin. You try desperately to hold still though we both know you want to flail about like a madman. I let the point hover above your skin. I drag it slowly through the air down toward your cock.

You scream again for help. You presume, man-child that you are, that you can read the thoughts of an adult. You thrash now with such fury that I know you have convinced yourself that I plan to separate you from your precious and sainted peter. I could if I were simpleminded enough to doubt that you are mine. But I know that you are. Besides, this god does not need such dramatic sacrifices. Only a little blood and I am content.

So I take your dick which is my dick and I tug the sound slowly out. I will not tear assunder what is mine. Once I let it fall to the floor with a loud metallic clang, you are awash with pain. You keep shouting that I have cut off your dick. Your voice climbs higher and higher until you shriek in tongues. Somewhere in my unconscious I understand your babblings. There alone dwells the tender spirit of my Holy Ghost.

I stand and watch your cock jerk back and forth. The silver ring will not release its chokehold. I steady your dick with my hand and push the tip of the knife against the head. It is just a nick. But this bulb, fattened by its own blood, its skin mottled with uneven reds and purples like a ripe nectarine, oozes its rubicund juices. The blade has had the first bite of your fruit. The second will be mine.

I lap at the cut. I taste the tang of metal, like corroded pipes. Then I suck in the whole head and drink deep. My tongue washes back and forth at that precarious point where the head meets the shaft. You stiffen. I push my lips down the length of you and bite. I release and slide up. I slip your cock in and out of my mouth like a piston while I twist your balls. Your dick can get no harder. I wait for your rupture and it comes. I swallow and swallow and swallow.

In the distance, I hear you crying: primal and mindless and wracking sobs. I am happy for this brief moment between more moments. With the blood and come of you, my lamb, I have been washed clean. I have been born anew.

My love for you only grows harder.

The *Writer's* Life

As much as I delight in your welcoming ass, it is your voice that I am paying for tonight. You sit atop me and read my words—many more than these—back to me. You claim to be from London and I believe you. For your mouth's particular spinning of vowels and consonants raises my modest round tower to royal heights. Your sparsely haired thighs straddle my womanly hips while your disinterested dick sleeps on my gut. Your muscles—so close to the skin's pale surface—tense when I thrust to punctuate a line that makes you laugh or pause.

These moments of lightness belie the distance between our bodies pressed so intimately together. You have run half your race. I have only thirty brief minutes left with you.

I ask you to read another, darker tale. And while you recite it, I add, you must wake that cock of yours and have him ready to sing by our story's end. Since you are as professional as you are beautiful, you do just that until you come to the final period. Then, clutching my book in one hand and gripping me through the transparent wall of latex with your asshole, you chew your lower lip and jerk your dick so violently it looks as if you're shaking a martini. You spill, in biting, burning splashes, across my belly and breasts.

"Lap it up." You pull away from me to do it. "Tear out that page and wipe up what's left and put it in your mouth." You laugh again but indulge me. You too must know the high fever of a fetish. "Kiss me," I beg. You bend even closer to me. I swallow pulp, spit, sperm, and your tongue.

I am one with the Word. I am one with You.

Our time is up.

The Color Khaki

for C. M. Murchison

"**H**ey, nigga. Wassup?!"

Marcus George pursed his lips, catching every bit of his stillborn shout except for the brisk snort which shot from his nose into the mouth of the cordless phone. It could be only one man. His best friend. Louis Waters.

"Hey, Louis. How's my favorite fifty-somethin' homie?" He put a half-dried dish back in the sink.

"You know that weak-ass punk wit' the Day-Glo hair you've been peepin' at the Hole? Well, listen, nigga, I hear he's been dissin' you."

"Again, Louis, in English."

"Shit, nigga. Light-en up! Ooh, that's right. Yo' problem is you too light as it is!"

"Ha. Ha. Ha. So funny," Marcus said as he toweled his hands.

"Just tryin' to keep it real."

"Un-huh. You keepin' it real all right. Mighty real." Marcus walked out of the kitchen to sit down on the stool on the other side of the still-wet counter. This was going to take some time. Everything with Louis did.

"Now can I finish tellin' you what I heard?" Louis insisted.

Marcus shifted uneasily on his stool as a dull ache began pressing behind his right eye. It had been a long day already and he wanted to delay the inevitable bad news—Louis was too happy for it to be any other kind—until the vague pain rolled to the back of his head. So he decided to torment the messenger until he was ready to hear the sad tidings.

"Hey, I'm gettin' old, my brotha. Can you remind me where we first met?" he asked.

"Don't you start."

"Answer me, nigga." Marcus could hear the strain in his own voice.

There was silence on the other end.

"Fine, Mr.-Keepin'-It-Real," he continued, "I'll tell you. Columbia. That's the university, blood, not the country. You remember?"

"Nigga, please," Louis groaned. "Get off of this mid-life crisis shit. I done passed mid-life long ago. Not as long ago as some people though. Some people who's fifty-six going on dust!"

"Tell me—is that diploma for yo' doctorate from *Harvard* still hangin' above yo' head in that office of yours over at the *University* of *California* at *Berkeley?* Y'know them both some mighty big schools I hear."

"Ah, shut up, Marcus."

"An' I heard the President of the U-nited States done gone an' made you a consultant to some governmental oversight committee. Lordy, chil', to climb that high y'musta whitened more than just yo' collar."

"Fuck you, Aunt Jemima," Louis laughed. "Standford's answer to John Maynard Keynes may think he's pretty smart, but I ain't the nigga puttin' on watermelon-colored Izods an' prancin' 'round the house when the curtains are closed."

"I'm hangin' up now. Bye." The hardwood floor gave up a sharp echoing screech as Marcus pushed the stool from the counter and stood.

"Wait—wait, Marcus G. C'mon."

"C'mon what?" Marcus snapped.

"The little punk at the Manhole."

"Yeah, which one?"

"Don't which one me, girl. I know you know who."

"Spit?" Marcus asked as he sat back down.

"See I told you you knew who it was."

"And?" Marcus began to drum his fingers lightly against the countertop. He knew it was time for Brother Louis to spread the Bad Word; his eye had felt much better after he'd said the boy's name.

"Well, blood, it looks like carrot top went and tried to tear Bernie a new one."

"What?" The drumming grew quicker, louder.

"You know. Bernie? The only other brotha in that *honkey*tonk."

"Yes, Louis, I'm well acquainted with Bernie." He stilled his hand. "We profiled his software startup in my class."

"Well, kiss my big black ass...."

"Wait. Wasn't that how *you* met Bernie?"

"Ooh-whee. Ain't you hysterical tonight, Chicken George. Yes'm, Chicken George loves his mens young—and hung—and...."

"Louis," Marcus interrupted. He had to get the conversation back on track. Ever since their brief fling at Columbia as undergrads in the Sixties, he'd learned that Louis was brilliant, in many ways, but easily distracted by every dazzling new flare of his synapses.

"What?"

"What'd Spit *do* to Bernie?"

"That spindly little muthafucka. Y'know, I have to deal wit' white folks' children all week long. Why, if my ex-bitch Kelvin wasn't rulin' the Pendulum on Fridays like she was the fuckin' Queen of Nubia, I'd be there instead of hangin' out wit' you and Bernie at their shitty little clubhouse. All I have to say is thank God for all those fine brothas at Rimshot. Lord, I live for Saturday night in Oaktown...."

"Louis," Mac coughed out his name. He tried to distract him back to their conversation. "Why's Spit a 'spindly little muthafucka?'"

"Y'can't tell by lookin'? Nigga, you need to start wearin' those granny glasses of yours when we go out."

"Louis!" Marcus slapped his hand down hard on the formica.

"Fine. You ain't gonna like this. But Mad Jack's fuckin' that friend of your beloved Spit. Y'know, he's one of those Ridiculous Faeries named Scalawag or some such shit. Should be Skunkweed. Tell me somethin': why is that white folks get all obsessed 'bout purity and then forget to bathe?!"

"Louis, you were talking about Mad Jack."

"I ain't forgot!" Louis shouted. "Y'know, his taste in white boys's 'bout as bad as yours."

"Yours in black boys ain't much better, my sista."

"Nigga, don't start wit' me."

"I wouldn't have to if you'd ever finished telling a goddamned story!"

"Okay, okay. Chill, Marcus G. Gettin' all riled up like that can't be good for a man of yo' age."

Marcus played his trump card and refused to speak.

"Fine. Be all high and mighty wit' me, Dr. George. Here's the 411. Your Spit told that Skankyrag that he'd run into Bernie at the MacExpo over at the Moscone Center. It seems Spit dresses up windows on the web and was wanderin' around pickin' up fashion tips when he collided wit' Bernie and his entourage. Well, like a few other boys at the Hole, Spit had it bad for our Bernie and wanted a taste of his cane—both of them, if y'know what I mean. They even set up one of those play dates you both are always goin' on about."

Marcus flinched; he wasn't jealous of Bernie. Envious, yes. Bernie could make bloody art of even the flattest white ass. But jealousy wasn't possible when they were the only two black leathermen in the bar. (Louis liked the look of leather and nothing more.) No, what stung was the realization that he might be as much of an object to this boy as this boy was to him.

"But that all changed when Spit saw Bernie in his workclothes. And y'know Bernie. He's definitely the creative type—for Silicon Valley."

Louis paused to chuckle knowingly. Marcus knew better than to ask why and kept silent.

"Nothin' too nerdy from what I hear. Bernie had on that black shirt of his wit' those big golden Chinese dragons breathin' fiery red curlicues all over the fabric and some khaki pants. Now who else do I know that has a bad jones for khaki?"

Marcus snorted another long breath into the receiver.

"You ain't makin' this much fun, baby."

"Neither are you."

"Awwh," Louis cooed into the phone. "Well, here's the good part for me and the bad part for you. Seems khaki makes Mr. Spit see red. I can't give you his exact words. Y'know how those grungy-ass boys like to mumble. And these are second-hand mumblings courtesy of Mad Jack's boy. But it goes somethin' like no self-respectin' black man and, certainly, no badass muthafuckin' nigga top, would ever wear Dockers."

"He said *that*," Marcus sputtered.

"So I heard. Why? The word of a black man ain't good enough for you?!"

"Just the word of a *particular* black man...."

"What?!"

"Louis, I've known you for almost forty years...."

"So?!"

"And I know you're prone to embellish...."

"Prone! Baby, when I'm prone I do a helluva lot more than embellish."

"I know," Marcus laughed.

"Don't sweet-talk me."

"You know what I'm sayin'."

"No. But I know what you mean."

"Louis," Marcus interrupted.

"Don't 'Louis' me, bitch."

"Louis,...."

"No, no, it's too late to apologize. You wanna know the real deal, Marcus Robeson George. Fine. Here it is. Mad Jack said it sounded somethin' like 'Men worth doin' don't do Dockers.' You happy. As for my *embellishments*, Uncle Tom's gonna have to ask his Little Evil herself if they's true or ain't they."

"Louis,...."

"Don't interrupt me no more, nigga. You still ain't heard the worst of it."

"It gets worse?"

"Fool, you know it always does."

"Oh, God."

"That's right, baby. Start prayin' now. Cuz your Spit did—*for a fact*—walk right past Bernie like he didn't see him. Like a three-hundred pound badass muthafuckin' nigga wouldn't stand out at a computer expo! And then he flaked on their playdate. Mad Jack told me so and I asked Bernie and he said it was true. The boy was a no-show. Had no idea why, and I'll be damned if I'm gonna clean up that muthafuckin' punk's shit and tell Bernie the few weak-ass words Mad Jack told me. You like that damn boy so much you can do it."

Louis paused to cluck his tongue and sigh fiercely, as if this mean mistreating had happened to him and wearied his already burdened soul.

"So?! What you gonna do *now*, big bad Marc Daddy? Especially when your Spit finds out 'bout your dirty little counter-revolutionary fetish. Shit, nigga. Bernie's got nothin' on you!"

Marcus grimaced. What predictable, old fools they'd become; in twenty years, they'd gone from classmates to roommates to lovers to best friends who happened now to be two of the most respected economists in the country. And every Friday night they carried on over the phone like tonight. No different than two righteous sisters who sit next to each other every Sunday, stiff as gravestones, and then rush home to call each other and let the shit fly as they catalogue the trespasses—fashionwise and otherwise—of the congregation.

Without asking, Marcus knew that Louis was in his home office, probably wearing some new FUBU sweatpants getup and swiveling in his state-of-the-art desk chair under the watchful eye of the framed D'Angelo poster. And that his wide nose had to be nearly flat because his wider mouth was grinning like mad into the empty air spinning around his head. Why? He knew that too. Because Louis could "see" that Marcus was perched on a stool at his kitchen counter, wearing his latest purchases from the J. Crew catalog, contorting his face with that odd combination of grimacing, blushing, and rolling of the eyes he did every time Louis nailed his black ass, like now, to the floor.

"Do I have a cap?" Louis shouted into the phone.

Marcus, startled, yelled back, "What?!"

"Huh?"

"You said you had a cap."

"No, girl, Bernie asked if I *had* a cap. Then I asked her, 'Why? Do Miss Daisy need me to drive her to the Piggly-Wiggly?' A cap. Please. I only wear hats. And who the fuck sent me these links?! Like I'd ever shop there. Might as well go down and buy my leather at the GAP."

"Louis."

There was no answer. Just mumbling and clicking. Marcus' clairvoyance hadn't been so precise tonight after all. Louis had been doing more than just spinning and grinning in his chair; he'd been online, reading his email, and probably browsing chat rooms, all while trying to carry on this old-fashioned conversation by phone.

"Louis!"

"What?!"

"You goin' to the Hole tonight?"

"Huh-low, girl. Why do think I'm emailin' Bernie what *not* to wear tonight?"

"Good," Marcus said. He began to repeat the word absentmindedly as he wrestled with himself. He knew, down to the squeaking joints between his bent knees, that he wanted this boy bad. And he knew that Spit— always eyeing every man in the bar with his studied-yet-disconcerting gaze of nonchalant defiance until he'd catch Marcus matching his cold look and quickly turn away—wanted Marcus down to his bright blue boy balls. But before Marcus would even let that self-styled punk suck his dick, let alone ride it, and certainly before he'd ever let them kiss, he'd have to insist on some intensive remedial tutoring. There was a flash of images. His fattening cock thumped around in his madras boxers and plain-front khakis. Then he heard Louis. He was interrupting him, calling him back.

"What you goin' on 'bout?"

"I said," he stalled until he'd fully returned, "a professor's work is never done, is it Dr. Waters?"

"No way, baby. It may be summer but I was rippin' an' runnin' all day at Berkeley. Then the Bay Bridge was backed up to the muthafuckin' toll plaza and...."

"It was a rhetorical question, Louis."

"Oh. Well, forgive me, Dr. George. I forgot how serene life could be at Stanford."

"Don't start, Louis."

"Me? Whaddabout you? What you gonna do 'bout Spit?"

"I was coming to that before you interrupted...."

"Well, I ain't interruptin' you now. Get to it, nigga."

"Jesus, Louis."

"Don't you start blasphemin', boy. What would your granddaddy say 'bout that?!"

Marcus laughed as he caught a glimpse of the Reverend George gripping the pulpit, his glasses catching the light from the stained glass windows and reflecting the eternal twirl of the overhead fans, his clean-shaven face, as smooth and dark as Great Aunt Regina's homemade molasses pie, subtly reddening. This was going to be some fiery sermon. And, before the image faded, he was sure he heard him say, "What dark times these are, my brothers and sisters, when from out of the mouth of babes come curses against Our Lord Jesus. Can I have an amen?"

"Amen," Marcus murmured out of habit. Louis laughed now. Marcus caught himself and added, "What I'd intended to say was that I guess I'll have to teach our young Mister Spit just how mean a muthafucka a nigga in Dockers can be."

Louis harrumphed. "I wanna see that day."

"You will, baby. Starting tonight."

"The Manhole after eleven?"

"Sounds good. Oh, and tell Bernie to stay away." Louis tried to blurt out something and Marcus stopped him. "Just tonight. I'll explain later. I'm gonna need your help."

"You always do, Marcus G. You always do. Peace." Louis hung up.

Marcus pushed *END* and laid the phone, face-down, on the kitchen counter. Then he sighed.

• • •

White men. What was it with them? Lord, if that wasn't the question of the ages. He felt his ancestors sigh now. And what must they think of him? Especially his recently passed-over mama. Her baby boy reddened with shame. But he was fifty-six, dammit. Time to be honest about who he was and what he wanted. Wanted since he was a small boy sitting in the hard pews of Baltimore's Olivet Baptist Church, under the harder eye of the Reverend Isaiah George, Sunday after Sunday.

Men. He liked men. That was it. Known it since he was a little boy, fooling around with his two copper-skinned and red-headed cousins, James and LeRoy. End of sermon. Okay, he especially liked white men. The end. But wasn't no one's fool. Not at all. He'd known like every other black man, woman, and child in that congregation, cooling themselves with printed fans from Brewster & Sons, Funeral Home—the company name, address, and phone on one side; a portrait of Our Lord Jesus on the other—what evil-spirited sons of bitches white men could be; it wasn't like he got it up for Bull Connor or George Wallace. Now that was going beyond the pale. No, it was simply that from a young, young child he'd taken the good words to heart and fallen in love with that kind face he'd seen everywhere he turned.

What a friend we have in Jesus.

He was fifty-six and had never told a living soul that, not even— especially not—Louis. But the ancestors knew. And now his mother was one of them. But how did he go from loving his sweet Lord Jesus with all his heart—his first and still greatest love—to wanting to thrash the living daylights out of an immature brat named Spit?

It hadn't been planned. That much was certain. Desire might have laws like economics, though nowadays he suspected the fixity of either, but Heaven help the fool who tried to predict its up- and downturns.

It was just something unconscious that, despite all his anguished prayers to be washed clean, stuck to him and, with time, became conscious. A conscious choice. A conscious pleasure. A conscious delight.

One day, he was sitting in his grandparents' parlor, listening to Mahalia Jackson testifying from out of the speakers of Reverend George's phonograph and wishing, innocently, to sit beside his Lord in the upper room. Next day, he was lying alone in his own upstairs bedroom, thinking impure thoughts about fierce and gentle young men like James Dean and the Attorney General, Bobby Kennedy. Later, Louis would often wonder aloud why Marcus never chose to lay down his burden and follow The King. But Elvis knew too much of the world. It was the other-worldly ones. The ones too innocent or weak to belong to this world. These were the men he dreamed would one day take a closer walk with him.

How he longed to watch over them, to cover them with the shadow of his mighty wing, to lift them up before they dashed even their foot against a stone. How he'd bawled when they'd died.

And it wasn't, he argued with Louis time and time again, because he believed they were special or better. It just surprised him when white boys died. By his twenties, all he'd heard about, all he'd cried over, was black boys dying. Boys from school, boys from down the street, and boys in faraway places like Mississippi. He'd come home from little Joe Goode's funeral or read about Emmett Till's lynching and get mad and then go mad, wanting to bust up everything in sight. But there was just too much pain around it to get sad. He'd just get that look his father did if he and his brothers and sisters ever asked him about what is was like to fight in World War II.

Hey, daddy, daddy, did you ride in a boat? Hey, daddy, daddy, did you fly in a plane? Hey, daddy, daddy, did you kill anybody? Hey, daddy, daddy, did they give you a parade?

But these white boys, why did *they* die? They were the children of The Man. Or so it seemed. Yet, they were so different from other white folks. Like they didn't belong any more among them than he, some days, felt he did among black folks. They just seemed so unprepared for this world and its cruel, cruel ways. Much like he had been when that old man had wrinkled up his already shriveled face—he looked like a bitter old white raisin—and shouted at him a word he'd never heard. And he'd run all the way home to ask his mama what it meant. And, she, smiling to hold back tears, had taken him aside to explain the Devil's ways. But these boys, it was obvious no one had ever bothered to take them aside.

Of course, losing so many friends throughout the Eighties and Nineties, the death of any boys, even white boys, stopped surprising him. Until he heard about Matthew Shepard. Until he saw him. He was so ashamed of how upset he got. After all he'd been through, after all he'd witnessed.

Louis couldn't understand what was wrong with him. "What you gettin' so upset about?" he'd said the night his friend, only a few months into his year abroad as a visiting professor at the London School of Economics, had called him—a small voice, breaking with emotion. "You seen plenty a white boys die. Hell, every boyfriend you ever had is dead." But Marcus just kept crying into the phone. "Why you surprised, Marcus G.," he'd said sharply, frustrated that Marcus was worked up again over another white man, frustrated that he couldn't put his arms around the old fool. "This is how faggots died before AIDS and that's how they gonna die after they find a cure. Of course, by then, there won't be a nigga or a fag left alive on this earth." Louis prided himself on being a realist. It had made him a world-class economist.

Marcus couldn't answer him. It had begun as just one more in a growing processional of gray days in London until he'd received an email from a former student and followed the links back to a growing string of articles. He read of Matthew's long night and finally saw his blurred little face, and he was a boy again crying for these white boys, so like Our Lord Jesus, who kept coming down from heaven and getting the holy crap beat out of them and sent right back.

If he'd been a black man, he heard Louis say long after they'd hung up and from deep within his own aching head, you wouldn't have shed a tear. If he'd been a black man—and if he'd been a black and same-gender-loving man and fool enough to be in Wyoming after sundown—then Louis was right because he would have expected such a violent death, probably one that was even worse. Hadn't some cracker morons just tied a brother to the back of their rusted old Ford pickup and dragged him across the great state of Texas till his days-dead body fell apart? And for what? Because they were bored on a Saturday night.

But these boys, these innocent-and-pure-and-good-looking white boys. The kind of boys he imagined white women would pray to have for son-in-laws, for sons. It just shocked him every time how fragile they were, how easily they died. Far too gentle for this world. And, God, that Matthew, that delicate, doe-eyed boy, he didn't have a prayer.

It was Good Friday all over again and no chance of any angel coming to roll death's stone away. That boy was gone and that was it. So Marcus kept crying through the night until he had to leave for his first class.

Days later, he thought he saw Matthew Shepard. The murdered boy was sitting across the lecture hall as a colleague catalogued, with painful dispassion, the First World's many sins of omission committed in Russia's forced conversion to a free-market system. He was staring earnestly at him. Marcus strained to refocus his eyes. The boy wasn't Matthew Shephard after all—he was bald and dressed like an imagined centerfold in W.A.R.—and his look was far from earnest. He wasn't sure the skinhead was outraged or aroused by his presence until he winked.

After the lecture and over pints, Marcus decided, as he got many long, lingering looks at his small childlike mouth and wide upturned nose and large, watery brown eyes, that his appearance was less that of a footsoldier for the Aryan Nation and more that of a beatific and, upon speaking his name—Andrew, mischievous cancer patient. This doctoral candidate at the School of Economics was short and slight, but hardly frail—in mind or, as Marcus would learn forty-five minutes later in the hallway of Andrew's flat, in body.

It wasn't until a proper fortnight had passed, on their fifth date, as their tongues rolled languidly in each others mouths and Marcus slowly pushed Andrew's suspenders off his shoulders and Andrew gently released each button from Marcus's fly, that the good doctor was finally introduced to the English Vice by his sweet-faced boy who said, upon freeing the last bit of metal from the cotton's embrace, "You know what I'd really like now...."

Marcus pulled his mouth away from where it had been sucking on Andrew's neck.

"You want me to spank you until you cry?" he said uncertainly.

"Yes."

All Marcus could think of was the terror of waiting for his granddad to return from the backyard with a switch or his dad to finish unloosening his belt. "I'm gonna beat the black offa ya," they'd said their separate times, echoes of the other in so many ways. Then they'd kept their promise. It hadn't happened often, but enough—enough that he wouldn't have wished it even on his worst enemy.

"Like with a switch?"

"Oh, yes." Andrew nearly bounced up and down on the couch and clapped his hands. "But you're not ready for that...yet."

"Yet?!"

Marcus' eyes grew wider and whiter. He'd obviously given Andrew the wrong impression. The roughest sex he'd ever had was in his last and longest relationship with Steve. Maybe once or twice, when Steve had been healthier and their love-making more spontaneous, more vigorous, Marcus had slapped him on the backside right before he came. But he always felt embarrassed. He thought he must have looked like a little boy playing rodeo cowboy, bursting out of the chute on a bucking bull. And Steve had usually put in his two quiet cents about Marcus' improvisation and turned away when it was time for their perfunctory post-coital cuddle. And now this angelic-looking boy wanted to be spanked until he cried—and, Lord knows, what else after that.

Then again, that boy had a fine behind—mighty fine. Each cheek could and had fit perfectly in the palm of his hand. Looking back now, he realized how brilliant a mind reader Andrew had been that night. Certainly as brilliant as he would prove to be a teacher. For, by the time Marcus' thoughts had returned from their wanderings, the boy was naked and stretched over his lap. And with that—and a coy request of "Please, sir, spank me very hard"—Marcus began two semesters of serious study at Andrew Marlowe's Homeschool for Sadists.

The pupil took to spanking quite well. When he called Louis next, half-hoping the realist would try to talk him out of this newest madness, and told him how he'd slapped a white boy's ass till it was red like two cherry tomatoes and his own hand ached and he'd loved every moment of it, all his best friend had said was "'bout time" before spending the next thirty minutes telling Marcus about this "fierce muthafucka" he'd met at the Pendulum named Kelvin who was riding his "sweet, black ass" to glory almost every other night.

Without his best friend's discouragement, Marcus advanced quickly from hand to paddle to hairbrush. It was the leap from spanking to striking, from kinky tourist to earnest pervert, that proved to be the true test not only of his newly learned education but of his newfound faith—in Andrew, in himself, in the soundness of their desires and their minds.

They were well into another round of Headmaster and cheeky boy. Andrew was being especially insolent—driven by the pride of how beautiful his gift of a red silk cravat looked against Marcus's throat and how much Marcus, despite his initial protests that it made him look like David Niven in a minstrel show, glowed as his boy had wound it around his neck and tucked it within his shirt. The Headmaster now inquired of the boy the nature of his latest offense. The bold pupil inched as close as he could to his stern inquisitor and spat out a snide comment, drizzling the Headmaster's skin and beard with flecks of spittle. There was only one proper response to such an affront and it was delivered to the rude upstart with the back of the elder's hand.

But the blow, though not unwanted nor unexpected, had been too strong. Andrew snapped back onto the bed and bounced twice before falling to the floor below. When he could get his head above the mattress, Andrew saw Marcus standing stock still with a near-cartoonish look of horror on his face. When Marcus saw Andrew, his hand holding up what must be his broken jaw, he collapsed to his knees with a hideous cracking thud, crying and swearing he would never harm him again.

After two weeks of Andrew's persistent coaxing that his jaw was not broken—though it did hurt and that was how he liked it—and that he loved rough sex—much rougher than anything they'd done so far—and that he fancied Marcus for a natural—to which Marcus replied, "You mean natural savage," and Andrew had added, with a lusty smile, "Ah, I knew you were the answer to my prayers"—the Headmaster and boy were giving it another go. The wayward student, naked and bent over his just-inspected bed, was pleading with his disciplinarian to administer his punishment with more force.

"Please, Sir, strike me harder." The ends of the deerskin flogger collapsed in a messy pile on the boy's ass. "Please, Sir, harder." The fluttering tips landed with a more distinct sound of gravity this time. "Hit me, you dumb nigger."

Marcus felt the wind go out of him, as if he'd been punched squarely in the gut. The flogger hung limp from his right hand.

"What did you call me, Andy."

"Sir," he shouted as forcefully as he could, to brace himself for what he was about, he hoped, to receive, and to remind Marcus their games were far from concluded. "I called you 'a dumb nigger,' Sir. And if you're not as dumb as you are dark, you'll thrash me for the piece of skinhead shite I am."

Shite. What the hell kind of word was that, Marcus thought. It just sounded wrong. Charmingly and ridiculously wrong. So, Marcus did what he'd done the first time he'd heard that word and figured out what it meant. He laughed and his swift-rising anger evaporated. "Nice try, Andy."

"Then let me have my punishment, Sir."

Marcus threw the flogger over his shoulder and let it fall across Andrew's back. The boy barely flinched.

"What in bloody hell was that? You call that a thrashing?"

"That's enough, Marlowe," said Marcus, struggling to regain his character.

"No, Sir, it's not. You're black. As pitch. As night. And that means once upon a time your kind came from out of the fuckin' shadows of darkest Africa. Land of the bloodiest savages…"

"Stop baitin' me, boy. I said that's enough."

"But there was nothing bloody or savage in that horsetail of yours flicking flies off my back. Some angry black man you turned out to be…"

"Listen here, boy." *Listen to me*, Marcus thought. *I sound so unconvincing. This is so stupid. I can't do this.*

"Well, c'mon, nigger. Beat me. I can take it. I'm not like all your other white boys. I'm not fuckin' likely to go and die on you!"

And that was all Marcus remembered Andrew saying. The rest—dropping the flogger, snatching up the riding crop, gripping Andrew by the scruff of his neck and pushing his head down onto the mattress, walloping his bouncing ass and squirming thighs with the crop—it all felt far-removed from his own body and out-of-focus, like a half-remembered dream that vanishes slowly upon awakening. The sounds of his own shouts and the boy's screams and the thick whistle of the descending leather warbled about his ears and faded as if heard from under a great body of angry water.

He awoke to find himself sitting on the floor, cradling Andrew in his arms, both of them sobbing. He felt surprised and relieved and excited. Through Andrew's clever taunting and willing sacrifice, the dam round Marcus' deepest anger and lust had been breached. He had raged until he'd run dry. And both men were still alive.

Alive. Both of them. Very alive.

At that moment, the scales dropped from his eyes. He was born anew. Marcus had found a new calling. His own way to serve his sweet, sweet Lord. He would make strong the meek, blessed though they might be.

And he had.

In the few years since he had met Andrew at the lecture in Damascus Hall, since he'd tearfully matriculated from Marlowe's Homeschool with an open invitation to return each summer for further post-graduate work, Marcus had left his healing mark on the pale hides of boys on either side of the Atlantic. And now, he had come to a new twist in that road. He was going to make straight, so to speak, the crooked. Take the rod to a spoiled child. But he had to hurry, he thought as he lifted his ass, sore from the unforgiving flatness of the stool's oak seat, and stood. He had only an hour to dress—how would the boy know he was there to minister unto him without his collar?—and find parking.

• • •

Marcus strode through the leather flaps hanging in the doorway and knew immediately by the smells of the dimly lit place that he'd entered a sex pig's garden of earthly delights. It had that unmistakable musk: the aroma of freshly polished leather mingled with the strong funk of ripe, unwashed denim, and was sharpened by the pungency of cigar smoke (for this was a bar of smoking as well as sexual outlaws) and sweetened with the odor of beer-scented sweat and piss from an overcrowded room of horndogs on the prowl. He could be in no place other than San Francisco's infamous Manhole.

The eyes of those in the know, the alerted ones, fixed on the hulking presence standing beside the pooltable. Like Kemet, the name ancient Egyptians gave to their land, he was known to the denizens of this bar, to the whole South of Market demimonde, simply as "The Black:" the Black Marc Daddy; the Black Knight; the Black Man.

And what a man he was: a linebacker in leathers; 6'3" tall and 250 pounds solid. He wore his biker's cap pushed forward, the brim shading his eyes, small, clear, and intense like a predatory bird's, and pointing the viewer's gaze down to his long and strong nose, his high cheekbones, and his well-trimmed beard which was going white, making his thick lips look fuller and his broad jaw stronger and his sepia skin darker. He'd wrapped a gleaming black leather jacket around what he could of his wide shoulders and arms, but it looked more like a picture frame for his chest. And there were few men in the crowd staring at him at that very moment who wouldn't have admitted he was built like the proverbial brick house, and letting it all, maybe not hang, but certainly bulge out in his tight white tee and, as their eyes happily dropped, well-faded Levis.

Unaware that he was the object of such especially keen interest tonight, The Black Knight ignored the men watching him and looked out over their heads as he scanned the bar for the one he'd come for. There, he thought. Annie Lennox wailed out overhead that she needed a man; Marcus agreed. He walked until he stood a few feet from a group of boys hanging around the pinball machine, until he too was illumined by its strobing glow, never noticing how certain men had quietly stepped to either side of him and pulled the soon-to-be-clued-in along with them.

In the center of the boys jerked and gyrated Spit. He was a few inches shorter than Marcus and a good hundred pounds lighter. Or as Louis liked to say, "he's built like a beanpole and almost as smart and, Lord, nearly forty years younger than you, Methusaleh."

Marcus had to admit, as he observed him for the first time without interruption, that he looked pretty scrawny. His gray-green T-shirt—in the seconds his body came to rest, Marcus was able to read that it said "Extra Fancy"—had been worn down to that state of fuzzy translucence which occurs in cotton just before it disintegrates and it clung all the tighter to his concave chest and spindly arms. His battered camouflage pants were held up by an orange extension cord that he'd coiled several times around his hips and cinched in one enormous square knot. The makeshift belt was close in color to the shade of his tightly buzzed hair—the only easy-to-spot indication, in Marcus' eyes, that he was a fag; that and the fact he was in this bar.

And he did look younger, decades—*Fuck you, Louis!*—younger. His skin was smooth and still refusing to be pulled out like taffy in gravity's sticky hands. It didn't hurt that it had never seen the sun; it was paler than any undead's. And his long, squarish head made his nose all the smaller, turned-up, and boyish. Then there were his eyes—large, almond-shaped, and heavy-lidded in the classic stoner fashion. Louis had said they made him look like a cartoon character and called him "Dopey Dick" until he learned his name was Spit and had done just that with his mouthful of beer. To Marcus, they gave Spit an endearing appearance, like that of a sleepy child found wandering in hallway late at night, lost between the bathroom and his bed.

This moment would have been perfect, Marcus thought, as he grabbed Spit's jangling arm and yanked it toward him, if the boy had been a flick or two away from the machine's all-time score. But he refused to look at the blinking and buzzing box; that would have been a fortuitousness so poetic that it could only ever occur in fiction. Still, it did have some very sweet seconds.

Before the silver ball had spun past the flippers and vanished, Spit had tried to throw a punch at the "fuckin' asshole" who'd pissed on his wild times with Bo and Luke Duke in Hazzard County; opened his eyes wide enough to see who it was; majorly blanched and swerved his fist to avoid the Black Knight and stumbled into his arms. The Black Knight had then promptly spun the punk around, pinned him in a full nelson, bent him forward until his bony ass was grinding up against Marcus' swelling crotch, and force-marched him deeper into the bar through the waiting path of silent men.

When they arrived, fifty-six seconds later, in front of the john, Marcus released Spit long enough for him to stand up before slamming him into swinging door and pushing him into the center of a small dark room made all the bleaker by its black walls and a single red light bulb. Half-dressed bodies tugged at their pants and scrambled for the door. Even Ol' Kris Kringle, a naked bear with a flowing beard like his namesake who sat each night in the furthest toilet until his hoary pride and glory was as yellow as an Easter egg from California's multi-vitamin-enriched piss, hurriedly closed his door out of respect.

God, Marcus wondered, *who doesn't Louis talk to.*

He jerked Spit down onto his knees before the trough. He was shivering, just barely. "Boy, you've been eyeing me for months," he growled, lowering his voice to a deep, bone-rattling bass. "Well, tonight is your lucky night. I've decided to find out if you're worthy. So c'mon, snowflake, pull it out. If you can soak yourself before I'm done emptying this," he pulled his own dick out and enjoyed Spit's eyes growing slightly whiter, "then I'll give you the last shakes of dew from my big...black...lily."

Marcus lifted his dick and pissed; the stream battered the metal sides of the trough and echoed off the walls. He could hear Kringle whimpering in his stall. When he'd nearly drained himself, he turned and saw that Spit had his camos down around his thighs and was sitting in a growing puddle. He aimed his weakening stream at the boy's chest and said, "Open your mouth." Spit closed his eyes as if he'd fallen into deep prayer. "Boy, did I tell you to do that?! Stick out that bitter tongue of yours." And with that, Marcus dropped a small necklace's worth of amber pearls on his curling tongue.

Marcus glanced down past Spit's mouth. His tongue wasn't all that jutted out eagerly from the boy. He had one of those long, thin dicks, made all the longer and thinner because it was now hard enough to twitch and bounce on its own.

"You just may do, punk," Marcus said as he rearranged his dick within his jeans and turned for the door. Spit scrambled to get up. Marcus had to bite his lips to keep himself from laughing at the ridiculous sloshing sound. And this must have looked like a terrifying grimace to Spit when The Black Knight spun around and pointed, his hand shaking with fury, at the ground and shouted, "Stay," for the punk crumpled to the ground. "You'll leave when I'm gone."

Spit gave him a look of wide- and watery-eyed soulfulness, like the accusing gazes of those old, abandoned dogs in the newspaper ads the SPCA runs each week. And it might have tugged more at Marcus' heart than his cock if this bratty punk had been a whipped dog, *his* whipped dog.

All in good time, Marcus said to himself. *If you follow the divinings of that stiff dick of yours, maybe a week. Maybe two.*

"What?" he replied out loud to Spit's silent question. "You think I was gonna take you to the backroom or maybe just fuck you upfront on the pool table. Give you somethin' finally *worth* braggin' about. Like hell. Here."

He threw his card on the floor. "You'll get to this address next Friday at 10 p.m. Not a minute before. Not a minute after. I expect to see your skinny ass there or don't even think of showin' it again in this bar." He paused to look at the punk's ghostly white knees, splitting the already-wide rips in his pants. "Hey, boy." Spit bobbed his head. "If I was you, I'd get that card outta all that piss before the ink runs." Marcus turned for the last time and, as he pushed against the door, he heard Spit splashing about furiously in his own urine.

The Black Knight appeared in the doorway. The room was silent. A statuesque man with a bald head the shape and color and sheen of those ornamental oak balls at the bottom of a banister, distinguished by a prominent nose that seemed to be balanced on a thread-thin goatee, and wearing a fluorescent orange jersey, two sizes too large, stepped out of the crowd, raised his long arms over his head, and clapped his hands. Louis had spoken. Every other man, all save Spit's very confused friends, joined in. The DJ began to play—most likely, Marcus imagined, with a little bit of prior encouragement from his forever bold soul sister Louis—Tina Turner's cover of "Under My Thumb." The

Black Knight smiled and, uncharacteristically, bowed. "That's for you, Bernie," he shouted over the music as he parted the crowd, passed Louis who was nodding his head and saying "Well, all right now. Well, all right," and headed for the door.

• • •

Marcus hit the *OPEN* button and the carousel rolled out. He pushed the tip of his thick finger in the tight hole of the CD and lifted it out and up to its case. Then again. Until he'd picked it clean. No Patti or Aretha or Lauren tonight. And no—*which one is this?* (he had to squint hard without his reading glasses)—Parliament—*oh, that's where that went*—either. He'd take the boy aboard the Mothership if, and when, he proved himself worthy. Tonight, Marcus had planned a trial by a different fire. This had to be a very heavy scene. So he filled each slot with Nat King Cole and pushed *CLOSE* and then *SHUFFLE* and *ALL DISCS* and then *PLAY*.

First came that syrupy staple of late Big Band, two dozen strings gliding and sliding their way through the song's intro. Nelson Riddle was at it again. It was as ridiculous as it was unneeded. Like draping a sling with pink taffeta bunting. Then came those warm-as-brandy notes out of the King's mouth and, as his voice had done the first time Marcus heard him sing "When I Fall in Love" forty years earlier, it turned him into gooseflesh.

He turned and walked across the room to turn off the overhead light. The man in the mirrors that paneled the opposite wall smiled back at him. He was tall; he was dark; and he was very handsome in his skin-tight pink Izod that he'd tucked into a brand-new pair of Dockers. What he couldn't see, because of the couch, were the Bass Wejun loafers. He looked down, drawn by the glints from the mint-condition pennies tucked into each tongue, and then back up and across at himself once more.

"Damn, I look fine tonight," he said before flinching. The doorbell had rung out and startled him. He looked around the room at the various clockfaces: 10 p.m. in the kitchen; somewhere between 10 p.m. and 10:05 p.m. on the wall in the living room; and 9:59:54 p.m. on the high-tech gizmo Louis had bought him that sat gathering dust on the shelf above his CDs.

"Good boy."

Marcus took a deep breath and walked cooly over to the front door and flicked the overhead light off.

"Prepare to meet your Black Knight, Spit," he said to himself. And from somewhere deep within his head, Louis answered with, "More like Black Night over Kennebunkport." He almost told the door to "shut the fuck up" when he heard the opening strains of "Orange Colored Sky." "Now that's what I call serendipity-doo-dah," he said out loud. He unlocked and then opened the door, expecting to see a shock of orange hair.

Instead, he got a shock. Spit had dyed his hair daffodil yellow in honor, Marcus rapidly guessed, of their first "date." And they both were wearing pink shirts! Spit's was a fairly clean tee with "Subtonix" written in bleeding blue letters across the chest. Marcus puzzled over the words, but whatever the odd look on his own face it was nothing compared to Spit's. The boy stood frozen with his bloodshot eyes open wide enough that Marcus could finally tell they were green.

"Um, I'm sorry, bro'," stammered the punk. "I think I got the wrong house."

"Who told you to speak, boy?" The preppy reached out and grabbed the multiple piercings of the punk's left ear between his thumb and forefinger and pulled him inside. He then pushed him toward the couch and, when he'd turned around after locking the door, saw that the back of the punk's shirt read "rip your heart out."

"With pleasure, Spit," Marcus said softly as he walked up behind him. "With pleasure."

Spit halted when he hit the wall of pink muscle. Marcus was once again in front of him.

"On your knees, boy. Now."

Spit collapsed onto the carpet.

"Hands behind your back. That's it. Let 'em rest on that little bitty white ass of yours."

Spit looked up earnestly and almost smiled.

"So, boy, you here for my dick…?"

"Yes, Sir."

Marcus grabbed Spit's jaw in his hand and squeezed his thin pink lips together with his free hand.

"Don't interrupt your elders, boy. It's rude. You hear?"

Spit nodded his head. Marcus kept both his hands in place.

"I said, you here for *my* dick or did you come lookin' for Shaka Zulu's mighty spear?"

He let go of the boy's mouth and waited for his answer. The boy, in turn, looked at Marcus' face quizzically, searching his unmoving scowl for even a clue on how to answer.

"Well, boy? We both know you here for black dick. Am I right?"

Spit started to nod, then stopped.

"What's wrong, snowflake? From what I hear, you usually got lots to say. I just want to know if you here for my black dick or you just come 'round for some of that gargantuan gangsta manhood the homeboys are always clutchin'?"

Spit blinked nervously and his skin turned—amazingly, Marcus concluded—a shade paler.

"Did I lose you? Use too big a word? 'Gargantuan'? It means big. Like all us bucks is s'pose to be. And my black dick is big alright," he said as he rubbed his crotch until he could grab his cock throught the khakis. "Sho' nuff. But I don't know if it's big enough, or black enough, for you, young Master Spit? Cuz Lord knows it's gonna have to be a whole lotta both in a getup like this. I mean, look at me. Look at me, boy! How much of a badass muthafuckin' nigga top do you think I can be in these goddamned Dockers?!"

Spit could have only looked more comical, Marcus thought, if the little beads of sweat sliding down onto the forehead of his beet-red and bug-eyed face had slipped together, just like in one of those Busby Berkeley dance routines, to form the word "BUSTED."

"I know you got a tongue in there, boy. I seen it lap up my piss last week."

"I'm sorry, Sir," the boy finally blurted.

"Yes, you are. But I'm not the one you gotta apologize to. Am I? Besides, that doesn't answer my question, does it? I wanna know why you here. Is it to see *me* or do you just wanna peep my Clarence Thomas?"

Marcus watched the space between the boy's eyebrows furrow.

"Don't stare at me like you don't know what I'm talkin' 'bout? You just come to get it on with my long dong. Take a ride back to the plantation on my big black donkey dick. That's right. You know what I'm talkin' 'bout, punk."

Marcus slammed the butt of his palm into the punk's chest and pushed. Spit almost rolled over backwards. When he'd righted himself, his nose and mouth were an inch from the fly of the Dockers.

"Yeah, that's it, boy. Take a whiff. Smell it. It's all packed away in there for you. You know what I'm talkin' 'bout. Thirteen fuckin' inches of black meat. Thirteen. That *is* the devil's number. And black *is* his color. That *is* your dream, boy, ain't it? To have the devil dick you down. Ain't it, snowflake? Cuz I'd hate to see that dream deferred on a count of pair of a preppy pants that are only a shade darker than you."

"No, Sir. Shit. I mean, I...I don't know, Sir." Spit choked out the words and hung his head. Marcus was certain the punk was about to cry.

"Good boy," Marcus said softly, as he patted his bristly head. "You may be worth fuckin' after all."

The boy looked up. Relieved. Eager. Ready.

"Don't get your ass in the air yet, Spitrag. I said you 'may be worth fuckin'.' I'm still not sure. But if you do everything—everything!—I tell you to do tonight. Then next time, I'll take you back to my bedroom, throw your heels up to Jesus, and fuck you bowlegged *and* stupid. And that's sayin' a lot, isn't it, boy?"

Spit replied by biting his lower lip—to keep from grinning or letting out a whoop, Marcus guessed.

"I'm talkin' to you, boy. You better answer or get the fuck outta here."

"Sir?"

"I said it'd be hard to fuck you even more stupid than you've already been, wouldn't it boy?" Marcus bent down, put his hands in pits under the punk's arms, and lifted him to his feet.

"Yes, Sir," Spit said from within his shirt as Marcus pulled it over his head.

"And you've been sayin' some pretty stupid shit lately, haven't you, boy?" Marcus gripped the boy by each butt cheek—*well, all right, Spit...you've got some cushion for the pushin' after all*—and knelt. He untied the boy's boots and pulled off one and then the other. Then he peeled off and tossed the socks over his shoulder.

"Yes, Sir."

"And why is it, boy," Marcus said, pressing his palm up and into the crotch of Spit's pants as if he were about to lift him over his head and spin him around, "that all the smug ones who think their shit don't stink cuz it's made outta solid gold—like you, boy—end up bein' the dumbest...." Marcus had heard the faint crackling sound of the fabric when it had touched his hand and now he could smell it. *Spit, you romantic little wanker. You haven't taken these off since we met.* "And the stankiest."

Thank you, Jesus, Marcus thought as he unbuttoned the boy's pants, *you made him leave that extension cord at home. As you know, I wrote student evaluations all day and, the way my joints are burnin', I'd never've gotten that knot and these buttons undone.*

And then he dramatically punctuated his last spoken sentence by yanking Spit's pants to the ground.

"Goin' commando, are we?"

"Yes, Sir."

"Did you think you'd get lucky or you just eschew underwear cuz it chafes with your punk aesthetic?"

"Sir?"

"Oh, right. Big words. You's stupid. I forgot." He paused to get to his feet. "I'll keep it simple—simple like them sweet little ol' darkies in a Stephen Foster song." He threw his hands up to frame his face and grinned. "Oh, doodah day!" Then the hands and grin just as suddenly dropped away. "But mind you, boy, I'm only gonna do this once. Cuz there ain't nothin' simple 'bout me—or my friends."

"Yes, Sir. I'm sorry, Sir."

The naked punk snapped to attention, his dick giving Marcus a floppy salute. Marcus sighed. Either this boy was a recovering military brat or he'd watched way too much porno.

"Yes, boy," he said as he inspected him with a brief downward and then upward glance, "you sure as shit are. And you gonna pay dearly for it. But, if you do right by me tonight, Spit, then there'll come a day when you *will* eschew a helluva lot more than just underwear."

Marcus tapped his chest.

"Now, it's your turn. Boy, don't look at me like that. You can't be that dumb. Get over here and undress me. But you gotta use that filthy mouth of yours and get *my* clothes wet this time."

Spit hurried over and got a mouthful of the pink cotton and began to suck with the blind, silent fury of a leech. He sniffed loudly and gulped down more of the shirt. As if following a scent, he wriggled along Marcus' chest until he found the fat stub of a happy and hard nipple. Then he grew still again.

"Since you such an expert on niggas...." Somehow, through his nipple that was sweetly crushed between the boy's lips, Marcus felt Spit cringe. "Especially nigga tops, you must think I like this shirt so cuz it looks just like a juicy slice of watermelon."

"No, Sir."

He thwacked the boy on his yellow head and pushed him back into his chest.

"Did I tell you to talk, boy? You here to worship. So get to it."

Spit had released his bite on Marcus' nipple to go and suckle, with a series of nips of his teeth and jabs from his tongue, at the other. "That's good." The abandoned tit throbbed and stung as the wet cotton weighed down on it and grew hard and cold. "Oh, that's real good, boy."

Marcus paused to wince and then exhale in one loud, shaky breath.

"Like I was sayin', you probably think I like the color pink cuz all us muthafucka nigga tops like watermelon. Well, you'd be wrong again. A good, sweet slice of watermelon is red. Like your ass is gonna be when I'm done slappin' the shit out of it next time. Oh, yeah, bite *down* on it, boy!"

He cupped the back of Spit's head and tried to shove all of his stinging pec into the punk's mouth.

"No, no, no," he sighed. "I like the color pink cuz it reminds me of assholes. Not a full grown one like you. But this one."

Marcus laid his hand on the crack of Spit's ass. He pushed his middle finger deep between the warm and full flesh of his cheeks and rubbed the tip slowly around the soft ridges that puckered his hole.

"You know the pink I'm talkin' 'bout. Like the inside of your hole. Once I've gotten a few fingers in it and push my big pink tongue all up inside it. Once it's really opened up. Like it's ready to blossom. Like it's almost ripe. That's when I stick my big black dick in—fast and hard." He shoved his finger in, up to the knuckle.

Spit lost his grip in all his squirming and when he bit down again, he had the stiff knot of fabric that was the green alligator between his teeth. He shook his head back and forth and nearly tore it from the shirt as Marcus flexed his finger deep inside the boy.

Marcus chuckled as he watched and then whispered toward the bobbing head, "That's what I'm gonna do to you next week, boy, *if* you do right by me tonight." He felt little warm, wet pricks around his left knee. The head of Spit's dick was slapping up against it and leaving behind a trail.

"You sure got a thang for Izods, doncha, boy?" Marcus gently kneed the boy's cock and Spit detached, his lips raw and red, and looked up. "It's time for you to go south," the preppy said to the punk before he pulled his own shirt off. The punk licked at the retreating Izod, following the hem into the preppy's sweaty armpit and up along his bicep until it was out of reach.

Marcus tossed the shirt on the floor and pushed Spit back down along his chest and stomach. Spit lived up to his name and went wild, like he was trying to lick the kink out of each and every hair. Then his mouth reached the edge of the Dockers.

"Don't stop till you've reached the floor."

When Spit had tugged the last wet argyle sock off, the boy looked up and Marcus locked eyes with him. The preppy grabbed his own balls and started tugging on them.

"Get up here and start kissin' these pants. And don't give me any of those little dry-mouth baby bird pecks. I want you to kiss them like you drownin' and you gotta breathe oxygen through your lips, through your tongue, and the only air that's fit to breathe is trapped in every fiber of this pair of Dockers. You hear?"

Marcus' body relaxed, his hand gave way, as he felt the pressure from Spit's mouth, his nose, his whole face, mashing themselves against his cock and balls.

"My, my, my, Spit, you got quite a mouth on you. Now I want you to run that tongue of yours all over my crotch. Get it up there against the zipper. That's right. Now find my dick. That's it. Use your nose. Smell. Now suck it through the fabric. That's right. Take the cotton in your mouth, boy."

"I'll help you with the belt." He unfastened it. Spit alternated tugging on the brass buckle and tonguing the interlocking strands of dusky brown leather.

"Shit, boy, you gonna lick the weave right outta my belt. Save some of that spit for what's behind zipper number one." And Marcus undid his fly and let the Dockers fall. Spit chewed and yanked on the cuffs of the pants like an undisciplined puppy. Once he'd dragged them out onto the floor, he leapt back up onto his knees and lunged for the waistband of the Madras boxers. He gripped it in his teeth and pulled.

Marcus began to laugh, and, when Spit dropped the shorts onto the floor and lifted his head, he laughed even harder. The little pup looked like he'd been kicked. For where Spit had expected to see a strapping black man buck naked, there stood Marcus with his legs straddling the floor and his arms akimbo and his fists resting on his hips. It was a pose that did just as it was intended to do and drew all Spit's attention to the jock which stood between a boy and a dick. A jock whose pouch was a garish patchwork of paisley tie tips that Marcus had spent several late nights handsewing.

"You like? Cuz you should. I got somethin' special in here for you, boy. Somethin' long and smooth and colorful."

Spit's heavy, fleshy eyelids fluttered with interest and moved back so the boy's eyes could see better what Marcus' hand was freeing from the overstuffed

The Color Khaki

pouch. He lifted his whole, huge hand over the edge of the waistband and let it drop. It unfurled down to his knees.

It was long, yellow, and made of silk. It was floridly awash with turquoise and pink paramecia. Marcus had remembered their first date as well.

"It ain't no amber wave, but you still ain't convinced me you much of man yet neither. C'mon. Show me I ain't a fool to wanna fuck you. Take it, golden boy. Take it all in your mouth. That's it. Eat up."

As Nat King Cole plaintively sang "Nature Boy," Marcus looked down on his own poor boy, licking and chewing and devouring and choking on the paisley tie, like a wild, starved animal. Marcus pulled away and the tie unraveled out of Spit's mouth. He crawled after it and tongued his way to the edge of the waistband.

"Un-unh," Marcus said as he pressed him palm against Spit's forehead. "That's all you gonna see tonight. I said you gotta earn the right. And you still gotta a ways to go. A long ways."

He pulled away again and the tie hung soggily, clinging now and then to Marcus' leg as he grabbed the pants and the shirt off the floor. He dropped them in front of a very confused looking Spit.

"Here. Take 'em and lay 'em out on the floor. Like they's a body on the floor. Like a body makin' snow angels in my carpet."

Spit hesitated and then scooted out of the way before Marcus' hand could box his ear. He laid the shirt down first, smoothing out the wet and wrinkling patches. Then he delicately placed the waistband of the Dockers at the edge of the shirt and stretched out the crumpled and tangled legs. He glanced up to determine his success in Marcus' expression.

"Now lay on 'em," Marcus said after their eyes met.

Spit continued to stare.

"You heard me. *Lay down on them.* That's right. Like you gonna fuck that body makin' snow angels in my carpet. Get that hard dick of yours right smack-dab in the middle of them Dockers."

He did. Promptly.

"I'm gonna go easy on you, boy. Since you like leather so damned much, here." Marcus placed one of the loafers under Spit's face, then pushed it and the boy down onto the shoe with his foot.

"Go on. Kiss it. That' it. Get *all* of it wet." He gave Spit's butt a little tap with his foot. "And get *these* to bouncing. That's right. Fuck those Dockers. Fuck 'em like they're the sweetest hole you ever gonna get."

Spit stuck out his tongue and poked at the tip of the shoe, like he was uncertain it was really leather or the same quality of leather that covered the round, steel toes in those motorcycle boots which Marcus had heard he lived to polish. Marcus pressed the boy's tongue, mouth, nose, forehead deep into the loafer. "I said, 'Get it *wet.*'"

Spit lapped the sides, the vamp, the tongue of the shoe with broad, wet strokes. Marcus watched his head bop in time to the steady bounce of his ass. He watched the muscles clench and release in his neck and along his shoulders and down his back and around the dimples in his butt cheeks. He watched his jaw widen to get all of his tongue inside the shoe or bulge as he chewed on the leather. He watched how tightly he pressed his eyes together, like he was squinting to see the stitching in the shoe or hold in all the pleasure he was getting from banging a pair of khaki pants.

God, this is actually gettin' me hard, Marcus thought.

He freed his dick from the tightening knot of ties and looked at it. It *was* big. An honest eight inches. But it *wasn't* black. He'd never seen a black dick that actually *was* the color black. And he'd seen some pretty dark dick back in the day.

He turned his cock in his hand and, as it stiffened, a familiar question from childhood returned. Can't white folk see colors as clearly as black folk? He used to look around him—hell, he still looked around him—and he'd seen an amazing palette of browns—every shade imaginable. But never once had he met a black person who was black. Not even his colleagues from Africa. Maybe as dark as that light-swallowing brown in those little tiny cups of coffee he'd drunk in Egypt or that amazing inky blue on the Cape Town horizon at midnight with a full moon overhead. But never *negro*, *niger*, black.

"*A thick bar of fine dark chocolate or a heavy block of polished mahogany.*" *That's how he'd once described his dick. It was a rather pornographic wish-you-were-here-baby letter to his then-lover Joel, away for the summer on a research grant. And Louis, of course, had read it before Marcus could mail it.*

"*Why if it isn't Mrs. See herself,*" *Louis had said as he propped himself against the doorwell, waiving the letter overhead.*

"*What you goin' on about now, Louis?*"

"*Fine chocolate, my ass.*"

"*Well, yes, if I remember correctly it is.*"

"*Don't try to sweet-talk me, Mr. Hershey-Bar-between-his-legs.*"

"*Jesus Christ, Louis! Give me that. You weren't supposed to read that.*"

"*Then don't put* it *where I can find* it."

"*Louis!*"

Louis stopped rustling the papers and brought them down as if he were going to read them once more — out loud.

"*Mahogany,*" *he harrumphed as his eyes glanced over the page and back up to Marcus.* "*Don't flatter yourself, Miss Ross. It ain't nothin' but an ol' chewed-on switch of black willow that's got a dab of cheap-ass chocolate puddin' stuck to the end of it.*"

"*Well, you always seemed happy enough to eat it. Two or three times a night.*"

"*Not no more. If I had to put it in my mouth right now...*"

"*Which you ain't.*"

"*Got that right. Cuz it would taste real sweet at first. But when I pulled it out, all I'd taste is the bitter. In fact, I can still taste it.*"

"*Well, that's your own damn fault. Cuz you were the fool who kicked me to the curb for Mr. Black Power.*"

"*Don't start....*"

"Listen to him," a voice echoed inside Marcus. He looked down and his dick was looking pretty hangdog. "Keep your eyes on the prize, son." And below his cock, there it was. Spit's bright-white butt. Looking a lot like a pack of Hostess® Sno Balls®—*damn, I shoulda eaten somethin' for dinner, nerves or no nerves*—all shiny from the light hitting the untorn plastic. Shaking in their rack as a tremblor gets ready to roll through the convenience store, dropping everyone and everything to the floor. Yes, there it was. Spit's ass. Rounder, smaller, and sweeter than his scrawny frame and baggy clothes had led Marcus to imagine. Rump-a-pump-pumpin' those goddamned Dockers. Hard and fast.

Too hard and too fast.

"Hey." He held his foot so Spit's ass hit it on the upthrust and then foot and ass went down together and stayed down. "You drillin' for oil?"

The boy was breathing too quick to answer immediately. Eventually, he got out a "No, Sir."

"That's right. Now I wanna see some passion. I wanna see a lot less pound and a lot more ground." Spit lay still. "You know, grind those skinny hips of yours." He traced a circle on Spit's ass with the ball of his foot. Then he pressed his foot deeper into the muscle and dragged it and the boy around in a long ellipse. "That's better. And more pushin' too." He shoved his foot into the crack of Spit's ass and pushed, his toes sliding down as Spit slipped forward along the resisting fabric until Marcus was almost standing on the boy's balls.

"And make some noise, boy. Hell, if you was a real wasp, I'd hear your wings hummin' while you're stingin' me." He rubbed his toes around the back of the punk's surprisingly unpierced ballsac until he got a moan. "That's a start. Remember, this ain't no chore. You s'pose to be givin' those Dockers the fuck of their bland life."

Spit rolled the weight of his body over the Dockers and his dick slowly. First side-to-side and then up and down. Then again. Memorizing the moves of Marcus's foot. He lifted his hips high enough so that only the bottoms of his balls rested on the pants. Then he dropped on them in one crushing thrust and groaned from the back of his throat. He started to rub against the floor with continued and varied bucks and grinds of his hips. The sounds he made grew higher in pitch and more urgent in tone.

"Never in all my born days did I think I'd see a scrawny-assed, nigga-lovin', faggot punk makin' sweet love to a pair of khaki pants. I guess you can take the boy out of Connecticut but you can't take Connecticut out of the boy. Ain't that right, Chad Myers?"

Spit's head bolted up while his hips kept bucking and grinding. He tried to turn toward Marcus but Marcus had his foot down on Spit's neck so fast that the raised tooling on the shoe dug into the side of his face.

"Who said you could look at my dick, Chad? Remember, you earnin' that right tonight."

Marcus spat loudly, twice, into his hand and rubbed his slaver up and down his cock. He spat again and wetted his dick so that even Spit could hear it—over Nat's graceful crooning of "The Very Thought of You"—sloshing as it slid back and forth in his hand.

"Chad. Good ol' Chad Myers of Darien, Connecticut. Pleased to meet you, son. That's right, Spit. Never underestimate us old folks. Mad Jack smokes a lot of weed, but he always remembers what Scalawag tells him. And then Jack told Louis and Louis told me and I told Bernie. You remember Bernie, Chad, don't you?"

Spit had stopped fucking and lay eerily still. He was shuddering like he was cold, like he was crying. Marcus pushed down harder on his neck.

"Boy, did I tell you you could stop fuckin' your daddy's Dockers? If you ever wanna get near a black dick again, especially this one, you'll rip those pants in half with the golden shrimp fork the Good Lord gave you? You hear me?"

Spit mumbled something into the leather toe as he rubbed his head against the shoe.

"Wha'd you say, boy?" He lifted his foot high enough so Spit could raise his face and open his mouth to groan, "Yes, Sir."

"What, boy?"

"Yes, Sir!"

"Then get to it."

Marcus hacked in the palm of drying, burning hand.

"So, like I was sayin', I told Bernie and Bernie's a real whiz on the Internet. He did a little diggin'. So why'd you come west, boy? Couldn't get it on with the maintenance crew at Phillips Andover after you gradu-ated? Didn't wanna spend another summer drivin' into Bridgeport every Saturday night? You get to college and find the negroes a little too uppity for your taste? Hunh? The brothas in New Haven too real for you? That why you on your second year-abroad from Yale? Yale, Chad. That's a good school. I'm disappointed they never taught you what 'gargantuan' means."

He spat forcefully. Like he was disgusted.

"Yeah, we black boys learned there's quite a gargantuan silver spoon shoved up your punk ass. Oh, yeah, Chad. There's an idea. Yes, indeed."

Marcus spat again.

"Bernie's fuckin' fortieth birthday is tomorrow night. Oh, God. I think my gift'll be lettin' him have a go at your two scoops of vanilla. Let him shove an even bigger…a fuckin' mandingo-sized…silver spoon up your ass. Yeah. One that's been sittin' in the freezer for a couple of hours. Yes. Oh, yes. That'd be sweet. Sweet. Ah, sweet Jesus. Too bad you can't see what I can, Chad. You should see how hard my big…black…dick is. And I got it pointed right at your back, boy. Oh, God. If you weren't rubbin' a hole in those fuckin' pants, Chad, you could see I'm gonna come. Oh, yeah. I'm comin', Chad. Oh, God, Chad. You wanna see white flight, boy. Just…wait. Oh, God. I got your white power, Chad. Here's…your…muthafuckin'…white…power,…Chad!"

Marcus watched his cum splatter across Spit's back. The boy writhed and flopped atop the Dockers like he'd been scalded with acid. The groans and grunts had given way to a frantic string of whimpers.

"Oh, God!" Spit coughed out. "I'm coming. Permission to come, Sir! Oh, God…."

"Spit it out, Chad," Marcus said as forcefully as he could despite being winded. "Spit it all out."

The boy thrashed obscenely and collapsed into stillness. Marcus nodded his head approvingly as he pulled up the end of the dangling yellow tie and wiped his dick with it. He then pushed his spent manhood back into the jock.

"Not bad, Chad. Not bad at all. You catch your breath there and then it's time for you to go."

Spit raised himself up on his arms and turned to give Marcus an even better version of the dying dog stare he'd used on him in the bathroom of the Manhole.

Marcus laughed.

"You listenin' to me earlier, boy?"

"Yes, Sir."

"You ain't actin' like it. Why you gettin' all mopey and dopey on me."

"Sorry, Sir."

"Yes, we already established that. Now listen good. I told you if you did right by me tonight and did everything I told you to do I'd bring you back here next Friday and fuck you stupid. Is it next Friday already?"

"No, Sir."

"Do you wanna get fucked stupid?"

"Hell, yes—Sir!"

"Don't get cocky on me, Chad. You too ugly to fuck when you get all cocky. You hear?"

"Yes, Sir."

"Good. I want you to wrap those Dockers 'round your sticky privates like they's a diaper. You heard me, boy. Gird up those loins with your preppy diaper. And put the rest of your damn clothes on too. Well, go to it, Chad. Get dressed."

Spit stood up and straddled the soiled pants. Without a word, he started to dress. Thank God, he wears those baggy pants was all Marcus could think.

After ten minutes and two false starts, Spit was done.

"Come here," Marcus said as he stood next to the apartment's door. Spit approached, stiffly and slowly. When he was close enough, Marcus grabbed him by both arms and pulled him into a tight hug. He bent his lips toward the boy's ear and whispered, "Now, here's the hard part, Spit. You listening? Cuz I can feel your dick gettin' all eager and upright on me."

"Yes, Sir. I swear."

"Don't be swearin' till you heard what you gotta do next."

Spit nodded and the feverishly warm skin and cold metal studs and rings of his ear grazed Marcus' lips.

"First, you gotta wear your Dockers just like you got 'em on now all week to the bar. That's right. Starting tomorrow night, you gotta show up and strip down to your dirty diapers and your boots. And tomorrow's Bernie's birthday, like I said before. You remember?"

"Yes," he whispered.

"Well, you're my gift. And that means you gonna do whatever Bernie tells you to do to make things right between you two. And keep things right between us."

Marcus exhaled gently into the boy's ear before resuming with a distinct clip in his voice.

"You do all that and you'd better be back here next Friday at ten o'clock sharp. We will begin your education then in earnest. At that time, you will refer to me as Dr. George and you will be have a pen and notebook handy at all times. I will then give you a dictionary, a reading list, and the rugburn of your life. You think you can handle all that?"

"I'll try, Sir."

"Don't try, boy, just do." And Marcus pulled his mouth away from Spit's ear and placed it firmly on his lips. The boy's tongue felt even better inside Marcus' mouth than it had outside on this skin of chest.

With a little reluctance, Marcus pulled away and said, "Go on, now. Go." He unlocked and opened the door. "I'll see you tomorrow night."

"Yes, you will, Sir. Good night, Sir."

"Good night, Spit."

He closed the door and slid the lock into place and then waited. There it was. Cackling. Lots of it. But from a very deep-voiced henhouse. The louvered doors to the living room closet swung wider apart and out slipped Louis, nearly dropping his camcorder as he doubled over in laughter.

"Oh, girl," he said when he could finally breathe. "As much as I hate bein' in any closet, this," he took a deeper breath, "this was worth it. Oh, Lord— white power!" The cackling was pushed aside for some gut-busting, tears-at-the-corners-of-the-eyes guffawing.

"Fine, you go on and let it out, Sister Waters," Marcus said as he leaned back against the door. "I wanna see what you have to say in the heat of the moment come Monday night."

"Oh, mercy!" Louis said as he dabbed at his eyes. "Don't worry. I ain't stickin' my _big black dick_ anywhere near that young Republican. But I gots just the spoon."

"Oh, I bet you do. Just remember, Mr. Spike Lee, to bring your masterpiece to the Manhole tomorrow night," Marcus said as he walked past Louis into his bedroom to get his robe.

"Nigga please, you even have to ask."

There was a loud laugh from the bedroom.

"And when the fuck am I gettin' one of those paisley jock strap thangs?" Louis shouted as he sat down on the couch. "Shit, you are one crazy ol' muthafucka, Marcus G.,…"

"And that's why you love me," Marcus said as wandered into the living room, tying his robe.

"Who said anythin' 'bout love?" Louis muttered as he raised an eyebrow and then his cellphone. And, on cue, Marcus grimaced and then switched off the CD player just as the strings slid into full stride in "Stardust."

There is no way in hell I'm lettin' you in here next Friday night, he thought as he sat down in the armchair beside the couch. Next Friday night. He was going to slap some serious sense into that boy's itty bitty booty and then get all up inside it. He closed his eyes, sat back in his chair, and watched the previews of coming attractions.

"Marcus G., what you still grinnin' 'bout?" He opened his eyes and looked over to see Louis punctuate his sentence with a flourish of rolled eyes. "That bony-assed fool left here half an hour ago."

"Nothin'."

Louis went back to whispering even more animatedly into the phone. Marcus couldn't stop smiling. He was falling for a runaway white boy from Connecticut named Spit of all things. And if this punk showed up tomorrow night wearing his Dockers diaper, he was going to be rocking and roping and slapping and strapping him all night long next Friday. Well, that's if the punk didn't run out when he saw tonight's video playing throughout the bar.

Damn, I can't wait for it to be tomorrow night, he moaned to himself. They were going to be talking about Bernie's birthday for years to come at the Manhole.

Then he sat up, slowly. Something cool was blowing on the back of his neck. He swore he heard laughter again. But Louis was sitting on the couch, gabbing away on the phone in his special, hushed, girl-sit-down-and-hear-what-I-have-to-say voice. There it was again. Laughter. Or the echo of it. Several voices. Then the unmistakable gravelly belly laugh of one, and only one, person. His mama.

Somewhere in heaven, his mama was laughing her ass off. Hopefully, with him and not at him. Well, at least, he thought, the ancestors aren't sighing anymore.

Lord, just wait till they see what happens tomorrow night.

"Hold on, hold on," he heard Louis say from far away. "What the fuck you laughin' 'bout, old man? And don't nothin' me now."

Marcus just kept looking at something in the distance, something which Louis craned his neck here and there to try and see. And he kept laughing.

"What's wrong wit' you? Don't tell me you in love wit' the Great White Dope?"

Now it was Marcus' turn to double over.

"Ah, shit, Bernie," Louis yelled into phone wedged between his ear and his shoulder. "Nigga, this is all *your* fault."

The Story of the I[1]

for Kiki Carr

Je ne suis pas une **femme**,
je suis **un monde**.

—Flaubert,
La Tentation de saint Antoine

It should be my story. It is my story.

Forgive me. One may think me no more than a voracious maw, and I am that, but I am also well-bred. Let me introduce myself. I am *le Con de Simone*.

If you thought I meant the sex of de Beauvoir, then put this *feuilleton* down immediately, you ill-read fool. Hers will always be second to the

---

1   Translated from the French by Lord Auch Vey.

sex of *my* Simone. *Moi.* The Cunt.

Ah, yes. Now you remember her. That French girl with an insatiable fondness for straddling—bicycle seats, toilets, girls, boys, eyes, even the dead.

Yet, this story is *my* story.

After all, who had to stare for hours into that toilet while Simone's head raced elsewhere and nowhere? Who could never look away from that white bowl? Another egg broken open and dropped. The water spitting up on me, into me. Below, there it floats, boiled and bored, among the dozen others in their vast porcelain shell. And who had to choke on plates of milk and skinless bull balls? Who had to grip that rickety bicycle's seat between her lips? Who had to endure the repeated blind thrusts of that idiot boy's epileptic member?

I will tell you who. Me. The Cunt. I was both hero and heroine. It is my story.

Not Simone's.

Certainly not the boy's.

Least of all, that inanimate, insignificant eye's.

You doubt me?

What dry-lipped bitches you are!

Sadly, you are not alone. Even M. Bataille—the creator of my laconic world—acknowledges me personally but once. He calls me a swamp. Sweltering, abuzz with insects, strewn with decaying moss and rotting weeds, afloat with reptilian eyes and filled with the crooked teeth of crocodiles.

Me—a swamp! Should I be flattered by his attempt to allude to what I can only imagine he thinks is my deadly, chthonic beauty? Why? Am I no more than a backdrop, like the sewers of Paris, for our literature's miserable, ever-male protagonists, our Jean Valjeans and Inspector Javerts, to wade through while they gaze only, longingly, at each other?!

Ah, yes. The male gaze. It forever haunts me.

Even in my name I am branded with the masculine article!

I could retch.

If I were a forgiving cunt, I might make some allowances for the oversights of the reader or the obsessions of an author. But I am, as one may clearly deduce from all I have written so far, not.

No, not at all.

But do not fear, dear reader, for I save all my dark fury for the noble academics of our country. They, most of all, have perpetuated the lie. They have robbed me of my story.

And now, with the swiftness of a guerilla strike, I shall expose them. For, like the Church in centuries before, this fraternity is no more than an insidious collection of charlatans in cloaks. They may not turn wine into blood or bread into flesh, but, I promise you, they *do* have their own sleights of hand.

Their greatest deceit? I will tell you. They have cleverly obscured the origin of all their so-called vast, so-called venerable wisdom by stabling it in the cavernous halls of the Collège de France[2], by grooming it with long, black robes, and by renaming this animal—a beast so simple that even Adam could have named it—"hermeneutics."

Surely you know "hermeneutics." Perhaps you've petted it at the children's zoo. It is a goat. Its keepers feed it pages and pages of books. And the goat tells them what it tastes. When it grows tired of talking (and even a goat, unlike an academic, grows tired of talking), it drops its answers out in a rain of pellets. Marbles of turd for these boys to play with. That is all.

And when it ate my story, what did the goat tell them?

That mine is the story of the eye and its endless transmogrifications and transubstantiations. But of course, o sagacious goat, that *is* the story's title. Could it be more plain and simple?

Idiots.

I cannot forgive them. If I had hands to get upon them, I would skewer and roast them *and* their goat. But I do, sincerely, pity them. They are, after all, men—better still, French men—in thrall to a talking goat. Worse, these sad, old pomposities are dying off, leaving behind legions of

---

2   You obviously are not French and therefore, I not only feel inexplicable sorrow towards you, but see no reason to explain this reference. For even the smallest French child would have never bothered to read this simple footnote. Why, you ask? You are as ignorant as you are inferior. It is for the most elementary of reasons: the French do not footnote; that is the English vice.

beardless fools who are no longer content to confine their madness to the asylum. No, they have the zeal of evangelists, besotted with the ecstasy of The Word Made Flesh. And so, in France, we must once again witness the lamentable march of a children's crusade—this time: holy, triumphant, semiotic.

Semiotics. My lips spit disgust at this meaningless word. If one wants to take a good, long shit, squatting out ropes and ropes of words, say so. None of this hollow politeness.

Semiotics! Oh, a word a thousand times more obscene than our rustic "hermeneutics." What these boys mean is no more than a constant stream of semaphore to other pre-pubescent males. A stream of their own excretions and ejaculations.

In my case, they obsess over the eye, a jiggly blob of symbolic semen. Forever these adolescents, with their still-pupating penises, talk of the sperm's sign, signifier, and signified. Like a little "x" they scrawl as if to say—yes, a brilliant French male mind was here. And yet, the story is not of *an* eye but of *the* cunt.

What? you protest. But you are negating the gaze. There can be no literature without the gaze. What of the gaze? you ask. The eye?

Impotent simpletons! Does one honestly think I need the slimy eye of a dead priest stuffed between my already full lips?!

I see much more than any man has ever suspected. Do not listen to the Jungian barkers calling you to witness the hijinxs of another freak in the carnival of Dionysus. "Behold, ladies and gentleman," they beckon, "the unconscious feminine! She animatedly devours *puer* and *senex* alike and yet knows not what she does."

Really, are we French, even the stupidest amongst us, so foolish as to believe this nonsense? Do we not know, down to our wine-dark marrow, that only Americans consume without consciousness?

I tell you this for the final time: I am not the empty socket you imagine me to be.

And thus, I urge the men of France, especially her scholars, to consider the following: if one really wishes to know what a French cunt signifies, by all means, ask a French cunt!

I am here. Uncurl your bound mind. Rise up and walk. Look for the cunt. I am here.

Le con, c'est moi.

I am here. Close your sun-dazzled eyes and smell me. Come and enter my dark cave. Only in the quaking heat of my blackness will you ever be able to open your eyes and see.

Come. Enter my dark cave.

Find me. I am the oldest oracle. More ancient than the Sibyl at Cumae or the Pythia at Delphi. Come and sit atop my smoke. I will tell you what you need to know.

I am here.

Come. Hear all of my story.

I will enlighten you.

Sheldon Smalley Meets His *Satan*

for Louise Mock

Every time a world ends, the first and only warning comes in a dream. It would be no different tonight as the Rev. Sheldon Smalley lay down by the rivers of *Celestial Seasonings* Sleepytime® tea and dreamt.

• • •

He stood at the corner of Post and Montgomery, sometime in the night, maybe midnight, maybe 3:30 a.m. The battered gray blanket of fog had been pulled over the city once again. It bunched up in lumps in some parts; it was threadbare enough in others to see the stars beyond. Mercury lamps gave that comforting radioactive amber glow to every water droplet from the rivulet of piss flowing toward his shoe to the sky's underbelly overhead. Nothing unusual. He was downtown in the financial district. Except the streets were too still. Not even the telltale *pock pock, pock pock* of leather-soled heels striking concrete. Not even the distant clattering of a stray shopping cart. Not even the slow thudding heartbeat inside a signal box to announce the nearby traffic light would change.

Everyone must have fled. Those with homes to the suburbs. Those with apartments to anywhere they could afford. And those with nothing, to whatever doorways that remained unbarred.

No, it was so still because everyone must be asleep. Except for maybe a few stray bands of office cleaners wandering on random floors in the random office buildings circling him. Nothing seemed unusual. Yet everything felt off.

First, he'd never, before now, stood on the corner of Post and Montgomery in the middle of the night. He might have driven through this intersection or somewhere like it during the hours normal people went from here to there. To be honest, he'd have been driven rather than driven himself. He'd been driven most everywhere since his television ministry had been picked up by several cable markets. It didn't really matter. The point was that he wasn't the kind of man who stood on deserted streets some time in the night—long after he was sure he'd be asleep and long before he was sure he'd be awake. He had no idea what time it was. He only knew this was night. A foggy night.

Maybe there should have been some cars. That was it. It wasn't that he was the only living soul. No, there were no cars, not even parked. That was what was odd. No, it certainly wasn't that he was alone. He was surrounded by office buildings, stone-and-metal boxes and cartons. Nondescript but comforting. For each had a window here or there or maybe a whole floor lit up. He couldn't be alone. There had to be others. Go toward the light. But which one? There were hundreds of them. Which one was the right one? Where could he find help? But why did he need help? He didn't really feel in danger. A man who'd accepted Jesus Christ as his lord and personal saviour?! How could he! And this man, as unworthy a sinner as any other, had not only been saved but embraced. Given a special task even. And he shared this wonderful secret love with millions as he spread the good word every Sunday, at 6 a.m. on stations in Los Angeles and San Diego, at 7 a.m. on stations in Fresno, Sacramento, Stockton, Bakersfield, and Redding, and at 11 p.m. on two stations here in the Bay Area. And that was only California! He was his master's humble servant. He was the Rev. Sheldon Smalley. What on earth should he be afraid of!

He wouldn't have admitted it, not even here in what might have been his subconscious, that as his eyes widened and his upper lip and wrinkled brow began to sweat, he was slowly turning into one of those hellbound heathens he'd always chuckled at in those Chick Publications he used to pass out by the handful, before the Lord called him to labor in a larger vineyard—a televised one—hung with millions of souls ripe for the saving.

He was beginning to panic. Who was watching him? He was all alone. He'd thought. Now that was all he hoped. But why? Which way should he go? Why did he need to move at all? He felt he'd be safest if he never moved—not even an inch—from where he stood. But he had to get away from the eyes. How many? Two, at least. Maybe more. A dozen. Maybe many more. Maybe every plate of glass in every building could see him. And behind each of these eyes were other eyes. Why was he so nervous about being seen? He'd been before the camera for years. Preached before thousands. Why now would he be afraid? Perhaps he'd buried years of stage fright, and tonight, here on this street corner he couldn't remember getting to, it had decided to surface. One enormous, *grand mal* panic attack no longer content to run silent, run deep.

No, it wasn't his imagination. These eyes were different from the millions before tonight. They weren't holding him with love, with respect—maybe, occasionally, even with awe and attraction. These eyes stared. Worse, they smirked. *Eyes that smirk will leer* he thought he remembered some great aunt whispering to him as a child. Yes, they were leering now. Then they laughed. A slow chuckle first. They knew a secret. A secret he should have known too, like his fly was undone. A secret that, if they'd liked him, even felt sorry for him, they'd have told. A common courtesy. But there was nothing kind about these chuckling eyes that now laughed louder until they screamed. He moved that inch now. He didn't care about safety if it meant listening to howling eyes all around. Evil cartoon hyenas circling closer and closer.

Music. Beyond the eyes, he heard music. Faint thudding. As if a radio with some super bass contraption were playing as loud as the driver could bear in his car, windows rolled up, passing several stories below a locked window to an apartment humming with air conditioning. It came from the corner across the street. The building stood alone from the others. In fact, it was a building while the others were boxes of steel, concrete, glass, stucco and Sheetrock. It was not one shape, but a collection of angles and curves. Some of the stone was smooth and unblinking. Other bits curled into garlands or congealed into ancient masks for gods, for warriors, for even the occasional misplaced farm animal. Window arched beside window with an identical layer below and above. On the inside of this Roman aqueduct, curtains faded by a thousand suns gathered on each side of each window into the embrace of an emotionless winged brass cockroach. And both of these bugs looked up to the center of each arch where a small wolf's head blossomed, the lone bud left on a leafless trellis. All the windows, all the stonework pulled Sheldon toward the pillared portico. The garlands quickly grew thicker and the masked menagerie more menacing. Blank stares became scowls, maybe even sneers. The music too was changed. Less muffled. Thumping was no longer thumping. *Pa pa pa da, pa pa pa dum. Pa pa pa da, pa pa pa dum. Pa pa pa da, pa pa pa dum, dum, dum.*

He went up the three steps through the center pillars. On the marble floor before the door was an oddly stretched circle. Even a simple geometer would have known it was an ellipse. Not Sheldon, however. He'd been forbidden to study much within the liberal arts. His parents had strongly taught him, hands on usually, that if it wasn't mentioned in the Bible, it not only wasn't worth learning, it just plain wasn't. Yet here an ellipse lay, smugly carved into the stone and inlaid with yet more burnished brass. And circling its outer rim like charms on a bracelet were figures and scribbles. And there were more scratches within the heart of the unacknowledged ellipse. To the simple geometer, these symbols were more arcane than most would like to admit. To Sheldon, they were undecipherable.

Once he'd passed over it, Sheldon pushed his way through the revolving glass-and-yet-more-brass door into the lobby of what must have been, by day, a bank. The ceiling had retreated even further away from him. There, squares honeycombed within squares within squares within circles within squares yet again. An educated liberal, or more likely a liberal education, would have whispered into his mind's ear—*early overblown Roman basilica*. But he stared at the ceiling unaware, for neither had followed him past the door—the one unlikely to have this dream in the first place, the other unable to ignore the inscription in the ellipse.

The air, as still as stone, smelled of brash polish and cigarettes. The music had grown loud enough to make its presence known. It was all that moved other than perhaps his heart—no, too faint—the near-soundless snorts were coming from his almost-trembling nostrils.

Ooompa. Ooompa. Ooompa. Ooompa. The music had changed beat. It was quicker and closer. It came from the doors far across the white marble floor with the gold flecks that matched the white wood-and-gilt trim of the ceiling and the forest of hundreds of pillars and posts. The music sounded nice. Certainly nicer than the howling eyes outside. He wouldn't go back. So he walked forward. The *clack clop clack clop* of his dress shoes on the tiles was almost too loud. He tried to ignore the emptiness he felt all around him as he crossed what felt to be miles of marble.

The echoes reminded him that just that morning—was it really that long ago?—he'd clacked along with a crowd of journalists, lobbyists, politicians, and well-wishers through the corridors of the state capitol in Sacramento. His idea—and he warmed just thinking this—his idea to turn the Defense of Marriage Act into a constitutional amendment had been hailed as an act of political genius by friend and foe alike. He'd learned the hard way not to quote chapter and verse from Deuteronomy or II Corinthians at every public forum. He'd learned to curb his usage of favorite phrases like "Adam and Eve, not Adam and Steve," "abomination," "pedophile," "child molestor," "culture war," "Satanic lesbian witches," "mental illness," "God's divine retribution." Sure they'd been crowd-pleasers. But he was out to wow a much larger crowd now. Of course, he wanted to stop the radical homosexual agenda dead in its tracks. Who didn't? But there was something greater in the "Endangered American Families Amendment." It was time that Christian soldiers all across this great land knew there were other generals in God's army besides that cherub Ralph Reed. And they *had* begun to take notice. Why already just today he'd had breakfast with the Governor and lunch with the Assembly Speaker. It was only a matter of months before he'd be praying with the President in the Oval Office. Yes, he was going to make it to the mountaintop this time.

After hours, days, a million *ooompa*s, he made it to the other side. The white-washed and gilded doors reached up to be closer to the still-retreating ceiling. He turned the knob and pushed one of the doors back. The room beyond was as dim as the room he stood in was bright. The air smelled even more of cigarettes. All he could make out was a vast desk that like everything around him had white wood and gold trim. He closed the door. When he did, the music stopped. He was startled at the stillness. Except for the ugly desk, the enormous room was empty. He began to walk toward it when he heard a click.

He turned as he heard the door open behind him. He wasn't alone. He'd been right about the eyes. That was the last thing he remembered believing clearly. For when his own eyes took in the person in the doorway, time and synapses and whatever else that usually ran smoothly derailed. Seconds and thoughts began to tumble from the track one by one. It was just like any other accident. The event happened in an instant; the effects would play themselves out forever.

He stood looking down on an old Mexican cowboy. Maybe he wasn't Mexican. He looked Mexican. For Reverend Smalley, this was anyone with brown skin and black hair living south of Texas—all the way to the tip of Patagonia. In fact, his only attempts to acknowledge any Latino presence in San Francisco had been to avoid the Mission district, day or night, to fight Army Street's renaming to César Chavez, and to ignore his wife while she watched that Linda Ronstadt special on the local PBS station.

Despite this doubt, he was certain, very certain, even in such dim light, that the man was very old and very little. Old was an epithet he was becoming used to, but little he'd understood all his life. Sheldon was no more than five feet three inches himself, except in the eye of the television camera. But now he no longer felt alone or small. In fact, this new arrival made him feel physically, morally, and racially superior. The man pushed the large black leather sombrero back off his head till its stringy little arms clung around his neck. As Sheldon's eyes focused, his thoughts began to blur even faster.

This he might be a she.

The face was both childlike and ancient, an odd combination he'd seen before in the features of the newborn and the nearly dead. Forehead and chin were broad and round while the cheek bones and nose were sharp and narrow. The skin thickened and cracked with wrinkles around the eyes and mouth, but it ran as thin and smooth as an onion's over the cheeks and forehead. It was not one color, not one shade, more a desert ridge of layered reds, oranges, grays, blacks, blues beneath a surface of sun-stained brownness.

If it was a he, then he had the faintest black moustache and a few whiskers on his chin. But these slight hints of masculinity combined with the jet black eye shadow and mascara convinced Sheldon this he must be a she—or worse—a pathetic female impersonator.

He could observe her face so well because her hair had been pulled tightly behind her head into a bun, a miniature version of the sombrero now sleeping on her back. It was dyed. Black. No, he thought, darker even. As dark as when one walked, as he once had, out of a too-brightly lit cabin into the forest. Alone in the too-dark-darkness, too blinded to see any other shapes. Only sense their presence. Feel their shadows. Smell their closeness. Her whole small body was covered in leather dyed that same shade of too-black black. If pressed to describe her style of dress, he would have had even more difficulty than he'd had with naming geometrical shapes. To Sheldon, she simply looked like a member of a malevolent mariachi band or a motorcycle gang.

As his eyes had eventually adjusted to the dark outside the cabin so he could see the millions of stars in that night's sky, so now he began to notice little grinning silver skulls buttoning every hole and studding every seam. He stopped. He could only stare. A large silver phallus, a gargantuan *milagro*, pointed out from her—*please, let it be a her*—crotch.

He trembled. He was confused. *What is it? What does it want with me?*

Her bony hands moved. They were speckled with liver spots and silver rings. They reached for the phallus. Sheldon's eyes had never moved from it. Suddenly all he could see were the blue threads of her veins, barely hidden beneath the skin. He couldn't tell if she'd unscrewed the phallus or unbuttoned it or slipped it off like a garter. All he understood was that it was glinting in her hands and then he heard it thunk hard on the edge of the desk. She turned toward him again. He realized her pants were not pants but chaps like a cowboy's. And beneath them was only her well-worn flesh. Where the lone silver bullet had stood was only a tuft of pubic hair the color of steel wool. *How disgusting, that whore is flashing me,* he thought. The head of his penis, however, wobbled like a pink marble in a nest of white string.

He was shocked. Here he was, the Reverend Sheldon Smalley, trapped in a room with some perverted old Mexican hag. He tried dismissing her from his thoughts with every name he could curse her with, and he knew many from his childhood in Fresno. But none had any effect on her presence. She was different. She was not of this world. She was an affront to the laws of nature. God's very laws! Such an abomination in the sight of the Lord could only be a demon, a servant of Satan.

Now, Sheldon was angry. Why hadn't Satan come himself instead of sending this old maid to terrify him?

Satan. Just the thought of him puffed Sheldon up with the confidence he needed to confront whatever this thing was. He would use His words to drive out this spirit. "Devil," he bellowed in his Sunday best, "thy name is legion, and, in the name of our Lord, Jesus Christ, I cast you out."

"Nice try, padre," she smiled as she looked directly into his eyes. "But I'd save that exorcism for the next available herd of swine. I'm fresh out since I scared away today's delegation of California Republicans. Forgive the form, it wasn't intended for you. But it always scares *la mierda* out of former Governor Wilson."

Sheldon paled.

"Oh, I'm so sorry, *pobrecita.* Petie's session ran over and I had no time to change." She'd stopped now that she'd reached the opposite side of the vast desk. She turned toward him, lowering her eyes and her presence. They both stood downcast. "Perhaps, I could fold some laundry—*¿Sí?*—make breakfast for your children—*¿Sí?*—or I could just sit silently slapping out tortillas—*¿Sí?* Would you like that, *don Sheldon?*"

She opened a humidor that had sprung fully formed from the field of green leather on the desktop. She took out a cigar as fat as a baby's thigh. She held it out toward him. He shook his head and his backcombed hair, a white shell covering his pink skin, wobbled to decline the offer as well. She lit up and pulled in several drags.

"Care for some scotch. No? How about some blood of Christ. Oh, how Catholic of me! Forgive me." She whispered to her fist, now parallel to her face. Her thumb, jutting out from it as a bony lower lip, moved. "*Ego te absolvo.*" She looked up at Sheldon and smiled. "Let me guess, you'd prefer some grape juice in a paper shot glass."

He tried to scowl through her as she puffed away.

"Don't judge me, Reverend. No one I cared for was exploited in the creation of this masterpiece." She rolled the cigar between her thumb and forefinger as she exhaled. "I have a little plantation not far from here where little fair-skinned old men, just like you, shrivel up in the sun almost as fast the tobacco leaves." She offered it toward him once again.

He said nothing.

She began the long walk around the desk back to him, a demonic Rudolph, the cigar's burning tip lighting her way.

"So, *¿qué tal?*, Smalley." She ran her hands along the lapels of his gray polyester suit while she whispered, "My, my, my. The latest in urban puritan. Don't you look dour. Just come from a witch burning?" She jerked him down toward her teeth and spit out, "You know you've been fucking with the wrong side, don't you?" She let go.

"Ah, but that's why you're here isn't it." She wiped her palms along her thighs, then shook them to flick off whatever still stained them. "First things first. We'll get to the fun stuff later. Would you be more comfortable if I changed into something less comfortable for me? I could take the shape of Carrie Nation. Now, while I must agree with you, Shelly, that an axe *is* an amazing fashion accessory," she paused. "You—no, I guessed right—you have no idea who she is. Cotton Mather? John Calvin? Zwingli's definitely out then. How about good old *Miss Diet of Worms of 1521*, little Marty Luther." Her leathers cracked and popped as she clasped her hands together. "Oh, my god, here I stand..." she pleaded heaven-ward with the subtlety of a silent movie star. "I can do no more. Poor little old me, just 95 theses and a prince's army, ready to kick the holy fuckin' ghost out of anyone who disagrees with me." She turned her glance Sheldonward. But her black eyes met only the stern stare of his blank, bloodshot, blue eyes. "Isn't there any other disgruntled Protestant zealot you'd recognize besides yourself?

"No words when the camera sleeps, o holy one. Well, then I'll just keep this form. It suits my mood." She jumped onto the side of her desk with a *thwack* as the leather of her pants greeted its kin stretched across her desk. "Welcome to your nightmare, *señor* Smalley. Would you like it hot or mild? For here or to go?" She laughed softly so that only the sides of her darkened lips, the color of wet clay, slipped upwards.

"I know. You can't take your eyes off me. You never thought someone non-white and over twenty-five could look so hot in leather. Surprise! And there are many other things of which you've never been aware that you will be soon. Of course, *mija*, if you listen to your spider grandma, they'll only hurt in all the right ways in all the right places."

She locked eyes with him, then looked down into her lap knowing his gaze would follow hers. She spread her legs even wider as she slowly slid back another inch from the edge of the desk. Sheldon's pink marble rolled from one side of the nest of white string to the other. "It's a dick. You want to hold it?" The marble rolled still. "Go ahead, touch it." She crooked her right index finger under it, raising its head, then she straightened her finger and it flopped back. "It won't bite. I will." Sheldon's own pink little head rose up over the edge of the nest. It wasn't a cold marble after all. It was a just-born bird, hairless and hungry, that raised its little gaping mouth up and up.

"You look confused, *mi amor*. We've been talking about dicks. Mine, not yours. Or do you prefer the more clinical penis—yes, yes—how insensitive—this clinical penis doesn't bite. No teeth. See. Nor my vagina. Disappointed, eh, *mija*? Perhaps since *abuelita* is so old, all the teeth have fallen out. I can read the headlines now—*Travesty or Tragedy in the Underworld: Rev. Sheldon Smalley gummed to death by a vagina-no-longer-dentata*. Story at eleven." She held her cigar like a microphone and spoke into the smoking end. "Then at last, then at last, thank god almighty, then at last, my Smalley, you'd finally get a teensy-weensy taste of the fame you've mistaken for heaven."

He emitted a harrumph that sounded very little like a harrumph and very much like a heavy fart muffled by a thick mattress or a cushion in a chair. *She is not Satan,* Sheldon thought. *I will sit here until he arrives. Sending some minor demon, really. Lord, strengthen me to endure this trial. With your angels watching over me, Father, I will not break. I will not falter. I will not betray you. Sinner that I was and always have been, Lord, I'm yours now. Tell me how I can serve you here.*

"Disgusting." She put out the cigar in her palm with one swift twist. "You think your god's going to come rushing over for that half-assed attempt at prayer. Smelly Shelly, honey, you make one pathetic bottom. Throw your whole soul into it. Burn with praise or fear or desire." She pointed the blackened end of the cigar at him. "No, no, *mija*, I didn't say burn those you fear or desire. Burn *with*. *With*, dear." She finally laid the cigar to rest in a brass ashtray that had sprouted from the desktop as magically as the humidor.

"Reverend Smalley, you may find this an odd question, considering your profession and all, but do you know what an angel is? Right, right, a white person with wings." She slapped both her palms flat on the desk. The sound echoed. "Wrong. A being so awake to the desire to create that it burns. You could become an angel, still, instead of what you're settling for. Think about it. You could be your very own burning bush." She let both her hands slide well behind her and she leaned back on her arms. "I'm no shrink, Rev., but I'd say it's time to turn off that old projector of yours. Otherwise someone might kill you before you kill them."

He squeezed this idea into a little gunmetal-gray box and then stuffed that between the oatmeal-gray layers of what a coroner would later claim was a brain.

"I felt that," smiled Sheldon Smalley's satan. "Daddy's little girl was listening."

The gape-mouth birdie stirring in Sheldon's pants almost peeped. A peep that, if it had happened at all, would have, sadly, been drowned out by his loud-mouthed mind. *There she goes again, that old wetback cunt, calling me girl.* "Get thee behind me...."

"Oh, here we go again. All those lines from the Mount of Temptation story you've waited your whole pastoral life to use against the devil." She swallowed a yawn. "But answer me this: What could I offer you that you haven't already sought and taken? Power over the kingdoms of earth? Wealth? Fear? Death to your enemies? You have no need of a satan. You're the one who's everywhere. Your armies, the herds of the righteous, are legion. Me?" She lightly kicked the desk with the backs of her boots. "I'm here alone. Able only to inflict a little pain, a little remorse, a little poetic justice long after the deeds are done. Where's the terror in that?"

They sat silently staring at each other while her kicks kept track of the passing minutes.

"Why am I here?" he said as his whole body finally blinked. She stopped kicking.

"It was time one of us had a talking with you, and I manifested the short end of the stick."

He asked again. "Why am I here?"

"You've been here before, many times."

"No, I haven't. I've never stepped inside this bank before."

"Bank? You think you're in a bank?" she looked puzzled at the simplicity of his statement. Then she glanced around the underworld and laughed. "Ah, yes, the decor. Welcome to First Infernal. Will you be opening or closing your account today?" She laughed softly, encouragingly, hoping Sheldon was just playing dumb. He remained silent. Her face slowly hardened into a mask of pity. "You really have no idea where you are." A chair of white wood and gilt trim with a green leather seat and back now crouched beside him. Sheldon sat.

"Hell."

"Hell? This is your heaven. Surprise number two! All those years of wasted torment and tribulation, finding and seeking. I've found your kind bore easily of open desires. You've never enjoyed any pleasures on earth unless you stole them when you thought I wasn't looking. So I redecorated. I bulldozed the garden of earthly delights and buried everything under a hearty schmear of concrete. Haven't had a complaint yet."

"Why would I want my heaven to be a bank?"

"Don't ask me. You're the Protestant."

"If this is heaven, where's Jesus?"

"Like he'd want to hang out with a bunch of uptight assholes in a bank."

"I sympathize with you, demon. You will never look upon the glorious face of the Lamb of God."

"What makes you think you're not looking at that very face right now?"

"You sicken me."

"Me? You're the little infectious disease. Not me!"

"Tell Lucifer I will speak only to him."

"Oh, and all I get out of you is your name, rank, and favorite serial killer?"

"I will only speak with Satan."

"Not in."

"Where is your master?"

"I am my lord *and* my master."

"What is your name?"

"Why? Do you want to report me to my supervisor?"

"What is your name, bitch?"

"That's definitely one of my favorites. I have as many others as I have forms.

"Like Beelzebub. Mammon. Satan."

"No, no, no! What is your obsession with Satan, padre? You always want to talk with 'The Man,' don't you? Even when it's obvious the man's been gone for several spins of the cosmic wheel. Still you and so many others keep feeding that concept with your energy. I myself have no idea how I first, if you believe in such things as first, got here. All I'm certain of is that each year I grow a little stronger. Thanks to all those prayers of fear and hope from all those people you and your kind have taught to believe they are no more than powerless pawns in a devil/god champion chess match. They hand it over to me, and I hate to see energy lie around idly—puritan energy will do that to you. So here I am—buffer, butch, and bent on giving my children a good time."

Sheldon ignored the bristling of the hairs on his balls and spoke, "You mean you're in charge?"

"I'm, more or less, the zoo keeper."

"So you are Satan! Or the son of Satan or daughter or something!"

"When are you going to get it?! This isn't hell. I'm not Satan. I'm just the embodiment of your unwanted fears and passions."

Sheldon recited the Twenty-third Psalm.

"Great. Yet another love letter to god. Of course, it doesn't really matter. It's all falling on deaf ears." She smiled as if remembering a private joke between herself and a lover. "Deaf ears. You humans, I swear you'll personify anything, even the void."

"God knows all, sees all, hears all."

"Then he has an awful response time. Worse than 911 in a quote-unquote bad neighborhood. When, old man, was the last time you remember him doing a walk-on? And I know why. Aren't you the least bit curious?"

Sheldon sat unmoved.

"Nice imitation of a stone tablet. C'mon, Friar Tuck, don't you want to know? I know something you don't know. I know something you don't know." She had begun to kick the desk again. "Ah, the silent treatment only works if I couldn't read your every thought. And since most of your thoughts are someone else's and since we've had this conversation a million times in a million different forms, I'll forgive myself for cutting to the chase and telling you all the answers." She stopped kicking to preface what she was about to say.

"This ain't hell. I'm not Satan. He hasn't been in since four—no, I think it was five, yes, five—worlds ago."

Thus the devil spake to the televangelist and then spake some more.

"God and Satan, dear boy—dear little malignantly mutated egg of your mother—they were lovers the whole time. All of this," she threw her small arms out wide until her leather jacket creaked, "was to get the other's attention, stir the other's passion, a game, a way to pass that which for them never passes. But they grew bored and left this universe so many long agos for another. Why not? This play has happened so many times. And it will over and over again. So now there are no headliners hanging around. Does it matter? Sometimes some blob gets to your level, sometimes it evolves well past you. But you and I always end up having the same conversation about the same topic: good and evil. It never gets scripted differently. No matter the matter, I always get caught up in some version of this passion play for particles."

She paused and noticed him. He looked bored. Actually, his small blue eyes, small even behind his thick glasses, looked disconnected from his brain. They didn't roll or shake. They didn't twitch. They didn't do anything.

"C'mon Shelly. Don't blank out on me, *mija*. Right, right, take me to your leader—the one hung with a Y chromosome. Okay. I'd hoped to avoid that. Walk with me, my teensy weensy tiny whiny one. Your spider grandma is taking you to a fiesta!"

Anything would be better than this, he thought sleepily. He followed the black leather dot as she bounced down a long, even darker hall. The music had begun again. *Ticky ticky ticky ticky ticky ticky, ticky tat, ticky tat.* He could hear trumpets and laughter. They stood before doors even wider and taller and whiter than before. He guessed from the noise, hoped, there must be hundreds of people on the other side.

"Before we go in and party your life away, let's finish the talk we've both come here to have. It's fine by me if you don't say anything. I'm beginning to enjoy having all this air time to myself. Amazing, isn't it? I once was blind but now I see why you've always avoided any televised debates. So wise for one so stupid, my Sheldunce!

"Good and evil, or let's bring it down to your level of intelligence, me and not-me. It really is that simple for you, isn't it? I'll admit that keeping conscious of the multiplicities of multiverses—*ave, maria* that's a tongue-tier—anyway, keeping conscious of all those multis is a learned skill, hard-won, definitely. But you and your kind have sealed off so many cubits in your brain with pitch that all you've left yourselves with is a leaky boat big enough for two, and only two, of every kind. But, baby, the flood's over. You can come out of the ark now. Hell, your kind has been stumbling over dry land for millennia."

She kept speaking out loud to herself, very out loud to herself, so Sheldon couldn't help but overhear.

"Two. Two. Rarely ever is it more than two. Existence either comes down to one, two or, on a good day, three—though it's usually just three-in-one. Father. Son. Holy Ghost. Maiden. Mother. Crone. Hecate's three crossroads. But they're all roads. Only variations on a single theme. Yet a forest isn't just the same tree cloned over and over. There are conifers and deciduous. There is grass and dirt and animals. Rocks. Streams. Mud. Shit. All this," and she winked coyly at him, "and much, much more, is a forest. And as below so above. The universe is much more than a huge black box with a gas problem. But it's always more fun to search for Euclid's point-that-has-no-part or Lucretius' unsplittable atom. Or God and Satan. Or the three little bears!

"So I'll spare you the trouble of discovering what I've learned. I'll just tell you. You probably won't grasp it. Even though, like you, it's very short and very simple. But I don't care. I'm sick of waiting for you and yours to get it. The secret is this: It's the odd that makes any of this bearable. The fourth dimension. The sixth sense. The queer. The other. But you want to pretend it away. Better yet, closet it. Best of all, kill it.

"I'll admit you're not alone. You have many friends stupider and smarter than you. Even your enemies are usually in favor of a dualistic pissing contest. Just one where they get to piss on you once in a while."

He harrumphed again. This harrumph sounded worse than the one before but Sheldon still heard the peep from his growing ugly red bird. He fidgeted and then tried to halt his glasses' attempt to slip quietly away. He pushed them all the way back to where they'd been before he'd ever entered this madhouse.

"Please prove me right. I thought you harassed my queer children because you were willfully stupid and unaware of all the other possibilities. That you needed an easy mark to win you friends and fame. Someone to rally the wagons 'round now that the 'Injuns' are dead, the buffalo skinned, the forests cut down. Where to take your 'pioneers,' your 'freedom fighters' next? I know!

Down the yellow brick road!

"Still won't talk? And don't give me any more of that 'I'm just a handpuppet for the Lord' bullshit. Don't lie to me. You've never even had your wife's pinky, let alone anyone's hand, up your asshole."

Sheldon grimaced. The bird stood up in its nest and squawked. He asshole squeaked. His eyes stared forward at the door. As if they were just two people—*well, one person and some thing*—in an elevator. He waited for the doors to open so he could get out and this creature could descend to another floor.

"Don't you ever think about what you're trying so hard to destroy— the treasures, the worlds. No, it's Ferdinand and Isabella do Spain all over again. You'd rather live without eyes than have to see anything different from yourself.

"Do you know anything about the world you're working so hard to conquer? Have you touched it, tasted it, smelled it? *¡Chíngate!* Now you've got me doing it. Shrinking all possibilities down to a lump solid enough to make a sound while it rattles around in the head.

"Do you know what the dirt of a fuckin' faggot forest tastes like? Before a rain? After? Do you know what a bulldyke sunset smells like? Ever listen to the music of queer sex? For a solo instrument. A duet? A full flaming orchestra!

"No. Your mouth, your mind are filled with the hates of another. No choice then. No responsibility. Just let go and let God. Or at least his legally appointed guardians on earth. What do you believe, Smalley? What do you want? If I offered you the gift of my ass," his tough old bird stretched the length of its neck, "and you would be very unwise to refuse it, would you desire to bite it?" The bird shook its neck. "Lick it?" It grew even redder in the face. "Wipe it? Fuck it?" Much more of this and the old bird was going to crow. "Do you know what desire is? Have you felt it flow full on—no longer struggling to push past that rock you've rolled before it?"

His eyes, those scratched, unwashed Plexiglass windows to the soul, still looked only at the door.

"But perhaps you do know. Perhaps I've misjudged you after all. Tell me, torturer to torturer, you *do* enjoy it. You *love* to fry up the souls of your enemy like some psychotic short order cook for Christ."

The doors flew open. The guest of honor had arrived.

Sheldon's heart fell. No men. Only more women. The bird jumped up and down. Even in the band. It then jumped up onto the edge of the nest.

Sheldon was the only man. When would Satan arrive? He was beginning to wonder when God would. Then he stopped still and his eyes twitched. *Neither would have made Ralph Reed wait*, his inner agent whispered. Now he knew just how minor league a fallen sinner he was.

"All these goddesses have names, many names each, none of which you'd know. Should, but you don't. So tonight we're all going by names you'd recognize. No, no. Don't get excited. There's no one here by the name of Baal or the Whore of Babylon. Innana. I saw that. You know what I mean." Sheldon looked to where she'd turned. He saw a woman with dark skin—they all had skin darker than his—layered in gold. She was wearing the brightest, darkest blue eye shadow he'd ever seen. She looked familiar. Maybe he'd seen her at one of his famous revival meetings.

"So I'd like you to meet Prop 67, Prop 188, Prop H, No on M, Measure 4, Amendment 2, Rider to Senate Bill..." One after the other passed by. It was worse than Halloween in the Castro. The things he'd seen those cold nights trying to save souls paled before these horrors. Maybe he'd stumbled into the lesbians' secret masquerade ball. What day was it? Was it October? Or April? Some of the women even flashed him as the old Mexican had. He grew sick.

It seemed like hours. Maybe a day or two passed. Sheldon was growing tired. He exhorted his soul to stay alert for when Satan arrives. *She's just wearing me down to tip the balance in favor of her master.*

"My, what a busy boy you've been," she said, pulling him close. The introductions were over. The band had returned, filled with a second wind. But since he didn't know his tito from his puente, it was all just loud horns and drums—blaring horns and pounding drums. The line of women began to circle them like a snake coiling.

Finally a man had appeared. A dignified older gentleman in a gray pinstripe suit walked toward them. Perhaps this was his bank. Perhaps it was Satan. Then Sheldon noticed he was bearing a silver tray loaded with small shot glasses. Each one burned like a fancy dessert in a French restaurant. His wife would have been impressed.

"I don't think you've met the board members of the United Fruit Company." She continued to play hostess and started to introduce them. Then she changed her mind and picked up a glass. "Don't worry if the irony hurdles over your little balding head. It's a private joke between me and *centroamerica*." She tried to pat him on the head but he pulled away. "Oh, now where did the CEO go? Ah, yes, there he is. No, child," her bony brown hand was amazingly strong as it gripped his chin and tilted his head back. "He's up there."

An old man hung from the ceiling. He didn't hang heavy with death like a convict on the gallows, a human pendulum of a clock that had stopped ticking minutes before. He dangled like a gaudy plastic earring decorated with warring primary colors and bright feathers and strands of crêpe paper. Then the shock fully snuggled its way deep into the remaining marrow of Sheldon's bones. The old man had been stripped naked, hog-tied with a few leather straps, painted, feathered, crêpe-papered, and suspended from a mirrored ball in the ceiling like a *piñata* in the tackiest Mexican restaurant ever!

Sheldon tried not to, but he kept looking. He could no longer deny he was hard. A smaller mirrored ball dangled from a shiny hook piercing the head of the old man's orange-painted penis. Very hard. Sheldon winced and quickly looked elsewhere.

That man's mouth. A red ball had been shoved in and a piece of gold shiny fabric wrapped around it and the rest of his head. Above his silenced mouth, his eyes spoke. They screamed as they bulged like the sideways eyes of red-orange-gold fish. Eyes so large and wide and detached. As if they'd been glued on in the last few minutes rather than taking their own sweet eons of evolution to swell.

This can't be real Sheldon told himself. *God is just testing my faith. The Lord will rescue that man just like Daniel. The Master will come skipping along the water or dance out of the conga line snaking tighter and tighter beneath the man. Just like Peter and Paul in prison, the earth will tremble, the band will stop playing, the women will stop conga-ing, and the chains will drop safely to the ground.* He'd be free. Then he, all the other old men, and Sheldon, under the command of their mighty Lord, would lay waste to Hell.

This image strengthened him. He turned to her and announced, "Whatever you threaten, witch, my final place is in heaven with my sweet lord, Jesus. Whether I go tonight or I wait until the Rapture..."

"The rapture? Oh, baby, have you got a long wait ahead of you. Girls, correct me if I'm wrong, but I heard it was scheduled to happen right after the true Messiah comes, the matriarchy is restored, and Walt Disney raises himself from the dead." The music stopped suddenly for a rim shot. Then it began again. The women clucked and brayed just as he imagined the whores of Satan would.

Sheldon felt odd. He couldn't move. And he was looking down, down where he'd been standing before. The women were looking back. Where had all those shiny silver sticks come from?

"Sheldon, I know you have other dreams than driving the queers into the Pacific. Our little St. Patrick of Fresno, eh? And in the future, men who look and think just as you do will hold parades in your honor and drink bucket after bucket of weak beer until their faces turn the same sickly shade of green as their plastic hats. And when the party's over, all that remains is that stale smell of piss. Face it, my dear, their illegible writing's all over the wall."

The *bleat, peal, squeal* of trumpets. His shoulders burned. The *ticky, ticky, ticky, ticky, ticky* of drumsticks on metal. His arms were being slowly uprooted from their sockets. The *pa, pa pa da, pa pa pa da, pa pa pa dum dum dum* of hands bouncing off the taut bellies of drums. It was getting harder to hear over all the *din, da da din, da da din, da da din* of the music and the *da umpf, da umpf* of his heart. He couldn't feel his legs. He was cold. He was sore and afraid.

"Your vision leads here and nowhere else. All the pain and death you will cause. For this. Choose again, *mija*. I can't keep my friends from trying to knock out the sweet meats and other goodies inside you forever."

At that, the bird leapt forward, cock-a-doodle-doing, leaving the hard little eggs behind in the nest. Someone else noticed too. An old voice shouted, "Look. His right nut knoweth not what his left nut doeth." Sheldon's devil grandmother turned toward the voice. She smiled. *That Baubo*, she thought, *always the party animal.*

Sheldon tried to speak now. Anything. But he couldn't. Something was stuck in his mouth. The Reverend's dick rejoiced. It had finally been severed from that dour mash fermenting upstairs in the skull. In fact, it hadn't been this red and round in decades. This was better than that first hit of Viagra. Better even than two bottles of Viagra downed in one swallow!

"Face it, Rev. You're no Ricardo Montalban and I'm no Roddy McDowell and this is no *Fantasy Island* morality play. You're in real deep shit and I'm trying to scoop you out though everyone around me keeps screaming 'Flush!' C'mon, *mija*. Listen to your spider grandma."

"Enough, Ereshkigal," said a shadow from the edge of the circle. "He's chosen."

"*¡Ay, mierda!* Fine, Smalley. I tried." She shrugged her shoulders and all her leathers sighed with her. "Well, ladies, it's puritan *piñata* time!"

• • •

Sheldon awoke. Screaming. Miraculously, he'd simultaneously spermed and pissed the bed.

Beloved of God

and Man

"for **love** is strong as death"
—The Song of Solomon

As it came to pass and Judas closed his bleary, gray eyes and pressed his stone-dry lips to His own, He thought of another kiss. His last kiss with John. His choicest morsel. His Beloved.

In the dancing shadows beneath last night's sputtering clay lamps, He had pulled His Beloved aside. The others had filed downstairs. He could hear Peter scolding the good man of the house over their Passover meal. "It was not fit for The Master," he shouted. "Your bread was stale and your wine bitter."

He smiled. Every act now meant so much more than it seemed. His Beloved smiled back. His lips were the purple of overripe grapes. And his wine-stained teeth had the silvery glint of those fish, aglow in the oddly angled light of late afternoon on the Galilee, that He'd once seen gasping and flopping across the net-strewn floor of His Beloved's father's boat.

He leaned down into the browns of His Beloved's eyes. And He saw the terra cotta walls of Jericho. And He saw the russet sawdust in Joseph's shop. And He saw the dark-as-honey hair of His mother. And He saw the umber waters of the Jordan in his cousin John's still darker hands. And He saw the tanned leather of Peter's sandals. And He saw His Beloved's body: the chalky dust of the road now wet with His spittle and the uneven ochers of that sweet and familiar skin burnished by the perfumed oils He would wipe over him with His hair.

He leaned in even closer, resting His forehead gently against His Beloved's. And like the lily, arching its open mouth unto the sun, His Beloved's mouth rose up to His own. And His Beloved's tongue, a startled dove, flew into the cave of His mouth, fluttering from wall to wall and from ceiling to floor to ceiling. And His own tongue leapt up like a hart, fleeing from the hunter, only to find itself caught in a firm, warm net. And they were as one, locked in an embrace tighter than that between Jacob and the wrestling angel, licking the honeyed wine from each other's lips and beards.

He pulled His Beloved's body into the hollows of His own like a breath. And He held him. And as He felt His Beloved's rod and His own staff rise up together like two cedars of Lebanon, wide in girth and towering in stature, he whispered to the gaining shadows in the large upper room, "Thank you, Father, for this last cup of wine, sweetened with milk and honey, before I must drink the fated bitter cup."

He stumbled.

His whole face throbbed from the slap of the soldier's leathered hand. And He opened His eyes and looked for Judas. The disciple stood in the shade of a tree, his pebbly eyes still blinking as if he were looking directly into the sun. He moved toward Judas but found Himself bound by the hands of others. And then He heard His back crack and He felt it almost break in half like the withered branch of a dead mustard tree. And His head fell to His chest. Another soldier had shoved the blunt end of his spear into the small of His back. The hands of others pulled Him away from this garden, from His Beloved.

It had come to pass.

Memento Mori

for Dr. Andrew Campbell

> "And sure in *language* strange she said 'I love thee **true.**'"
> —John Keats
> "La Belle Dame sans Merci"

Julian straddled Suetonius and his twelve Caesars over the arm of the chair. Little baby jackbootie, or Caligula as he was known to the troops, had tired of waiting for the poison to do in dear grandpapa Tiberius, the murderer of his mother and brothers and a good third of Rome, and so he'd finished the wheezing emperor off in his bed with a silken pillow.

Roman imperials.

As a boy, Julian had shuddered at their operatic antics. Stiffened even. But tonight, he was a much different, much older man, and their catalogues of excesses struck him as just that. An inventory of desperate attempts by the all-powerful to spend, as lavishly as possible, the gilded hours remaining in a life they'd proven pointless by taking it countless times through countless tortures. A final and glorious and hollow huzzah before they too were reduced by the hands of others to shadows cowering slavishly in the kingdom to come: the realm of endless death.

Roman imperials.

They were the Old World's masters of rendering the obscene ordinary.

And if that was all one had wanted, why need he trouble the shades of the ancients, he'd asked himself. Mightn't one have read more modern accountings from Bataille or Cooper? Sat out the rest of this Saturday night like a fly on the pages' white walls? Below him, Sade's bored great-great-grandchildren throttle a priest; the holy father ejaculates and expires; minutes later, they're at it again, greedily shoving his just-severed eye up the twat of the prettiest one. Or, a new world away, bored suburbanites in southern California drone on as they ring up a pizza and a hustler whom, later, they will gut from the arsehole up.

Instead, he'd passed these post-prandial hours re-reading blood-and-thunder tales of the elderly Emperor Tiberius waving away crying, screaming boys about to be flung from the cliffs of Capri now that he'd tired of them as much he had of ruling the earth. No more campaigns, abroad or in the Senate, for the son of Augustus. No more banquets for kings and adopted rivals. No more trips to the circus through the sweltering cesspool of Rome. No, he had retired. He would be the simple imperial rustic, tending the gardens of flesh he cultivated throughout his villa. The court and Caligula, in exchange for their continued longevity, could come to him, to this chalky outcropping in the Gulf of Naples, crawling with sure-footed old goats. And there they would find him, as content as any paranoid with the power of life and death over everyone on earth except himself, winnowing his "minnows"—the sons of slaves and senators, fathers of future emperors even, whom he made, each day, nibble between his divine legs, two wax-yellow candlesticks, while he thrashed about in his marble pool.

The old pervert.

Both of us.

There was a muffled, hissing gasp from the fireplace as the three small flaming logs collapsed closer together. Julian followed and shifted his weight from one hip to the other, letting the leather creak, then sigh. He was sitting in the most comfortable piece of cowhide he owned. A red leather wingback. A chair.

He sipped at his gin and tonic. He swirled it in the cup of his mouth. The clear heat of gin. The piquant sting of quinine, mollified by the burst wedge of lime. He looked down at the gilt tracery tattooed over Suetonius' back.

No matter the sadist, no matter the domme—he'd returned to his musings now that he'd swallowed—exceeding excess seemed to be the ultimate goal for literature's *perverterati.* Push so hard that, finally, some outraged divinity would appear and thrash the existential angst, that small grey leech sucking on the spleen, out of the offender's system. So much Sadean effort to prove there was some deeper meaning to anything, everything. To prove no man is an island, but an isthmus.

But the gods never did come to Tiberius or the Marquis. Because they never were. Or because they too were dead and dying. Or perhaps absence was how they announced their presence. Regardless, no cosmic force showed up to stop them save physics. For in the end they all, even emperor and aristocrat, died. Death alone, the blunt magistrate and gaoler. Death, the ultimate and opposite reaction to every one of life's outbursts.

Julian yawned and looked up at the spines on the shelf for another book to read. He blinked his eyes to focus on the titles. He started mildly when the fat blocks of ice slid back down and hit the bottom of the glass. A chime of several flat notes. Nothing as majestic as a glacier sloughing its skin into a fjord.

A fjord full of ice cubes. Scandinavia one vast gin and tonic. Fire and ice and several lime wedges.

Obviously, he chided himself, the time had come to get up and remove all the Grieg from the CD carousel. And, regrettably, he added, this would have to be tonight's last drink.

He sighed. How tired he'd become. In all the senses of this elastic word. For here he was—Julian Francis Aidan Gibbon, the Fey Dom, the Scourge of SOMA, and that was back when San Francisco's South of Market district truly was a leatherman's garden of earthy delights, growing thick and wonderfully twisted from plots named the Tool Box, FeBe's, the Ramrod, the No Name, the Barracks, the Brig, the Slot, the Ambush, the Hothouse, and Handball Express—thirty-plus years later, sitting at home on a Saturday night and dispassionately reading of others' debaucheries as if he were following a saga of debits and credits in a bank ledger.

Not only had he grown old and ill, but sickness and age had softened him with their repeated handlings. Left him like one of his gram's quilts which she'd stitched as a new bride and then used to swaddle her four children and fifteen grandchildren. *No, worse.* Left him, a drooling dotard wrapped in a blanket of infirmities, on senectitude's cold doorstep. *Good. A few synapses still fire.* A man no more a menace to other men than Karenin, Russia's greatest cuckold and Anna's cipher of a husband, who also sat at home on Saturday nights, while his beloved Anna and her beloved Vronsky were out painting the town a pre-Soviet red. In repose, for an hour after dinner, the old Slav would cut his quiet, calm way through the pages of Baudelaire's *Les Fleurs du mal.* One poem, one flower, each night.

Or, in one's own pathetic case, the life of one Caesar.

Get a grip, man, he exhorted himself. *Your edge hasn't dulled that much. That's the drink talking. Yes, yes,* he nodded to no one. *Besides, unlike Tolstoy's sorry bastard, you know exactly where the love of your life is.*

He nodded more vigorously.

The love of my life.

It will be 366 days tomorrow. A year and a day. Our anniversary. Our first.

And, most fucking likely, our last.

Stop it, Julian. You're getting sour and melancholy. Too much gin and black bile. What would Galen recommend for such excesses? A purging no doubt. Then a bleeding. He grinned wanly. *Well, then, that's what I'll do: Mourn tonight; celebrate tomorrow.*

He tipped all his weight on to his right hip so he could reach out his arm and abandon the empty glass on the dark wood ledge of the bookshelf. When he rocked back, he flinched. A quick sting and a string of weakening echoes. A drunken charley horse staggered its way up his left calf. He looked towards the riding boots, gleaming as he lifted one slowly off the other.

Mustn't scuff.

The boy had polished them for a good hour before serving him tonight's supper of grilled salmon with a soy and ginger marinade, sautéed new potatoes, steamed green beans, and, fittingly, a Caesar salad.

Now his right leg, which had fallen asleep under the weight of its sinister twin, bristled at being jostled awake. Julian gripped the arms of his chair and pressed his well-cared-for nails into the skin below the golden studs fastening leather to wood. And as the ache ripened from sharp to sweet, he rolled the right and then the left boot off the ottoman and dug the heels of his palms into the padded arms of the chair and pushed all of his six-foot-and-190-pound frame up.

With a sluggish resistance, his own blood laboured the length of his neck to his brain. He ignored the resulting dizziness and righted himself by locking eyes with the reflection in the gilt-edged mirror above the fireplace's mantle. It was a dignified face that met his gaze. One of elegant symmetry which had retained its grace while witnessing and enduring much in its many years.

In the center of it stood a nose that was striking in its solidity and straightness. It resembled a temple column that held aloft the broader, heavier entablature of the forehead. The marble had been yellowed in the persistent California sunlight and etched and nicked and faintly spotted and stained by that vandal, Time. Beneath his brow and resting on the thin ledges of his cheekbones were two narrow eyes. Despite their size and the coolness of their pale blue colour, they managed to evince a genuine warmth and even a bit of good-natured mischief. And further steadying these features was his magnificent white beard that fanned out from his face like a constantly tended topiary.

Indeed, the face impressively called to mind, said various British and European expatriates and the rare American he'd met who was a student of history, that of King George V's doomed cousin Nicky, Russia's Czar Nicholas II. If, that is, the Czar had a been a better, or, at least, more cunning ruler and lived long enough, as Julian had, to see his own red hair grow roan and then white.

Julian smiled and brushed back from his forehead the few strands of his thinning hairs that pomade and gravity failed to hold in place. Here he was thinking again of imperials. And somehow it seemed appropriate tonight. For hadn't the Russians once claimed that Moscow was the third Rome?

He paused. He caught a glimpse of something as he'd gazed past his image in the glass. There it was in the shadows cast by the fire and the creases following in the wake of his collapsing smile. A skull. The grinning skull of the tombstone.

The *memento mori*.

"Remember you too will die," it says. Until it too is reduced to dust.

Of all people, he did not need to be reminded of death.

Memento mori.

His secret nickname for himself since the diagnosis. The words he'd heard whenever he lingered too long in looking at his old man's face. Sober, he would have known better. He let his eyes fall down through his beard to the base of his neck; he tucked the black silk of his ascot deeper into wide V created by the topmost button of his red—again, silk—smoking jacket—a coveted find in a vintage clothing shop; he smoothed the lapels and then dropped his hands to tug at the hem. His eyes followed and relaxed, dissolving as they stared into the lustre of his custom-made black leather jodhpurs.

When he felt sufficiently becalmed, he crossed the room and stopped the Grieg in the middle of the "March of the Trolls." He rifled through the rows of what appeared to be little plastic books and extracted a choice. A single collection of Erik Satie's "*Trois Gymnopédies*," "*Embryons Desséchés*," and "*Gnossienes*."

After he tucked the CD into its bed, Julian looked back at the chair and down at the ottoman. It was shivering. The few weeks of October's summer were over. Julian had tried with tonight's pitcher of gin and tonics to tempt it to return. But, as he watched the tiny, involuntary spasms ripple across the ottoman's hide, he knew it wouldn't be long before this night's cool air would chill and grow damp enough to cling to his own skin like icy, wet wool. The winter rains must be only a few miles offshore.

He clicked a button and the delicate and sombre music of Satie, dead after all these years, began to play. As he set down the remote—*such an ugly thing*, he concluded, *black plastic skin suppurating with rows of brightly coloured boils*—he glanced at the tip of his right boot. A scuff. A lone scratch of cuneiform in the black clay of his boot.

Damn. This just won't do.

"Come here and lick this blemish from my boot."

The ottoman scuttled across the reds and blacks and blues of the Persian carpet like a beetle without its shell. In fact, its only carapace was made of leather the colour of the chair and it tastefully contained what would have been, otherwise, a comic display of flopping genitalia.

The head of the ottoman bobbed at his boot's tip. With its shock of onyx hair, it was hard for Julian to tell where one began and the other ended. His eyes moved out over its back, white as a bleached bone, encircled at its waist by a small strip of leather as dark as dried blood.

Bleached bones and dried blood.

Why this ottoman of mine is the very height of sepulchral chic.

He smiled and winced simultaneously.

Anytime the grave and; by inference, its digger, Death, were mentioned openly nowadays, he would shudder imperceptibly.

Julian was sobering quickly.

Death. Pallida Mors. *My old colleague. My forever foe.*

How utterly crafty It was in Its plans of attack. It never followed through on Its frontal assaults. The body's walls were often stormed, its gates rammed and battered, and then, when Death held the field, It retreated—to the amazement of any eyes left to watch from the battlements—beyond the horizon. Days or months or even years later, under night's shadows, always under night's shadows, It would come back.

Would sneak through some unlocked tower door or ungated sewer drain, waking the inhabitants from their dreams only to slay the weak and enslave the hardy. And the killing and pillaging would continue until the body's castle was a cold pile of broken rocks to be left behind.

A monument to the fallen.

A boundary proclaiming, "Thus far and no farther."

A cairn.

A *memento mori*.

A shiver sprinted the course of Julian's body.

It was as if Death had never forgotten the horrifying marvel of the Greeks destroying Troy. Certainly, It must have been happy for the plains and rivers and hills flush with bodies. But the real trophy It took back to Its bone-carpeted cave was that final plan of battle so vicious in its cunning that It preferred never to use another when It worked without the decimating hand of man: to come in the final assault as a surprise, an odd-shaped, often undetected, gift to be wheeled within and opened inside the safety of the body's warm, bloody dark.

But why did Death shake him so tonight? Surely he had seen It lay waste to a body a hundred times as a surgeon. And just as surely he'd stood by, helpless and broken and finally resigned, as the old greedy guts had carted off the remains of more than two hundred friends, lovers, tricks, and even enemies he made in his second youth along Folsom Street. His beloved dead.

But any queer his age—he would be sixty-four in December—who had lived in San Francisco as long as he had—he moved here from the UK in April 1967, almost thirty-five years now—had their own roster of fallen comrades that was the equivalent of three or four fat address books. This might have been cause enough for tonight's third and final drink, even for tonight's elegiac mood, but not for tonight's fear.

No, he shuddered simply because it was *his* time. The master trickster with an inhuman love for the absurd had tagged him and he was IT.

It.

Dying.

He, Dr. Julian Gibbon, a physician and a faggot, who had outwitted and outlived so many of the City's on-going plagues—in his case, heroin and speed, AIDS and depression—was going to die. Soon. And from a throat cancer that four years ago had decamped under the white flag of remission only to sneak its way back in through the marrow of his bones.

A throat cancer from all the cigarettes and then the cigars and then, until his last inhale five years ago, the ever-brimming bowls of English-blend tobacco in his cherished pipe. Each one a little burning crutch on which he'd stumbled about after cleaning up twenty years ago. Each burning crutch crippling him. So odd. So bloody cliché. And so like Death. Forever heavy-handed with the irony.

A throat cancer against which he'd ransomed everything within and without his body's walls to vanquish. Until one day his doctors had told him of his Pyrrhic victory. It was going, going, and then, gone. Right as rain until two weeks ago. Now, as the cancer led its slow-moving triumphal march through the streets of his bones, all that was left to him was to wait. Wait for the pain. Wait for the painkillers and palliative care. Wait to waste away—a hollow man drowning in morphine. Yet another of Odysseus' lost sailors who would dine and die amidst the Lotus Eaters.

He released the breath he had been holding behind his bitten lips.

There was still time before that, he reminded himself. Several weeks. Maybe months. Perhaps a year. Miraculously two. Time enough to train his ottoman.

The *membrum virile* to his *memento mori*.

His boy.

His Sid.

Julian moved his boot out from under Sid's mouth. He eyed the toe. It glistened under all the drying spit. The scuff had been lapped up long ago.

Only once before had he seen a boy be as reverential with the toe of a boot. But boot worship was *all* Mike would do, Julian had learned the second and final time they'd played together. The first, Julian had been so smitten with him that he forgave him his limited repertoire: Mike began by wetting the leather from heel-to-toe and kept at it for nearly thirty

236

minutes while Julian watched transfixed, as he had never seen a boy moan and buck so by licking an impassive boot, then he'd shot, unbidden, and whimpered and begged for his "fuckin' hot liege and lord and master" to shower him with his "lyrical seed," which Julian obliged, and then the boy sucked up, vociferously, whatever stray notes had splattered across the tip of his lord's boot until he came all over again and finally curled up at his liege's feet, falling fast asleep.

Julian simply excused it as exhaustion from his demanding public performance earlier that evening. For he'd picked him up—this swiftly rising poet with but one impressive chapbook under his belt, so to speak—after he'd read from it, naked, at a standing-room-only "literary" event. A production at San Francisco's queer equivalent of Carnegie Hall called "Naked Boys Slamming." A "no-holds-barred look at the up-and-coming stars of SF's red-hot queer poetry scene." A glorified rent-party to stave off eviction and keep the dot hounds at bay for another month.

Julian had found most of the poems not to his liking. And the same for the poets. They were no more than a chorus line of third-string strippers and hustlers who fancied themselves the second coming of Rimbaud. And each read more angrily than the next from his grocery list of banal observations and indictments. Until Mike. Julian couldn't remember a word he'd said. And later, when he rued their meeting in the cold light of their unhappy parting, he would agree, snickeringly, with a certain critic's acerbic reason as to why:

> "Mike D'Urbanville's body is such a work of art that the listener welcomes all the sophomoric inanities which tumble haltingly from his mouth: 'Deep in my tight/young/manboy's/greedyhot butthole/your milky spray/of kosmicstarstuff/harmonically converges/with my soul/we/are/ONE!' All for the chance to gaze a little while longer at this genetic masterpiece."

Masterpiece indeed.

The young poet was a marvellous, living pastiche of classical and Renaissance art: his head was tousled with curls that gave way to contrasting, angular features which, at first, conjured up the dramatic visage of

Michelangelo's *David*, but with continued observation of the slight fleshiness in his checks and the flowering fullness of his lips evoked the rich, smouldering carnality of the Emperor Hadrian's deified lover Antinous or the smirking wantoness of the rough trade who modelled as gods for Caravaggio; his shoulders, arms, torso, and legs were that perfect meeting of plain, smooth, muscular lines which the ancient Greeks had borrowed from the Cretans who'd lifted it from the Egyptians when they carved their statues of the divine youth, the *Kouros*; his genitals were too elegant to be described as mere cock and balls and too much for any early Christian art critic's fig leaf; they were, in fact, worthy, Julian believed, of a mural of their own in Pompeii's whorehouses.

Julian was besotted that first night but not sated. For he had not had the opportunity to appraise these pornographic wonders to their fullest extent. And the boy's ass, as yet, remained uncatalogued. Thus, he insisted that Mike return for a second and more prolonged session of art appreciation. Within several wordless minutes after his arrival, the poet was naked and again on all fours before Julian's boots, licking them in time to the rapid yanks he was giving his dick.

"That's enough spit and polish, my beautiful bootblack. They're gleaming. Instead, stand up and let me have a go at that dick of yours. I can see you enjoy a rough touch so…"

Mike sat back on his knees, locked eyes with Julian, and said calmly, "This isn't gonna work out."

"What isn't?"

"This. You know. Us."

"Oh, I see." Julian's body tightened as he wrapped it in a rope spun out of all Mike's possible reasons for rejecting him.

"Sorry. I gotta be honest here."

"Please."

"I only went home with you because I thought you'd know Thom Gunn."

Julian paused to comprehend the words that had tumbled so not-haltingly out of the boy's mouth and then spoke. "Oh, you did."

"Yeah."

"So, why'd you come back tonight?"

"I forgot to ask last time."

"Well, that *is*...honest."

"Hey, nothing personal, you know. It's just the leather jacket and boots—you know you've got fuckin' hot boots."

"Oh...well...thank you, Mike," Julian stammered out as he waited for his brain to connect with his tongue; he'd never had such a surreal conversation and been sober.

"So, I looked at your clothes and then I heard your accent."

"Accent?"

"You know. It sounds English-like."

"Well, yes, that would be because I lived in England for thirty-odd years before I moved here."

"Exactly!" Mike shouted as he slapped his hand on his thigh. "I knew it. Just like Thom Gunn. He's my idol. Fuckin' swear-to-God, it's true. I'd do anything to meet him."

"Obviously."

"Yeah," he smiled, merrily unaware of the poisonous barb Julian had shot into his sinewy flesh.

Julian lowered his eyes and sighed. The boy was no longer as beautiful as before. So be it, he concluded. If one wished to slaver over Thom Gunn's boots that badly—and perhaps Mike just might suck out some poetic abilities through the soggy leather while he was at it—who was *he* to prevent Lancelot from his grail quest.

"So, do you know him?" the young knight asked. His dick stood upright and insistent, twitching in anticipation of Julian's answer.

Actually, Thom's number *was* in his address book. But Julian held his tongue, and his temper. After all, it wouldn't be much of a quest if one just gave Mike the master poet's number or simply drove him over and fobbed him off on Thom's front step. For before one could mutter, bitterly, in the din of the slamming door, "And Bob's your uncle," this errant knight would be frantically attempting to scale the walls and make poor Thom his daddy.

"No," Julian replied with an icy smile.

"Oh." The boy now lowered his eyes, reflected, and looked up at Julian all the more earnestly, enticingly. "Are you sure?"

"Quite. But I'll make an inquiry at the next meeting of the Anglo-American Leathermen's Club."

The beauty's face grew terrifyingly red.

"Hey, dude! Don't go all crotchety on me, okay. I was just being honest."

"Yes, as only a native-born Californian can."

"Whatever, old man. I don't have any problems with who I am."

"Pity."

"You know what, fuck you!"

Mike started to snatch up his clothes and shove on his shoes then pants then remove his shoes then retry with his pants then shirt then shoes. He stood and, as he hobbled towards the door, jamming his left heel into his flopping sneaker, he mumbled, "fuckin' ol' fart," over and over. Meanwhile, the fuckless old fart had a growing, sinking feeling that he'd not only been cast into outer darkness but had become the inspiration for a new poem which might be read aloud to a future room of old fools that would include a few of his still-living friends.

He watched Mike fumble with the doorknob and when he saw his back turn, waited for him to give his parting soliloquy.

"Every time I was licking your boots, I was thinking of Thom Gunn's. That's the only reason I came."

Yes, we've already established that, Julian thought as he flashed him a backhanded V. Mike looked confused. He'd probably misread it as a peace sign or the Vulcan salute. And the harder he tried to decipher it, the more agitated he became. "Fuck you and your mind games, man," he blurted before running down the outside steps.

Julian sighed once more and plodded towards the open door. When he'd reached the threshold of his house, he stood silently, looking on as the boy fumed off into the chilly June night, a veil of steam thrown over his head.

"*Ab asino lanam*," as the Romans had once said. Or, one cannot gather wool from an ass—no matter how fine. But the finest arse of all was yet to come that night. And now, over a year later, it was arcing enticingly into the slowly chilling air of his living room.

Julian tapped his ottoman in its kneecap with the other boot. "Make this one just as wet." It disappeared under the bouncing, black hair.

Their relationship was odd, even to his colleagues. *Always the queer fish*, he whispered to himself so as not to distract the devoted bootblack. He could see their faces. A line of grim men. Not the others at the hospital who'd grown grey with him, and eventually under him, when he'd become Chief of Staff. But his few remaining perverted peers: all elders now to the New Guard; all old men to each other; all once nervous boys, burning with earnestness and lust, who'd learned to top from the stern hands of the Old Guard themselves.

The Old Guard, he sighed anew.

Men as different from the present day *Mr. So-and-So Leather*s and their attendant *so-and-so leather boy*s as medieval inquisitors from massage therapists.

Then he saw *his* face—a face that he would always fear and love. A face forever scowling. For even when he *had* smiled, his brush of a moustache hid that subtle upturning of his lips. *Dear Robert. Dear, dear Robert Wicks.* The only man he would ever willingly, and fondly, call Sir.

And though Julian wasn't sure if Master Wicks would have approved of how heterodox, even eccentric, his own methods of mastery and discipline with Sid were, he was certain that he would have understood, without explanation, why this relationship was so important to him. For Julian was more than just this boy's top or his daddy. He was his *magister*. A Latin double entendre for both teacher and master. A dusty word from a dead language he hadn't written in or even read much from since he'd gone to university at Oxford. A dusty word from a dead language which he was using to teach a 28-year-old boy about a dying world—his own.

The *magister* reached down into the thick hair and twisted his fingers through a clump. "Enough." He tugged the hair and the head and the boy until they all sat, kneeling, at his feet.

"So, my young Turk…" Julian paused to clear his swelling throat. "You've been such a good ottoman tonight that I dare any of my friends now to tell me you will prove to be fickle and feckless like so many other boys in San Francisco."

The boy smiled. It was a smile that took shape in degrees. A slow curving at the ends of his mouth. Then his upper lip was drawn up like the big red curtain in the movie houses of Julian's childhood. The rows of teeth, choreographed by a skilled orthodontist, shyly took the stage— their white costumes a bit browned and worn from all the smoking they did while waiting in the wings. It was so awkward, self-conscious, and yet very sexy.

Still.

Not just the first time he'd seen it at Dr. O'Hearlihy's party.

My God, and here I believed one drank to forget.

Another fundraising event. This time, for the hospital. A tasteful event in O'Hearlihy's even more tasteful home. A reproduction of a repro- duction. A Spanish-Moroccan villa built for some forgotten starlet in Bel Air that had been rebuilt for an unknown and unmissed executive in the thick of St. Patrick Woods. That posh enclave on the seaward side of Twin Peaks, those two humps of a hill, The Great Wall to the landed gentry like the good Dr. O, which keep all the freaks that the outer world considers to be San Francisco corralled in the snake pit on the other side.

Yet, somehow, a freak the likes of Julian Gibbon had managed to scale the wall and stand among the self-appointedly normal.

And, to his surprise, he was being cruised.

By one of the waiters, no less.

He was the tallest person in the room—somewhere close to 6'3" or 6'4", Julian estimated—and he had the commanding natural brawn of a rugby player who needed neither pads nor helmet. He had a large, squarish head with a thick jaw. His black hair had been slicked back from his forehead and cut close at the sides which made his wide eyes, thick, broken nose, and thin lips seem huddled in the centre of his face. His neck was beefy but easily outdone by the breadth of his shoulders coupled with the width of his biceps and forearms. All of which were barely contained in his short white jacket. He stood in the corner by the bar with his back against the wall and his wide hands clasped before his crotch as if awaiting a penalty shot in a game of football. His eyes darted from the bartender pouring the drinks to the milling crowd. His lips trembled and the bartender laughed at whatever he'd nervously muttered.

The waiter seemed desperate to sink from the notice his physical presence commanded. Until he had the tray of drinks in hand. Then he assumed a confident stance. He would calmly navigate the crowd and make pleasantries as he served the cocktails and took new orders.

Julian was fascinated by the contrast.

And so, when Mr. and Mrs. Steuart had finally mingled onward, he looked back to the corner where the hulking waiter had been standing his nervous guard. He was there again. But this time, he was eyeing Julian and almost, faintly, grinning. Julian was intrigued. He'd never gone in for the athletic "all-American" type before and the disinterest, until now, had been mutual. Then again, there was something not quite right about him: the ebony colour of his hair that could only come from a bottle; the paleness of his skin that, even if he were just a weekend athlete, should have been a fading shade of brown by this time of year.

Julian smiled and raised his hand towards the suspected jock, beckoning him with a crooked finger. The waiter nodded and advanced quickly.

"Can I get you something to drink, Dr. Gibbon?" he said cheerily.

Julian's expression stiffened. He was blindsided by the stranger's unexpected use of his name. "How do you know my name?" he said curtly once he'd recovered.

"I asked around," he answered and, with that, the curtain raised on his smile for the first time.

Julian was captivated. For there was a striking transformation of the waiter's face once he smiled. It took on an unusual delicacy for someone with such traditionally masculine features. He also noticed his eyes were a nearly luminescent grey. It was all rather hypnotic. Like he'd encountered a fey giant from a children's fairy story.

"Well," Julian replied, the prior coldness in his tone melting hastily, "I'm at a distinct disadvantage then because I am completely unaware of *your* name."

"Sid."

"A pleasure to meet you, Sid."

"Thanks. You too, Dr. Gibbon. Can I get you something to drink?"

"Yes, Sid, but only if *you* call me Julian. I prefer the informal." *The little lies we tell when we cruise*, he thought. "We're in California after all," he added.

"Okay, Julian. What will you have?"

"A gin and tonic, please. With Bombay."

Sid made a grimace, as if to keep his gorge down.

"Something the matter, dear boy?"

"Sorry. No. Nothing. It's just not what I'd have with all this heavy pâté and brie."

At that moment, Julian, if he hadn't found Sid so inexplicably alluring, would have snapped, "But you're not me, are you?" Instead, he delighted in his bluffness. "A sentimental favourite," he replied. "I'm afraid I have rather unorthodox tastes." He punctuated this last statement with a wink.

Sid was smiling so hard that Julian couldn't determine if it was the strain of his muscles or genuine excitement that caused his cheeks to redden so. "Well," Sid stammered, "we're *all* in the right city for that." Then he quickly turned and headed for the bar.

A word came to mind as he watched the broad white back disappear in the crowd. An odd word. Rather precious. Like this Sid. *Ensorcelled.* And that is what he'd done to Julian. Utterly.

And so it was no surprise, to Julian, that, when Sid returned with his drink, Dr. Gibbon would brazenly—for a wine-and-cheese fundraiser where aging widows outnumbered the canapés—leave his drink, a large tip, and his card on Sid's platter with instructions to meet him at a coffee-house the next day at nine in the evening. He then kissed him on the cheek and made his way through the crowd and to the door beyond.

The following night, the giant was already waiting outside Sweet

Inspirations—the coffeehouse were so many blind dates between men in San Francisco begin and often end—when Julian, always ten minutes early, made his way up Market Street. The bulk of Sid's body was draped in a black wool greatcoat, and he looked every inch the Victorian undertaker, save for the missing silk top hat. He was anxiously shifting his weight from foot to foot until he recognised that the character flying up the sidewalk—outfitted dramatically in a burgundy cutaway leather coat, black shirt and ascot, grey leather waistcoat, and black leather pants and boots—was none other than his date, Julian. At that, he grew still and straightened up to his full height and gave a wolf whistle. Julian stopped a few feet in front of him, made an elaborate flourish in the air with his right arm, and bowed from the waist.

"Wow!" Sid exclaimed. "Don't you look...*dandy*, Dr. Gibbon."

"You were warned, my dear, that I have rather unorthodox tastes. And please, Sid," he said as he placed his gloved hand tenderly against his check, "call me Julian or I will be forced to turn my coattails and run."

"Coattails? Do you mind doing a turn for me, Julian? I have to see them."

"A student of fashion?"

"What?! You're a surgeon *and* a psychic?" Sid asked with impish grin.

"I guessed it?!"

"I start next spring," he answered. He motioned with his hands for Julian to turn around. The good doctor indulged him with a swift pirouette that let his tails fan out for a brief moment. "Nice...nice," Sid appraised as he clapped his hands.

"I can be," Julian laughed. "I'm also freezing. So, how about some hot coffee for you and tea for me."

When Sid sat across from him with his mocha, Julian was able, at last, to slowly and pleasurably scrutinize the boy's face. Again, he was mesmerized by his eyes. Pale and pellucid. Like transparent stones. And how his features, which looked, at first glance, like they belonged to some dogged boxer, would be overtaken by such gracefulness whenever he smiled—as he did now.

Julian returned the simple gesture and then spoke before the fast-accumulating silence could become awkward.

"So, Sid, a fashion designer is it?"

"Some day. I hope." Sid took a large gulp of his mocha.

"In the meanwhile," Julian continued as he poured out his tea, "a waiter."

"Yeah. Though last night was special."

"Indeed."

Sid lowered his eyes and chuckled.

"What…what I meant is I usually wait tables in a restaurant."

"Which one?" Julian enquired.

"Boulevard."

"Well, well. That's a damn fine one."

"You've been?"

"Once. But now I'll need to come again." Julian raised his cup and blew at the surface of the tea, never once taking his eyes away from Sid's. He took a slow sip and put the cup down. "Are you also an actor?" he asked, synchronizing perfectly the arching of his right eyebrow with the upturning of the same side of his mouth to signal—in case there could be any doubt left—that the games had begun in earnest.

"Excuse me?"

Julian leaned across the table, leading with his outstretched finger. He stopped at the edge of the eye. Sid didn't flinch. *Impressive*, Julian thought. He touched the lid, tracing the outline along it.

"Don't tell me this is kohl?" He showed the boy the smudged tip of his finger. *There it was again. That smile.*

"Let me guess. You're Egyptian royalty?"

"Close. Goth."

"Ah, less Cleopatra and more Lord Byron."

Sid's smile broadened. Julian was growing excited. He hadn't had to explain who either was.

"Actually, I prefer Shelley," offered the boy.

"Percy Bysshe?"

"No, Mary."

"Yes, yes, of course. Frankenstein. I take it you have a fondness then for monsters."

"Not after Egon."

Julian raised his eyebrow alone this time. *Here we go 'round the rebound bush?*

"His real name's Jackson. He's my ex. We broke up six months ago. He'd laugh his bony little ass off if he heard me calling myself a Goth. Always said that no matter how white I got my skin or how long I grew my hair or how much black clothing I owned, I'd never be anything other than second-rate punk trapped in a dumb jock's body."

He paused, raised the over-sized cup that seemed dainty in his hand, sipped once, then again, and returned it to the saucer without a clatter. Julian waited, delighted by this beautiful giant taking such an effete pause for dramatic effect. As Sid dabbed at the sides of his mouth with the tiny paper napkin, he resumed, "He always called me..."

"Sid Vicious," blurted Julian, eager to return to their flirtatious banter.

"Too obvious. He wants everyone to know he's got a masters in comparative lit."

"So, what?" Julian pressed. "Sir Philip Sydney?"

"Nope."

"Sidney Sheldon?"

Sid shook his head firmly enough, but there was soft clouding in his eyes. A second of hesitation. Julian suspected he didn't want to blow their so-far promising date by admitting he knew who neither was.

"Sid Vacuous," he said in a solemn monotone.

"What a dreadful pun," Julian tittered. He quickly changed his expression when he noticed Sid remaining stone-faced. "And what," he added, "a jealous little cunt you saddled yourself with."

"I really hated him after I looked it up."

Julian noticed Sid had paused once he caught Dr. Gibbon eyeing him from his face to his crotch and back. He wondered if the lad could also see the subtle tenting of his leathers from across the table.

"As far as I can tell, notwithstanding the sad facts that I'm sitting far too far away from you and am an old man with only five, waning senses, your talents, dear Sidney, appear to be very real and substantial."

Sid blushed; Julian was smitten.

He watched the swift flitting of Sid's irises from side-to-side as the boy tried, Julian imagined, to think of some worthy, perhaps even saucy, retort. All that came out, however, was, "You're not *that* old."

Julian guffawed. "Geologically speaking, no I am not." He could see Sid was mortified by his faux pas. He was so charming when humiliated. He decided to be merciful and get them home where they would need less words—for now.

"Perhaps you would allow me a closer inspection."

Sid nodded.

"Somewhere where the lighting isn't so industrial. Somewhere all candlelight and shadows? Goths like that, yes?"

The young man pushed his chair away from the table and stood at a relaxed attention, his coat hung over one arm.

"Good." Julian rose slowly and moved closer to Sid's face until they were nearly eye-to-eye. If the boy hadn't seen the pronounced arch of his dick as he gotten to his feet, Julian was sure he must feel the warmth radiating from it now, suffused as it was with hot and quickly coursing blood and pressed squarely against his thigh. Julian lifted his arms and his hands gripped Sid by the shoulders. Easily, he spun the boy about. He then raised his mouth to Sid's ear. "Off we go then, boy," he whispered and swatted him once on his rewardingly full and firm arse.

He started.

He'd heard something at the edge of earshot.

Forgotten but familiar music.

And before Julian could remember any further from their first night, those mournful, disquieting siren sounds brought him crashing against the present's shore. It was Satie's *"D'Edriophthalma"* with its brief echoes of Chopin's "Funeral March." The room—larger, quieter, and colder—blurred into focus. Whatever heat the alcohol and memories had generated in their combustion was fast evaporating; his cock no longer strained against the tight animal skins which had confined it; it had retreated instead for the dark fires deeper within the body; besides these, it had curled up and now slept.

They may be playing our song, Death, but I'm not ready to dance.

He winced; he had been fiddling, unawares, with his pinky ring and jabbed one of its hard, metal corners into his other hand. It was a square-cut onyx set in silver. It and the small, round carnelian ring on Sid's outstretched hand below were the only symbols of their intricate relationship as *magister* and *discipulus*. They only wore them when both wished to undergo the rigours of higher education. Otherwise, they rested together inside an elaborately carved and gilded box that sat upon the bedroom dresser.

To signal his desire for a painstaking examination the following night or approaching weekend, one would leave—as Julian had yesterday—the other's ring on his respective pillow before bed. For a less formal and perhaps more hurried tutorial, the *magister* had simply to thrust the *discipulus'* ring upon his finger whenever and however he found him or the *dicipulus* would appear in the self-made sartorial splendour of his leather jock and kneel with his head bowed and the ring held aloft in the palm of his hand. If the master took up the ring, the games began. As for the pupil, he was allowed to reject his ring once every six months and could force the ring upon his master once a year for the *Saturnalia*, that ancient Roman feast in December where anything went—even an enlightened master serving his own slaves.

Six months.

A year.

Julian snorted and rubbed the sore spot in his hand. Those rules had been made when they both believed they would spend the rest of their lives together. And now—"O irony of ironies," Julian muttered aloud—it looked as if they would easily keep this most difficult of vows. For neither had imagined how short a life together could and, in their case, *would* be.

Theirs—and he rued this very realization—was fated to be a relationship of surprises to the imminent and bitter end.

He refused to think of that cruelest one a minute longer and willed himself to remember an earlier and most pleasant one that had resulted in many more of its kind. It had all begun with an innocent but providential discovery the morning after their second date.

Julian and Sid were breakfasting in the sun and shadows of the kitchen in

Julian's flat. The apartment itself was a rambling series of redwood-floor-boarded and wainscotted and bevelled-glass-windowed and plaster-rosette-festooned rooms in a mammoth whitewashed Victorian that had once been home to a mayor of San Francisco. Through the seven-foot windows beside the table cluttered with dishes and plates and cups and one tea- and one coffeepot, they could look down into the garden of browning wildflowers or up into the dark green canopy of the neighbouring pine: a tree so enormous that it appeared the house was only an odd nest in its gigantic, soughing branches.

Julian turned away from the window to find Sidney staring at him and chewing his toast and trying to grin between bites. He swallowed and spoke. "I was going to take a leak this morning and I wandered into your little room by mistake."

"Little room?" Julian asked, pausing before taking a second swipe with his spoon at the eggshell enthroned before him.

"Yeah, the one with the leather shop inside it."

"Ah, yes. Of course. The closet. Dear boy, I assure you there's nothing special about it. This isn't Bluebeard's castle. It's simply a walk-in closet."

"That's about the size of my bedroom."

It was Julian's turn, at last, to blush. He had yet to see Sid's apartment and was now embarrassed by his cavalier tone. Two fucks and he'd already stumbled over their first tripwire: income and class.

"Oh, *that* room," he countered, trying gallantly to undo the damage. "How careless of me. I warned you I was old and thus capable of forgetting far too many a thing. Forgive me, my sweet Sidney. And now that you've discovered my attic, I'm afraid I can never allow you to leave."

"Your attic?" Sid said wryly.

"Yes, my attic. The forbidden room which holds the portrait of my true likeness."

"Oh, yeah. *That* attic, Mr. Gray. I guess I did."

"And what, pray tell, do you think of my shadow, sir?"

Sid smiled. "I'd like to meet him. Maybe play together with some of his toys."

Julian raised his eyebrow, a gesture that allowed him to pause and choose his words carefully. *Intention is something so foreign nowadays*, he thought; *the fantasy within the unfulfilled promise is what is preferred.*

"An easy enough wish to grant," he said finally. "But be careful before you make it in earnest. I'm not altogether certain you understand just what it is you'd be inviting upon yourself."

As Sid grew very still, Julian became aware of how truly physically large and powerful a presence the boy was. He looked a bit stunned. Hurt.

"This is San Francisco, Dr. Gibbon. I've been tied up before. Even spanked."

"How terribly charming."

Sid put his fork down with a hard clank on the plate. "You're mocking me."

"No, not at all. I sincerely meant what I said: It would have been a terribly charming sight. But I want you to know that if I ever *were* to spank you, there'd be nothing endearing nor amusing about it on your end—if you'll pardon the unavoidable pun."

Sid flushed. The room was silent but for the compulsive warbling of a bird from somewhere deep within the pine.

"Promising," Julian murmured, disrupting the stillness. "Quite promising."

Sid looked up and met the doctor's eyes. Neither looked away; neither blinked.

"Shall we play a game, then, Sid? Clear the plates and meet me—naked and on your knees—outside the 'attic' door in ten minutes."

With a loud and sudden screeching scrape, Sid pushed his chair away from the table and began his education.

And once more a sound outside of memory's earshot returned Julian to the present: the low, giddy burbling of his own suppressed laughter. That and the pleasurable discovery that his dick was again hard and pressed against the leather.

"Enough," he said to both himself and Sid. There followed the rough staccato beat of him clapping his hands twice.

"Arise, my loyal and steadfast ottoman, and stand before me." The ottoman stood, eyes respectfully, coyly, downcast. Julian took the broad chin, smooth except for a peppering of stubble, and tilted it until the eyes of the pupil met those of his master. "Shall we play a game then, my pet?"

Sid beamed. *"Ludamus, magister mei."*

"Good. A round of 'Tiberius' Minnows.' But I have no desire to wait while you draw me a bath. Besides, in honor of tomorrow, I think Saturnalia will come early this year." He knelt with a deliberate slowness—to mask the difficulty of the act—and, when the searing in his joints cooled, took Sid's large hand in both of his and pressed the ring against his lips. "Tonight, the emperor shall have the supreme good fortune of swimming and nibbling between the wicked minnow's legs."

He slipped his hands around Sid's thickset middle to seize his arse, gripping deeply into the soft but muscular fullness of each cheek, steadying himself as he leaned his face into his crotch. He nuzzled his nose and mouth against the leather pouch before whispering in a low growl, "How cruel of me." Unclenching his fingers, he hooked them around the band of the jock and began to tug the elaborate leather underwear to the ground. "You have been *so* still for *so* long. Holding in *all* that wine I forced you to drink at dinner. I will let you take a piss. Here."

He pointed his long and knotty index finger to his mouth; Sid seemed to hesitate—perhaps, Julian suspected, he was confused or suspicious since his *magister* had never switched roles mid-game; his master, however, was driven to impatience by his own avidity and took hold of the boy's well-shaved balls and yanked; Sid lurched and then staggered the step forward.

"Piss," the emperor commanded.

The minnow eased the head of his cock against, and then through, the hole made by the slight parting between his master's lips. Julian felt him tremble as the delicate and inflamed skin brushed beneath his moustache. *Patience*, he counselled himself and opened his mouth wider.

It was not the biggest dick Julian had entertained; Mike, the bare-naked, boot-licking bard, had taken that prize, in several categories—for this decade. But this was the stoutest mouthful of flesh and blood he'd ever swallowed. Even now, when flaccid, it weighed on his tongue and rubbed against the roof of his mouth, pushing gradually, as it swelled, towards the edges of his cheeks.

It stopped, grew still, quivered, then spurted violently; his mouth was completely full.

He gulped the warm rushing water with all the muscles in his throat. He strained and snorted like a maddened animal as he fought to continue swallowing and keep from choking and sputtering the piss over himself, his silks and leathers, his freshly cleaned rugs. But his urgency was more about lust than pride in his cocksmanship or fastidiousness regarding his person and place. He simply, desperately, wanted to drink Sid in—every wine-embittered drop that bit into his gin-scalded tongue.

Hadn't Sid pledged himself to him a year ago?

Wasn't there little to no time remaining for them?

He would have him all tonight.

Julian was sober now, awake, and alive.

And when there was no more piss and Sid's dick had shrunken—slightly—and softened—noticeably—like an emptied wineskin, Julian opened his mouth as wide as he could and took the whole of it—down to the base of the shaft and a few strands of pubic hair—between his lips. He slid back and forth, clamping down hard with lips while caressing the cock's warm underside with the flat and then the tip of his tongue. It burgeoned appreciatively. And when it could stand without the wet encouragement of his mouth, he let it twitch in the modest warmth of the firelight while he busily sucked on his boy's balls. Eventually, the master returned to the hardened cock and alternately licked it with his tongue and grated it with his teeth before he gave way and let Sid pummel his mouth and the back of his throat.

Soon, Julian could feel the welling within Sid's dick; he reached for his balls, wrenching them down before they could pull all the way back, cocked like the hammer of a gun; he spat the fat, red dick from his mouth. He wanted to watch the boy beg, plead for relief, for the mercy of the little death.

But it was too late. Sid's entire body was rigid. Julian barely had time to look up at his face—the eyes were white beneath the agitated lids; the lips and chin tremulous; the cheeks and forehead and throat flushed—before the skin around his own eyes and mouth was hot and gluey.

"How bold," Julian hissed. "Are you planning a slave rebellion, my young Spartacus?"

"Lord, forgive me," he said in Latin, opening his eyes, the corners of his lips rising upwards. "I knew not where I was shooting."

His Lord laughed. *I must remember that*, he thought. *There are rewards that even I never imagined by having a pupil translate the Vulgate and Catullus simultaneously.*

The laughter also encouraged the largest drops of semen to begin a fast slide down Julian's forehead. It appeared—*well, at least from Sid's vantage*—that they were anxious to swim once again with the rest of their brothers on Julian's cheeks, now the florid colour of raw salmon meat after all his recent, vigorous exertions, and within his matted beard. Sid dropped to his knees and licked them away. He dragged his tongue across Julian's cheeks and nose, bringing on more laughter. Then he sucked at the damp clots in his *magister*'s beard until he was at the fan of hairs beneath Julian's lower lip. He licked the lip once, then nipped and tugged at it until Julian kissed him.

Sid pulled away and smiled, his eyes never wavering from Julian's. He was beckoning, taunting, his master to reach over and kiss him. To come and take him fully by the gentlest force.

Julian reciprocated, however, with a glassy stare and an even more absentminded grin.

He had been struck. He'd heard the high-pitched whistling scream of the falling bomb first—just as he had as a child during The Blitz. Then he'd shuddered through the inevitable explosion and rain of dust. And now he was shell-shocked.

It hadn't been the impudence of the *discipulus*—which the *magister* had always found endearing before and would now if he weren't so addled. It had been the kiss itself. He'd thought himself sobered until that moment. But only the clear and constant and pressing heat from Sid's lips had evaporated melancholy's grogginess.

And it had also blown up from the rubble of the even dimmer past of adolescence a line from a poem. One of Catullus' that he and Sidney had yet to study. "*Miser Catulle*," it began. "Poor Catullus." It was that Roman dog's half-hearted attempt at regaining a proper patrician stiff-upper-lip after he and the immortal Lesbia had broken off their clandestine affair. Despite all the initial righteous blustering, his manly resolve deflates by poem's end and he's left alone and maudlin, asking, "*{Q}uem basiabis? cui labella mordebis?*" "Whom will you kiss? Whose lips will you bite?"

How he'd commiserated with Catullus' the first time he'd deciphered the poem. It was 1952. He was sixteen and would not meet his first love, Alex, for another year. How he'd burned to answer that question. And now, here on the eve of his death, he could. At last. With certainty. With finality.

For Sid—his dear, dear Sidney—was more than a trick he'd grown fond of. More than a beloved subject or pupil or boy. He was simply beloved. *His* beloved.

The full weight of this night toppled onto him.

He was in love for the last time in his life.

And this, most likely, was not the eve of his death but of their only anniversary.

He knew what he must give him. He reached across and grasped the startled boy's head with both hands, tugging his ear towards his waiting lips.

"I cannot wait for tomorrow, minnow. I must give you your gift tonight. Are you ready to receive it?" The ear bobbed against Julian's mouth as the head nodded enthusiastically. "Good. Then I will tell you what it is. A simple gift. I shall mark you as mine. And then I will take you as mine. I will bring you to the edge of where I am going. And, in the frenzy of our fucking, I will destroy you and bring you back to life and you will be forever mine and I forever yours."

It was Julian's turn to pull away and smile. He watched his wide-eyed boy shudder, his dick frantically jerking with joy. "Happy Anniversary, luv. Now go and get my medical kit...and those long strands of pearls...you know where to find them since you wore them last...and bring my red flogger and the single-tail...and throw another log or two on the fire before you leave."

With more crackling and popping than the fresh wood charring in the fire,

Julian got to his feet. Another pair of feet, bare and squeaking along the floorboards, thudded at the other end of the flat. A door opened, followed by a muffled curse and then, most likely, the slamming of the very same door; silence; and then more thuddings before another door squawked on its hinges. It would be a several minutes before Sid returned laden with the "trimmings" for his package.

Julian hobbled over to the CD player next to the window. Even in the day he would have seen just the lowermost branches of the pine and the shadows they cast. Tonight, they had vanished into the dark; there were only the dim watery reflections of him and the room's furniture and the intense wavering of the fire's light within the glass.

He turned away, anxious not to repeat his earlier experience with the mirror, and busied himself with the selection of new music. He loved to fuck to a score; it reminded him of some of his happiest memories at sex parties long past—especially The Catacombs. He replaced Satie with a recording of Glück's opera *Orfeo ed Euridice*. The overture commenced; he felt himself, and the spirit of this evening even, in both the giddiness of the strings and the sombreness of the trumpets and timpani.

He crossed the room to close the door—there was still a subtle but growing bite in the air—and moved on towards the couch nearest the fireplace, picking up the dark green blanket and spreading it in front of the fire and tossing down some pillows for his knees this time.

That final exertion warmed him enough that he was willing to remove his ascot and jacket. Since his diagnosis, he'd become reticent to strip; he not only felt his age but double it. He postponed the necessary look-down at his body, which he would have to take if he wanted to undo his pants, by painstakingly folding the silk clothing and primly arranging it on the arm of the couch.

When the pain in his lower back began to sting at him like an upended hive of bees, he stood up. His shoulders rose and fell with his sigh; he looked down. He let out a long, single breath through his nose. He recognised the body as his own: lean, tight, even the outline of his musculature remained—not as prominent as twenty, thirty, forty years ago; but still there. He ran his hands along the contours of his arms and through the white hairs across his chest. It was his skin that had changed, was changing, the most: growing coarser, thick with wrinkles and veins and spots in varying shades of brown, that would in time—time he did not have—begin to thin and droop. It was already sagging where his belly met the edge of his pants.

Time to let everything that's going to hang out hang out.

He bent over and unfastened the inner lining from his jodhpurs; he was left wearing a gentlemanly pair of chaps and a codpiece—not quite the ensemble for polite society, but modest enough for the leather bake sales that passed for street fairs nowadays. Propriety, however, would hamper what he had planned so he removed, with a few resounding snaps, his codpiece as well. His heavy balls dropped first; his dick was soon falling apace but, being longer, took longer to descend completely; all were lowered center stage, dramatically, from white clouds of pubic hair overhead, like some fantastic prop that sets even the most staid of opera audiences to wild applause.

At that, the door opened and his beloved returned.

"On all fours, boy. Your master needs a writing table."

There was the crash and clatter of the surgical kit and the pearls and whips hitting the floor. Both men dropped onto their knees; Sid scrambled to turn himself about in the thickening folds of the blanket; and then Julian surged—his arm coiling around the boy's vast chest, his hand straining for his thick neck. Julian's dick—instantly, alarmingly, miraculously rigid with blood, like he was sixteen again—leapt with him. Pushing its way between Sid's thighs. Jabbing at his dangling, exposed balls. Poking its blind way up the shaft of the boy's cock and across his tightening stomach.

Naked, sweating, almost orange in the flickering light, his prick between his boy's legs, Julian imagined they must appear like an ancient Greek vase painting of the lover chasing his beloved. A final lunge and his hand was at the boy's throat; he'd caught him.

The old man's hairy and hoary chest bobbed on the smooth, muscled surface of Sid's back like a skiff adrift on a mildly agitated sea. Roughly, he pressed the bristles of his beard—still sharp from yesterday's weekly trimming—into the

Memento Mori

skin of Sid's neck as he bit it. He laboured to expel his own hot breath as he swallowed more of the pliant flesh, so fragile he could detect the blood's steady trembling as it frantically rushed away from the pressure of his mouth.

"I'm going to write you a love letter," he whispered through the skin. "Actually, I'm going to write it *on* you."

Julian felt himself quickly rise and fall and rise and fall as the boy took in a series of deep, shuddering breaths. He let the skin drop from his mouth, gave it a farewell lap, and bit, gently and firmly, into the lobe of Sid's ear, licking the bit of flesh caught between his teeth. Sid stopped breathing; Julian released the ear and pressed his lips against its opening. In nearly inaudible sighs, he spoke.

"The words are not mine, but the sentiment is. And when I'm done cutting it into your back, I'll read them to you. And you will give me the gift of hearing you translate my handiwork. And if I am pleased with your gift, and I have no doubt I will be, I will give you the other part of your gift—a delicious and painful fucking that will make you swoon from the pleasure of it."

Julian turned his head away to search for the single-tail whip. Without releasing his grip, he stretched and fumbled to reach it and twist it into the tell-tale shape of a noose. He waved it before Sid's face, whispering one last time in his ear, "I promise it."

He slid away from Sid, dragging his dick along the underside of his impromptu writing table, until he sat on his haunches, staring contentedly at his boy's glistening back and butt.

"That should have gotten your blood flowing. But I want my ink mixed just right. So, give me…three sets of…ten pushups. Now, please."

As Sid pressed his body against the blanket, against the cold floor beneath, over and over and the shadows surged around the walls each time he lifted himself before the fire, Julian took the longest strand of pearls and knotted it loosely. He struck it against Sid's shoulders. Once. Twice. Thrice. And, on the next strike, it broke; pearls clacked against the floorboards and wainscoting; they rolled down the rivulets of muscle in Sid's back; they drooped and fell from Julian's hands into the blanket's creases.

But of course. The tragic omen. Oh, how ironic. How perfectly symbolic. How well plotted and placed. Very droll, Death.

"Keep on," he said aloud. He brushed the stray, stuck pearl from Sid's back as it rose to his hand. Each still had their lustre; they were "nacreous" as Master Wicks liked to say when he would hold up to the lights of his dungeon the drying droplets of Julian's come, smeared along the squarish ends of his fingers; it was the string within that had frayed—unseen and unmissed until now.

Once again, I guess I'll have to make do with the strand the fates have dealt me.

He chortled to himself as he nabbed the flogger and gave his beautiful, not-dumb, and not-that-winded jock a few whacks. "That will do now. You may stop." He rifled through his kit for some antiseptic swabs and a scalpel. And as he wiped the cloth against the skin, he noted, even in the dim light, the fading latticework of past whippings.

My palimpset—pale and smooth—is ready.

He gripped the scruff of Sid's neck and said, "Be still, my pet. Your *magister* has much to write."

He tore into plastic around the scalpel's blade; his own dick danced alone in the air; the muscles at the edges of his writing table flinched. He swatted at the rear legs of the table to open wider. Between them, he rearranged his pillows and himself. He leaned in and began to recite in his head. Outside him, Amor sang to Orpheus that the gods had been moved to pity by his grief for his dead love, Euridice. They would allow him to wade into the Underworld and ferry her home; but he could neither look at her nor explain to her why he did so or he would lose her forever.

Julian pressed the glinting tip of the blade into the skin and dragged it downwards; it slid through it effortlessly. There was a near-silent hiss from the boy that, in time, would grow into a quiet, blissful humming.

The *magister* cut beam after beam, buttressing each in a variety of angles against the next, until he had his first row of words in Roman capitals. He'd carved half his way through the next line before the letters above began to darken. The sightless, blue blood was hurrying to fill the vacuum near the slits, rushing to the light, to the oxygen, to become the red of unpolished rubies and garnets.

As he cut on and as Orpheus sang his way past the Furies and into the gardens of the blessed in Elysium where he begged his beloved to return with him, the poem bled. Swelling polyps above ripened and burst. Beading down the back like wine streaking along the curves and indentations of a rich drunk's ivory goblet. Or tears of the undead as Julian remembered Sid calling them. He cut around them; he cut through them; and when he was almost to Sid's waist, he was done.

He put the scalpel down beside the openmouthed bag. "Listen well, *discipule*," Julian said before sucking his thumb and forefinger. "I shall only read this once."

He bent forward and ran his tongue across the first line; and with the drying blood encrimsoning his lips and beard, he spoke the words aloud. And he did the same for all the lines that followed:

> *Vivamus, mea Lesbia, atque amemus*
> *rumoresque senum seueriorum*
> *omnes unius aestimemus assis.*
> *soles occidere et redire possunt;*
> *nobis, cum semel occidit breuis lux,*
> *nox est perpetua una dormienda.*
> *da mi basia mille, deinde centrum,*
> *dein mille altera, dein secunda centum,*
> *deinde usque altera mille, deinda centum;*
> *dein cum milia multa fecerimus*
> *conturbabimus illa ne sciamus*
> *aut ne quis malus inuidere possit*
> *cum tantum sciat esse basiorum.*

Julian sat back; his mouth and beard were stained a hue of red that was almost brown. "Now it is your turn, *discipule*." And slowly at first, his voice growing deeper and stronger with each line, the writing table spoke:

Let's live, my Lesbia, and let's love

And not give a flying fuck

For the hissing gossip of grumpy old men.

Almost out of earshot, Julian could him them grousing now, muttering "unsafe, unsafe," huddling around him, propped up on sticks far stronger than their own bones. All his life, when these same men and he were younger, they'd shouted "unclean" to him and everyone he'd loved, chasing them like lepers, into the hills, to the brink before the sea. And here they were again, saying "Unsafe." From what? Death? Death was so close Julian had asked the doctors to provide him with an ETA. He feared nothing from the boy.

The sun can set and rise again,

But once our brief light fades

There is only night, one unbroken sleep.

So give me a thousand kisses, then a hundred more,

Then another thousand, a second round of a hundred,

Then still more, a thousand and then a hundred,

And when we've racked up many thousands

We'll make those old farts loose count

Royally screwing their plan to total up just how many kisses we have

So they can use that ol' evil eye to drain our account dry.

Julian sat silent but smiling. *Brilliant*, he thought of both the student's translation and his own penmanship. For he had carved more than one of his favourite poems, more than his own epitaph, a *memento mori* with a literary flourish. He had cut into living stone a greeting to future travellers that would pass this way, a memorial to their love that would last as long as the scars. And if he made it to their second anniversary, he would cut it afresh. Open it up to seal it further.

He cleared his throat. "Here and there you took some liberties with the letter," he said as he leaned across Sid's left leg to retrieve the unbroken strand of pearls and the single-tail whip and arrange them on his own right side. "Still you managed, and under some duress, to capture the spirit of the old rogue." He slapped him hard on the ass. "Very good. Now, present so I may give you the rest of my gift."

The boy knelt down onto his elbows and spread his legs further apart until Julian could see his favourite entrance to the underworld.

"Good," he said, stopping him by placing his hand on Sid's cool cheek. Then, Julian sighed. A contented sigh. His first tonight.

Here, at long last, was a precious moment, rare as it was rarefied, when that inestimable Greek adjective, *callipygous*—καλη πυγη, *kalê pygê*, beautiful buttocks—could be invoked, offered up as a hymn of both artistic and salacious praise. For thanks to Julian's constant tutoring, both men knew what the word meant—intimately. There was no need to haul out the OED or search for the often-errant magnifying glass. There was no need to rely on pedestrian comments like "nice ass" or "cute butt." Or worse, the standard drivel of pornography:

What mouth-watering mounds!

Such rock-hard globes!

My, what tight, smooth buns you have!

Buns. Now there was a word that took him back to nineteen-seventy-something. A word that had fallen out of favour. Like bum. Too queer. Schoolboyish. Schoolgirlish, actually. Subsumed by the primacy of ass. Even arse was now spelled as ass back in the UK. Another casualty of *Pax Americana*.

But that did not matter. These were not buns; they were neither small nor doughy soft. They were not mounds. Not even globes: twins in close orbit, mirroring the other's spherical perfection. They were undelicate, wide, fat and almost boxy from muscles that deserved the word "slab".

Pack a hundred pounds more on Sid and take away some muscle and they would have been Rubenesque. And still as juicy. Still as fuckable.

For they were and he was callipygous.

Julian stared down at his hand spread against the broad cheek and another forgotten word came to mind: *chiaroscuro*. Here was the perfect interplay of light and shadow. The darkness of the ring's obsidian, the veins and spots on his own hand covering the whiteness of these moons, brilliant with their own light, unpocked and unmarred unlike the satellite stone whirling along in the earth's wake. Only the faint traces of his former landings on the surface. The near-imperceptible scar of a knife's tooth or whip's tongue.

Chiaroscuro.

Callipygous.

There were no other words more perfectly fashioned to paint this moment. Julian reverentially bowed his head and licked at the opening to merry hell.

No stubble.

Good boy.

"Good callipygyous boy."

They both laughed.

"On such a special night, my dear Sidney, I believe an orifice such as yours—so welcoming, so well-trained—deserves more than just a wham or a bam. Now, now. Don't fret," Julian said as he patted each beautiful buttock and then pinched them. "You shall receive the pummelling which you have so valiantly earned. But with a certain flourish that truly says, 'Happy Anniversary, my beloved.' Behold! It's okay, Sid. You can turn around and have a look."

And Julian posed again and waited to watch Sid's expression as he took in his dick; the eyes grew wider than he'd even hoped once they'd seen what the *magister* had done: he'd gone and wrapped the length of his cock with the strand of pearls—letting it coil three times around the base—and anchored it in place with a now quite swollen and knobby condom.

"Again, I say to you, '*Voila!*' I give you—well, I will very soon—the Marie Antoinette of French ticklers. A shimmering beauty to behold and a searing pleasure to endure. Prepare to make way for the Queen."

"*Ave, Maria*" was all Sid could muster before he lowered his head and took a very deep breath.

"Yes, yes. Full of grace, my dear. And soon you will be. I promise. Patience, boy," Julian said and he extracted the lube from the kit and drizzled it over his hands and Sid's asshole. He slid one, then a second finger, in; and he followed it with one, and then another, from his other hand. He plunged them all deep until he could add an extra finger from each hand; Sid was ready; the gates had been swung open wide enough.

He pushed the tip of the condom against the gently sighing mouth. It widened and he felt the crush of the pearls around the head of his dick. It was an intense, unusual, and exciting pain—certainly for him and he hoped his boy. He thrust forward, slowly, and the pain clenched and burrowed its way into every inch of his cock.

He wanted to shout—perhaps not so loudly as Sid; he was still English at moments of extreme pleasure and pain, no matter how long he'd lived in America—and he almost did. Then he stopped still. Orpheus was singing *"Che farò senza Euridice?"* It was his favourite aria from the opera.

Euridice has died again. She was alarmed by Orpheus' silent treatment as they stumbled along in the dark caves out of the Underworld. She'd pleaded with him to answer her, even look at her. And eventually, heart-sick, he did and, as warned, she fell dead at once. He has lost his beloved twice now. And this aria was his exquisite lament before he tries to kill himself and join her.

What shall I do without my Euridice?
Where shall I go without my love?

As the otherworldly voice of the countertenor sang, he began to build up a rhythm that matched the slow, delicate, mournful procession of the music. *Fortunately*, he thought in the clear moments when the necklace and the muscles of his boy's ass where not squeezing and grinding his dick, *I will never know what I would do without my Sidney. All I must do is remember this night. This moment. This is us. And I must make certain he never forgets our anniversary as long as he lives.*

He rammed his cock and the coils snaked tighter and bit at him fiercely. "Body remember." The line from the modern Greek poet Cavafy echoed in head. No longer could he hear the music outside himself. Only these words. As clearly as he felt the pain. A sharp, gnawing, tearing pain whose origin he knew and understood. He wanted more of it, more of this moment, as much as he could take, as much as he could give. He had to etch—*no, burn*—this second into his brain so it would be the clearest memory—the memory that would leap before his mind's eyes at that instant when the cancer fully conquered him and he choked on his own madly multiplying cells.

He pulled his dick out as far as he could and lunged. Finally, he could yell. He did it again. Sid bellowed and pleaded with him in several languages. The desperate, driven urgency of his boy's demands made Julian thrust even more furiously. He fell onto Sid's unsteady back—one of the boy's arms was tugging at his own dick—and reached out to seize the whip; he didn't have much more time to keep all of his promise, to give all of his gift. As the two men bucked closer and closer together, Julian threw out the end of the whip and wrapped it once around Sid's fat neck.

He tightened it: he had to catch him; to catch up to him; to keep him from galloping away; to drag him back to the little deaths they were both destined for; and perhaps he could pull him into the greater one with him, that night which is a perpetual sleep, *perpetua una dormienda*; perhaps…perhaps…perhaps.

The whip slackened and the boy's neck drooped. The beloved's body quaked and buckled; his arm gave way and he lost some of his consciousness and all of his come. And with that, Sid's hips tightened and his muscles contracted, squashing and smashing the trapped dick until Julian was spilling broken strands of his own body's pearls.

When he'd been released from the convulsions of ejaculation, Julian found himself clinging to Sid, both of them panting feveredly. And Orpheus and Euridice had also been reunited since Glück had decided to rewrite the myth's ending and have the gods show even more uncharacteristic mercy by bringing her back to life a second time. They danced and sang about the triumph of love; and as they did, Julian helped Sidney hobble down the cold hall to the bathroom.

There, he sat the boy on a towel he'd placed on the icy toilet seat. He turned the faucets of the tub and let the water pour out. The room grew slowly wetter and warmer as he removed the sagging condom and pearls. He tenderly removed Sid's ring, placing it on the sink and then adding his own. He sucked on the naked finger and kissed the heel of the palm before he bit, playfully, into the fleshy Mount of Venus beneath his thumb and Sid's eyes—quickly—grew less cloudy. Holding the boy's head against his blood-smeared stomach, he stroked his damp hair and then raised him up so he could kiss his eyelids and forehead and lips. With a bit of awkward contortionism, he lifted the larger man's arm around his shoulder, helped him into tub, and turned off the water.

Now, he let himself sit on the toilet seat. He looked at his boy, squatting, letting his arse bob on the water, wincing in anticipation of the water's sting across his back. *Such a pair we make. The Goth and the old goat.* Julian's eyes teared. Before Death finally pushed him from its chalky, calcified and cancerous cliffs, he would cherish and tend to this one, his last beloved minnow, with as much passion as he'd had for Alex some forty-odd years ago.

Alpha to omega. Alex to Sidney. The alphabet of loves was complete.

He knelt in over the tub and grabbed the not-long-to-be-white washcloth. As Sid leaned towards him, Julian stopped to kiss the blood from his back. He dipped the cloth into the rose-petal-red water. The needles of the pine tapped at the upper pane of the small, steamy window. They had a message to deliver to the lovers within: The rains had come.

Winter is here. For me. And for our sad, doomed species.

He sighed with great weariness and watched his cloth-covered fingers drink in the blood through their cotton mouths. He stopped washing Sid's back to listen to the boy's hushed, fluttering breaths. Suddenly, he wanted to laugh out loud at himself for his epic moroseness. *If there is any hope for this renegade strand of savage, balding apes*—a voice far within him sang as he washed and rung out the rag—*it lies within that one act where we are our most divinely insane, violent, and extraordinary; where we are truly obscene; where we are most ourselves.*

It lies in the sweet, bitter madness of love.

A love like ours tonight.

Love at its most queer.

"Hail, Love, we who are about to die salute you," the old man sighed, smiling as he pressed the cloth against his boy's back again and watched it redden.

"*Ave, Amor, morituri te salutamus,*" the beloved responded to his lover's call, his words faintly echoing off the wine-dark water.